ISBN: 978-1710242522

Yomatri: A Hero's Journey

Written by: Javon Manning

Editor: Stephen Delaney

Associate Editor: Pamela Manning

Cover Art and Aridnemeki Map: Nilanjan Malakar
www.youtube.com/thegeekartist

Author Photo: Jacob Ngui

Interior Layout: Michael Nicloy
Nico 11 Publishing & Design,
www.nico11publishing.com

Printed in The United States of America

Acknowledgments

Writing my first book has been a fun and exciting adventure for me. I feel like I've learned a lot simply with grammar and punctuation. But more importantly, it's taught me how to better see the real world and understand people as a whole.

I don't think any of this would be possible without my mother, Pamela, who was there with me on this massive project from day one nearly 13 years ago. Mom, I knew you saw something in me from the beginning, and you never let me lose hope on what a great story this could someday be. You stuck with me through the toughest of times: helping me edit chapters night after night, discussing story concepts, reading through confusing parts and finding a way around them, and so much more. You mean the world to me, and I'll always love you for that.

I'll always be thankful of my father, John, who really got me off my butt at 10 years old and forced my friends and me to stop playing video games one hot summer day. And then came the first time I started developing the character of 'Yomatri'—originally called 'Yodoriki'—and building a universe around him. Only two years later, I self-published this character in 7th grade, which was an incredibly rewarding experience. I thank my dad every day for being an awesome parent and doing something so simple.

I'm eternally grateful for my cover-artist, Nilanjan Malakar, who was able to bring Yomatri to life with his incredible artistic ability. You were honest, dedicated, respectful, and you made sure to understand the characters in my story to the absolute best. I admire you for your patience and hard work in knowing that I wasn't going to be happy until we got the front cover and the map of planet Aridnemeki exactly right.

To my editor, Stephen Delaney, who also helped so much with bringing this story to life in terms of how it was written — making it fun and enjoyable to read, serious at times, descriptive, and also interesting to say the least. You were so patient and understanding with me sending you revisions and e-mail after e-mail whenever I needed help or didn't understand something, and for that, I'm forever thankful.

To my interior designer, Mike Nicloy, for really trying to understand this book from the inside-out and giving it the medieval, young-adult fiction feel. You always made sure to get everything right and formatted this thing to give it that final touch it needed.

To my siblings. To my big sister, Kara: for always supporting me through the countless delays of releasing this book and encouraging me to keep going no matter what. To my older brothers Jamar and Devere: for always willing to talk with me about the story if something didn't make sense. Whenever I had a question mom or my editor couldn't answer, whether it be big or small, I always knew who to call for help.

A very special thanks to my friends Morgan and Isaac. Without question, you both took on the challenge of proofreading one of the earlier versions of this book.

You guys were straightforward, kind, and gave really great suggestions and comments to improve the overall quality of the book. Both of you opened my eyes to new directions I didn't even realize I could take this story to. Whether I had to text you guys or talk in person, you both were always there to help.

To my longtime friend, Jacob Ngui. You knew I was really stressed the day I came over to your house in hopes of fixing a big plot hole in my story. By talking things out with me, it really helped to get my thoughts out both verbally and on paper. Not only that, you were always there if I had a question afterwards whether it be something silly or the randomest thing in the world. It gave me confidence to move forward with the book, and I'll always thank you for that.

To two more of my great friends, Bronyta Holmes and Ryan Wisth: thank you both for also taking the time to help me with the big plot hole I was really struggling with. Even though you guys didn't know much about the story because I didn't want to spoil it, both of you were always able to give me insight on how I could improve that part of the book for the better.

And lastly, to all of my friends, family, and fans not listed here: I can't thank you guys enough for all your support, your honesty, your words of encouragement and so much more. This book has definitely changed my life, and I honestly don't where this story would be today without all of you. I'm very pleased with what it has become. But no matter how long you've been on this journey with me, this book is for you. Thank you, everyone!

Thank you Morgan, Isaac,
and my mother, Pamela, who read it first.

YOMATRI:

A Hero's Journey

by Javon Manning

TABLE OF CONTENTS

PROLOGUE

Master Zorhins – Commander-in-Chief, the Hero Alliance
(Narrating)

Y ears ago on a mysterious planet known as Aridnemeki (AIR-rid-Nuh-Meh-KEY), composed of twelve enormous continents called "kingdoms," there existed a great time of peace. Collectively, the twelve kingdoms were ruled by high-ranking, powerful individuals together known as the Allied Nations.

All of the kingdoms held a mystical, elemental power contained in the form of a crystalline rod. Each of the ancient rods represented one of the twelve elemental forces: fire, water, electricity, wind, earth, sky (flying), shadow, metal, energy, healing, magic, and light. The crystals acted as a source of great power, for whoever controlled them all would be unstoppable.

After a dispute over power between several members of the Allied Nations, they became divided and the balance of peace amongst the Aridnemekian people had been lost. As a massive group of vicious and evil marauders, the Aridian Army, began to form, chaos broke out throughout the twelve kingdoms.

A band of brave, unlikely heroes retaliated and came together, calling themselves the Hero Alliance. Together, they worked to defend the Aridnemekians from the threat of danger and to restore peace to the twelve kingdoms.

Despite their efforts, a massive war erupted which threatened to destroy the entire world. The Aridnemekian civil war continued over a span of many years, unleashing chaos and destruction across the alien planet.

When many of the Aridnemekian people realized the planet's future hung in the balance, the twelve crystals were sent out into space to protect their world from further destruction. Several warriors from both sides of the war searched the stars and dozens of planets throughout the galaxy in search of their precious rods.

Eventually, the two sides stumbled upon a new world where they began to find traces of mystical energy emanating from its atmosphere—Earth! We, the Hero Alliance, have now found ourselves here on planet Earth in search of the twelve crystals ...

CHAPTER ONE:

LANDING HOME

In the far reaches of outer space, stars, asteroids, planets, and other celestial matter hovered all around. Without warning, something flew past countless bright stars. It appeared blue and crystalline like a comet. The object flew with purpose, making its way to planet Earth as if it had a mind of its own.

The cometlike entity soared towards the large planet at an incredibly high speed. As it approached, the object became a hardening orb. It entered the planet's atmosphere, growing hotter and hotter by the second as its velocity gradually decreased.

On Earth, a white and blue light descended from a cloudy dark sky toward a snowy New York City. In the vast metropolis, tall buildings loomed high over thousands of people who walked the busy streets.

Today, it was quite cold outside, and many individuals wore long coats, hats, and mittens to keep warm. Hundreds of cars drove through the heavily packed streets, and there was constant honking and commotion amongst citizens.

Although it was only several hours past noon, the wintery weather made it seem very much like nighttime. All kinds of sparkling, vibrant Christmas lights in addition to large colorful billboards contributed to the city's grandeur.

In Times Square, thousands of people began to notice the cometlike object in the dark winter sky. As it flew by, they pointed up in astonishment, attracting the attention of many others. A few individuals quickly pulled out their cell phones, hurrying to try to record the incredible sight.

At last, the mysterious object—which now looked very much like a round pod—roared across the city. Several tiny chunks of metal from the pod's surface ripped away from the ship, appearing as glowing fireballs hurtling toward the planet's surface.

Swiftly, the pod cut through the windy clouds with a trail of black smoke and flames. Down below, hundreds of people covered their heads and ears, fearing the worst. A few of them were forcefully thrown off their feet.

Moments later, the podlike entity crash-landed in a wooded area of Central Park. It smashed into the ground, blowing clumps of dirt, snow, and large chunks of icy rock high into the air. Within seconds, the pod came to a complete halt in the Earth's rugged land.

Many citizens called local news outlets and began dictating events as they'd unfolded. After only thirty minutes, it seemed that every reporter on the face of the Earth was covering the crash-landing.

Thousands of New Yorkers watched the incident live on TV. At an apartment in Sunnyside, Queens, a teenaged girl and her mother were absorbed in the story. The teenager turned up the volume on a large flat-screen TV and listened more carefully as a blonde reporter spoke in front of the camera.

The reporter gaped, her eyes wide; she carried a microphone while interviewing dozens of civilians, police officers, and firefighters standing around her. Soon after, the woman gave the audience a brief message:

> ... To recap, here in Central Park, it appears the authorities have discovered some sort of alien space pod or small spacecraft that seems to have come from another planet. From what my sources are telling me, the authorities are not entirely sure as to what the object is or even what planet it came from. At the moment, though, the police are taking many precautions and are now investigating the matter. We will bring you any new information as we get it ...

The girl's mother took a sip of her hot chocolate, then said, "That sounds pretty interesting!"

"Yeah, I know! We should go down there and see if we can find out more," the young girl replied. Immediately, she and her mother both grabbed their jackets and rushed to the park.

At a house in Forest Hills, a husband and wife were also watching *Channel 6 News*. "Hey, Luke, what's that you're watching on TV?" the wife, a woman named Miya, asked while she boiled pasta for spaghetti.

"The media's saying some orb-shaped thingy from outer space landed in Central Park just a few minutes ago," Luke responded.

Immediately, Miya turned a dial on the stove to a lower temperature and went over to her husband in the living room. "Wait, really? No way!" she said while studying the screen. "I bet that's him! When we last spoke, he told me he'd be coming home today. Honey, we have to go ... now!!"

Luke and Miya were overjoyed at the thought of their son returning home from space camp. Properly known as the Space Camp Federation, it was a once in-a-lifetime program offered by NASA. The camp itself was a large battle station in outer space run by alien life-forms who sought only to protect the galaxy from danger.

It was their duty to maintain peace and prosperity. To help achieve that goal, beings from any planet would be randomly selected to come and train, hoping to one day become warriors, heroes, and leaders.

They would help in the intense fight against the dark forces of evil, being taught how to defend themselves in mortal combat and on the use of futuristic technology. In addition, once old enough, the trainees would be allowed to take part in massive battles on land, in water, and up in the stars.

When not on the battleground or in training, they'd learn a lot about outer space, sometimes being able to study fun subjects like astronomy. Once in a while, the trainees would get to do other exciting things like piloting fast and powerful spaceships.

Immediately, Miya and Luke left their house. They jumped into their red minivan—one of the two vehicles they owned—and headed to the park in Manhattan. Around forty minutes later, the two parents could see crowds of people ahead of them, the space pod the center of their attention.

A fair number of armed law-enforcement officers, firefighters beside them, investigated the mysterious scene. Nearby, a mass of police cars and fire trucks with flashing lights were parked along the sidewalk.

After parking the van, Miya and Luke hurried toward the crash site, where some people were huddled together, their brows furrowed, while others talked in short bursts and pointed.

With great caution, civilians crowded around the pod, now partially embedded in a fairly deep crater in the ground. Police worked diligently to maintain order and keep the crowd under control, forcing some individuals back.

"What do you think it is?" a redheaded woman asked.

"I have ... no idea," said a man with dark-brown hair and a scruffy beard.

Studying the alien vessel closely, the man noticed, behind a dark ovoid glass surface, a dim form that looked very close to a human's sitting inside. It seemed to be sound asleep, but at the moment, nothing was for certain.

One NYPD officer nudged the bearded man aside and upon closer inspection, realized that it was in fact a human being lying inside the vessel!

Suddenly, Luke and Miya emerged from the crowd. They pushed people aside trying to get a closer look at the space pod. Miya—a very tall, slim, and beautiful woman— wore a navy jacket, jeans, and a red Santa hat, revealing long brown hair that flowed down her back.

Like his wife, Luke, a tall man with short blond hair and fair skin, was dressed in a dark winter coat and jeans. He sported a freshly-shaven face with a clean haircut.

"Stand back!" one of the male officers surrounding the pod demanded.

Miya screamed, "It's okay, it's okay! I'm pretty sure that person inside knows me!"

"Who are you?!" a female officer snapped.

"We're his parents!" Luke yelled, trying to calm the situation. "Please ... don't hurt him."

"Wait a minute. How do you know who the person inside the pod is anyway?" the male officer asked, tightening his brow.

There was a short pause.

"Because I'm his mother," said Miya. Many of the officers lowered their suspicions and looked on curiously. She continued, "His name is Yomatri (Yuh-Ma-TREE) Yotaroshi (Yaht-uh-ROW-Shi). He was part of the space camp program sponsored by NASA three years ago."

"Yes, and he's only fifteen. Please be careful," Luke added. After a moment, he and his wife were allowed to get face to face with the damaged metal pod.

Looking a bit confused, Miya knelt down and examined the pod, noticing a red button on a side console. She pressed it. A glass panel slowly lifted, releasing a mechanical, gassy hiss.

Sparks popped out of broken fuses inside the vessel as the crowd watched with amazement. Luke stayed close to his wife. Both of them cautiously inched forward.

Lying back in his seat, the boy wearing gloves, a hooded jacket, jeans, and a pair of goggles around his neck suddenly woke and rubbed his eyes. He tried to get up, but then remembered that he was fastened in with leather seat belts.

Luke glanced over to his son's right side and noticed a backpack lying against him.

Meanwhile, the boy unbuckled the seat belts and lifted himself from the crashed ship, carrying his backpack with him. Seeing that he was a bit weak from the trip back to Earth, Miya and Luke helped steady him as he planted his feet onto the ground.

He was a fairly tall, strong, and handsome teenager with spiky brown hair and blue eyes. Instantly, Miya recognized the boy she knew and a smile formed on her lips. Wiping away tears of joy, she and her husband felt very relieved to see him after three long years.

Miya quickly pulled her son into a tight embrace. She was a very kind mother with a soul as warm as fresh pumpkin pie. She never yelled at her son, even when he was younger, and always gave positive vibes towards other people she interacted with.

"Oh my God, Yomatri, it's so good to finally see you again! You're back … on planet Earth. You're home," his mom said.

Noticing a dazed look on her son's face, Miya paused to see if he was understanding her. Yomatri rubbed his eyes and slowly recognized the female voice.

"I am?" he asked tiredly, eyeing his parents. His stomach growled with an intense roar, as he was very hungry from the long trip home. Luke and Miya grinned, and more words came from their son's mouth. "Mom? Dad?"

"Yes, you're here. You finally made it," his father added, giving his son a warm hug. The crowd of people surrounding the three of them had erupted in cheers and applause.

"You've grown so much over the years!" Miya said.

Yomatri smiled. Immediately, it hit him that the two human beings standing before him were really his parents—the people who'd cared for him all his life.

After embracing his mom and dad, Yomatri paused. He turned and began walking a few steps nearby in the snow. The teenager slowly breathed in some of the fresh cold air, then exhaled deeply. Looking up at the sky, he noticed the moon, which appeared bright in the semi-dark winter sky.

Yomatri also looked around and took note of his environment, which was mostly snow and plants. The falling snow really caught his eyes.

The teen then glanced down at his feet which were now covered in heaps of snow. He began to remember how Earth's land used to feel on his feet when he was younger.

Everyone else looked on, curious.

Yomatri removed the goggles from around his neck and tucked them away in his backpack. Luke took a short, closer look at the bag and noticed some of the contents inside: several packets of nonperishable food, a set of photos, and a strange metallic device.

After a second, Yomatri glanced back over to his parents. He smiled. "It feels so good to finally be back home," the teenager said.

Miya smiled back. "That's good to hear. We're so happy to see you."

Minutes later, the crowd of New Yorkers had gathered together and sang Christmas carols as it was Christmas Eve. After almost an hour in the cold, the police gave Yomatri's parents permission to take their son with them.

Miya drove home, humming the long-forgotten Christmas carols along the way. The brisk tune of "Jingle Bells" was engraved in her memory. The red van, which she'd received as a present in the past, was her favorite vehicle. Although it was very old and outdated, it had served its purpose well.

Luke, on the other hand, had been given a sturdy, four-wheel black Jeep by a great friend of his many years back. He always seemed to have more than enough money to make ends meet.

Miya's early life was quite the opposite. Her mom was a stay-at-home parent, and it was difficult growing up because only her father worked. However, it was not all that bad now. Miya enjoyed being able to stay home herself, while her husband worked at a film company in the city.

Luke spent most of his time in a studio drawing concept art for all sorts of science-fiction films. Because of his excellent technical skills and ability to always meet deadlines, he was well-loved by many of his coworkers. He made a lot of money for his family and was always able to provide for both his wife and son.

Miya and Luke didn't raise the type of kid who always held an outstanding grade-point average; however, they did manage to raise a nice, charming teenager with a unique personality. In addition to having high hopes for his future, they were proud that he was chosen by NASA to attend space camp for his bravery, willingness to learn, and hard-working nature.

While riding home, Yomatri stared out the van's side windows and recalled his parents walking with him around the neighborhood and showing him new things. Although he was glad to finally be home from camp, he missed the old times of being a kid who loved to play outside every day.

As the family of three pulled into the driveway of their two-story house, Miya stopped the van and parked. After taking her keys out of the ignition, she opened the door and stepped outside.

Her foot landed in a pile of snow and icky, muddy slush. "Oh, come on," Miya complained, her sock now soaking wet.

Walking up the cobblestone driveway, Yomatri noticed that the front lawn was completely covered in sparkling, white snow. A long strand of vibrant Christmas lights was strung across the front of the house: blue, red, green, and yellow.

Several bushes, trees, and other small plants surrounded the residence—all of them covered in thick, heavy snow. Near one of the bushes, a large American flag billowed in the wind, attached to a metal beam fastened to the house.

Miya closed the van door and noticed Luke and Yomatri patiently waiting for her at the front porch. She was always the last one out of the car and it was typical for them to wait, even in the past.

Moments later, the three of them walked into their large house. A massive staircase towered just inside the entrance. On the main level near the front door was a mat covered with a cluster of shoes.

"Hey, sweetie, you can take your shoes off over here," Miya said to her son, pointing at the cluttered mat.

While he removed his shoes, Yomatri became astounded by the Christmas tree in the nearby living room. He adored the tree, which was littered with beautiful ornaments and strands of bright lights.

Yomatri then looked all around the house, taking in everything in sight. He got the feeling that although he was finally back on Earth, his house hadn't changed much in three years.

Briefly, the teenager recalled moments when he and his space camp comrades would share large meals together and have lots of laughs. After dinner, they often trained in a large courtyard and practiced with exciting, futuristic weapons.

Suddenly, he came back to his senses. Miya noticed a frozen expression on her son's face. "Is everything alright, honey?"

He sighed. "Yeah, everything's fine." The teen shifted his gaze back to the Christmas tree. About ten wrapped presents surrounded it, but not all of them were for him.

Yomatri dropped to his knees and picked up a red, box-shaped present with a green bow while Luke closed the front door and took off his shoes. The moment he placed his finger on the bow, a hand smacked his.

It was Miya, squatting beside her son.

"Honey, it's not Christmas yet," she laughed.

"Oh." Yomatri turned, his expression curious. "Wait, what day is it then?"

"It's Christmas Eve. Tomorrow, you can open all the presents with your name on them. Sorry, it's tradition."

"Would it be okay if I opened one at midnight?" asked Yomatri. "At space camp, Admiral Kaiser (KY-sir) celebrated Christmas the same day we humans do. He's human just like us. Me and my friend Neo would always get to open one present at midnight, and then we'd have to wait until morning to open the rest."

Miya sighed. "Sure, you can open one, but only if you're up at midnight. By the way—this is probably gonna sound stupid—but who's Admiral Kaiser again? I tend to get him mixed up with other space camp people from time to time."

Yomatri set the present on the floor, smiled, and embraced his mother. "Admiral Kaiser's the leader of the entire camp, Mom. He's the best. I'll tell you all about him sometime."

"Oh, that's right ... duh," Miya replied; she tapped her forehead clumsily. "How didn't I remember that?"

"It's okay, don't worry," said Yomatri, chuckling, as he began to stretch. "Hopefully, I'll be up at midnight to even open a gift. I'm sooo tired."

"Well, hey, before you get too tired, do you at least wanna see your room?" Miya asked. "I feel like you'd probably want to see that after being away from it so long." Without her son seeing, she winked at Luke.

"Sure, why not?" Yomatri got up from the carpet and raced upstairs to the second floor.

As he slowly opened his bedroom door, he couldn't believe his eyes. Inside were multicolored balloons lying on his bed with a big white sign, hanging from the ceiling, reading, *Welcome Home, Yomatri!!*

The teen's eyes lit up and a big smile formed on his face. He glanced at a wooden desk near a window and noticed his old desktop. Next to it was a small chocolate cake and a set of old photos depicting him and his parents having fun out in Manhattan.

Yomatri hurried over to the desk and examined the photos, which immediately brought back wonderful memories for him. Suddenly, he heard a knock. The teenager turned to see his parents, who were expecting a hug.

"Surprise!!" Luke and Miya yelled, beaming.

Yomatri rushed forward and embraced them. "You guys, this is amazing! Thank you!" He glanced around his room, which looked almost the same compared to when he'd left for camp years ago.

"You're welcome."

✫✫✫

Later, Miya and Luke sat with their son at the kitchen table. Beside him was the backpack he'd carried home with him from outer space.

"Okay, so honey, tell us about your journey! We've been dying to know," said Miya.

"Mom, Dad, it was incredible! Honestly unlike anything I'd ever imagine. Thank you, guys, so much for letting me go on that trip—really. I know it was probably super hard for you both, but it was totally worth it."

"That's great! I'm glad to hear that," Miya replied.

"What all did you do there?" asked Luke.

His arms crossed, Yomatri paused for a moment to think. "Ummm ... I did a lotta studying for sure, like astronomy—learning about the stars and other planets out there in space. Even a little physics and chemistry here and there. Oh and uh, they taught me how to defend myself ... and I learned about all these futuristic weapons and gadgets they had!"

"Wowww, that must've been exciting," said Miya.

Yomatri added, "Yeah, it was pretty cool, I'll admit. Admiral Kaiser—the guy I was tellin' you about before—he and a bunch of other members of the camp let me pilot spaceships, tanks and all sorts of other stuff. But of course, with supervision!"

Luke creased his brow. "Wait, hold on ... so you've been in real battles?"

"Yeah, and to many planets out there in space. But the spaceships and whatnot was really just them showin' me what it was like. I never actually got to use 'em in battle. I wasn't old enough."

Luke sighed with relief. "Ohhh, okay. You had me worried there for a sec."

Yomatri gave a smirk, then jumped up from his seat and showed his parents the contents of his backpack, setting them on the table.

"What's all that stuff?" asked Miya.

"Nothing really—just food, old pictures, and some other stuff." The teenager then pulled out a small metallic device in the shape of a rod and pressed a tiny red button along its shaft. In the blink of an eye, the device expanded into a rusty, battered metal staff.

Luke's eyebrows rose. "Whoa! What's that?"

"My trusty staff. It's one of my favorite weapons I

used in camp. I was really happy that Admiral Kaiser let me take it home. It's kinda beat up, but it still works. Isn't it awesome?"

Miya and Luke didn't answer.

Without thinking, with a blur of motion, Yomatri swiped the weapon in the air. He paused after hearing a shattering noise, then slowly shifted his gaze downward.

On the floor was a broken glass.

"Oops—sorry, you guys," he said regretfully.

His parents stared at him with wide eyes, their arms raised. "It's ... okay," replied Luke.

Miya and her husband each became relaxed again, then took some of the photos from the table and studied them together. Yomatri leaned his staff against the wall and stopped to pick up the glass, using a pair of dishwashing gloves from a nearby cabinet.

"Whoa! Wait, so you've interacted with aliens and all sorts of other creatures from outer space," said Miya. "That must've been pretty neat. Was it scary? How'd you end up communicating with them?"

Yomatri took off the gloves, then sat back down. "It was a little weird at first, but I kinda got used to it over time. There were always translators around, so I never had to worry really."

Holding a photo in one hand, Miya eyed her husband. "It's really sad that this was only a once-in-a-lifetime thing, you know?"

"Yeah, it's crazy when you sit back and think about all this. I guess we were just lucky enough to have been selected," Luke replied. He turned his attention to his son who seemed lost.

Yomatri stared downward, blinking pensively.

"What's wrong, honey?" Miya asked, curious.

He shook his head. "Nothing—sorry, I was just thinkin' about what you guys said. Now that it's all over, it just feels so far away. It already feels like I've been away too long."

"It'll be okay ... don't feel so down about it," Miya said, then paused. "Maybe one day, you can go back?"

Yomatri looked up at his parents as a smile slowly formed from the corners of his mouth.

"We've missed you, buddy. We're really glad you're home," Luke added.

There was a short pause.

"Hey, to get your mind off this, how does making some Christmas cookies with me sound?" asked Miya. "It'll be a lot of fun, I promise."

"Sure," Yomatri responded. He and his mother got up and headed over to the fridge.

"Oh, this is so exciting!" Miya said, clapping her hands eagerly. She began gathering the dough, cookie cutters, plastic wrap and flour, and laid them out on the kitchen table.

Afterwards, she took off her jacket and began pressing down hard on the dough. Yomatri helped her while Luke went into the living room to watch TV.

Together, Miya and Yomatri made a variety of cookies, some shaped like stars, Christmas trees, and gingerbread men. Occasionally, they'd have a little fun by flicking flour and bits of cookie dough at one another.

Miya began to laugh uncontrollably after joking around too much and covered her son's face entirely in flour. He looked like a powdered mess. Yomatri tried to pretend being very annoyed but couldn't take himself seriously as he burst into laughter with his mom.

After two hours of making the cookies and preparing for dinner, it was finally time to eat. While Yomatri washed his hands, Miya took the cookies out of the oven and put them on a plate with paper towels over it. They weren't meant to be eaten until the next morning. In keeping with their Christmas tradition, Santa always ate the first cookie.

At the dinner table, it looked like Yomatri wasn't opening a present at midnight, as he was so exhausted that he fell asleep with his face smashed in the spaghetti and meatballs.

"Sure looks like someone's tired," Miya said, nibbling on a piece of garlic bread. "Isn't he just adorable?" She smiled and turned to Luke, who was now beside her.

Her husband smiled back, then got up and pulled Yomatri's face out of the spaghetti. After wiping off the red sauce, Luke gently carried his son over to a couch in the living room where, when he woke up, the Christmas tree would be staring him in the face.

Minutes later, Miya appeared with a soft blue blanket and laid it over him. She looked at Luke and smiled again, wrapping her arms around him while she leaned on his shoulder. It had been a long day for the Yotaroshi family, who'd just been reunited after three long years.

CHAPTER TWO:

A CHRISTMAS ADVENTURE

A winter sunrise spread over the city, bathing skyscrapers and other tall buildings in a warm orange glow. At home in Forest Hills, Yomatri slept calmly on the couch as beams of bright light seeped through various windows. Although most of the lights were turned off, the snow outside provided some visibility. In the living room, the Christmas tree shined with vibrant colors.

"Wake up, Yomatri! Wake up!" a voice was calling.

Yomatri, who felt his body being rocked back and forth, suddenly heard his mother's voice. His vision partially blurred, he sat up, knocking the covers off himself. He yawned loudly as he stretched. Then he rubbed his eyes and stared tiredly at his mother, who sat beside Luke on the edge of the couch.

"Merry Christmas!!" the boy's parents yelled.

Miya and Luke studied their son who looked very silly, but all they could do was laugh. Together, they joined in and gave him a big warm hug.

"Merry Christmas, guys," Yomatri said, smiling. His voice was a bit weak, but he was definitely excited. After embracing his parents, he rubbed his eyes again and did a quick fix of his messy brown hair.

"You ready to open up some presents?" asked Luke.

"Yeah, definitely," his son replied.

Immediately, the three of them gathered around the Christmas tree, where Yomatri began tearing away at the wrapping paper like a little boy. Although he was fifteen, the kid-like nature in him had completely taken over.

His face was filled with joy and excitement, and he was very happy to get a brand-new laptop along with a pair of sleek red Bluetooth headphones and a handheld tablet. "Whoa!!" the teen exclaimed, studying his new gifts. He turned to his parents. "Thank you, guys!"

"You're welcome," Miya and Luke both said.

Almost thirty minutes later, Yomatri had already set up his new laptop while fiddling around with his tablet in between.

"Hey, sweetie, don't get mad at me when I ask you this, but, uh, do you still remember how to use that kind of stuff?" Miya asked, studying her son's actions. Luke glanced up with a strange expression, which caused her to snap. "Well, he hasn't been on this planet in three years ... I just, you know, thought I'd ask!"

Yomatri giggled. "Yeah, a little bit. I mean, some of it I forget. The tablet I kinda know how to use 'cause we'd use 'em all the time in space camp. But hey, while my laptop's downloading system updates and whatnot, you guys mind showin' me how to use these headphones?"

Miya seemed hesitant before responding. "Wait, are you being serious?"

"Well, you are the one who said the boy's been technology-deprived for the last three years." Luke grinned and Miya rolled her eyes.

"No, no, Mom, just the Bluetooth kind. I'm familiar with the earbuds. The Bluetooth's a little different if I remember correctly? Come on, you gotta give me some credit," Yomatri smirked.

"Sure, honey. It's really easy actually. Here, just look." Miya pulled out her cell phone. "Okay, so since these are Bluetooth, you just press this button here on the phone and hit 'scan'. But make sure you're also touching this button on the headphones at the same time so they can link, you know?"

As she spoke, Miya noticed that her son was paying close attention. Without warning, Yomatri took his headphones and his mom's cell phone into the kitchen. Miya and Luke shared confused looks, then followed their son who sat down at the dining table.

"You guys got some tunes for me to listen to?" he asked. Miya shook her head, then opened a music app on her phone. Meanwhile, Yomatri put on his stylish headphones and began jamming away to some funky music. "Ow!" he yelled, jumping up while banging his knee against the table.

"Well, don't blast the darn thing to max volume, my goodness!" Miya said, laughing hysterically. "What are you tryna do—blow a hole through your eardrums?"

Yomatri took off the headphones, grinning widely. "These things are insane! They sound great."

"Yep, and the good thing is that they're wireless, so you don't have to carry a really long cord or whatever with you everywhere you go," Miya replied.

"That's pretty convenient."

"Hey, Yomatri, do you by chance still remember how to use a cell phone?" Luke asked, curious.

"Do I remember how to use a cell phone ... are you kidding me? Do you know who I am?" the teenager said in a sarcastic tone, pointing a thumb at his chest. He laughed awkwardly, then wavered between a smile and a frown. "No Dad, I'm afraid I don't."

Luke snickered. "Well, here, come on over. Let me show you a little somethin'." He took out his own phone and showed his son through several of the apps—*phone, messages, calculator, settings,* and *Internet.* He also gave him a quick lesson on how to text, send messages, and use mobile data when not on Wi-Fi.

"Hmm ... seems pretty simple. It's like a tablet for the most part. I'll just have to keep using it to get more comfortable, I guess."

Luke replied, "Yep, it's not too bad. You'll be fine."

"You wanna learn a thing or two about computers really quick?" asked Miya.

"Yeah, sure, why not?"

Moments later, Luke and Miya stood over their son's shoulder, reteaching him how to use a computer. Yomatri pointed at a round dot at the top of his laptop screen. "Wait, so this is called a what again?"

"It's a webcam. You can use it to talk with or video-chat people who might live far from you or whomever, really. Even someone from a different country if you wanted," his mother responded.

"Ohhh, that's pretty cool, actually." Using the touchpad, Yomatri navigated around the main screen, studying it closely. "Man, there's so much you can do on here! It'll take me a while to remember all of it, but I think I'm getting the hang of it."

"Yeah, you're doin' fine, kiddo." Luke smiled. "We can show you much more later on."

"Definitely," said Miya; she turned to her husband. "Hey, honey, don't you think now's a good time to open up the presents we got for each other?"

"Yeah, for sure."

Yomatri got up and joined his parents as the three of them reentered the living room. He and Luke sat on the edge of one of the couches.

Miya dropped to her knees beside the Christmas tree, beaming. "Ahh ... this is so exciting!" she said, rubbing her hands together. "Is it okay if I go first?"

"Yeah, of course. I don't mind."

"Alright, uh, let's start with this one." Miya handed him a small box-shaped present with a red bow.

Luke tore off the wrapping paper, seeing a deluxe shaving kit that included a holiday-themed razor, body wash, and a tube of shaving gel. "Heyyy, this is nice! I have always been asking for one of these now that I think about it. Thank you, honey!"

"Yep, and I know you're always on the go with work and stuff, so I don't know—maybe this'll help for when you get ready in the morning?" said Miya. "There's also a little $50 gift card to the movies tucked in at the bottom 'cause I know you really like goin' there in your free time."

"Yeah, no kidding. Maybe one day all three of us could

go together and see a movie."

"That'd be fun!" Miya insisted.

"I agree," her son added, smiling. He pointed to another present with his father's name on it. "What's this really big one over here?"

"Oh, here, lemme see it," said Miya. She took the rectangular-shaped box from him and passed it to her husband.

Luke unwrapped the present, seeing a 126-piece art set that included drawing pencils, markers, oil pastels, and more. His eyes widened. "Niiice! This is just what I needed actually, especially for work. It'll help me a lot. Thanks!"

"Yeah, definitely," Miya responded; she turned, grabbing the last present with her husband's name on it and handing it to him. "I also got you this. I think you'll like it."

Luke opened an all-black box and pulled out a smaller box from within. His and Yomatri's mouths dropped opened when they saw it was an aqua blue water-resistant smartwatch. "Alright, now this is very cool! And you even got it in my favorite color too!"

"Isn't it pretty neat? I know you're really big into watches and thought this might fit you."

Yomatri interrupted, "Wait, why does the box call it a 'smartwatch'? How's it any different from a regular one?"

"Well, sweetie, it's good that you asked," said Miya. "You can actually use it to text or call people ... play music ... track your calories if you're workin' out. It's also got a built-in calculator. Dad could even use it to pay for something if he doesn't have his debit card with him—I mean, all sorts of stuff."

Yomatri's eyebrows rose. "Hmph. That's really cool, actually. I didn't even know those existed."

"If you want, I could let you check it out sometime, kiddo. Don't worry, I got you covered." Luke winked at him, then turned to Miya. "But hey, honey, I really love all my gifts—thank you."

"Yeah, of course! I know you said you didn't want too much, but I thought I'd get you at least a few things."

Yomatri rubbed his hands together. "Now I'm really excited to see what you got Mom, Dad."

Luke chuckled. "Alright, let's get this party started then." He got up from the couch and handed his wife a fairly heavy box-shaped present with a gold bow. "You're gonna love this, I'm sure."

Her face beaming, Miya set the present down onto the carpet and began tearing away at the wrapping paper. "Awww, honey … this is great! I can use this all the time," she said, studying the box containing a 15-piece copper cookware set, which included an assortment of pots and pans, spatulas, measuring cups, and more.

"Yeah—I saw it as I was walkin' in the store and I just thought, 'that's perfect for her,'" said Luke.

"That is really neat, I gotta say. And we all know how much you love to cook, Mom," Yomatri added.

"Yeah, no kidding." Moments later, she opened up a medium-sized present and pulled out a limited edition makeup set with a foldable light-up mirror.

Luke pointed and said, "Now this one I got because I know you like to wear makeup from time to time, especially when we go out for a dinner date or whatever."

"I love it!" said Miya. "It's got everything I'd really need. And it's limited edition too? Look at you gettin' all fancy over here."

Luke and Yomatri shared a laugh.

"Is that everything?" Miya asked, glancing around. A cluster of torn wrapping paper surrounded her.

"Wait, there's one more gift," Yomatri stammered. "This really big box over here."

From a nearby drawer, Luke grabbed a pair of scissors and turned back to his wife who'd already began opening the present. Miya soon pulled out a soft, colorful heated blanket; she unfolded it and examined it. "Heyyy, this is neat! I think I know why you got me this, actually."

Luke grinned and set the pair of scissors aside. "Yeah, because you always mention how you get cold from time to time in the winter."

"You're right, I do tend to say that a lot. But honey, I really love my gifts! Thank you so much," she said, standing up to give him a hug and a kiss on the cheek. Pausing, she checked her wristwatch. "What time is it? Oh, almost 8:30. I'm gonna make some food, you guys."

"I like the way you think, Mom."

A little over an hour later, Yomatri took a break from his new gifts and stopped in the kitchen. Luke was seated at the dining table, reading the daily newspaper with a cup of hot coffee to his side.

Miya had prepared a large breakfast: sausages, pancakes, eggs, and bacon. Yomatri couldn't resist the urge to chow down on a home-cooked meal because like most teenagers, he loved eating. At space camp, most of the trainees were forced to follow a strict diet so they'd be strong and fit for battle.

"Ummm ... what are you doing?" Miya apprehensively asked her son.

"Nothin'—just snaggin' a piece of bacon. What are you doin'?"

"Ah! Ah! Ah! You most certainly will not!" Miya snapped, slapping a crispy piece of bacon from his hands. "You have to wash your hands first and then get a plate to eat on."

"Look at what you did! You just ruined a quality piece of bacon! Now it's collecting germs and getting all infected."

Miya snickered with a spatula in hand. "I'm serious! You'll be fine."

Yomatri shook his head in disbelief. Moments later, he returned to the kitchen and noticed his mom munching on a piece of bacon without a plate or napkin to eat on. "Wait, so what's that all about?" he asked, pointing at her with a confused look.

"What do you mean? I'm the mom. I can do what I want," Miya responded. Yomatri glanced at his father, who simply shrugged his shoulders.

Minutes later, the three of them gathered at the kitchen table to eat. They enjoyed talking to one another and remembering old times. Still, like all great things, breakfast had to come to an end.

Yomatri was the first to finish eating. He got up and set his plate in the sink. "Hey, Mom, what time is it?"

Miya checked her wristwatch. "Almost 11:00 now. Was

there something you wanted to do today?"

"Wait, I just remembered—it's Christmas. What about you guys? Are you doin' anything today?"

"No, I don't think so. I mean, we might go out, but that's about it," Miya replied, exchanging a glance with Luke. "I know ... it's a little weird. Your father and I were just gonna wait until New Year's to have a big celebration with everyone. It'll be fun, I promise. A lot of people from the family are actually really excited to see you."

Yomatri nodded. "Would it be alright if I went out into the city by myself—maybe to Manhattan? There's so much I wanna see."

"Yeah, why not? I'm sure it'll be okay," said Luke. "Maybe you'll meet a new friend or somethin'."

"Honey, are you sure? Some things are still new to him," Miya whispered to her husband. "I mean, how's he gonna get there? I don't know if that's totally a good idea."

"Aw, come on, Mom!" Yomatri begged. "I know I just got back from a really long adventure, but I promise I'll be safe."

"I don't know ... the last time we saw him, he was only twelve. And, he's never really been on his own," Miya said to Luke, tapping her chin. "I guess I'm just a little concerned for him."

"He'll be okay. He's fifteen. I think he can handle it," Luke assured. "He can take your phone in case there's an emergency. And I'm fine with letting him use my metro card to get around with the subway." He turned to his son. "You remember how to get there, right, Yomatri—to Manhattan?"

"I'm sure I'll figure it out; don't worry."

Miya sighed and shook her head. After a moment she handed Yomatri her phone and Luke's metro card. With a faint smile, she said, "Alright, alright. Just remember to be safe, honey. And call us if you have any questions."

With a cheerful grin, Yomatri stared at his parents while awkwardly scratching his wrist. Luke and Miya looked at each other, confused. When they glanced back, their son had already darted upstairs to his room.

He scrambled through his wooden dresser and eventually found a hooded jacket and an old pair of gloves. In a matter of seconds, his entire mood had changed. Having been gone for three years, he was very excited to see the world again.

After quickly tying a pair of black-and-white shoes, Yomatri raced back downstairs. He yelled good-bye, hurrying out the front door without closing it. At last, he was ready to begin his new adventure all alone, out in the marvelous city of New York.

Yomatri sprinted through his beautiful neighborhood filled with trees and houses of all shapes and sizes. As he ran faster and faster, he felt the cold wind slam against his face, remembering how much fun running was during his younger days.

Abruptly, he came to a stop after nearly falling on the slippery ice. He looked up and studied the winter sky, noticing a light snowfall. The teen then stuck out his tongue, trying to catch some of the snowflakes while simultaneously grabbing at them with his hands.

Around him, several individuals standing in their yards

and on the sidewalks had noticed Yomatri and gave him very strange looks. The boy glanced back at his fellow neighbors and ignored them. He smiled and for a moment, was finally beginning to feel back at home.

✫✫✫

Later, Yomatri ended up on a busy street in Manhattan. As he walked, he passed by many groups of people from all walks of life. There was lots of chatter, and the constant commotion of cars and taxicabs honking at one another could be heard in the distance.

Multiple buses waited alongside the sidewalks ready to pick people up. Almost everything in sight was buried in thick white snow, but fortunately, the temperature was slowly climbing above forty degrees. In the sky, the sun shined brightly, casting a thin light across the city.

Yomatri continued looking around and began to remember more from his past and about New York. During the summers as a kid, his parents would always take him on morning walks throughout Forest Hills, sometimes to the local bakery for a donut or anything else he might've wanted. In the evening, they'd stop at food trucks and occasionally go to the park for fun.

His attention back on the present, Yomatri eventually arrived at another crowded street. Across the walkway amidst a slew of New Yorkers, he noticed a very pretty, slender girl. He glanced around, his eyes alert. Instantly, he wanted to meet her.

She was a bit shorter than him, had brown skin, green eyes, and curly dark hair. Dressed in a red, padded winter jacket and tight jeans, the girl waited at a street corner while listening to music.

Suddenly, across the street, an electronic pedestrian light turned green and Yomatri ran after her, pushing others aside. Watching closely, he noticed her walking into a bakery just several meters down a sidewalk. He quickly followed her inside and waited for a few minutes towards the front.

Inside, the smell of cinnamon, cake, and coffee wafted heavily through the air. While cashiers took numerous customer orders behind a counter filled with bagels, muffins, cookies, and many different pastries, waiters and waitresses attended to tables all around.

The curly-haired girl sat down at a table close to the center and rested a backpack against her chair. While she took off a pair of earbuds and placed them in her bag, a server walked by and set down a glass of cold water.

Only seconds later, Yomatri joined her at the table, which was filled with napkins, food advertisements, and a set of eating utensils.

"Hello? ... Who are you? ... ," The girl's voice trailed off, her mouth hanging agape. It felt kind of strange to have some weirdo sitting across from her.

Yomatri stared, all googly-eyed—only seeing her beautiful face in vibrant detail, surrounded by a mirage of flowers and bright colors. He was definitely in la-la land.

Beginning to feel uncomfortable, the teenaged girl glanced away, eyes suspicious. Slowly, she took a sip of her water, her eyes back to watch Yomatri's every move.

All of a sudden, she spat out her drink in the air away from him and immediately, dozens of customers glanced over. She and Yomatri gazed boldly at the staring customers and tried to keep calm.

As the guests returned to their meals, the curly-haired girl quickly wiped her mouth. "Wait a second. I know you! You're that funny-lookin' space kid—the one from the news, right?!"

With a puzzled expression, Yomatri mouthed the words *funny-looking* to himself. He closely examined his clothing, trying to understand where he went wrong. At one point, he took a quick whiff of himself, making the girl laugh.

"Wait, why are you smelling yourself? You don't stink. You're fine. I was just kidding," she added, smiling. Yomatri didn't answer. "What's your name?"

Yomatri cleared his throat, trying his best to keep a straight face. He grabbed a toothpick from a small jar on the table and twiddled it between his fingers. "Name's Yomatri. That's what they do call me nowadays at least."

The girl chuckled and was already amused by his personality. "My name's Miyuki (MY-you-KEY)! Hi, it's nice to meet you."

They each shook hands, instantly forming a friendship.

"That's a pretty cool name; I like that," said Yomatri. "Tell me a little bit about yourself, Miyuki. Do you live here, in Manhattan?"

"No, no, I live with my parents in Queens. I go to high-school there, at Arrowsmith High. Once in a while, I'll come here if I'm really bored or have nothing to do. But I do enjoy the food they serve here too. It's sooo good. To answer your question, though, I live like twenty, twenty-five minutes away from here," she explained.

Yomatri's eyes lit up. "Oh, cool! Hey, I live in Queens too—in Forest Hills."

"Nice," Miyuki said; she tapped her chin while gathering her thoughts. "Ohhh ... how would I describe myself? I really love shopping, dancing, oh and uh, hangin' out with my friends. I'm also a big fan of sports—soccer, tennis, basketball, volleyball—you name it. I don't, uh, know if you know what those are."

"Of course I do," Yomatri responded, looking away. He started to redden. Miyuki caught on to his shyness but didn't say anything.

Suddenly, the two of them were interrupted by a waiter with short black hair who carried a pen and small notepad. With a smile, he said, "Merry Christmas! May I take your order?"

"Oh, we're not ready just yet. Maybe in a few minutes?" Miyuki insisted.

"Sure, not a problem; take your time," the man responded as he walked away.

Turning to Yomatri, Miyuki said, "I just have to say ... that was quite an interesting way to return back to Earth with the whole space pod and everything in Central Park yesterday."

"Wait, did you hear about me on the news? Didn't you say that before or somethin'?"

"Yeah, and I was actually there—at the crash site," she responded, then paused. "I was just wondering, though ... are you from here? Were you born on Earth?"

"Yeah, I mean, as far as I know, unless my parents have been lying to me my whole life and I'm some sort of alien," Yomatri answered. He and the girl grinned at each other.

"But why the pod and everything? Where exactly were you coming from?"

"Space camp. It was this really neat program I took part in that NASA offered when I was younger. Took me a few days to get back home. But I went there for three years … learned a lot … and now, I'm back here on Earth."

Breath taken, Miyuki responded, "Really? That's awesome! Wait, tell me more. What all did you do there?"

"A bunch of different things, really—learning about the planets and whatnot in space … the stars … a lotta training and fighting. I mean, I can tell you all about it whenever really."

"Yeah, you totally should! That's super cool."

"Definitely," Yomatri replied, then paused. "Hey, I know this is totally random of me, not that I'm tryna change the subject or anything, but, uh, are you on winter break or something?"

"Huh? What do you mean?"

"You said you were in school—that you go to high school. Are you on a holiday?"

"Ohhh, yeah, yeah—sorry. I'm on winter break. I don't go back for another week or two, I think."

A brief silence ensued and Yomatri didn't know what to say next. He glanced around awkwardly while Miyuki took out her phone to check her social media.

"So, Yomatri, what are you doin' today, you know, for Christmas?"

"I'm not really sure yet, honestly. Probably nothing."

"That sounds awful. No family coming over or anything? I mean, come on, it's a holiday."

"Nope, don't think so," he responded, shaking his head. "I asked my parents about it before I came here, and they didn't really say much. But I think we're definitely gonna do somethin' for New Year's, though. I'll have to see. What about you? Are you doin' anything today?"

"I don't know, honestly. I'm like you, I guess. My parents are actually out of town, believe it or not. They left just last night. And they won't be back for like another two weeks, which sucks, but hey, what can I do?" Miyuki responded, before there was yet another brief silence.

"Hey, I know this is totally weird of me asking you this since we just met and all … I'm sorry … you don't have to answer this, but ummm, do you wanna go ice-skating with me today by chance?"

"Wait, what do you mean? Like now? Like at this very moment? It's kinda early, don't you think?" said Yomatri.

"Nooo, I mean later in the day, silly. At night or something. I don't want you to be totally bored with your holiday. I mean, you should at least have some fun—unless you have space camp jet lag or somethin'."

"No, no, that sounds good to me." Yomatri giggled. "Did you plan on doing something now, though?"

"Sure, I'd love to! There's lots to do in Manhattan. We could hang out together or something. I really wanted to get out and maybe go to the mall or wherever to spend a few gift cards my family got me as presents. There's actually one not too far from here that's open today, surprisingly. You can come with me if you'd like."

"Don't you think it'd be weird since we just met?"

"No, not really. I mean, you seem pretty cool to me. You're actually kinda cute, too."

Yomatri blushed. "Okay, sure. I'd love to hang out with you, but I'd have to let my parents know first. I kinda forgot how to use this thing already." He pulled out his mother's cell phone. "My dad showed me a little, but there's so much to it."

"Here, I can help you out," Miyuki insisted, offering a hand. "Let's call your parents really quick and exchange numbers. Then, do you wanna hang out?"

"Yeah, sure, that sounds fine," Yomatri replied. Miyuki smiled as she got up from her seat, taking her backpack with her. " ... but wait, weren't you gonna order food or somethin'?"

"I was, but I'm not really that hungry anymore. Plus, I'm here all the time; it doesn't matter. I can come another day. I'd rather hang with you, especially since you're free," Miyuki said as Yomatri also got up. "Here, come on. Let's go before the waiter comes back."

After leaving the bakery, the teens continued down the sidewalk. "Okay, so, Yomatri, what kinds of fun things do you like? Are you into any sports at all? Or maybe reading? I just thought I'd ask to get to know you a little better."

"Oh, no, no. I hate reading. That's probably one of my least favorite things to do. In terms of sports, though, I love all of 'em, really. My favorite would have to be soccer, but my dad despises it."

"Wait, really? Why's that?" she asked with a smirk.

"How would I put this?" Yomatri said; he paused to

gather his thoughts. "I remember he always used to tell me that he doesn't really see the point of watchin' a bunch of grown men kick a ball around for ninety minutes. I mean, he'll watch it sometimes, but if he does and no one scores the whole game, it makes him reeaally angry."

Miyuki snickered and shook her head. "That's ... pretty interesting."

"Yeah. He's more of a basketball guy."

Moments later, the two of them arrived at the girl's car sitting outside in the parking lot. Yomatri's jaw dropped and his face had "awestruck" written all over it. "Whoa!! Is this your car?" He was amazed by the sleek, pearly-white Lexus RX. Examining the vehicle further, he noticed an "I Love Pandas" sticker on its left bumper.

"No, silly, it's my dad's. I'm just borrowing it," Miyuki said, giggling. She took off her backpack and threw it in the backseat, which was littered with plastic drink cups, tossed receipts, and several empty bags of potato chips.

"And he trusts you with this?"

"Yeah, I guess so," the girl replied, shrugging her shoulders. "What about you? Can you drive?"

"No, no, I'm only fifteen. I really wish I could, though. You're so lucky."

Miyuki entered the vehicle and unlocked the passenger door remotely with her keys, letting him inside. "Hey, sorry about the mess," she said, seeming a little embarrassed. "It's not usually like this."

"Oh, it's fine. Doesn't really bother me," Yomatri insisted, putting on his seat belt. "I'm honestly just thrilled to be in such a nice car."

Miyuki smiled. "Alright, well let's go have some fun."

✧✧✧

Later, amidst the hustle and bustle of hundreds of surrounding New Yorkers, the teens walked through a busy shopping center, its length illuminated by strands of glowing lights and other fancy decorations.

Long marble staircases spiraled high to the mall's second and third floors where some parents chased their tireless children. Most people were dressed in hats and heavy winter jackets; some of them spoke on the phone while others chatted with one another.

An enchanting melody played over the speakers and together, Miyuki and Yomatri walked down a narrow stretch with various stores and shops to each side.

His eyes filled with wonder, Yomatri looked all around, studying everything in sight. "This place is amazing! There's so much to see and do. You could like spend an entire day in here."

"Isn't it pretty cool? I love coming here, even when it's not Christmas," Miyuki responded. For a moment, she paused, suddenly noticing a bath and beauty shop down the hall. Pointing, she continued, "Hey, let's go in there really quick."

The teens stepped inside, hit by heady fragrances. An assortment of perfumes, lotions, scented candles, and bottles of soap were stacked on shelves and displays throughout the store. At the front registers, cashiers rung up customer purchases while salespeople assisted guests all around.

"What made you wanna come here?" asked Yomatri.

"My mom loves stuff like this!" Miyuki responded, looking at the various products. "What do you think I should get her?"

"Hmmm ... well, if she's into candles, maybe you could get her one of those. Here, smell this one," he said, taking a lemon lavender one from a high shelf and handing it to her.

"Mmmm! It smells good."

"Yeah. You could also get her some perfume or lotion—there's all sorts of stuff here, really. But I'd just keep it simple."

"That's a good idea," the girl responded. Minutes later, she and her friend returned outside. "That wasn't too bad. Wasn't really that expensive. I think my mom will love it, though."

Yomatri gave a thumbs-up and then, they continued down the hall. At one point, the teens paused in front of a large bookstore, noticing a variety of Nutcracker dolls, packages of candy canes, and different sets of gift wrap on a small table.

Yomatri's eyes shifted to a plastic tin containing an assortment of snacks. "This looks pretty neat. And it's not that much either. Only eight dollars."

Miyuki's eyebrows rose. "My dad loves these things! It's like a little snack tin." She picked it up from the table and pointed at the contents inside. "It's got everything. Peanuts, chocolates, pretzels, candy, popcorn ... oh, I have to buy it."

Yomatri glanced off to one side. "Yeah, I think you

should. That'd be a really nice present for him." He noticed a display of men's wallets atop a small round table. Picking one up, he showed it to Miyuki. "What do you think about these? They look pretty cool, hey?"

"Yeah, but he's already got a nice wallet, I'm pretty sure. What about you, though? Did you get your mom or dad a Christmas gift? If you didn't, I know it's sorta late, but I could pay for you if you want."

"No, no, I didn't, but it's okay; don't worry about it. I'm sure they're just happy I made it home safely from space camp. I'm here to have fun with you."

"Alright," Miyuki said, frowning. She glanced up and paused, noticing children running up and down the hall, some of them with cones of ice-cream in their hand. Pointing, she said, "Hey, look at them! They look like they're havin' a lotta fun."

Next to a video game store, some of the kids huddled around a tall glass cabinet display containing pristine trading cards, action figures, and other toys.

Yomatri sighed, a half-smile on his face. "Man, I miss those days—being able to do whatever you wanted without getting in trouble ... not having to worry about anything, too." He turned his attention away from the kids and faced Miyuki.

"Well, yeah, but I mean, now you can say that you went to space camp, which was really awesome, I bet," the girl said. After a brief silence, she continued, "What do you think about everything so far?"

"You mean like with the mall and stuff?"

"Yes. Are you having fun?"

"Oh, yeah, yeah!" Yomatri replied, then paused. He crossed his arms and glanced around. "The world feels … different."

"What makes you say that?"

"I don't know. Maybe 'different' isn't the right word. I mean, just seein' the kids play and have fun, I feel like there's a lot I've been missing out on while I was away at space camp—you know, simple stuff part of growing up. But so far, I definitely feel a little better about the technology and whatnot. Even getting around the city doesn't seem too bad. I'm kinda remembering bits and pieces here and there from when I was younger."

"Well, that's a good start. I guess I'd just say, don't sweat it too much. I mean, you've only been back for what, a day?"

Yomatri smiled. "Yeah, that's a good way to look at it, actually. Thank you, Miyuki."

"You are welcome."

CHAPTER THREE:

ANCIENT DISCOVERY

After leaving the mall, the teens headed back to Miyuki's car in the parking lot. In the sky above, dark clouds began to form.

"That was a lotta fun, I have to admit. We'll have to go there again sometime," Miyuki said to Yomatri, carrying several shopping bags on her wrists. For a moment she paused to unlock the car remotely with her keys.

"I agree. Here, lemme help you." He took the bags from her and set them down in the backseat.

"Awww, you're so nice. Are you ready to go ice-skating?"

"Yeah, definitely! Let's go."

☆☆☆

Later, Miyuki and Yomatri arrived at a large ice rink in a shadowy Manhattan park. Other people were there out and about with their families, but from where the teens stood, they looked small and unimportant. It was just the two of them, alone, surrounded by dozens of large, snow-covered trees. Vast bright lights illuminated the rink.

"It's a good thing we were able to rent our own skates from the rink," said Yomatri.

"Yeah, I agree," Miyuki responded, now wearing a fuzzy

knit hat and a pair of mittens. Glancing at her smartwatch, she noticed the time was now 7:15 p.m.

After putting on his skates, Yomatri took his friend by the hand and began to skate around the rink with her.

"Wait, so do you know how to skate?" asked Miyuki.

"A little bit. I think I just have to get a feel for it first and then I'll be good."

"Well, here, before you do that, let me show you somethin'. You stand there and watch," the girl insisted. She took the initiative of showing him various tricks of her own that she'd learned when she was younger.

Miyuki performed a variety of flips and slick slides. At certain points, she'd skate faster and faster, getting more daring with each move.

Yomatri eyes lit up. He was impressed.

Minutes later, Miyuki swung back over to him, sounding a bit out of breath. "How was that?" she asked.

"That was great! Where'd you learn all those moves?"

"Awww, thanks. I used to be somewhat of an ice-skater when I was younger. I mean, some of it I forgot, but most of it has kinda stuck with me ever since."

"That's really neat. You should teach me now."

"Here, come on, I'll show you." Miyuki smiled. She took Yomatri by the hand and skated with him for the next half hour.

Yomatri paid close attention to his new friend but couldn't get the hang of most moves. "This is so hard. I'll never learn any of this."

"It takes time, silly. You'll get used to it. Here, come

on, let's keep practicing." Again, she took him by the hand and together, the teenagers skated around the icy rink at a steady pace.

At one point, Miyuki separated from Yomatri who watched her closely. The girl began to increase her speed. "Wait, what are you doing?" he asked, suddenly sounding worried.

"I'm just trying to——" said Miyuki, who began to stumble while skating backwards; she started to lose control of her body and started freaking out. Unable to stop, she collapsed onto the ice with a hard impact, shattering the ground with a *crack*.

"Miyuki, are you okay?!" He hurried over to the injured girl as the ice beneath his blades suddenly began to crackle with each and every step.

Yomatri took another step just a couple feet away from Miyuki, and out of nowhere, his foot caved in. Instantly, he collapsed onto the ice and slid into the water beneath them.

"Yomatri!!" Miyuki shouted, reaching after her friend. The ice surrounding her body began to crack and crack.

Eventually, the ice had given way, and Miyuki too fell down into the water beneath the frozen lake. She screamed for her life, but no one could hear her.

In the water, the two teens were sinking fast. Holding her breath, Miyuki scrambled over to her friend to try and save him. Yomatri noticed the girl coming at him and reached for her but missed.

He panicked as he began to drop lower and lower in the water. Miyuki swam further downward after him. Yomatri was losing air and knew he had to take a breath again.

Simultaneously, Miyuki felt the same desperate urge.

With no other option, they both opened their mouths as their eyes widened. *They'd been able to breathe underwater!* The teenagers stared at one another and tried to swim for the surface.

Abruptly, the water rushed around their bodies and took each of them as if it had a mind of its own. Within seconds, Miyuki and Yomatri were lifted to the surface again.

Their heads shot up, both of them taking big breaths of fresh air. Exhausted, they eyed one other with fearful looks. Yomatri swam to the surrounding ice and was the first to get out, lifting himself up by his elbows.

Standing on even ground, he took Miyuki by the hand and helped her out of the lake. Their bodies were completely drenched and they were in much distress.

Yomatri yelled, "We almost drowned!" He and his friend were shivering. "I can't believe that just happened."

"Yomatri, I ... I'm so sorry!" Miyuki panicked.

He coughed and coughed while trying to regain his breath. "Please ... never take me ice-skating again, Miyuki. After that, I'm done."

"I'm sorry! I didn't know that this would happen."

Yomatri didn't bother to answer but turned to a new subject. "How did we escape that? We were pretty deep in there. I mean, we should be dead! There's no possible explanation."

"I don't know, but you're making me feel bad. Here, give me a hug or something," she begged, tugging at her friend's arm.

Yomatri, who was still frustrated, embraced Miyuki and held on to her tightly. Both of them paused, suddenly noticing that their clothes had quickly dried all by themselves.

Only seconds later, they separated and stopped shivering, realizing their bodies had returned to normal temperatures. The teens gaped at one another and then their clothes, shocked.

"What in the world?" Yomatri said to himself.

"Wh—what just happened?" asked Miyuki. "I ... I'm not that cold anymore! My clothes ... they're not wet!"

"What did we do?" His friend paused for a moment. "Miyuki, say something! We have to find out what's going on. This isn't making any sense." He took her by the hand and started to head off.

The curly-haired girl resisted and stopped on the ice. "What are you doing?! Where are we going?"

"Look, I don't know, but we need to get outta this place! We need to find answers," Yomatri snapped.

Miyuki sighed and gave in to her friend's demands.

Still holding each other's hands, the teens raced to the entrance of the ice rink, returned their skates, and later made it back to the car.

☆☆☆

After driving for a while, Miyuki pulled over along a sidewalk.

"Why'd you stop?"

"I dunno. I think somethin's wrong with my engine.

49

Do you hear that weird noise?" The two of them kept quiet for a second and listened closely, overhearing a series of loud rattles from the vehicle's engine. "That does not sound good at all. But I don't wanna keep driving. We might get into an accident or something."

"What are we gonna do then? We can't just leave your car here. It'll get towed."

"I'm not sure ... ," Miyuki said, her voice trailing off. She turned off the car and tried starting it again. Time after time she pressed the button to turn the vehicle on, but nothing happened. "Ahh—what's happening now?!" she asked with a grimace. "I didn't do anything. I don't know what's going wrong."

Yomatri noticed her starting to panic and tried to remain calm. "Wait, are you sure? Try it again."

"What are you, blind? I'm pressing it over and over—look!" Miyuki snapped; she sighed and felt hopeless. In a matter of seconds, she began to shiver. Even her coat didn't seem to be enough to provide warmth.

"It's okay, it's okay. Just calm down. We can get through this."

"Oh man, it's getting really cold!" Miyuki tried to stay warm by rubbing her hands together. At one point, she pulled out her cell phone and tried calling for help.

Yomatri did the same with his mom's phone, but they had no luck. No matter how hard the teens tried, neither of them could get service. Miyuki checked her smartwatch but noticed it had completely blacked out. Again and again she tapped it nervously, but there was no response.

"What the heck?!"

Meanwhile, Yomatri opened the door on his side and got out. Facing away from the vehicle, he looked up at the clouds. His eyes widened. In the dark winter sky were strange, colorful auroras: blue, green, red, yellow, purple, and orange.

"Where are you going? We have to——" yelled Miyuki.

Yomatri shut the car door. "What on earth is happening?" he whispered to himself, noticing snowflakes which suddenly began to fall from the sky.

Miyuki had gotten out of the vehicle and, while putting on her mittens, went over to her friend. "I'm not even gonna say anything. Nothing at all. That was just really rude of you."

"Wait, Miyuki—look!" Yomatri interrupted, pointing at the sky.

The girl glanced up, her eyes twinkling in wonder. "Whoa! That is pretty cool. Wait, what is that? What's goin' on?"

Out of nowhere, an explosion erupted somewhere far out in the distance. The teens grabbed one another tightly, flinching back.

"Yomatri!!" Miyuki screamed.

"What? What's the problem?" he yelled and turned.

"What do you mean 'what's the problem'? Did you not just hear that loud explosion? Are you deaf?"

"Yes, I did! Why are you going nuts?"

Miyuki stared at her friend with a puzzled look. "Hmm … I don't know. Maybe because we just almost drowned, it's freezing cold, we have absolutely no heat, there's bombs or whatever going off, and I can't get anything to work!! Do you not hear what you're saying? I mean, how can you be so calm during all this?"

"Don't worry. You'll be fine," Yomatri insisted.

All of a sudden, Miyuki's car roared to life. Immediately the teens turned around, their mouths gaping.

"Wh—what just happened? Did your car start all by itself?" Yomatri asked. "I thought something was wrong with it or whatever."

Miyuki shook her head. "I don't know! I'm just as lost as you are. Let's not stand here and ask questions, though. Here, let's get inside."

Both of them hurried over to the SUV. After getting in, they slammed the doors shut, feeling very relieved they at least now had heat. In just seconds, they were off and headed back to Forest Hills.

CHAPTER FOUR:

ARIDNEMEKI AND THE TWELVE KINGDOMS

Later that night, the teens finally made it back to Yomatri's house. Miyuki turned off the car and got out of the vehicle. Yomatri followed her, their breaths clouding as they each raced toward the front porch.

Gently, Yomatri opened the door, and he and his friend entered the house. For a moment, they stood still, trying to catch their breath. Yomatri then looked around for signs of his parents but found nothing.

Miyuki stopped in her tracks and scanned the rooms, noticing how beautiful they were. "This is a really nice home you got here," she said; she seemed much calmer.

"Thanks. My mom will love to hear that." Yomatri chuckled. Miyuki followed him into the kitchen and they stopped near a set of wooden cabinets.

"Where are your parents at?"

"I'm not sure, honestly. When I talked to 'em earlier today, I got the impression that they'd just stay home today, but I guess not. They should be back later, though."

Suddenly, the lights in the house flickered for a moment, and the teenagers paused, overhearing a strange creak coming from another part of the residence.

"What was that?" Miyuki asked worriedly.

"I'm ... not sure," Yomatri answered. "Let's go look." Miyuki joined him as they began heading towards the garage.

After taking a few steps, the teens paused again, then turned to the sound of an unfamiliar female voice: "Please do not be alarmed. There's nothing to be afraid of. We're not here to hurt you. We only want to talk."

Out of the shadows, a tall redheaded woman with long hair and fair skin slowly entered the kitchen from a nearby hallway.

Only seconds later, two other mysterious beings emerged from another hall on the opposite side. One of them was a man with spiky red hair whose left arm was formed entirely out of wood, while another man had robotic-like wings protruding from his back.

Soon after, a lady with short blonde hair wearing a skin-tight red battle-suit approached from the adjacent living room. Beside her was another woman wearing a headband, dressed in a green shirt and black tights. In her hands was a pair of charcoal-colored swords.

Lastly, a woman with short purplish hair wearing a pair of goggles on her forehead appeared out of thin air and stood close to the tall redhead. Simultaneously, the team of warriors slowly approached Miyuki and Yomatri from all sides. In total, there were six of them, and they all appeared extremely powerful.

Their hearts pounding, Miyuki and Yomatri stood still as they locked eyes with the mysterious beings. "Who are you? And how'd you get in?" asked Yomatri.

"My name is Captain Zeron (ZEAR-on). I am the leader of the heroes you see standing before you, Yomatri and Miyuki," the red haired lady said, gesturing to her alien comrades.

Her voice was resonant, and she sounded very calm as if she'd lived on planet Earth long before the birth of light. Dressed almost like a knight, her armor was blue and yellow in color. In her hand was a long metal sword with a golden hilt.

"Okay, I get that, but how'd you get in?"

"Through the, eh, back door. It actually wasn't dat hard," said the man with the wooden arm.

"How do you know our names?" Miyuki asked.

"I'll get to that," responded Captain Zeron. "The reason I've come here is because I have much to tell the two of you. My team and I originate from a planet torn by war, called Aridnemeki (AIR-rid-Nuh-Meh-KEY). And we've come here in search of many powerful items precious to our race."

Standing tall with his arms crossed, the man with the wooden arm spoke in a deep and intimidating voice. "Aye, Zeron, these the kids we been searchin' for?"

Miyuki flinched and grabbed Yomatri by the arm.

"Yes, why?"

"I like 'em already," the man replied with a smirk. Noticing Miyuki backing away even further, he continued, "Don't be scared, young lady. We ain't here to hurt you."

"I don't know if I can trust you. I mean, I only met you a few seconds ago."

The wooden-armed man shook his head. "Alrighty then. Well, I got a sorta weird question for you puny little things: either of you two know how to fight?"

"Yeah? I mean, that's mostly what I learned how to do while I was away at space camp," Yomatri responded.

Captain Zeron nodded as if she knew something.

"And I know I probably don't look like it, but in my free time I study kickboxing and whatnot, so I think I can handle myself," Miyuki explained. Bewildered, she shook her head. "Look, why is any of that important?! You guys need to start explaining yourselves!"

"Or what? You gonna hurt us?" the woman carrying the swords asked.

Miyuki tightened her fist. "I can do that."

Eyebrows raised, Yomatri glanced back and forth between his friend and the sword-wielding lady.

"Enough!" Captain Zeron ordered. Turning to the teens, she continued in a friendly tone, "You can trust us, Miyuki and Yomatri. I promise." She glanced over to the red-battle-suited woman and nodded.

The woman held out her hands as a blue light started to appear from her palms. Suddenly, a large hologram projected from the woman's hands and filled the entire kitchen with a three-dimensional map of a planet very similar to Earth.

Miyuki and Yomatri, completely engrossed, studied the hologram which pictured twelve large continents, each a different color.

"Whoa … ," said Miyuki. "What is all this?"

"My team and I are part of a larger organization—an army of powerful warriors who fight for the good of the galaxy called *the Hero Alliance*," Captain Zeron answered.

Miyuki and Yomatri eyed the alien warriors surrounding them and began to feel a little more comfortable now.

"Yep, and currently, we're fighting a war against a group of vicious and hateful individuals known as *the Aridian Army*," the red-battle-suited woman continued. "Their sole mission is to harm others and cause destruction through violence and torture."

"At first, this war started on our home planet, Aridnemeki, but recently, it's reached your world, Earth," Captain Zeron added. "And we need your help to stop it— to put an end to the threat and restore peace."

"Okay, so how do we go about doing that?" Miyuki asked.

"We need you two, to work together with the Hero Alliance and help us find the powerful items sacred to our people."

"What are they exactly? The items you keep talking about."

"Well, there's twelve of them. Essentially, they're very ancient crystalline rods, and they each contain an extraordinary level of elemental power," the man with the metallic wings explained.

"Wait, hold on a second. I'm lost," Yomatri interrupted. "Also, quick question: where in the world did all of you learn English? Because I am totally blown away!"

The red-battle-suited woman chuckled. "We've picked up radio waves from your planet, Earth. We've been studying it for quite some time now."

His arms crossed, Yomatri looked impressed. "Oh."

"Maybe I can help with your confusion, kid. Here, look at this map," said the woman carrying the swords, pointing to key items projected in the hologram. "So you can see that our world, Aridnemeki, is divided into these twelve large landmasses, okay? They're similar to what I think you humans call 'continents' here on Earth, right?"

"Yeah, that makes sense," replied Yomatri.

"Yep, so on this planet, you guys have seven, I believe. And well, back home, there's twelve of 'em. And we call each of them 'kingdoms.' Pretty easy to understand, right? We differentiate them based on whatever element is central to each kingdom."

"Ohhh, I get it. So, there's twelve kingdoms and twelve crystals. There's one crystal and one elemental force for each kingdom," said Yomatri. "And I'm guessing that these rods or whatever are what maintain the balance in your world?"

"Precisely," the woman carrying the swords answered.

"Okay, so you said there's twelve crystals, meaning one for each kingdom. But then you also mentioned these twelve elemental forces," said Miyuki. "What exactly are the names of the twelve elements?"

"Well, there's a lot actually. There's water, fire, electricity, sky ... which means 'flying' ... shadow, magic, light, wind, metal, healing ... there's also energy and earth," said the purple-haired woman wearing goggles on her forehead.

"Wow, that's a lot to remember." Miyuki chuckled. "What about this conflict, though, or war that you mentioned earlier? How'd that start?"

"Years ago on Aridnemeki, there existed a great time of peace. Together, high-ranking individuals—men and women from all over—ruled the twelve kingdoms," Captain Zeron explained. "They were known as the *Allied Nations*. During that time, the kingdoms worked together to resolve any issues and maintain the peace."

"Yep. But still, in the back of their minds, many of the Aridnemekian people knew that the twelve crystals were what kept the balance and all the power," the woman carrying the swords added.

"And several years later, there was discord within the Allied Nations and nothing could ever get resolved. People turned their backs on them because they felt disrespected and betrayed. So . . . they resorted to another way of getting what they wanted—causing tyranny," said the metal-winged man.

Miyuki shook her head, a look of sorrow on her face. "Oh, that's so evil of them."

"Yes, and it was then that a band of dangerous rebels had formed—*the Aridian Army*."

"They became obsessed with the idea of power and attempted to overthrow the government of the Allied Nations," the red-battle-suited woman said. "However, those who wanted to keep the peace retaliated and united together, becoming *the Hero Alliance*. That's us." She gestured toward her comrades.

Miyuki and Yomatri smiled.

"Eventually, though," the woman with purplish hair and goggles continued, "the Allied Nations was destroyed and forgotten. And now today, it's just become a war between the two sides: *the Hero Alliance* and *the Aridian Army*. But we need the twelve crystals to one day restore balance to the kingdoms of Aridnemeki."

"Whoa ... ," Yomatri and Miyuki said, giving each other impressed looks.

"Yes, so now that you understand the past, it's important that you understand more of the problem," said the Alliance captain. "The problem is that due to the war, these twelve rods have ended up here, somewhere on Earth. And we need you two to help us retrieve them. You see, if these ancient weapons end up in the hands of our enemy, we're doomed. There's no hope for Earth or Aridnemeki at that point."

"I'm not liking the sound of that," said Yomatri. "The part where *we* have to get them back."

"Well, of course, fighting a war will not be easy. It'll be scary for sure. But we'll keep you both protected. We can also help you both grow and learn over time," Captain Zeron replied. "My master has chosen you two to help the Hero Alliance."

"I don't know." Yomatri scratched his head.

"It's a lot to take in, I know. But understand that a war now threatens the Earth, and we desperately need to do something to stop it."

Miyuki was curious. "Who's your master?"

"He's a powerful and honorable man named Master Zorhins who's also the leader of the Hero Alliance. At the moment, he lives on a rocky island a few miles out from the city of New York with close to seven hundred stranded Aridnemekians. We call it, 'Ember Island'."

"What do you mean *stranded*?"

"When the conflict on Aridnemeki was getting to be too much, the crystals were sent out into space to save our planet from further destruction. Many of the Aridnemekian people, though not all, were forced to come to Earth and relocate, some of them to different continents around the world."

The man with the metallic wings added, "For us, it's impossible to get back to Aridnemeki, even with a spacecraft or ship of some sort. There's too many harmful energy fields present in outer space, given off by the twelve crystals as they traveled. The only way back to our world now is through teleportation or means of a space bridge."

Yomatri interrupted everyone, sounding doubtful. "I don't know if I can do this. Miyuki, I don't know what you're thinkin' but, I mean, who am I supposed to fight? And where am I gonna find these crystals?"

The man with the wooden arm spoke up. "Listen, kid, we're in the same position as you. We also ain't sure where any of da crystals are. And we don't know what da future will hold. We wouldn't've come all this way if we didn't think you and Miyuki could help us. Destiny's chosen you two to defend the world against a great evil."

After the woman in the red battle-suit turned off the projected hologram, a brief silence filled the room.

"So, what do you say ... about helping us?" Captain Zeron asked the teens.

Miyuki and Yomatri stared at each other, uncertain. Together, they inched away from the Aridnemekian warriors to form a huddle.

"Why are we huddling?" Miyuki whispered nervously. "We're only like twenty feet away from them."

The metal-winged man shook his head, grinning.

"I dunno. I think it looks cool. It also shows we're interested and thinking critically," Yomatri responded. Miyuki began to laugh. "Why are you giggling? This is serious."

Captain Zeron and her allies glanced at one another with very confused looks.

"Well, what do you think? Do you wanna help them?"

Yomatri took a deep breath. "Sure, I think it'd be fun. Maybe I was just overthinking earlier."

"Alright." She and her friend turned to face Captain Zeron. Standing side by side, the teens stared at the woman intently.

"We've decided that we'll help you. We wanna join you and the Alliance on your mission to help save the world. And we're willing to do whatever it takes," said Yomatri.

The Alliance captain glanced at Miyuki, who nodded. Immediately, the five warriors standing beside Zeron erupted in a series of cheers. The teens smiled at each other, feeling very relieved that they were doing something for the good of mankind.

"Thank you, Yomatri and Miyuki. This really means a lot to my people—honestly."

"You're very welcome," they both replied.

Suddenly, the Aridnemekians were interrupted by a ringing noise.

Captain Zeron took out a small round device from her

back pocket. "Oh, shoot. Master Zorhins wants us back at the island. Guys, we have to get going."

The five squad members clearly understood the situation and walked with their captain, who headed over to a window in the kitchen.

"Wait!" Yomatri stammered. "I just thought about something. You guys probably all possess some sort of cool elemental power. I mean, look at you. You guys are awesome. But what about me and Miyuki?"

"You already possess your elemental abilities. Your job now is to discover them," the Alliance captain replied.

"Wait, what? Wh—when did that happen? Tell me!"

"Those answers are for you to figure out."

Yomatri paused and stopped insisting. "Please don't tell me you guys are exiting through that window," he whispered to himself.

Moving her arms around in a graceful, circular motion, Captain Zeron conjured a ball of purplish energy which expanded into a round portal, leading to an unknown destination.

"Wait!" Yomatri called out. The team of Aridnemekian warriors turned around, confused. "You're leaving?"

"Yes, I'm sorry, Yomatri and Miyuki, but we must get going," the Alliance captain responded.

"But I don't even know what to do next or where to go," Yomatri fussed. "How's my journey supposed to begin exactly?"

"I want you to figure that out." Her smile flickered. "I trust you both very much and definitely believe you guys have what it takes to help us. Don't worry, this won't be the last time we see each other. I wish you both luck in your journey as you start your new life as heroes."

With a doubtful expression, Yomatri turned to Miyuki, who suddenly didn't seem so happy either.

Captain Zeron smiled back at the teens one last time before leaving through the portal. Waving good-bye, her comrades followed her, and in a matter of seconds, the team of Aridnemekian heroes had disappeared completely.

The portal faded into thin air, leaving the teens alone in the kitchen. Yomatri didn't like the idea of having to gather the twelve crystals with only the help of one other person. Although he was very worried, he knew the mission would be challenging but not impossible.

He watched Miyuki, who went over to the window where the Aridnemekians had disappeared, finding a partially torn, rolled-up piece of parchment on the floor. It looked thin and fragile, as if it were a thousand years old. Cautiously, she knelt down and picked it up, then showed it to her friend.

Yomatri also knelt down.

"What's this?" she asked herself.

"I don't know. Looks a little strange."

Miyuki unraveled a map with her friend beside her. They each studied it closely but couldn't understand a single word on it.

"Wait, this is New York, isn't it?" Miyuki exclaimed, coming to her senses. "Yomatri, this is a map of New York State!" She noticed several red markers placed in various locations around the state, while one marker out in the ocean in the corner of the map was green.

"Do you think Captain Zeron left this behind on purpose?" he asked, curious. Miyuki shrugged her shoulders. Pointing at the green marker, Yomatri continued, "Wait, why is this one a different color? All the other ones are red."

"I'm not really sure," responded Miyuki. "Maybe it means that that area is safe or something."

"Possibly. But wait." Yomatri shook his head. "Back to Captain Zeron for a sec. What do you think she meant by our powers? When did we discover them?"

"I have no idea. I honestly didn't understand that either," she replied, yawning. Briefly, she checked her smartwatch. "Excuse me. I'm feelin' really tired all of a sudden. I guess it is getting late."

"Whaaat? Miyuki, you don't sound happy at all. I mean, look at us! We're superheroes!"

The curly-haired girl stared at him incredulously. "Weren't you the one cryin' about having to help them save the world?" Suddenly, her phone started to vibrate. Pulling it out of her pocket, she immediately checked her text messages.

"What happened?"

"Oh, nothing. It's just my mom. She texted me asking where I'm at. Even though she and my dad are outta town, they always check to make sure I'm home by a certain time. It's pretty stupid, I know."

Yomatri chuckled. "That's adorable."

Miyuki rolled her eyes and mimicked him.

From outside, a wailing police siren could be heard in

the distance. The teens rose and rushed over to a row of windows in the living room and peeked outside. Together, they tried to figure out where the siren was coming from but had no luck.

Everything around them suddenly became silent.

Miyuki and Yomatri eyed each other warily, and it began to dawn upon them that war was looming.

They shared a warm hug.

Miyuki took a deep breath. "So, uh, I guess this is where it all begins, buddy," she said, gently rubbing her friend's back.

"Yeah, I think you're right. It definitely feels like it'll be a lot to take on, but I think we can do this."

The teens smiled at one another, trying to stay positive.

"I think so too. But hey, I'll catch up with you later. I've really gotta get going or my parents are gonna freak out," Miyuki said. Both of them headed for the front door. "I'll keep the map for right now. Sound good?"

"Yeah, that's fine. Do you think your dad's car is safe to drive, you know, considering what happened earlier?"

"I hope so. I don't think it was too bad, but then again, I don't really know. I'm gonna get it checked out, though, just to be safe. There's a guy I know I can take it to. He and my dad are good friends."

"Alright. Well, I'll, uh, see you soon, I guess."

Yomatri waved good-bye to his new friend and closed the door as she headed to her father's car. Moments later, he went upstairs to his room, gently shutting the door behind him. After grabbing a pair of earbuds from his desk drawer, he connected them to Miya's phone.

Stressed out, the teen crashed onto the bed, then started listening to music. He closed his eyes and tried his best to fall asleep, knowing his life was now forever changed.

CHAPTER FIVE:

KEEPING IT A SECRET

A few days later ...

Early one afternoon, while lying in his bed, Yomatri woke to a loud ringing noise. He reached over with one arm and shut off his alarm clock.

"Oh, shut up," he said, annoyed.

Moments later, the teenager sat up, knocking the covers off, and rubbed his eyes. As he yawned, he glanced at his alarm clock, seeing that it read 12:30 p.m. He then turned his attention to his closet nearby, noticing his backpack leaning in the doorway. Beside it was the rusty metal staff he'd taken home from space camp.

Yomatri smiled, then got up and walked over to the closet. Kneeling down, he slowly unzipped his backpack and took out a small leather hat with the words "Space Camp Federation" sewn into the side of it.

He also took out a set of old photos, some of them depicting himself, Admiral Kaiser, and many different alien creatures. Other photos showed him having fun during a birthday celebration up in outer space.

Yomatri sighed. "Man, I miss those days so much."

He glanced at his staff and took the battered weapon from the ground, then stood up. After twirling it around again and again, the teen continued to feel sad that his journey in space was now over.

Suddenly, his bedroom door opened. His mother paused with a surprised look.

"Oh, hi, honey. I just came to check up on you. What, uh, were you doing?" Miya asked, curious. Lowering his staff, her son looked away and didn't answer. "Is everything alright?"

Yomatri paused to think. "Yeah, I'm fine. I was just, um, thinkin' about space camp. You probably already know this, but I just really miss it sometimes, you know?"

"Awww, I'm sorry to hear that. Is there anything I can do? Did you maybe wanna talk about it?"

"No, not really," he responded, glancing down.

Miya frowned; she walked over and pulled her son into a warm embrace. "It's okay to feel down about it, honey. But I promise you ... things'll get better. Maybe not right now, but they will. I'm sure of it," she said, her expression hopeful.

"Alright," the teen replied, his eyes slowly shifting away from his mother. He turned and leaned his staff against the wall.

Miya continued, "If there's anything I can do, you know I'm always here for you. Your father too."

Yomatri nodded solemnly. "Yeah, for sure."

Moments later, he headed downstairs into the kitchen where Miya prepared a sandwich with bacon, lettuce, tomatoes, and mayonnaise. As usual, her husband sat at the dining table, reading the daily newspaper with a cup of hot coffee at his side. It was something he loved doing in the morning, as most fathers did.

Luke glanced up. "There he is!"

"Hey, Dad," Yomatri answered with a faint smile, sitting down across from his father.

Luke paused for a moment, studying his son. He took a sip of his coffee, then asked, "Everything okay?"

"Yeah, I'm fine—just a little tired, I guess."

Luke glanced at his wife with an unsure look.

Miya walked over to her son and set down a plate in front of him with the sandwich and a side of chips on it. "I made you a small lunch. All yours," she said, smiling. "Your father and I already ate."

"Thanks, Mom."

Miya nodded, then turned away and headed over to the fridge and grabbed one of the juice jugs from inside.

"Are you sure you're alright, kiddo?" Luke asked, his expression still uneasy. Yomatri took a bite of his sandwich. "I mean, not to be mean or anything, but you've kinda been sitting in your room a lot these past few days and haven't really spoken to me and your mom that much. Did somethin' happen?"

"No, no, I'm fine, honestly. I guess I'm still just, uh, coming to terms with Earth's way of life and whatnot after being away from it so long."

There was a short pause.

"Well, don't feel too bad about it, champ. I'm sure

you'll get used it pretty soon. Just ... give it some time," Luke said, giving his son a pat on the back. "By that way, I wanted to ask you—how was Christmas? Your mom and I have been so busy with other things that we never really got to talk to you about it."

Yomatri's heart dropped. "It was good, I guess," he said, his fingers fidgeting on his sandwich. He took another bite.

"Well, that's good to hear. Did you have fun with whatever you were doing? What did you actually end up doin'?" Luke chuckled. "I'm sorry, I don't mean to get all up in your business."

Yomatri tried to keep himself from laughing; he seemed a little happier. "No, no, it's okay. I was just, uh, exploring the city, really. Nothin' too big. But it was cool seein' all the tall buildings and whatnot again."

"Oh, nice!" Miya said, pouring herself a glass of juice. "We'll have to go out again like we used to when you were younger. Those were some fun times, actually. Did you by chance meet any new friends?"

Yomatri scratched his ear nervously. "Um ... no. I really wish I did, though. I guess I'll have to go out into the city again today to better my chances," he smirked. "Would it be okay if I did that actually? After I finish eating? There's still so much I wanna see."

"Yeah, uh, that should be fine. I'm sure your dad wouldn't have a problem with it," Miya said, glancing at her husband.

Luke shrugged his shoulders and turned to his wife. "Hey, the kid made it home safe, had fun, and didn't get into any trouble. I mean, what more could you ask for?" He and his son locked eyes. "He's got my ticket of trust if you ask me."

A half-smile on his face, Yomatri responded, "Thanks, Dad."

✿✿✿

Later that afternoon on an overpass, a long train winded its way along a narrow metal track. In one of the crowded passenger cars, seated beside a woman listening to music, Yomatri stared out a nearby window, his mouth agape. In the distance were rows of skyscrapers and other tall buildings with trees that appeared tiny mixed in between. A light snowfall fluttered down.

Gently, the train came to a stop at a busy platform within minutes. Yomatri stepped off as passengers entered and exited the vehicle all around him. For a moment, he glanced around, his eyes soon narrowing in on a sign that read "exit."

Eventually, he made it to Central Park and ran up to Miyuki, meeting her along a stone pathway lined with many tall trees, bushes, and other plants.

"Hey, there you are! It's so good to see you," Yomatri said, sharing a warm hug with her.

"Yeah, same! Glad you made it," the girl responded, dressed in a winter coat and tight jeans.

"Did you get your dad's car fixed?"

"I did. It actually wasn't that bad, but I told my parents about it, and they're fine."

Around the two teens, people were out and about

with their families, walking and chatting. Nearby, children chased one another with large sticks. A few of them worked together to build snowmen while others formed angels in the snow with their bodies.

The teens walked over to a small pond where they could chat in private.

"Hey, you remember when Captain Zeron mentioned that we already have our powers or whatever?" asked Yomatri.

"Yeah, but like I said, I didn't really understand it when she said it. I guess we just have to find out somehow and see what they actually are?"

"Probably."

"Try something, I guess—anything you can think of," Miyuki suggested. "Maybe it'll trigger them?"

"Alright, lemme see," said Yomatri. After checking to make sure no one was watching him, he turned toward the pond and held out both hands in front of him.

He waved them from left to right as small bursts of water formed just feet away, spurting into the cold air. One by one, the water droplets splashed on top of the icy pond.

"Whoa!!" the teenagers exclaimed.

Miyuki stammered, "Wait, hold on. That was awesome! I wanna try that." Like her friend, the girl pointed her hands out toward the pond but closed her eyes. She waved her arms left to right and thought of heat while doing so.

As she opened her eyes, the thick ice from the pond slowly melted and shattered, warm water flowing around it. Many people looked over but hadn't realized what just happened.

Breath taken, the teens exchanged excited looks. Together, they ran and hid behind a row of tall trees to continue their learning.

"Alright, whatever you did back there was so cool. I just really hope no one saw us," Yomatri said, catching his breath.

"Me too. That would not be good."

"I'm gonna try something else really quick."

Yomatri closed his eyes and creased his brow. His concentrated expression had relaxed after a moment, and a light breeze fluttered wisps of the teen's spiky brown hair. Imagining flying birds, he began to feel himself lifting a few feet off the ground.

"Whaaat?" Miyuki said, looking up at him while trying to keep her voice down. "How are you doing that, dude? You'd better get down from there before someone sees you!"

"I—I don't know … umm … just try to think of yourself flying or something!" replied Yomatri. "That's what I did."

Miyuki gulped; she closed her eyes, falling into deep thought. After a moment, she opened them and began to float in the air beside her friend. Struggling to stay afloat, she crashed into him. The teens stumbled to the ground and burst into laughter.

Both of them quickly rose and positioned themselves several feet apart. Miyuki slashed at the air as clumps of snow lifted from the icy ground and made their way to her friend.

Swiftly, Yomatri blocked a barrage of snowballs. Grinning, he playfully fired some of his own her way.

Miyuki jumped aside, then rose and kicked at the air. A rocket of snow fired its way toward her friend and Yomatri blocked the attack, bracing his arms up toward his face.

Mischievously, the teens had a quick snowball fight, using their newfound abilities to help them attack and defend. Water and snow splashed all around as they each fought hard, learning more about their powers by the second.

Together, they came closer and closer with their attacks until they stopped to catch their breath, falling into each other's arms. "Phew! That was a lotta fun, I have to admit," said Yomatri.

"Yeah. We're gonna have to keep this a secret from our parents for sure."

CHAPTER SIX:

BIRTH OF A HERO

Later, the teens walked through the park together.

"It's really awesome that we have these new powers," said Miyuki. "I wanna keep testing 'em already."

Yomatri responded, "Yeah, I agree, but part of me is still wondering how and when exactly we got them."

"I think I know," Miyuki said. She and her friend came to a stop and faced each other. "Do you remember when we were ice-skating a few days ago and almost drowned?"

"Yeah ... what about it?"

"Well, remember when my car was being really weird and we got out, and we saw all those strange lights in the sky?" she asked. Yomatri nodded. "And then Captain Zeron was talkin' about the twelve crystals or whatever that are special to their planet?"

"Yep—Aridnemeki, right?"

"Yes. My guess is that those lights were some sort of energy fields given off by the twelve crystals or something. And when we went down in the lake, our bodies must've adapted to the elements and helped save us from drowning. It's the only possible explanation."

"Stop it. There's no way that can be true."

"Oh yeah? You got any better ideas, mister?" Miyuki asked him with a smirk.

"I'll let you know if I think of any. But, no, seriously—how would she have known that that was the moment we received them or whatever? There's gotta be more to it. I mean, she wasn't actually there with us that night."

"I . . . don't really know, honestly. Now that you bring that up, that is a good point," Miyuki replied; she and her friend turned and made their way into the city. Minutes later, they stopped at a street corner. "Hey, I just thought about it—you still haven't told me about any of your space camp stories."

"What do you wanna know exactly?"

"Anything! I know this is probably a really dumb question, but was space camp like a boys-only thing?"

Yomatri snickered. "No, no, there were definitely girls there, both alien and human. But of course, the dorms we lived in, they were separated by gender."

"Ohhh, okay. Well, that makes sense. Were you allowed to date at all? Or were things sort of really strict?" Miyuki shrugged her shoulders. "I don't know . . . it's just a random question that popped in my head."

Grinning, Yomatri scratched his head. "Yes, you could date, which actually surprised me too. But if you did, it was always best to date someone who was, you know, human."

"Yeah, that's a good point when you think about it. I don't really know how being in a relationship with someone from like Mars would go."

The teens shared a laugh.

Suddenly, Miyuki was interrupted by something, and Yomatri noticed as she paused. Looking up at the sky, the girl's mouth dropped open. Her face seemed devastated, her eyes widening as she glanced at Yomatri.

Studying the sky again, Miyuki grew more and more nervous. "Hey, what are you, uh, lookin' at? What's wrong?" her friend asked anxiously.

"That," Miyuki said, pointing. She was so focused on the sky that she couldn't say anything else.

Yomatri glanced up. He noticed several dark clouds forming, but within seconds, he and his friend observed something new. In the distance, four alien pods, similar to the one Yomatri used to get back to Earth, appeared and seemed to be heading for the city.

Swiftly, the four pods picked up speed.

Hundreds of pedestrians paused in the crowded streets, overhearing the immense roar of the approaching projectiles. One of the pods crashed onto a snowy street with a massive impact, barely missing a few New Yorkers.

Large chunks of concrete were blown high into the air, pelting civilians and damaging neighboring buildings. In no time, groups of people were helping each other get up and escape the danger.

In the streets, several drivers had slammed on their brakes and put their cars in park. One after another, they rushed out of their vehicles, abandoning them. More and more citizens joined to help one another. Together they ran away, fearful of a sudden attack.

A second fireball came down and smashed into a car, ripping it apart as if it were a toy. The vehicle was engulfed in massive flames, causing a fiery explosion.

Various chunks of the now-destroyed car were thrown high up, and bits of glass and pieces of the vehicle began to hit fleeing pedestrians. Some of the civilians were struck as they dropped to their feet, unable to move.

Staring at the chaos, Miyuki noticed a woman with a bloody gash in her leg from a large piece of glass. The woman cried out, shaking intensely. Beside her was a man desperately trying to attend to her wound even with specks of blood on his own body.

Miyuki was shocked, unable to comprehend the scene unfolding right before her eyes. As pandemonium ensued, wailing police cars and ambulance sirens could be heard in the distance.

Not even a minute later, the third pod smashed down onto a sidewalk just outside a bakery, blowing its front windows inward. Inside, several waiters and waitresses, dressed in their white shirts and green aprons, were knocked backward by the force of the blast.

Eating utensils and food trays clattered against the wooden furniture. Parents embraced their scared children, desperate to make sure they were okay. Outside, the sidewalk had been completely demolished, small fires beginning to burn.

Near a bookstore, the fourth alien pod smashed into a group of parked cars, exploding on impact. Miyuki and Yomatri—only several feet away—were thrown back by the blast, the roar so loud that suddenly, neither of them could hear anything. In midair, Yomatri noticed his friend's eyes were closed.

Both teens were hit in the face by snow and bits of concrete as they crashed to the ground. Yomatri rose slowly, mustering just enough energy to get up. He looked at Miyuki, who was lying motionless on the street amongst dust and rubble.

His heart beginning to pound, the teen knew he had to help her even if it meant risking his own life. Yomatri rushed over to her, noticing his hearing had returned.

For a moment, he turned and glanced around to survey his surroundings. While panicked civilians continued to flee, police officers and firemen scrambled to the scene, hurrying to evacuate everyone to safety. SWAT officers, armed with heavy assault rifles, acted as backup.

In the distance, a dark figure had emerged from the shadows, standing in the middle of the street. Glaring as if it were after them, the figure paced slowly toward the teens.

Nervous, Yomatri turned back to Miyuki and began to pull her up. Putting one of her arms over his shoulder, he wrapped his own arm around her back. Eventually, Yomatri got his friend over to the side of a building. After gently leaning her against the brick wall, he kneeled down.

"Come on, Miyuki. I really need your help," the teen begged, shaking her left and right.

It took a good minute, but Miyuki finally woke after her friend had smacked her in the face so hard it left a red handprint on her cold cheek. Her vision was blurry for a second but returned to normal.

Noticing Yomatri's adorable face aside from everything else, Miyuki instantly hugged him, feeling a great surge of relief. "Oh my God, Yomatri! What's happening?" she said, her lips trembling.

"Good, you're awake. Now you can help me," the boy calmly responded. For a moment he seemed untroubled but grew more serious. "Look, I'm not sure what's goin' on, but I do know that we need to get those people to safety!"

He pointed to the fleeing pedestrians.

Miyuki turned around the corner of the building and peered down the middle of the intersection. Her eyes widened. Thick black smoke had billowed high into the air, coming from the fires caused by the crashed pods.

Squinting, she noticed the humanoid figure from earlier, now accompanied by a small team of soldiers. In his hand was a pointy, black scepter. Sporting a hooded uniform and a tattered leather cape, the humanoid looked much like a vicious sorcerer.

After a moment, the heavy clouds of smoke began to subside. Dressed in dark protective armor, the group of attacking soldiers carried long spears, scimitars, and swords. Like their captain, the dreadful sorcerer, they seemed intent only on killing and causing harm.

Together, the malevolent invaders marched onto the street without hesitation.

Yomatri turned to Miyuki. "We're gonna have to split up. I'll distract them, and you go and help those people find safety," he instructed, pointing again to nearby pedestrians. "I'm sorry, but you're in no condition to fight!"

Hiding back tears, Miyuki tried to show her friend that she was still brave. After giving him a quick hug, the girl raced to her feet and ran toward the fleeing civilians.

Yomatri stood up and glared at the band of soldiers in front of him. All alone, it was now time for him to do his part. Instilling terror, the evil sorcerer Shinzuki (SHIN-zoo-KEY) took command of the city streets. A dark facemask obscured the lower portion of his face.

Leading the attack, Shinzuki spoke to one of his men

in a deep, thunderous tone. "Alright, our target has been found. He's powerless, so we should have a clear shot at capturing him. I want there to be no mistakes. Go out and get him. Now!"

Near Yomatri's position, a police chopper hovered over the battleground. Using cables attached to long ropes, four armed police dropped to the streets. One by one, they detached their cables from the ropes and quickly readied their weapons for a fight.

Together, the officers worked as a team, surveying the area and neighboring rooftops to try to find trapped civilians or possible hostiles. After the "okay" was given, the men aimed their rifles at Shinzuki and his soldiers, who were several feet away.

Directly behind the four-man officer team, several police squad cars came to a halt, arranged so as to block off a portion of the street. More officers had stepped out from each vehicle and rushed over to their colleagues. Aiming their weapons, the men were ready to engage at any moment.

Yomatri, who was still hiding behind the brick building, looked on, impressed. Only seconds later, one of the officers had spotted him.

"Hey, kid! What are you doin' over there? You need to get to safety!" the man shouted.

The other officers turned.

Yomatri had emerged and dashed behind an abandoned car nearby, ignoring the man's demands. Immediately, two energy missiles shot toward the distracted officers. Fearful, Yomatri cried out and closed his eyes tightly, bracing his arms against his face.

He suddenly paused, noticing he wasn't feeling any

pain. Opening his eyes slowly, the teen became shocked by what was out in front of him. Miraculously, he'd protected himself and the officers with a large, thick body of ice.

A big smile had formed on the teen's face before realizing he'd forgotten about Shinzuki's second missile, which slammed into the police helicopter hovering over the battleground.

Having lost control, the pilots shouted in fear and the chopper spun off, maneuvering in continuous circles. As it plummeted, Yomatri turned back and leaped over the back end of a taxicab parked along the sidewalk. He crashed down into a pile of snow, safe for now.

Not even a second later, the helicopter smashed onto the street just in front of the armed officers. Its engine erupted in a mass of fire and smoke, the tail-rotor and propellers snapping off. Both of the pilots remained in the cockpit seats, motionless. They had been killed.

Peering over the back end of the taxicab, Yomatri stared at the catastrophe, horrified. He'd realized how relentless Shinzuki truly was but was also shocked by his own ability to effectively control ice and water.

Overhearing numerous gunshots, the teen flinched and covered his head. The officers unleashed a storm of bullets at the sorcerer and his men. Echoing all around was the roar of gunfire, and this was just the start of a grueling battle.

Yomatri glanced up, his mouth agape. It seemed that the bullets didn't affect the enemy invaders. The teen squinted, noticing his attackers appeared to use elemental shields to their advantage.

While trying to reload his rifle, thick snow and ice

smashed into one of the officers. Two other police were thrown into the air, snow and ice pushing up beneath their feet. One soldier pressed forward, using a dark magical force to throw the last officer backward into the nearby bakery.

The man crashed through the last remaining window, scattering broken glass as he dropped his weapon onto the floor. Their guns now jammed, there was nothing more the men could do. Together, they began to flee for safety.

Peering ahead, Yomatri wore a look of stunned disbelief. His eyes widened as a large blast of water rushed at him, but the teen dropped to the ground just in time. He'd outstretched his hand, summoning snow into his palm, which quickly formed into a sturdy, icy boomerang.

He gasped. "I don't know how I just did that, but we are not gonna ask questions right now!"

The teen stood up and hurled his weapon toward the enemy soldiers, clipping two of them in the head. Yomatri grinned and soon enough, the boomerang had returned to his possession. Tossing the weapon aside, he continued onward, racing toward Shinzuki, who stood firm.

Yomatri threw a punch at the man, barely missing him. The two of them fought rapidly, striking with swift punches and kicks. Abruptly, Shinzuki brought out his scepter and fired the weapon at Yomatri, who quickly formed an ice shield and braced himself with it.

Again the sorcerer fired with his scepter, but this time, the shot was too strong for his opponent.

A forceful blast of elemental energy had shattered Yomatri's shield to pieces. Shinzuki growled, unleashing a third burst of energy at the now-defenseless hero, knocking him backward.

Yomatri crashed into a parked vehicle and collapsed onto the snowy street. His body was scratched up, and he was in much pain. Trying to recover and catch his breath, he glanced up shakily, noticing the sorcerer had begun preparing yet another, more powerful attack.

"There's no stoppin' this guy," the teen said, staggering to his feet. Exhausted, he began to flee from his assailant. Behind him, pointy shards of ice pierced the dense metal of the parked car, barely missing the boy.

Clumsily, Yomatri slipped on the ice and fell to his knees. He quickly turned around, his heart pounding as he met the sorcerer face to face. Desperate, the teenager threw a punch at his opponent's head, but his attack was instantly countered.

The invader grabbed Yomatri's wrist, clenching it tightly. Knowing he was trapped, the boy screamed in pain. Shinzuki cackled and gripped the teen's other wrist.

With an opponent nearly three times his size, Yomatri was bewildered as to what to do. Again and again he kicked at the sorcerer's legs, but nothing seemed to affect him.

Civilians watched in horror.

Positioning the teen's body toward the bakery, Shinzuki had kicked him in the stomach at full strength. The teen flew back, stumbling on shards of broken glass as he crashed into the bakery with a hard impact. Knocking furniture aside, he landed beside the police officer who'd been wounded from the earlier attack.

His vision partially blurred, Yomatri took a deep breath and peered before himself, noticing turned-over tables and chairs lying all around. Outside, many abandoned cars and taxicabs were scattered throughout the wrecked streets. Tiny embers from the fires burning along the sidewalk had floated into the bakery.

Eyebrows raised, Yomatri knew time was running out and that he had to act quickly. He glanced down, noticing for the first time his leg was stuck under a large wooden post.

The teen shifted his gaze up at Shinzuki, his lip specked with blood. Around the sorcerer, groups of terrified civilians were threatened by the weaponry of the enemy invaders.

Yet again, Shinzuki took out his scepter and lowered it to a comfortable grip. Flanked by his eight remaining troops, the menacing sorcerer began to converge on the ruined bakery.

Using nearly all his strength, Yomatri lifted the wooden post off his leg and staggered to his feet, limping. Suddenly, two soldiers grabbed the teen by his arms and brought him before Shinzuki, dropping him to his knees.

A brief silence filled the air as the hooded invader stared into the teen's eyes. "Ahhh … so you're the boy the Alliance has desperately been searching for," the sorcerer said with a malicious grin.

Yomatri's heart pounded. "Who are you and what do you want?"

There was no response.

Shinzuki threw a forceful punch at his opponent. Weakened, the teen was unable to respond and defend himself. Out of nowhere, dense clumps of snow had formed into a large body of ice directly in front of him.

Startled, Yomatri was unable to move. More snow from the ground quickly formed into two shards of ice which levitated in the air. His eyes wide, he watched as the two shards impaled the soldiers holding him captive.

Angered, Shinzuki asked, "Who are you?!"

"An ally of Yomatri," a female voice responded.

Instantly, Yomatri recognized the voice. He turned and saw Miyuki, her forehead beaded with sweat. "You ignored my orders."

"Well, you were in trouble, so I thought I'd come back and help," she responded, smiling. Turning to Shinzuki, Miyuki was the first to attack as she rushed at him. The girl kicked and punched, landing several fierce blows.

At one point, the sorcerer caught Miyuki's leg and forcefully threw her onto the sidewalk just outside the bakery. Immediately after, he fired a ball of dark energy at the girl, just barely missing her.

Miyuki scurried back onto her feet. His face reddening, Shinzuki unleashed his scepter and fired numerous blasts of energy again and again but was unable to hit her every time.

"Ahh—I don't really know what I'm doing!" Miyuki panicked. Throwing both of her hands forward, she managed to encase her opponent's scepter in a thick coat of heavy ice.

In one swift motion, she knocked the weapon from his grasp, causing him to lose the upper hand. Shinzuki growled and threw a punch, which Miyuki intercepted as she thrust his hand down, stopping his attack.

Gritting her teeth, Miyuki punched him square in the

jaw. Yomatri dashed toward the sorcerer and assisted his friend, landing several lightning-fast blows. At one point, he delivered a powerful roundhouse kick, knocking Shinzuki to the ground.

The invader seemed to recover quickly. Standing up, he hurled a shadowy missile at Yomatri. In a flash, snow had formed on the teen's hands, hardening into thick ice. Brushing the energy rocket aside, Yomatri ran at his opponent once more.

Both of them fought fiercely, blocking and attacking in turn. Yomatri managed to gain the upper hand, using his water abilities to further assist him in the battle. For a moment, a flurry of snow had blocked the sorcerer's view, allowing Miyuki and Yomatri to deliver the perfect counterattack.

Together, the teens joined forces and socked their opponent in the jaw, knocking him back. Again the invader seemed to recover quickly as he stood up and hurled a spiraling bolt of dark magic at Miyuki. With poise, she dodged the man's missile and attacked full force.

Shinzuki fought back, punching right through continuous water blasts of water from the girl. At one point, he drew his scepter toward him, grabbing it as it flew in the air. Using his elements, he melted the ice encasing his weapon and slashed at Miyuki, who braced her arms up against her face.

From left and right, two pillars of dense ice rocketed out of the ground, but her opponent's scepter had slashed right through them. Taken by surprise, Miyuki was knocked down into the snow by the sorcerer.

Wincing, she landed shoulder first but managed to get up only seconds later. Again Shinzuki fired a powerful burst of shadowy energy at the girl with his scepter, knocking her right back down.

After placing his weapon into a back-holster, the sorcerer punched at Miyuki, who managed to grab the man's hand and stop the oncoming blow.

Unimpressed, Shinzuki used his other hand to bash the curly-haired girl across the face. Heavily exhausted, Miyuki couldn't withstand the punch; she collapsed to her knees, soon falling unconscious in the snow with her hair disheveled.

"Miyuki!!" Yomatri shouted.

Turning to Yomatri, Shinzuki began pacing slowly toward him. With the sorcerer now a safe distance away, several individuals standing nearby had rushed in to help the beaten girl from the ground. Yomatri angrily looked away and continued the fight, running head on at the remaining soldiers Shinzuki had brought with him. Having landed several fierce kicks and punches, the teen managed to steal two broadswords from one of the men.

Skillfully, he clashed weapons with his attacker, while just a few feet away, Shinzuki paused to catch his breath. Exhausted, all the sorcerer could do was watch his men get defeated. Miyuki was done for, and his only target now was Yomatri.

After finishing off the last soldier with a final slash, Yomatri turned around as a flurry of heavy snow hit him square in the face, tossing him onto the street. His swords clattered onto the ground as he was dazed by Shinzuki's attack. A flashing thought told him that the sorcerer shouldn't be taken lightly, and that being a hero was not all it seemed.

The teen slowly rose after what seemed like a million years, finding that his opponent was by no means ready to stop. *Yomatri wasn't either.* No matter what, he wasn't going to give up on the people he loved or the city he cared so much about.

"I underestimated you, boy," Shinzuki said to his opponent, who glared at him.

"Yes, you did."

Suddenly, a loud noise came rushing in behind the teen. He turned back and smiled, noticing a team of reinforcement police officers. Like before, the officers had gotten out of their vehicles, all of them clutching a heavy firearm. Together, the men formed a tight line of defense.

Furious, Shinzuki gritted his teeth.

The police aimed their weapons at him, firing carefully to avoid harming any injured civilians, but still, their bullets didn't seem to affect him. Shinzuki used an elemental shield to protect himself.

Using the last bit of his strength, the evil mercenary fought back against the officers, firing a torrent of dark energy straight at them. While trying to reload his pistol, one officer shouted, "Take cover!"

The missile slammed into a taxicab, engulfing the vehicle in a huge fireball. Breaking off into small groups, the officers continued their assault, trying their best to distract the sorcerer.

Nearby, Yomatri took a deep breath, then hurled a water rocket as his opponent. Shinzuki turned, his eyes widening as the missile took him by surprise, knocking him backward into the hood of a wrecked car. He tried to recover but was unable to fight any longer.

Altogether, the team of police joined back together and surrounded the sorcerer, their guns aimed. Beads of sweat dripped from the officers' foreheads as they glared at their opponent.

Panting, Yomatri remained still and waited for things to calm down. In the sky, a second NYPD chopper suddenly appeared, hovering high above the city streets.

"Stand down! Put your hands behind your head— now!" multiple officers repeated. The men kept their eyes locked on Shinzuki, who didn't move a muscle.

After a moment, the police moved in and began to arrest the enemy invader, pinning him to the ground and forcing handcuffs onto his wrists.

Yomatri glanced over to Miyuki, who seemed to be safe in the hands of civilians. He and his friend had put up an impressive fight, but this was only the beginning.

Minutes passed by like seconds, and people started returning to the area. A large crowd had gathered to give the two exhausted teens a great round of applause. All of them were happy that this madness was over for now, and that everything could return to normal.

Miyuki and Yomatri had managed to work together as a team, knowing they did the right thing. Their first mission wasn't easy, but through all this, it was evident that a set of heroes had been born.

CHAPTER SEVEN:

ONE LIE AFTER ANOTHER

Over the streets of Manhattan, a black police helicopter hovered in the sky amidst thin, wispy clouds. In the streets below, police officers held back dozens of reporters holding flashing cameras and carrying recorders. Various stationary firetrucks and police cars were scattered along the snow-covered sidewalks.

Throughout the ravaged streets were numerous abandoned vehicles, some of them, at that moment, being examined by forensic analysts. At the bakery, detectives investigated the damages, studying the building's broken exterior windows closely. Firefighters worked together to clear debris off the roads.

Meanwhile, multiple reporters spoke to various media outlets, elaborating on witness accounts of the battle. On televisions across the city, the story was being watched by millions.

At home in the kitchen, Yomatri and his mother also watched the story. While she poured milk into a cup, Miya leaned in closer to the news report displayed on a small flat-screen TV resting on a counter near the stove.

Her son, seated nearby, munched on a peanut butter and jelly sandwich. Using a remote, Yomatri turned up the volume and paid close attention like his mother.

On the screen, a female reporter from Channel 6 News relayed a brief message:

> ... Yesterday evening, a dangerous attack unfolded, endangering many people of our beloved city, New York. More than 70 people have been injured and at least two officers are currently reported dead. Officials have released numerous videos of the suspect along with many of his accomplices, who are currently not cooperating with police. Most of what law enforcement knows is merely speculation at this point. However, through recent evidence, it is believed that the suspect and his partners are perhaps from another planet. Authorities also believe that the men are after something but aren't quite sure. As for the teenagers who helped in the attack, they've not yet been identified, but police are asking that they come forward immediately. In addition, we are asking anyone with possible information related to this attack to please inform local authorities at once. We will continue to provide you all with updates as we learn more about these foreign fighters and our investigation continues ...

As the news report shifted to a commercial, Miya spoke after taking a sip of her milk. "Those must be some brave teenagers," she said with a surprised expression.

"Yeah, no kidding," her son sarcastically responded.

Knowing the truth, Yomatri tried his best to keep calm. He knew that even the slightest thing, such as his and Miyuki's faces appearing in the local newspaper, could reveal that he and his friend possessed ancient abilities.

Looking away from the television, Miya checked her wristwatch. "Hey, I'm gonna go to the store and grab some food for dinner," she said, glancing at her son, who took another bite of his sandwich. She paused suddenly, looking nervous. "Wait, what happened to you? What are those marks and cuts on your chin and neck?"

"Oh, those? Uhhh ... they're nothing, don't worry. Everything's totally under control, Mom." Awkwardly, he tried to cover wounds from the battle with his hands.

"Yomatri!" Miya said, raising her voice. "Tell me what happened. Did you get into a fight?"

"What did I just hear?" Luke called out from the living room.

"No, no—a fight? I would never do that."

"Then what happened to you?!"

Luke entered the kitchen. "What is going on in here? What's all the fuss about?"

Suddenly, the doorbell rang and everyone paused.

Yomatri's eyes snapped to the front door, his mouth hanging open. Nervous, he glanced back and forth between the front door and his parents.

"Who is that?" the teen asked, his heart pounding.

"I don't know," Luke answered, confused.

Frustrated, Miya glanced at her son, then turned away and headed toward the front door.

For a moment, Yomatri and his father locked eyes.

Eyebrows raised, Luke whispered, "What'd you do?"

"Uhhh ... ," Yomatri responded, unable to continue.

His father gave a smirk, turned away, and headed toward the front door. As he left, Yomatri jumped from the table, accidentally knocking his sandwich onto the floor.

"Oh boy," he said to himself. He glanced up, then hid behind a wall while trying to keep his cool. "I really hope that's not the police."

Peering around the corner towards the front door, he saw Miya who answered, but it appeared to be none other than his best friend, Miyuki. The teen sighed with relief as he dropped to the floor, still leaning against the wall.

"Hello, my name's Miyuki. I'm a friend of Yomatri and I just thought I'd stop by. Is he here right now?"

"Hi, Miyuki—welcome. I'm his mother, Miya. Please, come in. Yomatri's over in the kitchen," she explained, greeting the girl with a firm handshake.

Miyuki glanced at Luke.

"Hi, I'm Luke—Yomatri's father," he said, gesturing to himself. "It's nice to meet you."

"Nice to meet you too, sir."

In the kitchen, Yomatri quickly threw the rest of his sandwich into the garbage and his plate into the sink. Hurriedly, he washed his sticky hands and dried them on the sides of his pants, then met his friend near the front door.

"Heyyy, Miyuki. It's good to, uh, see you," Yomatri said, breathing heavily. "Why'd you come here?"

"It's good to see you too," she responded with a confused look. "Why are you outta breath?"

"I had some important things to take care of in the kitchen. But, um, seriously, what are you doing here so early?"

Miyuki checked her wristwatch. "It's not early. It's almost 3:00," she said, giggling. "But I don't know, really. I just thought I'd drop by and see how you were doin', I guess. Was kinda bored to be honest. You remember, though, right—I won't have school for another week or so with winter break?"

"Oh yeah, you did say that."

Seeming a bit more relaxed now, Miya interrupted, "Honey, you never told me you had a girlfriend! She's beautiful!"

"Mom!" Yomatri complained with an embarrassed pout.

"Is everything alright, kiddo?" Luke asked his son.

Eyeing Yomatri, even Miyuki felt he was acting a little strange. He was quickly growing nervous and shy. He hadn't expected his friend to meet his parents so suddenly.

"Yeah, uh, everything's okay. Couldn't be better!" Yomatri responded, scratching his head.

"Is it the itch? Has it come back to haunt you?" Miya whispered.

Miyuki snickered.

"What? No, Mom! No. That was years ago."

Miya turned to Miyuki and explained. "Miyuki, when Yomatri was younger, he had this really embarrassing itch at his friend's birthday party, and ohhh my gosh, it was terrible! He couldn't stop scratching, and everyone was watching. Unfortunately, he had to be removed from the party, but it was very funny. Let's just say it didn't end too well."

"Mom!" Yomatri yelled, his face red.

"Sorry, just tryna have a little fun," Miya joked. Pulling her cell phone out of her pocket, she checked the time. "Hey, I forgot—I have to get to the grocery store. But I should be back in a bit."

"Alright, sounds good to me," her husband said.

Moments later, Luke helped his wife search for her car keys, eventually finding them near the TV in the kitchen. After she'd left the house, he took the newspaper for today from a nearby counter and headed upstairs to his bedroom.

Miyuki and Yomatri regrouped in the kitchen.

"Hey, I'm sorry about the way my mom acted earlier."

Miyuki grinned. "No, no, it's okay. I've had it happen to me before. My mom used to do it all the time when I was little. That's why I could hardly ever have a boyfriend come over or just friends in general. I totally understand. Although, I have to say that that little story about you was pretty funny."

"Wait, so why do you have your backpack with you?" Yomatri asked, turning to a new subject. "Are you goin' on a mystical adventure?"

Miyuki chuckled. "Nooo, sometimes, I just like to have it if I wanna take a lotta things with me. I was never really the purse kind of girl. But in here, I usually just carry notebooks, pencils, and other stuff for school. My dad also bought me some flashlights right before the semester. I honestly have no idea why, though."

Yomatri shrugged his shoulders. "I wouldn't really know why either. Maybe for a school supplies list or somethin'?"

"Probably. But I also have that map Captain Zeron left behind with me." After resting her backpack against a chair, she continued, "Hey, that was some pretty awesome fighting we did yesterday. Good thing we made it out okay, too."

"Sshhh!" Yomatri said, even though Luke was upstairs. Miyuki furrowed her brow. Her friend continued in a whisper, "Yeah, Miyuki, you did great. Are you alright and everything, though?"

"Yeah, I'm fine … just a little sore. A few bruises here and there, but I'm okay for the most part. I guess learning kickboxing and other forms of self-defense with my dad back when I was younger really helped." Glancing at the TV, she noticed it was still on *Channel 6 News*, but the reporters were now discussing the weather. "What about you? I know it was super scary goin' up against that sorcerer or whatever he was."

"Yeah, no kidding. But I'm fine," replied Yomatri. "Have you told your parents about your powers yet? That's why I was acting so weird earlier, to my parents. I don't know if you could tell."

"Absolutely not. I could never do that. My mom would freak out. I don't really know how she'd take it. And yeah, I could definitely tell you were actin' a little strange earlier."

"Did you hear about what happened on the news? I think the authorities want us to come forward and everything. What do you think we should do?"

"Maybe we should, uh, just keep quiet about everything for right now. To me, that seems like the best option. I don't know about you, but I feel like it'd be really bad if our parents found out. We promised to help Captain Zeron and the Hero Alliance."

"Yeah, you're right," Yomatri insisted. "We've gotta help them!"

"Hey, you're too loud there, buddy," Miyuki whispered, grinning, as she held up a finger to her mouth.

Suddenly, the two of them were interrupted by a faint whistling noise. The teenagers turned and noticed it was coming from Miyuki's backpack.

"Miyuki, your backpack—it's glowing!"

She glanced at her friend and then snapped her attention to her backpack. Quickly, she opened it and took out the wrinkled map left behind by Captain Zeron. As she unfolded the dusty parchment on a countertop, the strange noise slowly faded.

"Is it trying to tell us something?" Miyuki asked, sharing a curious look with her friend.

Together, the teens leaned in for a closer look. On the map, a red marker in Westchester, New York began to glow with a vibrant aura. Suddenly, a shiny red light from the map shot into the air and formed into a three-dimensional hologram of moving images.

Yomatri and Miyuki backed up.

"Whoa!" they both said.

The hologram depicted a large forest in a very remote

area, filled with hundreds of plants and tall trees. Bushes and other weeds were scattered about, and dozens of logs and sticks lay still on the snow-covered ground.

Briefly, the hologram shifted to a large brick building set near the edge of the forest, many of its windows smashed open.

Miyuki whispered, "Why's it showin' us this random building? It kinda looks like it's in the middle of nowhere. And what's up with the forest?"

Yomatri furrowed his brow. "I don't know. I'm really confused to be honest."

Without warning, the hologram slowly began to fade. The teens shifted their gaze back to the map resting on the counter. Strangely, a bright light formed inside the parchment paper, connecting the red marker in Westchester to a spot in Forest Hills.

"Wait, hold on. What's happening?" asked Yomatri. He pointed to the spot in Forest Hills. "What does this mean? Is that where we are?"

"Yes, it has to mean that! I bet the map's tryna tell us to go there or something—to Westchester."

"Why would it do that?"

Miyuki shook her head, then paused to gather her thoughts. "Okay, I know this might sound a little funny, but remember how Captain Zeron was kinda tellin' us she wants us to be independent and find out how to start this whole 'savin' the world' thing ourselves?"

"Yeah ... but what are you getting at? How does it make any sense for us to go to some random building near the edge of a forest? You even said it looks like it's in the middle of nowhere."

"Look, I honestly don't know why the map's pointing us there. Maybe there's just some things we don't yet understand! But what I'm trying to say is that this seems like a clue of some sort. Even if it is just some random building in the middle of the forest or whatever, I don't think the map would've shown us that hologram for nothing."

"Possibly. That is a good point now that I think about it."

"Yes. And it looks like it's giving us directions or something. Yomatri, we have to go to Westchester to see if we can find out more!"

"How do you plan on doing that?"

"We'll find a way. Please, just trust me!"

"Okay, okay. How are we gonna get there at least? Have you ever been there? Because I definitely haven't."

"Yeah, yeah, a few times actually. I know the area somewhat. Very beautiful place. Once in a while, me and my family go there just for fun. Like sometimes, we'll take really long walks, maybe do a little sightseeing." Miyuki shook her head. "Look, that doesn't even matter! We can take my dad's car to Westchester and from there, we can continue on foot."

Yomatri glanced away with a reluctant expression, then considered her words. "Alright. We'll need to move fast then."

The teens froze as they heard footsteps coming downstairs. Miyuki quickly stashed the map away in her backpack. "That's your dad, right?" she whispered nervously.

"Yep, I think so. If he's got the newspaper for today, we gotta get it from him and throw it away. I'm scared it might have our faces somewhere in it because of the whole battle in Manhattan yesterday."

"Ohhh, okay. Gotcha."

Luke entered the kitchen with today's paper in hand. He paused and looked at his son, causing the boy's heart to drop.

Suddenly fearful, Yomatri tried his best to keep calm. "Hey, so, uh ... Dad, how was today's paper?" he asked, closely watching his father, who set the newspaper down on a counter.

"It was good, I guess," Luke replied, giving his son an odd look. Even Miya never asked him that question. He headed over to the sink, his back to the teens. Holding a black-and-gold coffee mug in one hand, he asked, "Where are you guys headed off to?"

"We were just gonna go ... into the city ... and you know, have some fun together," Yomatri answered.

Miyuki approached Luke from the side. Pointing, she said, "That's a reeaally nice mug you got there. Can I ask where'd you get it from?"

"Oh, this?" he asked, holding up the mug. "I've had it for so long, but I think it was at some old grocery store a few years back. I honestly don't even remember."

"Ahh, I see. No worries," said Miyuki. "I'm sure I can find one like it online for my dad. Believe it or not, he's super into mugs—like *really* into them. It's kinda weird actually." Behind her back, she gave a thumbs-up to Yomatri, who understood.

"Oh, okay ... sounds good," Luke replied, turning on the faucet. After grabbing a nearby sponge, he began to wash some of the dirty dishes.

Without his father seeing, Yomatri snatched the newspaper from the counter and threw it in a trash bin near the bathroom. He then joined Miyuki as they both tiptoed toward the front door.

Luke glanced over his shoulder and said, "Hey, Yomatri, I was gonna tell you something I was thinkin' about earlier. You know, you should try going to—" He paused, overhearing the front door close, realizing he was now all alone.

Together, the teens had successfully escaped outside and gave each other a relieved high-five. Deep down, Yomatri felt bad about lying to his parents. Although he couldn't tell them about his powers, he felt like all of the dishonesty would soon catch up to him.

CHAPTER EIGHT:

REBELLION

Westchester, New York

Tall oak trees, some with dead branches, loomed high over the snow-covered earth, bathed by a golden sun far out in the distance.

Down below, a small caravan of marauders dressed in protective armor over tattered leather robes paced through a large, remote forest. A few of the men were armed with spears and swords while others wore intricate metal masks.

Leading the group, one soldier held a small rectangular device in his hands that projected a miniature multicolored map of the environment.

"Are you sure the crystal is even out here?" asked a man wearing a bone necklace. "It seems like we've tried everywhere."

"Of course it's here!" the man leading the group snapped. He came to a halt and turned back to his comrades. "I know we've been searching a lot in the past few days, but it must've landed somewhere. We just ... have to keep looking."

"I say we go back to the hideout and start again in the

morning. The longer we stay out, the more likely it is we'll be noticed by someone."

"I agree," a third soldier interrupted.

There was a short pause.

"Let me ask ... ," the group's leader started. "Have either of you even stopped to think what could be ours if we were to find the crystal and hand it over to the Aridian Army? Honestly, just imagine."

"Yes, we have, actually, very much so. But regardless, I still say it's best we avoid any human entanglements. It'll spell a whole lot of problems—problems the five of us can't handle alone."

The group's leader shifted his angry eyes and pressed his lips together, then returned his gaze to his partners. "Alright, fine. We go back to the hideout for the day."

✫✫✫

A little over an hour later, Miyuki and Yomatri raced through bushes and feathery knee-high weeds coated in grimy snow. Maneuvering as best they could, the bottoms of their pants grew damp as they tramped between the brush and close trees.

A sudden harsh, cold wind blew violently. The teens covered their faces but pressed on. Together, they hurried up a small hill and came to a halt at the edge of the forest.

Miyuki glanced up at the winter sky, now slowly fading into evening. Yomatri did the same, then after a moment, he and his friend crouched down behind bushes and tall trees.

Peering between two trees, Yomatri noticed a large brick

building several hundred feet in front of them. Many of its windows were smashed open and graffiti was spray-painted along its vine-covered walls. In one of the corners was a tall stack of wooden pallets, once used for moving materials.

Miyuki took out the map from her backpack and unraveled the parchment, studying it closely. "I think this is it," she said, glancing at the building, which appeared to have been abandoned.

"Yep. Looks like we're in the right place. Now we just gotta find out how to get inside, I guess?"

"Yeah." Miyuki squinted and scanned the area with her eyes. After a moment, she spotted a brown metal door on the side of the building, then grabbed her friend by the wrist. Pointing, she whispered, "Here, come on. I have an idea. Let's go over there."

The teens were suddenly interrupted by what sounded like a group of soldiers trekking uncomfortably close to them. Keeping their heads down, they waited for the troops to pass. Minutes seemed to go by like hours.

Yomatri pointed at the men who were now further down a dirt road. "Look—those were the same kind of soldiers that attacked Manhattan yesterday!" he said while trying to keep his voice down.

Eyebrows raised, Miyuki responded, "Yeah, you're right. Wait, what are they doin' here? That's really weird."

"I don't know, but we need to get in that building fast, before someone notices us."

Miyuki nodded and slipped the map back into her backpack, which she then slung over her shoulder.

After checking to make sure the coast was clear, Yomatri

sprung up and followed her across a large courtyard, both of them trying their best to be quiet. Together, the teens stopped beside the brown metal door and took a moment to catch their breath.

"Is this how we get inside?" Yomatri asked, standing halfway bent down with his hands on his knees. His friend nervously turned the rusty handle on the door again and again.

"Yeah, I think so. I can't get this door to open, though. Might be jammed or something." Miyuki panicked, fearing they'd soon be discovered; she glanced around, not seeing anyone.

Turning back to the door, she took out a spare hairpin from her pocket and tried picking the lock.

"What are you doing?" Yomatri asked, curious.

Miyuki didn't respond but after several tries, she managed to pop it open. The teenagers rushed inside, gently shutting the door behind them.

"That was awesome. I'm impressed," whispered Yomatri. "Where'd you learn how to do that?"

"It's ... a long story."

Now standing in a dimly lit room, the teens glanced over at a nearby staircase, which towered high toward the building's second floor. Together, they tiptoed up the stairs and upon reaching the top, they turned right, noticing another door.

Miyuki paused. Eyeing her friend, she held up a finger to her mouth, then pointed at a square window on the door. Yomatri gently knocked against its metal frame.

In the other room, a nearby guard turned back, only seeing two silhouetted figures in the door's window. Opening it, his face immediately met Miyuki's fist.

Yomatri dashed forward and spotted another soldier several feet away. In a flash, he leaped up and threw a heavy punch at the man's jaw, knocking him unconscious. He and Miyuki then stopped to check their surroundings, noting things were okay.

Together, the teens grabbed both soldiers' bodies and dragged them out, closing the door behind them as they entered the room.

"Nice job, buddy," Miyuki whispered to Yomatri, bumping fists with him.

"Thanks."

"I still don't get what these soldiers are doin' here, but maybe if we keep looking, we'll find an answer?"

"Probably. I bet there's more of them somewhere. But we can't stay here and risk getting caught. Where do you plan on going next?"

"I'm not, uh, really sure to be honest. Here, follow me." Miyuki and her friend stood side by side as they cautiously approached a narrow corridor close by. For a moment, the teens stopped to survey their surroundings.

The floor was littered with grit, broken bottles, and shards of glass. Above their heads were multiple sets of dust-covered fluorescent lights, some of them dimming. Thin green vines ran along the ceiling while light from a row of windows along the wall broke through the darkness, providing some visibility.

"This place is givin' me the creeps. Looks like an

abandoned warehouse or something," said Miyuki.

"Yeah." Yomatri chewed his lip. Pointing ahead, he continued, "Here, come on. Let's keep moving."

Miyuki followed him, and together they hid behind a column of stacked packages set near the entrance to another hallway.

His forehead beaded with sweat, Yomatri paused, overhearing the sound of nearby footsteps. He peeked over the stacked boxes and immediately crouched back down as a group of soldiers chatting with one another had passed by.

He exhaled nervously, then turned to Miyuki. "That was close. I was right, though. There are more of 'em. But we can't stay here. It's too risky."

"Okay, well, where do you plan on going next?"

Yomatri peered over the column of packages again. This time he looked to both his left and right, finding that the coast was clear. Miyuki followed him into the hall, and they headed in the opposite direction of the soldiers.

Suddenly Yomatri crouched down, spotting a wooden door on the left side of the hall. He pointed as Miyuki's eyes followed. "Here, let's go this way."

"You don't even know where you're going!" the girl angrily whispered; she shook her head but followed. Gently, her friend opened the door and headed for the staircase.

Down the hall, two soldiers came to a stop.

"What was that?" one of them asked his colleague.

"I don't know. Must be nothing. You're probably just hearing things. Let's move on," said the other man.

Together, Miyuki and Yomatri tiptoed down the stair's

metal steps, trying their best to stay quiet. Eventually, they came to a halt and peered around the corner into a massive rectangular room, nearly half the length of a soccer field.

The teens examined the room, seeing that it was filled with clusters of old upturned furniture and shelving units. Large rusted metal chains hung from the ceiling, and on the ground were hundreds of papers and empty toolboxes lying all around.

Like the narrow corridor, windows along the wall provided some light. A few of them had been boarded up with panels of plywood. Towards the far end of the room, a small band of marauders conversed in an Aridnemekian language. To Yomatri and Miyuki, the language was a strange mixture of harsh, periodic consonants and airy vowels.

In the center of the room, more soldiers chatted loudly amongst themselves while other troops lay still, half-asleep, resting against its scarred concrete walls. Teenagers were scattered about, huddled together in small groups, their wrists bounded with electrified manacles.

Behind a large cluster of furniture and junk near the entrance, a teenager with fiery-colored hair awoke to the sound of close footsteps. Three other teens lying beside him woke up shortly after, immediately rubbing their eyes.

The boy with fiery hair squinted, noticing Miyuki and Yomatri hiding behind a brick wall. A few of the other teens in the room had noticed them, but out of fear didn't speak.

"This is really strange," Miyuki said softly to her friend. "I wonder why all these people are being imprisoned."

"Yeah, me too."

"Hey, you!" a mysterious voice whispered. Miyuki and Yomatri looked around disconcertedly. Eventually, they locked eyes with the boy whose hair was yellow, orange, and red. "Yes, you two—come here!"

Yomatri and Miyuki gulped, taking a quick glance at the guards in the center of the room. The men continued to talk and talk, and cautiously, the two teens approached the group, hiding amid the clusters of furniture and upturned shelving units.

Miraculously, the soldiers hadn't noticed them.

Miyuki and Yomatri studied the four teenagers, who all wore shackles around their wrists like everyone else. Although each of them had different-colored hair, they seemed to be related.

Holding up a finger to his mouth, one of the boys motioned for Yomatri and Miyuki to stay quiet. He turned and peered over the cluster of furniture. It seemed that everything was okay for now.

Miyuki took note of her surroundings, seeing several empty cartons of food lying on the floor beside her and the others. In a nearby corner, mice chewed away at crumbs of food. Looking away in disgust, she gently set her backpack onto the floor.

"Who are you guys?" the girl asked.

"I'm Sage," whispered the boy with fiery hair, gesturing to himself. "And these are my three brothers, Mako, Beta, and Zatch. We come from a planet called Aridnemeki." Miyuki and Yomatri noticed he had an unfamiliar accent. "Are you guys with the Alliance?"

Miyuki swapped a look with Yomatri. "We are now . . .

I mean, we met a woman named Captain Zeron. She's the one who told us all about the story of Aridnemeki and the twelve crystals."

Sage gasped with excitement and glanced at his brothers, who smiled back.

A thought suddenly clicked in Miyuki's head. Reaching into her backpack, she grabbed the dusty, partially torn map she'd found after meeting Captain Zeron and her team. As she unrolled the parchment on the floor, the brothers huddled around, studying it closely.

"What's this?" Sage asked, looking up at Miyuki.

"Can you help us understand this at all? It's a map from the Hero Alliance. It's a picture of New York, but that's all I can get from it. What do these red markers mean? Can you maybe tell us that?"

"These red dots here ... ," said Sage, "there's four of them marked within this place you call 'New York'. And this green one in the corner—it's some kind of island for the Alliance, but that's all I can understand from it. I'm sorry."

His brother Beta jumped in. He pointed at one of the markers on the map as he spoke, "This one here is where we are now—in a place called 'Westchester', I think."

"Yep, that's correct," Miyuki responded. "How long have you guys been imprisoned here by the soldiers if you don't mind me asking?"

"Only a few days," Beta answered.

"That's not too bad. But still, not good either," said Yomatri. "Are there more soldiers in other parts of the warehouse? Or is this it?"

"Yes, there are a few more, but we're not entirely sure on their, uh, whereabouts. In total, though, there's about twenty of us—you know, prisoners. The guards will shock us unconscious with these shackles on our wrists if we try to escape."

Miyuki looked horrified. "Is there a device or something to disable the electric charge in them, do you know?"

"Yes. One or two of the soldiers wear a small device on their hip that can disable and reactivate the charge with the click of a button. But that doesn't remove the handcuffs. That's where we'd need a key or something else to actually get them off. Don't ask how I know all that," Beta responded.

Miyuki nodded solemnly. "Here, this might help," she said, taking out a small hairpin from her pocket and handing it to him. "I used it before to pick the lock on one of the doors outside."

Beta smiled, then handed the hairpin to his brother, Mako (MAY-koh), a teenager with spiky blond hair. "He knows better than me about that kind of stuff," Beta said to Miyuki. "But thank you."

Yomatri glanced at Sage, then returned his attention back to the map. Pointing at it, he asked, "Is there anything more you can possibly understand from any of the red markers?"

"Ummm ... I could be wrong, but I believe they are, um, targets of some kind ... ," replied Sage, "places the Hero Alliance is planning to hit. Enemy bases probably. As you know, they're in search of the twelve crystals.

"Yes. Before you guys came here, we overheard the soldiers talking, and we think one of them might be nearby in the area—the Emerald," said Zatch, a boy with neat, short, sandy hair. "It holds the power of earth."

Yomatri's eyes lit up. "Wait, no kidding! Are you serious?!" he said while trying to keep his voice down.

"Now you're gonna get us caught!" Miyuki whispered, widening her eyes at him.

Suddenly, the six teens paused, overhearing soft footsteps and chatter coming from nearby. One of the brothers stopped to check the group's surroundings again, and after a short moment, he realized that the coast was clear.

Returning to the huddle, he gave a thumbs-up. "It's okay. A few of the prisoners are having their handcuffs removed by the guards because they have to go to the bathroom, I think," said Beta.

Yomatri nodded, then traded brief looks with him and his three brothers. "You guys, wherever that crystal is, we've gotta try to find that thing—fast."

"It might actually be somewhere in that forest, come to think of it," Miyuki said, sharing a look with him. "Maybe that's why the hologram was showing us it?"

"Possibly. That's not a bad thought."

"Wait, so why are you both here?" asked Mako.

"I guess this is a rescue mission now," Miyuki replied. "We didn't plan on it because we didn't really know what was goin' on here at first, but we're gonna save you guys, I promise."

"You're going to need some help then. We'll need to hurry up, though," Sage insisted, his eyes growing worried.

"Before you guys came here, the soldiers said that they were going to be doing a contraband search pretty soon. They might've already started."

"You guys know pulling off something like that isn't going to be easy at all?" said Zatch. "It'll take some time."

Suddenly there was a loud knock against one of the nearby pieces of upturned furniture surrounding the group. A guard armed with a baton, accompanied by two other troops, stared down at the six teens. Facing away from the men, Miyuki and Yomatri's hearts dropped.

"Just checkin' for contraband, maggots," said the man with the baton, his voice deep and menacing. Pausing, he studied the group's inhabitants. His eyes focused on Yomatri and Miyuki. "Wait a minute. I don't recognize you two. You don't belong here."

The other two troops closely eyed Miyuki and Yomatri, who nervously turned around to face the guards.

"Stop!" said the man with the baton. "Who are you?"

"We're prisoners ... of this, uh, fine abandoned warehouse of yours," Yomatri responded.

Miyuki face-palmed herself. "Oh my goodness."

"Arrest them," the man with the baton ordered.

Immediately, the other two soldiers forcefully pulled Miyuki and Yomatri away from the group and began to walk away with them, holding the teens tight by their wrists.

"Wait! Where are you taking them?" Beta snapped, rising to his feet. The two guards holding Yomatri and Miyuki stopped in their tracks and glanced back as the teens did the same.

"Quiet!" the man with the baton demanded. He kicked Beta to the ground and pointed his weapon at the boy as a warning. "There'll be severe consequences for the four of you. Remember that."

Around the room, many other guards heard the disturbance. Some of them, armed with bows and arrows, looked on with tense brows. The soldier standing beside Miyuki turned back around and shoved her forward.

"Move on!" he ordered. Having nearly fallen, the girl whirled around and elbowed the man in the jaw, causing him to collapse to the ground.

Yomatri tried to help, but the guard standing beside him tugged him back. Noticing a small gadget with two opposite colored buttons lying on the floor next to the injured soldier, Miyuki's eyes widened. Looking up, she glanced at the four brothers, her expression unsure.

"That's the device we spoke about! Press the green button!" yelled Mako.

The man with the baton swung at Miyuki, barely missing her. Dashing forward, she stomped down on the green button as instructed. Instantaneously, the electric charge in the shackles of all the prisoners had been disabled.

Again the man with the baton swung with his weapon, and Miyuki dodged. Nearby, Mako dashed behind a table on its side and used the hairpin she'd given him to pick the lock on his own shackles. After several tries, he managed to do so and successfully removed the handcuffs from his wrists. He quickly turned to Sage and did the same thing, freeing his brother in a matter of seconds.

In the center of the room, guards opened fire on the

six teens with their bows and arrows. Dodging the sharp projectiles, they tried their best to keep the plan going. The man with the baton swung at Miyuki a third time, but a bolt of thunderous energy electrocuted him, knocking him unconscious.

Mako scurried to his feet and kicked the man aside, stealing his baton in the process. He then charged at the soldier near Yomatri. Meanwhile, Sage used his fire abilities to melt the handcuffs off the wrists of his other two brothers, Zatch and Beta.

The other soldiers in the room continued to fire upon Yomatri, Miyuki, and the four brothers, who defended themselves with their elemental abilities. Working together, the six teens dodged oncoming projectiles and returned fire with the combined powers of water, electricity, earth and fire.

Shots of varied magical energy flew back and forth across the junk-filled room as dozens of explosions erupted. Nearby, the other prisoners cheered the heroes on. In the chaos, several enemy soldiers were obliterated by the strong force of their attackers.

As a team, Yomatri, Miyuki, and the four brothers raced toward the exit and dashed up the stairs, taking out additional troops along the way. More and more explosions erupted throughout the abandoned warehouse's narrow passageways.

Chunks of metal and bits on broken glass from overhead fluorescent lights rained down, but the six teens continued onward. Miyuki led the way, heading toward the door where she and Yomatri first entered.

Bursting the door open, she and her friends stepped outside into the snow, only to be surrounded by a battalion of ten armed hostiles.

"What are we gonna do now?" the girl asked.

"We'll have to fight them all one by one!" Sage responded.

CHAPTER NINE:

ALLIES OF THE ALLIANCE

Sage and the others eyed their opponents closely, watching their every move. Small drips of sweat ran down the sides of Sage's face. He knew the only thing standing in the way of him and the other Aridnemekians' freedom was the soldiers in front of him.

Suddenly, an enemy troop stomped his boot down. Yomatri's eyes snapped to the man's swift movement.

In a flash, the soldier lashed out at Sage with a sharp sword. Dodging the weapon, the teenager quickly overpowered his opponent with rapid jabs and kicks. He then went on the offensive, striking at many other marauders with a variety of powerful martial-arts moves.

His brothers joined in to help him, attacking full force with the combined powers of electricity, earth, and water. Sage intensified his fighting, knocking down enemy combatants left and right with a whirlwind of fireball attacks.

As a team, the six teens progressed forward and rushed into the main courtyard, taking cover from a hail of enemy fire. In a matter of seconds, more and more enemy troops appeared on the scene, and to the heroes, it seemed like they were now up against an army.

Standing by a tree, Miyuki took off her backpack and

gesticulated wildly, firing various ice and water attacks at enemy soldiers. Yomatri joined in, taking on many in hand-to-hand combat.

In the mayhem, Sage locked eyes with one masked troop. The soldier fired a large missile, barely missing his opponent as it crashed into a heap of snow.

Armed troops quickly appeared on both sides of the masked soldier and fired with a shadowy energy. Dashing behind a large rock, Sage hurled a swirl of flaming energy, the ensuing explosion taking out most of the soldiers.

Throughout the courtyard, some of the prisoners took cover behind anything they could as the battle unfolded. Others joined in, clobbering guards one after another, managing to steal their weapons in the process.

Next to Yomatri and Miyuki, Zatch manipulated multiple rocks from nearby to batter his assailants. Beta assisted, providing his brother with chunks of dense ice and snow.

More soldiers appeared out of the shadows, firing countless shots of energy at the heroes. The ground shook violently and fireballs roared all around, striking the snow and nearby trees.

Realizing Yomatri was in the line of fire, Miyuki rushed in and tackled her friend, shielding him from an oncoming missile. Together they crashed in the snow, then quickly recovered as they raced to their feet.

Spinning swiftly, Miyuki and Yomatri fired combined blasts of water. Their heavy attacks sailed through the air and slammed into two soldiers, wiping them both out.

The teens smiled at one another, then noticed that

more prisoners had joined the fight. A few of them had been killed by arrow shots to the chest, their bodies strewn among the others, and Yomatri and Miyuki quickly grew horrified.

Meanwhile, several prisoners hurled stolen grenades in the direction of the attacking soldiers. Explosions erupted all around, rocking the ground beneath everyone's feet. As enemy arrows rippled overhead, a group of inmates combined their elements, forming multiple, defensive walls from the earth.

Yomatri and his friends used this to their advantage, dashing behind friendly lines for cover.

"Are you good, my friends?!" yelled Sage.

"No—we need a different plan or something! There's too many of them!" Yomatri responded. Shots of dark energy and sharp arrows roared over his head. Smoke billowed as continuous explosions violently tossed up snow.

"We can do this, Yomatri! Let's keep pushing!" Miyuki screamed, covering her head. She turned left and saw Mako and Beta separate from the team to continue the fight.

Still hiding behind the war prisoners, Sage turned his head. His eyes widened. A fiery missile spiraled its way straight toward them.

"Run!!" Sage panicked. He and Zatch raced to their feet and jumped out of the way. A thunderous explosion erupted, wiping out the three inmates defending Yomatri and his friends.

Disoriented, Sage looked up and saw bodies; he felt instant sorrow. Lying in the snow, he glanced over at Miyuki and Yomatri, noting they were safe.

In the surrounding area, four more prisoners had been slain at the hands of enemy swords and spears. While shots of elemental energy roared back and forth across the battlefield, Miyuki and Yomatri got up and ran head on at a trio of soldiers.

Miyuki's water blast knocked one of the men down, but that didn't stop Yomatri from avenging the fallen prisoners. Leaping up, he spun around to land a powerful roundhouse kick at a second soldier.

He landed safely but was immediately knocked down by an assailant wielding a metal spear. As the man lunged at him again, a water rocket from Miyuki sent the man crashing to the ground. Yomatri staggered to his feet and hurried away with his friend to hide behind a tree.

Side by side, Sage and Zatch fended off a group of soldiers. Together, they fought bravely against the vicious marauders, striking and dodging with masterful combinations of fire and earth.

Rocks from the ground shot up and conjoined together, forming into a round, sturdy shield in Zatch's left hand. With it, he turned and bashed one of his opponents in the face, then continued on to the next.

At the same time, Sage knocked down several enemy combatants in hand-to-hand combat. Turning around, his eyes widened as a bolt of shadowy energy took him by surprise and knocked him to the ground.

More and more soldiers suddenly appeared, firing repeated bursts of dark energy at the teenagers.

Courageously, Zatch jumped in and shielded his brother from heavy enemy fire, his forehead beaded with sweat. He turned and punched at the air with his other hand, sending a barrage of snowy rocks at his attackers, finally wiping them out.

Panting, he then turned back to Sage and helped him from the ground as they pressed on.

Amidst smoldering piles of debris, Miyuki and Yomatri engaged a small team of enemy troops, attacking and defending in turn. Together, they punched and kicked at the men, landing several blows while using their elemental abilities to assist them in the fight.

Meanwhile, as shadowy projectiles and enemy arrows rained past them, Beta and Mako joined together to help two prisoners. Against a flurry of billowing smoke, one soldier armed with a crossbow had appeared from the shadows.

Weaving around piles of debris, the man closed in, firing one arrow after another at the brothers. Beta took cover and aimed his hands at the advancing soldier. In a flash, he manipulated the snow, sinking his opponent deep into the ground.

Standing nearby, Mako's eyes widened as yet more soldiers appeared on the scene. Looking up, he pointed his hands toward the gray sky, palms open. Mako closed his eyes and concentrated intently, waiting for the right time to strike.

Within seconds, his eyes flashed back open. He lowered his hands as a thunderous burst of electrical energy ripped through the clouds and jolted its way to his body. His eyes beginning to glow with an intense yellow aura, Mako fired a bolt of crackling lightning at the snow-covered ground.

A large shockwave rippled outward, violently shaking the ground out in front of him as showers of small rocks slammed into his opponents, knocking all of them to the ground.

"Woohoo!" Miyuki and Yomatri cheered, light shining off their faces. Nearby, the surviving prisoners viewed the destruction and cheered even louder.

Breathing heavily, Mako lowered his hands and scanned the area. As he locked eyes with his brother Beta, his eyes widened yet again.

"Beta, watch out!" he shouted.

Miyuki and the other heroes turned.

Out of nowhere, a small platoon of armed soldiers appeared and rushed Beta from behind. Beta turned around, but as several assailants aimed their bows at him, a barrage of fireballs came down with a sizzling crack, instantly wiping them out.

Stunned, Beta and everyone else looked over and saw Sage, standing in a battle stance near Zatch. Lowering his hands, Sage took a minute to recover from the exhausting attack.

"Is that the last of them?!" Zatch called out.

"Yes, I think so!" Mako replied.

Moments later, Miyuki and Yomatri regrouped with the four brothers in the center of the courtyard. In the surrounding area, the surviving prisoners came together and happily embraced, knowing they'd finally been freed. Afterwards, they worked together to remove the shackles from their wrists, using a key from one of the guards.

Around everyone, the battleground was littered with defeated enemy soldiers, stones, and various weapons. Thick black smoke billowed up while smoldering fires continued to burn.

"Hey, you guys, awesome job out there!" Miyuki said, pumping her fist into the air. "Where'd you all learn how to fight like that?"

Filled with joy and relief, Sage responded, "Thanks. We learned many years ago, back home on Aridnemeki."

"What about you two? Who taught you, you know, how to fight?" asked Zatch.

Miyuki glanced at Yomatri, then returned her attention to the others. "Oh, uh, it's a long story."

"That's fine, don't worry. I do want to say thank you, though, to both of you, for helping save us all. It means a lot to my brothers and our people," Sage said, then paused. "Can I ask, what are your guys' names?"

"I'm Yomatri," he said.

"And I'm Miyuki," the curly-haired girl added, gesturing to herself.

"Ah, okay. And you said that you're with the Alliance? If so, do you possibly know where we can find our leader, Master Zorhins?"

Yomatri was hesitant. His lips struggled to form words. "I'm, uh, honestly not sure how to find him."

A thought suddenly clicked in Miyuki's head. "Wait, I think I have an idea," she said, turning to Yomatri. "You remember that map we found after meeting Captain Zeron?"

"Yeah. Wait, why?"

"Well, I remember you pointing at one of the markers out in the corner of the map, away from the city. Might've been green or something. And then I suggested that maybe that area was a safe spot. That might actually be—I think she called it, 'Ember Island'?"

Yomatri paused to consider her words.

"Ember Island?" Mako asked, confused.

Miyuki turned to him and explained. "It's a place where there's supposedly a bunch of other Aridnemekians living there. If I remember correctly, Master Zorhins might also be there. But we were also told that the island is a few miles out from New York City. That's all we really know about it, though."

"Miyuki, I think you're right. You might be onto something," said Yomatri. "But how are we gonna get there? That's the thing. It's not like we have a list of instructions or whatever."

"I'm not completely sure. We'll figure somethin' out, though; don't worry. If I'm correct, we now at least have a faint idea of where it is."

Sage eyed Miyuki. "Is it possible my brothers and I can join you both in finding the Alliance and the twelve crystals? Would that be okay, do you think?"

"Definitely!" she replied, joining hands with him. "You guys are awesome."

The team was suddenly interrupted by the approach of a teenaged girl with dark shoulder-length hair. Behind her were four other younger prisoners.

"Hello. We just wanted to come and say thank you both, for saving us," the girl said, looking Miyuki and

Yomatri in the eyes.

"You're welcome," the two teens replied.

"It's a shame that not everyone could make it out alive, but that's just how war is. It's not always fair."

"Yeah. I'm sorry for what happened to the others," Miyuki said, her expression sorrowful. "At least you five are alive, though, right?" After a brief silence, she continued, "Do you guys have an idea of what you're gonna do from here?"

The girl glanced back at the warehouse out in the distance. "Well, this abandoned building or whatever—it was only meant to be a temporary living situation, at least from what I remember the soldiers saying. But I think, considering what just occurred, it might be best to leave this place."

"I agree," Yomatri insisted, exchanging a glance with Miyuki. "Even though this place is abandoned, at some point, the police are gonna find out what happened here and launch an investigation. And we don't wanna be around when that happens."

"If it makes it any better, I've talked this over briefly with the other prisoners and we've decided, now that we're free, we'll try to sort of blend in with Earth's way of life. From here, we'll try to make a life for ourselves—until we can return to Aridnemeki of course."

"That's not a bad idea," said Miyuki. Her expression grew nervous. "Are you sure you guys are gonna be okay, though? Like on your own from here?"

"Yes, we'll be fine, don't worry," the dark-haired girl assured her. "I'll look after the others, I promise. I'm not exactly sure how we'll do it, but only time can tell."

"Alright. Then my friends and I wish you guys the best." Miyuki shook hands with her and the other four prisoners. The Aridnemekian girl nodded solemnly, then waved good-bye and turned away as the others followed her.

Moments later, after recovering her backpack from the battleground, Miyuki and her friends regrouped.

"I'm surprised my backpack's fine given everything that happened," she said, slinging the bag over her shoulder. "But I was just thinkin'—that was kinda sad to be honest. I really hope things work out for them."

His arms crossed, Mako lowered his eyes. "Me too," he said, softly kicking a stone on the ground. "What do we do now, though?"

"Wait, hold on a minute," Yomatri interrupted, glancing at the four brothers. "When me and Miyuki met you guys, one of you—I don't remember who—said that you think one of the twelve crystals might be somewhere nearby, right?"

"That's correct—the Emerald. We overheard the soldiers talking about it in the warehouse before you guys came here," replied Sage. "I think now's the time to go search for it."

Yomatri and Miyuki looked on, their eyes hopeful.

"Wait, guys. Here, look," said Beta. Everyone else turned. Taking out a small rectangular device from his back pocket, Beta pressed one of the buttons, turning it on. "I found this on one of the soldiers."

"What is that?" Miyuki asked, knitting her brow. "Lemme see it really quick."

"I think it might be some sort of tracking beacon," Beta answered. Gently, she took the gadget from him and studied it closely, her friends huddling around her.

A map displaying a section of the forest was projected on a miniature screen toward the bottom of the device. Several spots on the map were red, orange, and yellow in color while other areas appeared blue and green.

"Hey, I've seen one of these before!" Yomatri stammered. "I used to learn about 'em all the time in space camp. But Beta's right, I think. This is probably one of their tracking beacons that they used to try and search for the crystal."

"I'm confused," said Mako. "What's the map for then? Does it do anything special?"

"Yep, so it's a heat map. They're actually pretty cool," Yomatri responded. Pointing at a tiny round dot in the center of the screen, he continued, "This must be where we are. And it's sorta showing us where the soldiers were when they were out looking for the crystal."

"But why all the different colors and whatnot?" asked Miyuki. "I'm a little lost too."

"I'll explain. Basically what a heat map does is, it represents data in the form of colors. It can be of any variables, but in our case, the map's based on, kinda like I said before—how often the soldiers were in a specific area over a certain period of time."

"How do you know that?" Beta asked, his expression unsure.

"Well, here, just look," Yomatri said, pointing at the round dot in the center of the screen. "This area around the warehouse is more of a darker color, and as it gravitates outward, the colors on the map get lighter."

"And what do the colors mean again exactly? I don't think you told us yet," said Sage.

"Yep, so just think of these lighter or 'cooler' spots of the forest as areas the soldiers didn't touch so much. And then, the darker or 'hotter' ones are basically the opposite. Those are areas they did have a lotta activity in," Yomatri replied, then paused. "Part of me is still kinda wondering, though, like how the troops knew to search *this* particular forest and why they couldn't find the crystal the first time around."

"Not completely sure how they knew to look here in Westchester, but it's a good thing they didn't find it," Beta insisted. "That would be very bad."

"I agree," said Miyuki. "But based on what you said, Yomatri, my guess is that the soldiers could only search an area within a limited range, you know, to avoid being seen by humans. Because if somebody did see them, who knows what would've happened. Maybe that's why this outer region of the map is a lighter color, like you mentioned?" She ran her finger along the edges of the screen.

"To me, that makes sense. I mean, there's no way they could've searched an entire forest. But now we know two things: we know that the soldiers could only search within a limited area around the warehouse, and we also have an idea of how much of that area they actually went through based on the heat map."

"Mmm-hmm. Those are two very big clues. Makes our job a little easier. Good thing we found this tracking beacon. Nice job, Beta." Miyuki smiled and glanced at him, then up at the sky. "We'd better get moving, though, you guys. It's gettin' kinda dark. Don't think we'll have enough time to search all the lighter spots on the map, but that's fine, I think. Let's try going east of where we are now."

Everyone else began to follow her.

✧✧✧

Later, the six teens paced through another part of the large, remote forest, passing by trees, bushes, and other small plants. In his hand, Beta carried the tracking beacon, which continued to display a map of the environment, most of it now covered with bluish, green spots.

"Do you guys think we're getting close at all?" asked Yomatri.

Climbing over a large log, Miyuki responded, "I don't know. Maybe. Let's just keep looking." Her friends followed her down a long narrow path, and eventually, the group came upon a large wall made up of various stones stacked like bricks.

Following the wall to the end and then peering around the corner, the teens paused, their faces registering shock. A large hole gaped between another stretch of the wall, appearing to be the entrance of a dark cave. Beside the entrance were clusters of weeds and several tall trees, some with thorny branches hanging lifelessly.

Miyuki glanced back at her friends, her heart beginning to pound. "Do we go in?" she asked them.

Yomatri looked confused. "I suppose? I'm umm … honestly not sure. It could be in there or it might not be.

Whatever you guys think is best."

"Let's give it a shot," Beta insisted. He glanced at the others, then toward the entrance to the cave, only seeing darkness in front of him. "We've got nothing to lose."

"Well, whatever we decide, I'm not leading the way this time," Miyuki said, shaking her head with a grin. "Nooo way."

Mako looked over at everyone else. "If we do go in, we're gonna need some light sources."

☆☆☆

Minutes later, Miyuki and Yomatri nervously followed the four brothers into the cave, heading down a flight of stone stairs. Above their heads, thick tree roots dangled from the rocky ceiling. In his hand, Zatch carried a handcrafted wooden torch that burned with a bright hot flame. Standing nearby, Mako and Miyuki held flashlights, which further illuminated the darkness in front of them.

"Hey, Yomatri, I guess those flashlights my dad bought me did actually come in handy," Miyuki said, chuckling. She glanced to her left, noticing a leafy moss which grew in between the cracks of the walls.

"Yeah, no kidding."

With his hands pressed against the cold walls, Sage led the way. He ordered, "Be careful, you guys. I know it doesn't seem like there's anything right now, but always remember to watch your step." Everyone else followed him, passing by several large spider webs.

"Hey, not that I'm tryna start anything, but, uh, how

again did we decide it was a good idea to go down into this cave?" Yomatri asked.

Mako tried not to laugh. "You were the one who said, 'whatever works best for the team', man."

"Well, yeah, but I wasn't actually expectin' you guys to go along with that." He shook his head. "Doesn't matter, I guess. There's no turning back now."

The six teens came to a sudden halt.

"What happened? Why'd we stop?" Miyuki asked, peering ahead with tense shoulders.

As her eyes adjusted, she realized that she and her friends were now standing in a massive underground cavern made up of many rocky formations. During a brief silence, small drips of water from gigantic overhead stalactites ticked on the cavern's rocky floor.

"We must split up," Sage insisted. "This cavern's too large for us all to search together. We break into groups. I'll go with Zatch. Mako and Beta, you both stick together, and Miyuki and Yomatri, you two make team, yes?"

"Are you sure that's a good idea? What are we supposed to do if one of us gets lost?" Miyuki asked, standing close to Yomatri.

"Just yell," Sage responded with a smirk. He pointed to the flashlight in her hand. "No, it shall be okay. Trust me. Remember, you have a flashlight."

"Can I hold on to the tracking beacon?" Yomatri asked Beta, who exchanged brief looks with his brothers.

Beta walked over and handed him the device. "Uh, I guess so. Not sure what help the heat map will be in this cave but have at it."

Yomatri and Miyuki nodded, then separated from the others. The four brothers broke off into their assigned groups and the search ensued.

"This place is really large, isn't it, Yomatri?" Miyuki asked, walking apprehensively with her friend through the mysterious, noiseless tunnels.

"Yeah, but I mean, this, this is awesome! We're in a cave!" Both teens suddenly paused, overhearing sporadic beeps from the tracking beacon.

Her brow furrowed, Miyuki approached Yomatri from the side. "What's goin' on? Why's that thing beeping?"

"I'm ... not sure. Are we near the crystal or something? Is that what it's tryna tell us?"

Eyebrows raised, Miyuki gasped. "Maybe you're right! It probably is. That'd make the most sense, I think. We just have to keep looking!"

Yomatri stopped to think. "If I'm right, I think that explains why the soldiers couldn't find it. It's kinda like you said before—they probably weren't in close enough proximity with the crystal. I just don't know why it wasn't beeping when we were at the entrance to the cave."

"No idea. Maybe it's somewhat broken? But I dunno. Come on, let's keep looking."

Moments later, Miyuki followed Yomatri, pointing her flashlight out in front of him. The teens progressed forward, moving cautiously with each step. At one point, they climbed over a small ridge formed from mounds of stone.

Taking another step forward, Yomatri's foot collided with a pile of heavy rocks, knocking them over the edge of a cliff and down into a massive steep pit just inches in front of him. After nearly falling, the teenager looked ahead, his eyes wide.

Miyuki rushed forward and pulled him back, wincing. Yomatri regained his balance. "Are you alright?!" she asked. "Did you not see that coming? I had my flashlight pointed right in front of you."

"I ... I don't know! Just ignore it. Listen ... I'm okay," he answered, holding the tracking beacon with a trembling hand. He paused to catch his breath. "Let's not go that way."

Miyuki stared after him nervously as he headed in another direction. For a moment, she panned her flashlight down into the pit and saw that it extended deep into the earth. Looking up, she returned her attention to Yomatri, who followed a stone pathway deeper into the cave. With tense shoulders, he led the way.

"Wait, Yomatri—don't go too far!" Miyuki yelled; she raced after him. After catching up, she continued, "I don't know if you should be leading the way after what just happened."

"It's okay, Miyuki. I'm fine, honestly."

The girl shook her head in disbelief, then shined her flashlight, illuminating the darkness ahead. While drops of water from the stalactites continued to tick the cavern's rocky floor, Miyuki cautiously followed her friend. Around them, a swarm of tiny bats fluttered by; the sound of them flapping their wings had echoed loudly throughout the entire room.

The teens flinched and came to a stop.

Miyuki glanced up at the ceiling and suddenly noticed tiny puffs of dust coming from the rocks. As she noticed more and more, her mouth starting to open as something dawned on her, several rocks fell from the roof of the cave.

"Yomatri, watch out!!" Miyuki screamed. She dashed forward and tackled him to the floor.

Heavy stones crashed to the ground, throwing up small clouds of dust. For a moment, the teens remained still, their faces dazed, as they considered what just happened. As the dust began to subside, Miyuki raised her head and batted her eyes at Yomatri.

"What happened now?! Did you not see that too? You were nearly just killed!"

His heart beating fast, Yomatri replied, "I don't know what's wrong! Maybe I'm just really nervous." Looking disappointed in himself, he glanced over at the tracking beacon lying on the ground nearby. Noting it was free of damage, he sighed with relief.

The device continued to ring with sporadic beeps.

Miyuki angrily shook her head. Later she and her friend turned a corner, now standing on a narrow stony ledge only a few inches wide. Pausing, Miyuki looked down: to her right, she could see nothing in the darkness beneath her.

As Yomatri edged forward, small chunks of rock broke off and dropped down into the shadowy abyss. With sweat dripping from his forehead, he stopped to regain his balance.

Miyuki's eyes lit up as she heard the rocks crash into a body of water. "You heard that, right? It sounded like water or something."

"Yep, I definitely heard it, but I am not looking down." Yomatri glanced ahead and spotted a wooden bridge connecting to a higher elevation of rock. In the distance was a faint hissing noise that sounded like rushing water. "Here, let's go there," he pointed.

Miyuki shined her flashlight ahead.

Together, the teens broke free from the stone ledge and slowly crossed the unstable wooden bridge, holding tight onto its loosely-tied leather railing. With each step, the bridge creaked loudly. On the other side, they came to a stop, noticing the beeps from the tracking beacon now came at a much faster rate.

"We're gettin' close," Yomatri said. "You mind holding this for a sec?"

"Yeah, no problem." Miyuki took the device from him and stashed it in a small pouch on the side of her backpack.

The teenagers turned and clambered up large rock formations covered in thick moss. After regaining their breath, they stood upright on an uneven rocky floor. Again, Miyuki panned her flashlight ahead. Standing close, she and Yomatri grinned tiredly, now overlooking an enormous waterfall shrouded in mist rushing toward a vast, murky pool.

"Whoa! You were right—this place is really large," Yomatri said in awe, staring out into the distance. Vibrant green and blue lights from the water's surface reflected off both teens faces.

"Yeah, no kidding," Miyuki replied, turning off her flashlight after realizing they could now see comfortably. The beeps from the tracking beacon now came at an even faster rate with lights on the side of the device flashing wildly.

Yomatri scanned the large, gloomy pool and eventually stopped, locking eyes with a bright green light glowing in the muddy water. "Wait a minute. What is that?"

Miyuki squinted. "What's *what*? What do you mean?"

He grabbed her by the arm and pointed. "That."

"You don't think it could be the crystal, do you?"

"It might be! We have to go down there ... now!"

Scrambling to the edge of the pool, the teens stopped near a large ridged rock formation carved into the side of the cavern. Miyuki bent down and scanned the water with her eyes, estimating that it was only about three feet deep. Taking the tracking beacon out of her backpack, she turned it off, then gently tossed both the device and her flashlight aside.

Together, Miyuki and Yomatri dashed into the water, a great feeling of wonder surging through them. Peering into the water, they studied the bright light, which appeared to be a jagged object shaped like a rod just over two feet in length.

Drawing tense breaths, the teens grabbed both ends of the strange item, each with two hands. As they tugged hard at the weapon, they kicked their feet at the bottom of the pool for traction.

Yomatri and Miyuki gritted their teeth, their necks straining as they pulled even harder. Tiny drips of water floated onto Miyuki's arms, hardening into thick ice. Hoping to gather more strength, she encased her hands in more ice.

Yomatri did the same.

Together, each with one hand, the teenagers grabbed the strange item and lifted it up firmly. It was sharp on both ends and very pointy.

"Whoa! Wait, so this is one of the twelve crystals!" said Yomatri. "The Emerald."

"This is insane!" Miyuki added, breathless.

"What is that? Have you finally found it, my friends?" a voice shouted from another part of the cavern.

Miyuki and Yomatri glanced up and saw Sage and the others standing on a rocky ledge overlooking the pool. As big, happy smiles formed on Yomatri and Miyuki's faces, they both stood up, dripping and soaked with water.

The teens raised the ancient rod, which cast a vibrant green glow, illuminating the surrounding darkness.

"Yes, we found it!" Miyuki screamed.

The four brothers smiled back excitedly. "Woohoo!" they each shouted, pumping their fists high; their yells echoed throughout the enormous cavern.

"YEAH!!" Beta yelled, clapping proudly.

Side by side, Yomatri and Miyuki each gripped the rod and repeatedly thrust the Emerald Crystal high into the air.

CHAPTER TEN:

CELEBRATION

Several hours later, the six teenagers arrived back at Yomatri's house in Forest Hills. After parking along the sidewalk, Miyuki got out from her father's Lexus RX. Her friends did the same, shutting the car doors behind them as they glanced at the residence, which was covered in sparkling white snow.

Miyuki approached Yomatri from the side. "Hey, I just thought about it ... we're probably gonna need a new way of carryin' that crystal or something." She chuckled. "It's too big to fit in my backpack."

"Yeah, that's a good point because putting it in your dad's trunk isn't gonna work forever. But I'm sure we'll find something out eventually."

Miyuki nodded, and the two of them turned their attention to Sage and his brothers who stared in awe at the strands of vibrant Christmas lights strung across the front of the house.

"Pretty colors," said Mako. Yomatri grinned, then turned to Miyuki, who seemed curious.

"Are your parents home?" Miyuki asked him.

"Yeah, I think so. Here, come on. Let's go." He led the way to the porch and opened the front door as his friends followed him inside.

While taking off their shoes, the brothers examined the clean, dimly lit two-story house, their eyes wide.

Yomatri glanced up. He could smell tacos—his favorite dinner—being prepared in the kitchen. In the living room, Luke was practicing guitar, a favorite hobby of his.

"Hey, Mom, I'm home!" Yomatri called out.

"Hi, honey, I'm in here," Miya replied from the kitchen. Miyuki and Yomatri entered the kitchen, and the four brothers soon followed.

Miya wiped her hands on a wet towel, turned a dial on the stove to a lower temperature, and stopped to give her son a kiss on the cheek. His friends stopped next to a set of wooden cabinets.

"Hello," Miyuki said to Yomatri's mother, waving at her with a smile.

"Hi, Miyuki," Miya responded, glancing at the four brothers. "Heyyy, I love the color of your hair!" she said to Sage who gave a thumbs-up. Miya then turned to her son. "Yomatri, are these more of your friends?"

Tapping repeatedly on the sides of his pants, he replied, "Yeah, I, uh, met them today, actually."

"Oh, that's nice," said Miya. "Where at?"

Yomatri paused. "Uhh ... in Westchester. It's like an hour away from here."

"I've heard of that place before." His mother looked at him unsurely. "What were you doing there?"

Yomatri's heart dropped.

Miyuki interrupted, "We were taking pictures!"

Miya furrowed her brow. "Wait, really? With what

camera?" She turned to her son. "I don't remember ever buying you one, Yomatri."

"Look, I'll explain later, Mom. Is it alright if my friends stay here, just for tonight? Not Miyuki, of course. But, uh, they don't really have anywhere to go."

"Are they homeless?"

Miyuki snickered and whispered to Yomatri, "Dude, your mom is hilarious."

"What? No, Mom—no, they're not homeless!" he snapped. "They just ... need some help. That's all. Please, just one night, I promise, and they'll be outta your hair."

Miya studied the four brothers, still feeling a little unsettled. Then she sighed but gave in to her son's request. "Sure, honey, I guess. But only for tonight. That's it."

"That's totally fine! Thank you. Don't worry, we won't burn down the house or anything."

"Please don't," Miya said, chuckling. "I'm glad to see that you're making more friends and everything, but you gotta give me a little more. Your friends—can they talk ... something?"

"Yeah, um, why do you ask? I mean, they have lips and teeth, and can form words. Ask them anything."

Miya shook her head, grinning. Sage and his brothers glanced nervously at Yomatri, then focused on his mother.

"Hello, it's nice to meet you all," said Miya. "Are you guys twins, quadruplets or something? What do we got goin' on here?"

"I'm not a twin, but they are," said Sage, pointing to Mako and Beta. "Fraternal twins. But we're all brothers."

Miya's eyes lit up. "Wow, that's a really strong accent in your voice! Where's that from? I've never heard it."

Miyuki and Yomatri glanced at each other, their eyes fearful. "Umm ... I wouldn't ask them about that, Mom," Yomatri interrupted. "It makes them nervous. Like *really* nervous."

"Is that so?" Miya asked with a smirk. "You said I could ask them anything."

Yomatri glanced at Miyuki who shrugged her shoulders, awkwardly looking away.

Turning back to his mother, Yomatri whispered, "Yeah, but that, Mom—come on now. I'm just saying that they get reeaally emotional when you ask that. You don't wanna make my friends cry the first time you meet them, do you?"

Miya grinned, raising her hands. "Alright, alright, I'll shut up. I'll believe you this time. Do they have names at least?"

"Yes, very interesting ones, actually," Yomatri replied. He introduced the brothers one by one. Suddenly, his father entered the kitchen, and everyone in the room turned toward him.

"Hey, everybody," said Luke. Miyuki and the four brothers waved and smiled. "Are these new friends of yours, Yomatri?"

"Yeah, Mom said it was okay for them to stay here tonight—just tonight; don't worry."

Luke studied the brothers as a puzzled expression formed on his face. He glanced at Miya, his look questioning. His wife shrugged her shoulders.

"Is something wrong?" Mako asked worriedly.

"No, not really," said Luke. "I'm just wondering, is there a reason all of you have different-colored hair?"

The four brothers—Sage, Mako, Beta, and Zatch— eyed one another, seeming confused. Miyuki and Yomatri didn't think they'd understood. Nervously, Sage and his brothers scratched their heads, looking away.

Seeing that no one was going to answer, Luke ignored the fact he'd even asked the question.

Miya glanced at her husband. "Hey, honey, did you wanna come with me to grab some stuff from the supermarket for the New Year's party? I forgot to get a few things."

"Yeah, sure. I don't really have anything to do." Moments later, he and his wife began putting on their shoes and winter jackets.

Miya took her car keys from a nearby counter, then turned back to her son. "Sweetie, the food's pretty much done. Just let it cook for a few more minutes and then you and your friends can eat."

As his parents headed toward the front door, Yomatri said, "Wait, Mom, before you go—I know this might be asking a lot, but would it also be alright if my friends came to the party tomorrow?"

"Sure, that's fine. I don't see a problem with that. You kids be safe."

The teens waved good-bye to Miya and Luke who walked out of the house, gently shutting the door behind them. Walking to the red minivan in the driveway, Luke paused and turned to his wife.

"What's wrong?" Miya asked, curious.

"Are you sure you're okay with letting those kids stay over for tonight? You didn't seem too sure about it in the kitchen."

Miya sighed. "I'm sure it'll be okay. I know we don't really know them yet, but they seemed fine to me. I just didn't wanna make him sad, I guess."

"No, that's okay. I was just wondering."

Back in the house, Sage and his brothers were seated at the dining table while Miyuki and Yomatri leaned against a countertop close by.

"Okay, okay ... ," Miyuki started, "I know you guys have told us a million times and I know Yomatri just said them a few minutes ago, but can you please repeat your names one more time—just to see if I have 'em right?"

"I'm Sage," said the tallest of the four brothers, a boy with spiky fiery-colored hair. His eyes were a strong red color and around his neck was a red, diamond-shaped pendant.

One of the brothers with spiky blond hair added, "And I'm Mako." Unlike Sage, he was rather skinny, and his eyes were a rich gold color.

"You can call me Beta," said the third brother, a handsome, muscular boy with dark shoulder-length hair.

"And my name's Zatch," said the shortest of the brothers, a teenager with hazel eyes and neat, short, sandy hair.

"Okay—Sage, Mako, Beta, and Zatch. Those names aren't too hard. Kinda cool, actually. I think it'll just take some time for me and Yomatri to remember them," said Miyuki. The four Aridnemekians smiled. "I know I probably said this before, but you guys were pretty awesome back there, in Westchester. Can I ask which of you guys has which element?"

"Sure. I hold the element of fire," said Sage, gesturing to himself. "My brother Mako wields the electricity element, Beta has the power of water, and Zatch uses earth. We were born with them."

Miyuki and Yomatri's eyebrows rose.

"Okay, so obviously you guys come from Aridnemeki, but where exactly?" asked Miyuki. "I remember Captain Zeron showed us a map of your world and she told us it's divided into these continents called 'kingdoms.'"

"I don't mean to be rude, but it's a lot to explain. You wouldn't understand," Sage replied, then paused. "But several months back, many of the Aridnemekian people were forced to come to Earth and reestablish their homes due to the war back on our planet. That included us, but we were here for a much shorter time, of course."

"Where'd you guys learn English if you don't mind me asking?" said Yomatri. "Captain Zeron said that she and her team listened to radio waves from outer space or somethin', and that she's been studying our world for quite a while now."

"It was kind of the same for us," Beta responded. "The war back home was becoming too great and we started to find traces of the twelve crystals here on your planet. As a result, the Aridnemekians thought it was a good idea to study your culture and learn your language since we knew we'd eventually be coming here."

Miyuki looked impressed. "That's really smart of you guys, actually."

Yomatri added, "Yeah, I agree. Your guys' English is pretty good for being from a totally different planet."

"Thank you," said Beta.

Miyuki turned to a new subject. "Alright, so obviously you guys had to come here because of the war and everything. But if you don't mind me asking, where are your parents? Did they not come with you to Earth?"

"A while back, when we were younger, our village was attacked, and many bad things happened," Sage explained.

"Yes. We managed to escape, but later on, we were captured by the Aridian Army. And we became prisoners of that abandoned warehouse in Westchester and . . . ," said Zatch, who suddenly stopped talking.

"And what? What's wrong?" Miyuki nervously asked, noticing a saddened look on his face.

"Our mother was killed in the raid, and our father's been missing ever since. We know not where he is. We don't see him since," Zatch continued, hiding back tears. "None of this feels real."

Yomatri and Miyuki's jaws dropped open.

"Oh my God," Yomatri whispered to himself.

"I'm so sorry to hear that," Miyuki said, feeling instant sorrow for the teenagers. She opened her arms, requesting a hug. "Hey, come here, you guys." Miyuki embraced Mako, Beta, and Sage as did Yomatri.

"It's okay," said Beta. "We don't like to think of our

past. It's too painful."

Both Miyuki and Yomatri suddenly paused, noticing Zatch who remained still.

Eyeing him, Miyuki looked concerned.

"It's fine," Zatch said, shaking his head. "I don't really like to do the, um, hugs."

Lowering her eyes, the girl nodded solemnly.

"That's the reason why we're in this war—to take revenge against the enemy, the Aridian Army," said Mako. "We must find Master Zorhins soon. Perhaps he can help us in the search for our father, maybe find answers too. The Alliance must regain possession of the twelve crystals."

"Well, we'll be here to help you guys with anything you need," Yomatri assured, sharing a solemn look with Miyuki. "You guys are our friends now. And we're a team. We stick together no matter what."

The four Aridnemekians looked on with renewed hope. Miyuki smiled, then stopped to check the time on her phone. Turning to Yomatri, she explained, "Hey, I've gotta get going. It's gettin' pretty late."

"Okay, no worries. By the way, I wanted to let you know, for the party tomorrow—you can come by whenever. But hey, before you go, what about the Emerald Crystal?"

"You can keep it. I'll go grab it from my trunk really quick." Moments later, Miyuki returned from outside with the ancient rod in her hand. She handed it to him and then glanced at the four brothers. "Also, that's very sweet of you to let them stay here tonight."

Yomatri smiled. Miyuki reached up to give him a tight

hug, then turned and waved good-bye to the brothers. After hearing the front door close, Yomatri froze and felt a big pressure weigh in on him. He felt he had to be a mentor figure for his four new friends, as they didn't have anyone to guide them any longer.

Coming back to his senses, he turned toward the brothers. "Hey, you guys, I'm gonna go downstairs really quick and hide this thing so my parents don't find out about it. There's this closet in the basement that no one really goes into anymore, but ... I guess that doesn't totally matter to you guys. Anyways, I'll be right back."

Minutes later, Yomatri returned to the kitchen, stopping beside the stove. "You guys hungry?" he asked, looking over at the brothers. The four of them nodded. Pausing to think, Yomatri tapped his chin. "Well, here, come on over. I can show you guys. Just, uh, tell me what you do and don't like."

"We know not what this is," Mako said, pointing nervously at the pot of ground beef.

"Right ... silly me. You're not from here. Why didn't I think of that?" Yomatri replied. He tapped his forehead clumsily. "Umm ... well, these are called 'tacos'. They're really good. I think you guys will like 'em. Here, try it." He handed them each a saucer and gave Mako, who was the first in line, a plastic spoon.

A pleased smile formed on Mako's face. "Mmmm! I really like this."

Yomatri grinned. "Then you're gonna love it when you add a shell and all this other wonderful stuff." He pointed to a round dish divided evenly into different sections containing lettuce, shredded cheese, tomatoes, sour cream, and olives. "Here, I'll show you guys."

After a short dinner, the teens gathered in the living room. In its center was a double-tiered glass coffee table with a colorfully woven rug underneath. Along one of the walls was a large flat-screen television resting on a wooden stand containing hundreds of Blu-rays and DVDs. Other walls were adorned with various family photos and a few art pieces mixed in.

"So, this is the living room. There's a couch, TV ... oh and, uh, there's board games over there in the corner if you guys are interested," Yomatri said, pointing. "But hold on just a sec. I'm gonna go upstairs really quick and grab some blankets. I'll be sleeping here tonight with you guys."

The Aridnemekians glanced around the room, examining their surroundings. After he'd returned, Yomatri briefly showed his new friends how to use the TV.

"Hey, Yomatri, I have question, about Miyuki," said Mako. "How long you know her?"

"Only a few days actually. We're just friends. Why?"

Mako shook his head and didn't answer.

Yomatri looked away, feeling a little embarrassed and confused. "Hey, you guys, let's watch some TV or something. Everything will be alright, trust me. You're safe here now."

Sage, Mako, Beta, and Zatch still looked anxious.

About an hour later, Luke and Miya had returned from the supermarket and after eating dinner, they stopped in the living room.

"You guys okay? Everything alright?" asked Luke.

"Yeah, we're fine," his son responded.

"Well, if you need anything, we're just upstairs," said Miya. She and Luke turned away and headed up to their bedroom, leaving the teenagers all alone.

Almost all of the lights in the house were now turned off, and the dishwasher hummed with a soothing murmur. As midnight approached, Yomatri showed his new friends how to play hand games like rock-paper-scissors, mercy, bloody knuckles, and hot hands. Even with having a TV to watch and tons of board games to play, he sensed that the Aridnemekians were bored and truly felt sorry for them.

As they continued playing, the brothers began to recall aloud intimate memories of themselves with their parents. Back during a time of peace, they remembered going out to hunt with their father, sewing with their mother and helping her cook, cutting down trees and gathering supplies for their village.

It was hard for Yomatri to relate to them because he'd never lost someone so important in his life. Looking up at the wall, he noticed the clock there read 1:15 a.m. Yomatri yawned and stretched, knowing that this was a moment he'd never forget.

✫✫✫

During the noon hour in the kitchen, Sage and his brothers helped Miya prepare for the New Year's party. Together, the five of them worked as a team, cleaning and setting up fast and efficiently.

Zatch swept the floor and Sage washed a few dirty dishes in the sink. Mako neatly cleaned and wiped down the furniture, while Beta replaced the garbage bag.

From a large box, Miya brought out many festive party favors: fancy hats, long beaded necklaces, party horns, and plastic champagne glasses. Afterwards, she brought up a variety of sodas from the freezer downstairs.

Yomatri woke to all the noise and entered the kitchen. "Hey, Mom," the teenager said, stretching. He went over and embraced his mother, who gave him a kiss on the cheek.

"Hi, honey. How are you?"

"Good ... still just a little tired, I guess. How come you guys are settin' up so early?"

Miya replied, "I don't think it's that early. Better to be prepared than not prepared at all, right?"

"I guess so." Yomatri shrugged his shoulders, then reached into the fridge for the milk and poured himself a glass. As he did, he turned toward Sage and his brothers. "Hey, you guys—you look beat."

Mako chuckled. "A little bit."

"Honey, I've gotta say—I love your new friends! They're so helpful. They clean up the kitchen faster than you've ever done," Miya said to her son, smiling; she patted him on the back.

With a smirk on his face, Yomatri rolled his eyes.

"Nah, I'm just kidding. You know I love you," Miya added, playfully nudging him with her elbow. "But hey, you guys should get ready for the party. It'll be time for it to start sooner than you think."

Yomatri giggled and tried to keep a straight face. "Mom, it's what, 12:15?" he said, glancing at a clock on the stove. "I think we'll be fine. Where's Dad?"

Miya grinned. "I think he went and got a haircut from an old friend of his. He should be back in no time."

"Oh, alright." Yomatri turned to the four brothers. "Are you guys staying for the party tonight?"

"I'm sorry, Yomatri, I didn't want to say this before, but we must get going," said Sage. "The Hero Alliance desperately needs us."

"The what?" Miya asked, suddenly curious.

"Uhh ... I'm not sure what he's talking about," Yomatri said, lowering his glass of milk. His heart pounding, he widened his eyes at Sage.

"What were you talking about, Sage?" Miya asked, as the Aridnemekian began to grasp Yomatri's absurd facial expressions behind his mother's back.

Sage nodded, then said, "I don't know, Yomatri's Mother. I don't know what I'm talking about."

With a very confused look, Miya stared at the fiery-haired teenager. " ... *Okay?*"

"He said he doesn't know, Mom. Look, remember what I said? You don't wanna make him and his brothers burst into tears. I mean, you almost did when you first met them. Like I said, they can get really emotional. And I mean *really* emotional."

"Is this some kind of joke?" His mother giggled.

"Absolutely not."

After a brief silence, Miya snapped her fingers. "Oh, wait! I forgot I have something important to do upstairs ... not that it really matters to you guys. I'll be back."

As his mother walked away, Yomatri widened his eyes at his friend again. "Sage!" he whispered loudly. "Are you trying to get me killed?"

"That is a very strong term you use and I don't like the sound of it," the Aridnemekian responded. "Your mother is a very nice woman and she would never do that to you." He and his brothers turned and walked away.

Bewildered, Yomatri shook his head.

✫✫✫

Later, the five teens played a board game on the floor in the living room. Suddenly, they all paused, overhearing the doorbell ring. Yomatri rose and headed for the front door as his friends did the same, following close behind.

Entering the next room, the teens were stopped by Miya, who paused at the bottom of the staircase. "Who's that?" she asked.

"I'm not really sure," her son replied. He turned and opened the front door.

"Hi, guys, sorry I'm a little early," said Miyuki, wearing a striped shirt with a black skirt and stockings. Over her outfit, she wore a woolly scarf and a thick jacket. Her sweet, tangy perfume filled the air. "Is it fine if I come in?"

Yomatri paused and took in her beauty. "Whoa."

"Hey, Miyuki! Yes, that's fine. Please, come in," Miya said. "It's good to see you again."

The curly-haired girl stepped inside the house, gently shutting the door behind herself. While she took off her mittens and a pair of heeled boots, Yomatri stammered,

157

"Hey, Miyuki, you, uh, you look really nice."

"Yes, you do!" Miya affirmed.

"Awww, thanks. It's just somethin' a little different," she responded, smiling. "I know Yomatri said I could come over whenever, but I just thought I'd stop by beforehand to maybe help out?"

Mako tapped Yomatri on the shoulder and whispered, "You should totally keep her."

"Huh?" Miyuki asked, overhearing.

"Shut up! We're not dating!" Yomatri snapped while trying to keep his voice down. He started to redden.

During a brief silence, Miyuki awkwardly looked around.

"Here, I can take your jacket," Miya said to the sharply-dressed girl. Briefly, she checked her wristwatch. "By the way, you're not too early; don't worry. It's only 5:30. The party doesn't start till 7 anyways. But if you want, there's a few small things you could help me out with in the kitchen."

"Yeah, sure!"

After the two of them had gone away, Yomatri turned to Sage. "Are you sure you can't stay, buddy ol' pal?"

"Ah, forget what I said earlier, my friend. Let's get ready for this party. We're going to have some fun."

In the kitchen, Miya began laying out the many kinds of food she'd prepared, which included trays of macaroni and cheese, spaghetti, beans, salad, and more. At the same time, Miyuki set an assortment of snacks on the counters: chips and dip, a platter of fresh vegetables, peanuts, chocolates, and even cheese and crackers.

Lastly, Miya brought out various cakes from the refrigerator: carrot, chocolate, and even a special cheesecake of hers. Meanwhile, Miyuki helped set the table and made sure everything was positioned correctly and in the right place.

"Nice job, Miyuki," Miya said, giving her a relieved high-five. "I think we did alright."

"Thanks!"

✿✿✿

A little over an hour later, Yomatri stopped next to Miyuki in the living room, wearing a stylish white dress shirt and black pants.

"Hey, I like your outfit! Looks good," the girl said.

"Thanks," he replied, rolling up his sleeves. "Hey, listen—I know my mom said the brothers could only stay here for one night. Would it be okay, do you think, if they stayed at your place after the party? Maybe just for tonight?"

"That's fine. My parents are outta town anyway. I don't think they'll find out."

Yomatri nodded. "Alright, I mean if you're sure you're okay with it. But thank you. I really appreciate you doing that."

"Yeah, definitely! Don't worry, it's not a problem."

✿✿✿

Loud music echoed throughout the entire house, now filled with members of the neighborhood and people from both Miya and Luke's families. As some partygoers clapped their hands in time with the music, others conversed in small groups throughout the living room and downstairs.

In the kitchen, Miya helped serve plates of food where more individuals spoke to each other. While some of the guests enjoyed their meals at the dinner table and on several couches in the house, many adults danced with their children.

Down in the basement near a bar filled with empty wine glasses, Luke taught Sage and his brothers how to play Ping-Pong. Nearby, Miyuki watched Yomatri dance with many of his relatives; she smiled while enjoying a slice of hot pizza.

On the couches, younger kids played video games on a large flat-screen TV. More people cheerfully danced with one another, whirling around the crowded, noisy basement.

As they continued with their game of Ping-Pong, Sage and his brothers watched the excitement all around them. Everyone seemed to move to the beat of the music, laughing and smiling.

Suddenly, Miyuki took a break from her meal and joined Yomatri on the dance floor. "You wanna dance?" she asked, reaching out her hand.

"Sure, why not?" He took the girl's hand.

"Do you know what you're doing?" Miyuki chuckled nervously.

Yomatri pulled her close. "Not really, no. I'm sorta just goin' with the flow. Here, come on!" Together, the teens danced happily with one another.

As midnight approached, the partygoers turned their attention to the flat-screen television, now showing Times

Square. Everyone in the house soon began the famous countdown ... TEN, NINE, EIGHT, SEVEN ...

The basement filled with drunken shouts while champagne and confetti were wildly tossed across the room. Yomatri couldn't help but grab Miyuki by the hand while smiling uncontrollably.

As the ball in Times Square descended upon the city, on the count of ONE, the whole world seemed to shout, "HAPPY NEW YEAR!!!"

CHAPTER ELEVEN:

HOMECOMING

Fireworks erupted high in the sky and the excitement in the streets of New York showed no signs of ending. Teenagers danced with one another and strangers hugged. In a Brooklyn prison cell just within the city limits, though, the atmosphere was somber as two inmates conversed in hushed tones. Other prisoners had begun preparing for bed.

"What is it, Master?" one of the men asked.

"I was just thinking, about the battle in Manhattan," the sorcerer, Shinzuki, replied. He shook his head. "Yomatri may have prevailed this time, but the crystal we seek will soon be in our grasp. Though, if he becomes too powerful, it may be even harder to stop him. That girl who helped him is also a person of interest. It seems she's had an influence already on the boy."

"You're right. But it's likely that he's not made contact with the Alliance yet. As you know, he's only recently returned to Earth."

"I'm aware. He's definitely been well-trained during his time in space camp. We'll need to change our tactics."

"What were you thinking of?"

"We'll need to prepare another battalion of soldiers using our help on the outside. Put our best men behind the front lines. The more you can get, the stronger our chances of defeating him will be. We will stop the boy and any new friends he might've already made. And then, with the crystal in our hands, we will begin to bring down the Hero Alliance."

"Yes, my Master." The man nodded respectfully. "I promise, I will not fail you."

✡✡✡

At home in Forest Hills the next morning, Yomatri was studying the Emerald Crystal that rested on the Ping-Pong table in his basement. Upstairs in the kitchen, Miya added the finishing touches to a big breakfast: pancakes, sausages, bacon, and eggs. Luke read the daily newspaper at the dining table with a cup of hot coffee to his side. Outside, there was a light snowfall.

Downstairs, the floors and counters of the basement were littered with plastic eating utensils and drink cups, empty paper plates, and more. In the center, Yomatri took the Emerald Crystal from the Ping-Pong table, holding it tightly with two hands. Inching several feet away from the table, he immediately felt the primitive object's heft—much like holding a metal staff.

As he twirled the jagged weapon around, the teenager closely watched its movement. He quickly spun around and pointed the ancient rod out in front of him, his eyes alert.

Yomatri paused and lowered the crystal to his side, holding it like a sword. Again he swung it, this time over his head in a controlled, fluid motion.

Gritting his teeth, the teenager repeatedly slashed at the

air while pacing several meters back and forth. He came to a stop, catching his breath as he drew the mysterious rod close to his face. With a tense brow, he studied the Emerald Crystal's strange shape and design.

Now holding it with one hand, Yomatri quickly spun around and slashed at the air again. Out of nowhere, the rod forcefully shot out of the boy's hand, throwing him to the ground! Yomatri's eyes widened.

He watched as the Emerald Crystal spiraled through the air, bouncing off the walls in quick succession. It slammed into multiple wooden chairs near the bar, knocking them all over, then shot back up toward the ceiling.

Yomatri dashed underneath the Ping-Pong table and covered his head, screaming wildly for his life as the rod bounced off the ceiling and raced past him. A burst of green, magical energy ripped through the air, violently shaking the Ping-Pong table.

Yomatri's eyes snapped to the crystal, which suddenly crashed to the ground, then rolled through an open door, into a corner of the laundry room.

Miya and Luke rushed downstairs and turned to see their son hiding underneath the table. "What happened?!" Miya yelled. She and Luke scanned the basement with its toppled-over chairs in the corner. "Why are you hiding underneath the Ping-Pong table?"

"What'd you do? Are you alright?" asked Luke.

Yomatri's panicked gaze shifted between his parents and the chairs near the bar. "I was ... just messing around ... and accidentally knocked down a couple of chairs."

Luke furrowed his brow and cocked his head. "What

were you doing—play fighting or something?"

"Yeah, Dad. What, you don't believe me?"

Miya and Luke shared confused looks.

"What was all that screaming for then? And those loud bangs?"

"I told you! It was probably the chairs falling. I was scared. That's probably what you're talking about."

Miya shook her head in disbelief. "*Okay ...* look, Yomatri, just clean up this mess and come eat when you're done. There's food upstairs." She and her husband turned away.

As soon as his parents reached the top of the stairs, Yomatri raced to his feet and ran into the laundry room. His heart pounding, he stared at the Emerald Crystal lying next to the washer and dryer. The teen came back to his senses, spotting a basket of clothes resting on a table nearby.

Quickly, he took several items of clothing from the basket and covered the crystal with them, then exited the room, gently shutting the door behind himself.

In the kitchen, Miya and Luke were clearly bothered.

"Hey, honey, have you noticed that Yomatri's been acting a bit weird lately?" Miya asked, sounding annoyed.

"Yeah, I didn't believe him when he said he was *"just messing around."*" Luke shook his head. "I don't know. I just don't like being too hard on him."

Miya sighed and crossed her arms. "I know, I don't either. But still, in the past few days, he's been acting really strange and awkward. I didn't wanna say anything, but I kinda noticed it yesterday, and the day before. Do you feel like I'm overthinking?"

"No, no, I've kinda noticed it too," her husband said. "You think space camp might have something to do with it? Or maybe that girl he really seems to like? What's her name—Miyuki?"

"Yeah, that's her. I don't know ... I think we should talk to him about it after breakfast."

Luke gave his wife a solemn nod.

✸✸✸

Later, Yomatri surfed the Internet on his new laptop at the desk in his bedroom. In one of the corners of the room was an old telescope with a framed poster of Earth's solar system leaning against it.

Suddenly, Yomatri heard a knock at the door. His parents opened it and leaned inside.

"Hey, honey, are you okay?" Miya asked. "Is it fine if we come in?"

"Yeah, I'm alright. By the way, I gotta say that was some party last night! We definitely have to do that again sometime," Yomatri replied, then paused. He turned around in his chair and glanced curiously at his parents. "But anyways, what's up, you guys?"

Miya and Luke entered the room, gently shutting the door behind them. As they sat down on their son's bed, they noticed a collection of photos from space camp taped to a wall behind his laptop.

"Listen, Yomatri ... ," Luke started, "don't take this personally at all, but recently, your mom and I have noticed you've been actin' a little strange around the house lately. And well, we just wanted to talk to you to see if everything was alright."

"We know it's sorta been rough for you, now that space camp's all over. And I know we don't talk much about it," Miya added. "Is that what's been bothering you?"

Leaning back in his seat, Yomatri crossed his arms and sighed. "Yeah, sometimes. It's okay, though, honestly. I try not to worry about it too much."

"No, it's not," Luke said, frowning. "I wish you could still be in space camp with your buddies and all, but I don't really know if that's possible anymore. How've things been going, though, since you landed back on Earth? Have you been adjusting to life here well?"

"Yeah, I'd say so. Things have been pretty good lately. Miyuki's been a really big help with that. She's shown me a lot around the city, the technology—I mean, all sorts of stuff. If I ever need help with anything, I can always count on her. We've actually been havin' a lotta fun together."

"That's good to hear," said Miya. "She seems like a really nice friend of yours—very respectful and sweet too. Do you like her?"

Yomatri gave his mother a shy smile and tried to keep himself from laughing. "I don't know, Mom. That's a hard one."

Miya grinned as she and her husband turned to the set of photos spaced out along the wall. Luke pointed to one of the pictures depicting a massive dome-shaped battle station hovering above a small watery planet bearing a single moon.

"Is that like your special headquarters or something—a base you reported to?" Luke asked his son.

"Yep, that's where it all began really. After the NASA spaceship left Earth, I remember that's where we landed. Took us about three days to get there. It's called Ark 128—the battle station I lived in. But in space camp, you gotta learn fast. They don't mess around."

Miya looked impressed. "That's pretty awesome, actually. I bet the three-day trip there must've felt like forever. But I honestly don't see how you did it because I definitely couldn't've lived there."

Luke chuckled. "I agree. There's no way I could live up in space that long."

Yomatri smiled. "You get used to it." He got up and pointed to a group of photos of him and his alien comrades training rigorously in an open courtyard. In some of the photos were commanders and other high-ranking individuals, who overlooked the trainees.

"What's that?" Luke asked his son.

"First day I got there, I had to have a physical assessment with a bunch of creatures and other life-forms I didn't even know. We trained a lot, though, about four times a week."

Miya nodded. "Yeah, I remember you told us about that—how you had to live with a bunch of aliens."

"Mmm-hmm. It was hard in the beginning, but I kinda got used to it over time. After training, we'd always have a small meal together, and then we'd get to do basically whatever we wanted if the commanders didn't have an assignment for us."

"Things like what?" his mom asked.

"I mean, we could visit the lab and use microscopes to study all kinds of unique creatures, dissect things ... maybe learn about the vegetation or wildlife of other nearby planets—anything!" Yomatri explained. From the wall he took a photo of a narrow corridor with rooms along both ends of the hall, handing it to his parents.

"What's this?" Luke and Miya asked, studying the picture closely.

"It's where I lived and slept most of my time there. There were four trainees in each room and everybody had to share. It's actually about the size of this bedroom. But it didn't matter if you were human or alien. They didn't care. You got mixed in at random, which kinda sucked."

"That's definitely gotta be a little scary at first," Miya said, her eyebrows raised. "But then again, you did say before that there were always translators around."

"Yep, so in my case, I lived with this guy named Neo and he actually became my best friend. We'd go on missions together from time to time—only in my last year with the program, though, because I wasn't permitted to go into battle until then. But he was actually raised there in space camp from the day he was born. He taught me some of the best things I know, honestly. Every day it was just repetition, repetition."

"What exactly did you learn from your friend, Neo?" asked Luke.

"A lot of things, really—how to survive, how to communicate with the natives and other life-forms ... how to defend myself. I mean, he also showed me where to go and what to do if I was ever lost."

Miya and Luke glanced at one another with impressed looks. Then his mother said, "You said earlier that from time to time, you and your buddies had assignments or something—but if there weren't any, it sorta just became free time. I'm just really interested, like what kind of assignments did you guys do?"

Yomatri paused to think. "We did, um, a lotta physical, virtual-reality training. That, especially, was something that really helped prepare me and my friends for the real test—fighting in outer space up against the enemy. That was the really scary part. Your life was always on the line."

Placing a hand on her forehead, Miya closed her eyes and shook her head. "Oh, honey, please don't tell me about that. You know I worry about you."

Yomatri giggled. "No, no, Mom, don't worry. It's okay. Maybe I worded it weird. Yes, going into battle was scary at times, but I was always protected, I promise. Here and there, I also did recon and stealth missions. Whenever I had Neo at my side, though, I was always a bit more relaxed. Usually, smaller-scale assignments were just simple things like gathering things for the commanders, cleaning the weapons and gadgets, helping fix things—stuff like that."

"And you said the top leader of the whole camp was this guy named 'Admiral Kaiser', right?" asked Luke. "I'm assuming he taught you and your buddies a bunch."

"Yeah, he was the best! I loved him. He let me do almost anything I wanted. Me and him would always talk whenever we were both free. But overall, though, the other leaders and teachers in the camp were great too. I mean, as a whole, they all taught me things like, you know, discipline, respect, and basic manners."

"Awww, that's really sweet, honey," said Miya.

"Yep, and they also showed me how to build up my confidence, which I'm still workin' on, and how to be brave—I mean, all sorts of stuff," Yomatri added.

"That's awesome. Ahh ... I wanna go to space camp now. It actually sounds like a lot of fun, minus the part about your life always being on the line," said Miya. "But I can definitely see why it means so much to you, and why you miss it a lot too. I see it as an experience you can sorta take with you for the rest of your life."

"Yeah, I agree. I'm just happy I got to participate in it and everything. But, really, I mean ... thank you, guys, again for letting me go on that trip."

"You're welcome," his parents said, smiling. After a brief silence, Miya asked, "Hey, Yomatri, not to change the subject or anything, but, uh, do you have my phone by chance?"

"I do actually. Is it alright if I keep it for now? Miyuki and I were gonna hang out later today, I think."

Miya glanced at her husband with raised eyebrows. "Sure, sweetie, don't let me stop you! Just be sure to answer our texts if your dad messages you." She and Luke got up from the bed and headed for the door, then paused. Miya turned back to her son. "And hey, just remember, we're always here if you ever need to talk to us about anything."

A smile slowly touched the corners of Yomatri's mouth. "Awww, thanks. Love you guys. Also, I'm really sorry about the mess from before."

"It's alright, don't worry about it. We love you too."

His parents smiled back as they exited the room, gently

shutting the door behind them.

Minutes later, while using his laptop, Yomatri felt his mother's phone vibrating in his pocket. He took it out and read a text message from Miyuki:

> Hey, Yomatri! Meet me by the bakery in Manhattan in about an hour. I sent you a link with the address in case you forgot how to get there! But I have something really cool to show you haha. Sage and his brothers are excited about it too :)

For a moment, Yomatri stared curiously at the message and then came back to his senses. Getting up from his chair, he went into his closet and looked through several piles of clothes lying on the floor.

Eventually the teen found a black-and-white hooded jacket with the space camp insignia—a blue and red rocket enclosed in a golden circle—on the shoulder.

After brushing his teeth and putting on a pair of tennis shoes, he took the backpack from underneath his bed and slung it over his shoulder. Yomatri then went down into the basement, stopping in the laundry room.

Beside the washer and dryer was a pile of shirts, jeans, and socks lying on the floor. Yomatri knelt down and gently tossed the clothing garments aside, seeing the Emerald Crystal, which shined its vibrant green color.

"Phew! Good thing they didn't find out about you, little buddy," the teen whispered. Lifting the rod up firmly in one hand, he continued, "Now how am I gonna fit this thing in my backpack?"

Yomatri gasped as out of nowhere, the ancient rod slowly shrank to a length half its original size. Having almost dropped it, he paused for a moment.

"What in the world?" He scratched his head. "Well, I guess that, uh, solves my problem. Don't really know what happened just now, but we are not gonna ask any questions."

Moments later, the teen carefully slipped the rod into his backpack and zipped it shut. He then slung the bag's strap over his shoulder and returned upstairs, stopping near his parents who were now watching TV in the living room.

"Hey, I'm gonna head out now. I'll be back later tonight," Yomatri said to his parents.

Pointing, Luke said, "Nice jacket you got there, kiddo. Looks really good on you."

"Yeah, I like it a lot too!" Miya affirmed. "Did you get that from space camp?"

"Thank you, guys. And yes, Mom, I did get it from camp. It is pretty spiffy, I must say." He chuckled and briefly examined his jacket.

"Well, since we've got nothin' to do, we'll be here just watchin' TV, I guess," said Miya.

"Oh, alright. I'll see you guys later then," the teen responded, heading toward the front door while waving good-bye to his parents.

✫✫✫

On a busy, snowy Manhattan sidewalk, Yomatri walked amongst groups of people dressed in hats, mittens, and heavy winter coats. A few individuals were out walking their dogs while others chatted on their phones. Every few minutes, the roar of a passing train could be heard in the distance.

As he continued, the teenager took note of various stores along the sidewalk—music, book, and souvenir shops. The smell of coffee and the constant sound of honking and commotion from irritated drivers in the streets filled the air.

Turning a street corner, Yomatri paused, noticing a white Lexus RX parked along the sidewalk. An "I Love Pandas" sticker was on its left bumper. He approached the vehicle and noticed Miyuki and the four brothers sitting inside.

Miyuki opened the passenger door and let him in. "Hey, you made it!" she said happily.

Yomatri smiled and put on his seat belt. After waving "hello" to Sage and his brothers, he responded, "I'm here! Why exactly did you want me to come here again? Wait, don't answer that. Can I tell you somethin' really quick?"

"Yeah, uh, sure, I guess," said Miyuki. "What's up?"

The four brothers listened in closely.

"Okay, so earlier today I was messing around with the Emerald Crystal in my basement because I was sorta, you know, curious to see what it could do. And I don't know what I did, but at one point, it like shot out of my hand and spiraled outta control and hit the wall a few times."

Miyuki's eyebrows rose. "Wait, really? That's crazy! What'd your parents say? Did they find out?"

"Luckily no," Yomatri said, laughing. "I guess the rod like flew in the laundry room or whatever and they didn't notice. I told 'em I was play fighting. And then ... they sorta got mad. But yes—good thing I didn't get caught."

"Yeah, no kidding. That would've been really bad. You have it with you, though, right—the crystal?"

"Yes, of course. Also, I guess it has the ability to like shrink and then go back to its normal length. I don't know how I made it do it, but that's how I got it to fit in my backpack. No more carrying it in the trunk," Yomatri replied.

"Oh." Miyuki looked surprised. "That's weird."

"Yeah. But anyways, what did you, uh, wanna show me?"

Miyuki turned and opened her backpack lying in front of her. After rustling through papers and other items, she pulled the map from her bag that depicted New York State and was filled with several red markers. In one of the corners of the parchment paper was a green marker.

Miyuki unraveled the map and said to Yomatri, "Okay, look. You're gonna love this. So, remember how we were looking for Ember Island and we didn't really have a good way of getting there?"

"Yeah ... did you find something?"

"Yes, we did! Here's what happened. So, me and the brothers were messin' around with the map late last night after that awesome New Year's party of yours and ... *dunn dunn dunn* ... we discovered a new marker of some kind! It's here, in Manhattan."

Yomatri looked confused. "Huh?"

"Here, I'll show you." Miyuki ran her fingers over the

Manhattan region of the map and a bright yellow marker appeared on the parchment paper.

"Whoa, that's cool! Wait, what exactly is it, though?" Yomatri asked, shifting his curious gaze between her and the map.

Miyuki pointed at the new yellow marker and turned sideways in her seat. A small paragraph of glowing Aridnemekian text expanded outward, enveloping the entire map. "It's some kind of message. Sage and his brothers helped me translate it. It's written in a language only they can understand. But basically, it says that we should meet them at this spot in Manhattan, which is like fifteen minutes away from here."

"Who's '*them*'?" Yomatri asked hesitantly.

Sage interrupted, "We think it's the Hero Alliance. They may be trying to communicate with us, using this map."

"How will we get there, to the spot you mentioned?" asked Beta.

"They gave us directions and everything. We just have to follow it, I guess," Miyuki insisted.

"You guys think Captain Zeron knows we have this?" Yomatri asked.

"Probably," said Miyuki. "It looks like whoever wrote the message ... they want us to meet them at this really old movie theater or something. I think it might be shut down or something. And then they said we'll be taken somewhere out in New York Harbor. I'm guessing that's Ember Island."

"Miyuki, you will take us there, correct?" asked Mako.

"Yeah, definitely. We have to get going, though. They're probably already expecting us."

While the four brothers put on their seat belts, Miyuki started the car. Then she handed the map to Yomatri and drove off.

✱✱✱

A short while later, the teens arrived at the parking lot of the closed-down movie theater. After turning off the engine, Miyuki and her friends stepped out from the SUV and looked all around, not seeing anyone.

Approaching the theater, the group briefly examined the large brick building, which appeared ancient and rusty, looking fit to fall apart at any moment. Once a place where parents and their children could have fun and spend an evening enjoying the latest popcorn flick, the theater was now dilapidated and forgotten. Long green vines ran along the building's aging concrete walls with many of its windows smashed open.

Miyuki took her eyes away from the theater and glanced around. "Is it just me or does this seem a little sketchy? I mean, of all places, why would they ask us to meet them here?"

"I'm not ... really sure," Yomatri responded. He and the brothers began walking through the vacant lot.

Miyuki soon followed.

Suddenly, she and everyone else came to a stop after noticing a large, black metal jet with twin thrusters parked near a willow tree. A ramp lowered to the ground, and a tall woman with fair skin and long red hair exited the ship.

178

Captain Zeron.

The teenagers gasped. As before, she was dressed resembling a knight, her armor blue and yellow. A pilot dressed in a navy jumpsuit had appeared just moments later. Beaming, Miyuki and Yomatri ran toward her, the four brothers following close behind.

"Captain Zeron!" they both said. After embracing the Alliance captain, Miyuki continued, "Oh my God, it's so good to see you! What are you doing here? Where's your team?"

"It's great to see you both again too. My team is actually on Ember Island right now. That's where we're heading. Are all of you ready to go?"

"Yeah, totally, why not?" replied Yomatri.

The Alliance captain looked on happily. Turning her attention to the four brothers, she asked, "You guys, who are your friends?"

"Oh, right. I actually remember their names for once— Sage, Mako, Beta, and Zatch," Miyuki said, pointing to each of them. "You guys, meet Captain Zeron, a strong, uh, captain ... in the Hero Alliance."

"Nice to meet you all," the Alliance captain said, smiling. "Are you guys from here on Earth?"

"No, we're actually Aridnemekian like you," Beta responded, then paused. His expression grew sorrowful. "Our mother was killed in a Fire Kingdom raid several years ago, and our father's been missing ever since."

The Alliance captain paused to think, then came to her senses. "Oh, wait. I think I remember that attack." Frowning, she continued, "Very sorry for your loss. We haven't learned

179

of any new information recently, but I promise you guys that the Alliance is still working very hard to find your father."

Mako smiled warmly. "Thank you, Captain."

Captain Zeron nodded. "Come on, you guys," she said to Yomatri and Miyuki after a brief silence. "Master Zorhins will be so happy to finally meet you both—and your new friends."

With the teenagers following close behind, Zeron and her copilot entered the large aircraft and headed into the cockpit. Miyuki and Yomatri each removed their backpacks and laid them under a row of seats in the middle of the ship.

Meanwhile, Sage and his brothers sat down together in a row of seats along the back end of the spacious cabin. While they strapped themselves in with seat belts, they conversed in an Aridnemekian language.

At the same time, Yomatri examined the ship's cabin. On a shelf above his head were multiple parachutes packaged away in black leather bags, a set of spare weapons, and a first-aid kit.

As the jet began to start, Yomatri turned to Miyuki, who was already buckling herself into a seat in the middle of the cabin. He decided to sit down next to her. Miyuki reached up and handed her friend a set of headphones with a microphone, and they each slid a pair over their heads.

In the cockpit, Captain Zeron and her copilot strapped themselves in. Afterwards, they both punched in commands on an overhead control console. Zeron then adjusted a microphone on her headset and flipped a switch to her side.

Miyuki and Yomatri watched as the boarding door next to them slowly began to slide shut. Glancing back at the four brothers, they both gave their friends an excited thumbs-up.

Moments later, the large Alliance aircraft began to lift off, pivoting its metal wings to its sides. Within seconds, it had soared off into the winter sky.

✫✫✫

As the ship traveled, Miyuki rested her head against Yomatri's shoulder, holding his arm tightly. In the back, the four brothers played electronic games on tablets provided by technicians riding along in the jet.

"Ember Island, this is transport shuttle 6854. We're a little bit under twenty minutes out from home base," the copilot reported in a microphone attached to his seat.

"Copy that. Whenever you can get them here is fine," an unknown voice responded in the mic.

In the cabin, one of the technicians tapped Yomatri on the shoulder and motioned for him to use the microphone in his headset to communicate. "So ... are you the kid they call, 'Yomatri'?"

"Yes, I am. What did I do?" the teenager responded, sounding a little worried.

"Nothing at all," the technician chuckled, already seeming to like the boy's personality. "It's just good that we've finally found you guys. Master Zorhins, our leader, has been waiting to speak with you and Miyuki for quite some time now. And it's nice you've made some friends already in your journey. Are you nervous at all about meeting him?"

"A little bit. But happy to be here!"

Miyuki looked over and grinned.

Yomatri turned away and leaned his head against Miyuki's. In the seats behind them, Mako drew a heart with his fingers and pointed. His brothers noticed and laughed softly.

Almost twenty minutes later, the Alliance jet soared at an angle, passing through thick white clouds. Yomatri peered out a nearby window, his face brightened by the soft red light of the sun. He turned and whispered to Miyuki, who was now holding an overhead strap for support, "We're getting close, I think."

Miyuki gave a thumbs-up.

In the cockpit, Captain Zeron and her copilot overlooked a stream of radars and geographic information presented on an LED screen enclosed by buttons and various switches. "I always hate this part," she said to her copilot. "You can hardly see anything."

Miyuki and Yomatri leaned in and looked ahead, tugging on the seats of Captain Zeron and her copilot. With the microphone in his headset, Yomatri asked Zeron, "Hey, Captain, where are we right now? It seems like we're getting really close."

"Yep, we're almost there actually. Right now, we're just passing through a secret portal to Ember Island, high in the clouds."

"Wait, what do you mean? I'm confused. What does the portal actually do?"

"It's basically sending us to an alternate dimension, which allows us to keep the island hidden from the outside world," the Alliance captain responded. "We can see New York City from the island, but if you were standing back home in the city, you wouldn't be able to see us."

Yomatri turned to Miyuki, smiling, as both of their eyebrows rose.

At the back end of the ship, Sage and his brothers looked out the side windows. Miyuki and Yomatri did the same as they sat back and resumed holding overhead straps. Their mouths dropped open as the ship cut free from the clouds and flew high over an enormous snow-covered island surrounded by a vast, pristine ocean.

"Whoa!!" said Miyuki and Yomatri, their eyes shining in astonishment.

Captain Zeron smiled at her copilot as she veered the ship past a forested hillside along the edge of the island, which was shaped like a crescent. After making a sharp turn, the jet hovered over a grassy flatland near the water and later touched down for a landing amid a swirl of billowing dirt and snow.

In the cockpit, Zeron's copilot flipped an overhead throttle switch. While the ship powered down, the Alliance captain said with clear relief, "We're finally home."

Yomatri and his friends hurried out of the parked jet, taking their things with them. Simultaneously, they all began to survey the serene landscape of the massive island.

Closing her eyes rapturously, Miyuki breathed in the fresh air, smelling forestry and woods all around her. With stunned looks, Yomatri and the four brothers stood near the edge of a rocky cliffside overlooking New York Harbor, which was filled with countless sheets of broken ice.

Captain Zeron stepped off the ship with her crew following close behind. She paused for a moment and studied the amazed teenagers. "Come, you guys. This way," she said, tilting her head in the opposite direction.

The six teens followed as the Alliance captain led them through snowy woods, the forest's fresh smell rising up in waves. While walking, Sage and his brothers stared in awe at the size and majesty of the strange trees, some of them very thorny with curled branches.

Continuing through the woods, the group suddenly came upon a stone pathway snaking up a hillside. Holding onto a bamboo railing, Miyuki and Yomatri's gaze shifted to three multicolored, four-winged creatures that swooped by and rose toward the top of a tree.

"Aw, those are cool!" Miyuki said, pointing.

Breath taken, Yomatri replied, "Yes, they are."

Eventually, the group reached the base of a craggy slope and paused at the sight of a monolithic statue resting atop an outcropping. The statue was of a woman in a strong combat stance holding a sharp longsword. Surrounding the woman were five other monumental statues of Aridnemekian heroes in action.

"Is that you and your squad mates, Captain?" Mako asked, turning to Zeron.

The Alliance captain nodded proudly.

"That ... is pretty cool," Miyuki whispered to herself, eyeing the unique sculptures—some of the Aridnemekian heroes wielding weapons which included maces and crossbows.

While the group continued their arduous trek up the mountain, they began to pass intricate dwellings built from mounds of stone.

Eventually, they reached the edge of a flat summit and Captain Zeron said to everyone, "Here, we can go inside now. I bet you guys are probably getting really cold." She pointed to a set of glass doors enclosed in a round rock formation.

Yomatri and the others followed the Alliance captain inside and walked through a narrow corridor carved out of rock. Numerous light fixtures mounted along the ceiling cast a bright yellow glow, illuminating the entire hallway.

The group followed Captain Zeron through a stone door on the left side of the hall into a lounge area where groups of Aridnemekians sat together at tables, eating and chatting. Towards the front of the room was a counter where drinks and snacks were dispersed. In the corner, occasionally erupting in loud cheers and complaints, Aridnemekian teenagers played board and dice games with one another.

Miyuki and the four brothers studied the room's unique architecture and its inhabitants. At the same time, Yomatri paused near a row of windows embedded in stone, seeing many leafless hanging branches from trees outside.

Looking down, he noticed dozens of stationary airships, some resembling helicopters, near the center of the island. He turned to Captain Zeron and pointed at the glass. "What's that out there?"

"That's the flight deck. The technicians and engineers down there—they clean the ships, make sure our jets run smoothly and look nice—stuff like that. But they also fix things or you might see them assembling new parts on an aircraft from time to time."

"Ahh, I see. That's really cool actually."

The Alliance captain took off her helmet, then replied, "Yep. And the good thing is that all of our ships are fully equipped with a special cloaking mechanism, enabling them to be hidden from the outside world. That's how we got you guys here unnoticed."

Yomatri looked impressed. He scanned the flight deck more in depth and noticed a row of windows situated just underneath it. Again, he pointed and asked, "Wait, Captain, what's that down there, in that row of windows underneath the flight deck?"

"Oh, that? That's just the main lobby. It's sorta like the central control center for this place. Lots of stuff goes on down there: pre-mission briefings, finding new ways to locate the twelve crystals, monitoring the weather for a specific day—you name it."

"That is awesome. It still blows me away that all this isn't necessarily not real ... it's just invisible to humans, you know?"

"Yes, exactly. Essentially, we can see what transpires in the physical realm, but nothing that happens here will ever affect the current state of the real world."

Meanwhile, Miyuki conversed with the four brothers while overlooking a blueprint of Ember Island mounted to a wall near the lounge's entrance.

"Are you having fun, Miyuki?" asked Beta.

"Yeah, so far! This place is so cool."

"Is this where we are?" Zatch asked, pointing to an area along the edge of the island labeled *East Wing*.

"I think so," said Miyuki. "It seems like this place has three levels. Looks like we're on the very top level, then there's a middle floor, and then a basement underneath."

"That is correct, little lady," a mysterious deep voice whispered into Miyuki's ear.

The girl flinched and turned around, only to see two members of Captain Zeron's squad: a tall man with spiky red hair whose left arm was formed entirely out of wood and another with robotic wings protruding from his back.

"Hey, I remember you!" Miyuki said, playfully nudging the man with the wooden arm. She reached up and gave the tall Aridnemekian a warm hug.

The being with robotic wings looked on, grinning.

"How you been, kiddo? It's great to see you again," said the red-haired man.

"Good! This whole 'saving the world' thing's been great. Here, meet some new friends of mine," Miyuki responded; she introduced the four brothers.

"What are you guys doin' here?" asked the robotic-winged man.

"We've come here to meet Master Zorhins," said Mako. "Do you know where he is by chance?"

"Ehh, last time we saw him … he was down in dat main lobby, over there where ya friend is lookin'," said the man with the wooden arm. He gestured toward Yomatri. "It's in da center of this island, on the second level. We can take ya there if you want."

Turning around, Captain Zeron locked eyes with the two members from her group. "Hey, you guys! Take the kids to the main lobby and show them around for a bit, would you please?"

The man with the metallic wings gave a thumbs-up.

As Yomatri began to walk toward the others, he paused and turned back to Captain Zeron who remained still. "Wait, are you not coming with us?"

"I'll, uh, catch up with you guys in a bit, don't worry. Go on, have some fun! Explore. My squad members will take care of you and your friends from here."

Yomatri nodded and regrouped with the others near the lounge's entrance.

✯✯✯

Minutes later, an elevator dropped to the second floor of the island. Together, the team of heroes exited the elevator into a spacious, curved hallway filled with dozens of bright fluorescent lights.

As the group walked, Miyuki and the others passed a variety of Aridnemekian people. A mixture of technicians, engineers, researchers, and scientists filled the busy hallway.

Yomatri paused to peer into several rooms throughout the hall. He stumbled upon a biology lab where groups of scientists dressed in lab coats worked at multiple microscope stations, studying samples of various specimens. Other lab workers typed away at computers and recorded data on large whiteboards.

Several feet away, Miyuki peered into a small armory

and took note of countless futuristic and medieval-looking weapons stacked high on numerous shelves. Staring in awe, she pointed at the armory, grabbing Yomatri's attention.

Eventually, the group passed through a set of automatic doors and entered a large, hexagonal-shaped room: *The Main Lobby*. Throughout the bustling lobby, office personnel wearing headsets worked hard at computers, some of them with hot chocolate, snacks, or candy at their side.

Large round consoles generated strange three-dimensional holograms. Other hi-tech machines displayed mission data. On a big monitor near the ceiling, the weather and current time was shown.

Technicians used drills to repair malfunctioned computers while other individuals recorded data using pens and clipboards. In the center of the room, a futuristic console projected a small globe of planet Earth. Huddled around the hologram, high-ranking officers and other commanders chatted quietly.

Standing near Miyuki and Yomatri, the four brothers examined the enormous room with awe.

"This is pretty cool, I'm not gonna lie," Yomatri whispered to himself.

Miyuki turned to the robotic-winged man. "Where's Master Zorhins? Is he here?"

The warrior with the wooden arm spoke. "Nah, I don't see him, but no worries. I got another idea of where he might be. Come this way."

Miyuki and her friends followed the two Aridnemekian warriors, and eventually arrived in a long hallway with windows along its sides. Stretched beams of sunlight shined brightly against the glass. Yomatri and his friends paused, noticing lines of armed guards standing on both ends of the hall.

The brave-looking soldiers, a mixture of men and women, stood tall and proud with different styles of colorful war paint drawn on their faces and arms. All were dressed in protective metal armor held together by leather straps.

Some of them wore feathered helmets and carried quivers of arrows on their backs. Many wielded long, sharp spears and held scimitars at their hip, while others carried longbows in their hands.

As the heroes passed, the soldiers bowed respectfully. Walking up a small flight of stone steps, the team continued through a set of automatic sliding doors into a majestic council chamber.

Sage and his brothers gasped, examining the circular room which appeared to have been built mostly from gold and other lustrous minerals. Mounted along the walls were numerous burning torches.

The brothers walked alongside Yomatri and Miyuki across a soft carpet knitted with rich yellow and red designs. After a short moment, the teens came to a halt in the center of the room, shifting their gaze toward a tall man with blue eyes and spiky blond hair similar to Mako's.

Wearing a long, fiery-colored robe, he sat comfortably in sturdy red chair with a gold finish. Seated next to him was a woman wearing a beautiful green dress with intricate designs and an ornate diamond on her ring finger.

Two other Aridnemekians—a woman with short

blonde hair dressed in a red skin-tight battle-suit and another in black tights wearing a green shirt—sat across from them in round cushioned metal chairs.

The red-haired man with the wooden arm turned to the teenagers and said, "Yomatri and company, meet Master Zorhins (ZOAR-ins), the leader of the Hero Alliance."

Simultaneously, Sage and his brothers began to bow before their honorable leader. Miyuki noticed and turned to Yomatri. She snapped in a whisper, "Bow!"

Yomatri grimaced at her but did so.

Master Zorhins stood up and focused his eyes on the six teenagers. His voice loud and clear, he spoke with a strong Aridnemekian accent: "Ah, it's so good to meet you all! You've finally made it." He warmly extended his hands as the teens stared into the eyes of the Hero Alliance leader.

"Hi," Miyuki and Yomatri both said with raised eyebrows.

Master Zorhins smiled. "Welcome to Ember Island."

CHAPTER TWELVE:

A HERO'S TEST

As Sage and his brothers sat down, Yomatri gasped.

"Mas ... Master Zorhins!" He shook hands with the Alliance leader, who had a smirk on his face.

"Hi, Yomatri."

"Hey, uh, it's a pleasure to meet you, sir. Oh my gosh, this is awesome! Wow."

Miyuki also shook hands with him, lowering her eyes.

"Here, come sit," said the Alliance leader, gesturing toward two chairs among a circle. Miyuki and Yomatri joined the four brothers, sitting next to them.

Master Zorhins sat down beside the woman in the green dress. Pointing at her, he said, "Everyone, I'd like you to meet my wife, Emma."

"Nice to meet you all," the woman said with a friendly smile. "Miyuki and Yomatri, we've been hearing a lot about you both lately—the battle in Manhattan and the rebellion at the abandoned warehouse in Westchester. Anyone who's willing to fight for the Hero Alliance is always welcome here."

"Thank you," Miyuki replied, sharing an excited look with her friends. "It's nice to finally meet you both too."

The red-battle-suited woman and the lady in black

tights glanced at Yomatri and Miyuki. "Hey, you guys. It's great to see you again," one of the Aridnemekians said.

The teens waved.

"It's like you guys are celebrities around here now," Master Zorhins said as everyone in the room shared a laugh. He turned to the four brothers. "Yomatri, why don't you introduce me to your friends?"

"Oh yes, sir! They're Aridnemekians, actually, just like you. Please meet Sage, Mako, Beta, and Zatch. They're the ones that helped us back at the warehouse to free the other Aridnemekians held captive there."

"It's an honor to meet you, sir," said Sage. He and his brothers waved.

"Nice to meet all of you as well." The Alliance leader grinned. "But that's good news. I'm glad you guys were able to launch a successful attack and make it out alive."

Miyuki stammered, "You wouldn't believe what we found there!"

Master Zorhins and the other Aridnemekians shared confused looks. Curious, Emma asked, "What do you mean? What is it that you've found?"

"We actually discovered one of the twelve crystals—in Westchester. The Emerald."

Emma and the other Aridnemekians looked stunned. Her brow creased, Emma asked, "Do you have it with you?"

Miyuki and the four brothers turned to Yomatri, who nodded. Rising from his seat, Yomatri slowly walked over to the group of Aridnemekians. He stopped before Master Zorhins and knelt down as he opened his backpack and took out the sharp, pointy weapon which cast a vibrant green glow.

Standing up, Yomatri briefly studied the object, watching it closely. All of a sudden, it had returned to its normal size—just over two feet in length. His expression resolute, the teen held the Emerald Crystal out in front of him.

Drawing a deep breath, the Alliance leader rose from his seat to accept the ancient rod. Immediately, the four members from Captain Zeron's squad erupted in cheers and applause.

Miyuki and her friends joined them.

Yomatri glanced back, his face beaming. He then faced the Alliance leader, locking eyes with him. "Well, what do you think?"

"What do I think?" said Master Zorhins, raising his eyebrows. "I think this is impressive! Thank you, Yomatri." He stopped to give the boy a warm hug and a pat on the back.

"You're welcome, sir, but I mean, don't give me all the credit. I couldn't have done it without the help of Miyuki and the brothers."

Master Zorhins turned to Miyuki and the others. "Thank you all. This really means a lot," he said, a tear streaming down his cheek. "As you know, this is a very sacred item to our people. We'll need to keep this well protected."

Emma interrupted, "Miyuki, you said that you and your friends found this in Westchester, but I must ask, where exactly?"

"Yeah, so it definitely wasn't easy, but we managed to

find it in a big cave in this, uh, forest not too far from the warehouse. Beta was a big help with that. He actually found a tracking beacon off one of the Aridian Army troops."

"Thanks, guys," said Beta. Turning to Emma, he continued, "Miyuki and Yomatri did a great job too. But we'll do our best to help find the other eleven."

Master Zorhins wiped the tear from his cheek and walked over to the red-haired man with the wooden arm. The Alliance leader handed him the Emerald Crystal, whispering in his ear as he did so.

The teenagers were confused.

Yomatri asked, "Wait, aren't you guys gonna lock that up or somethin'?"

"Yes, certainly, but later. Don't worry. It'll be okay, I promise," the Alliance leader replied. "I have to ask, though—how've your adventures been going so far, Yomatri, now that you and Miyuki possess these amazing abilities?"

"It's been a lotta fun, sir. I'd say me and Miyuki love being 'warriors of the Hero Alliance', I guess you could call us."

"Fantastic warriors of the Hero Alliance," Emma said with a grin. During a brief silence, Miyuki shared awkward looks with her friends.

Master Zorhins spoke up. "Well, I have to say it's been great to finally meet you all. I do have a surprise, though, so we don't have to stay in this boring room." Yomatri and his friends waited, very curious. "On behalf of myself and my wife, I'd like to give you all a tour of Ember Island."

"Sure, that'd be great!" said Miyuki. Immediately, she and the four brothers rose from their seats along with

Emma. Yomatri took his backpack from the floor and slung it over his back.

Emma turned to the four members of Captain Zeron's squad. "You guys will stay here and watch over the chamber, right?"

The warrior with the robotic wings answered, "Yes, ma'am, we can do that."

The six teens turned and stepped out into the hallway, following close behind Emma and Master Zorhins. "Are all of you ready to go on a short adventure?" the Alliance leader asked.

"Of course!" Miyuki responded.

"Master Zorhins, sir, I just have to say, my brothers and I are totally blown away by this place," said Mako. "Your palace and everything is incredible. Can I ask, how much did it cost?"

The Alliance leader chuckled. "Thank you, Mako. I'm glad you like it." He winked and continued, "Let's just say it was quite a lot."

Everyone paused as Captain Zeron suddenly appeared from down the hall and stopped near the group. "Hey, I'm here," she said to Master Zorhins. "Are you giving them a tour or something?"

"Yes—have you done that already?"

"Well, sort of, but I mean there's still a few things I'd like for them to see. I'll come with you guys this time." Peering into the council chamber, she noticed her squad-mates, who chatted amongst one another and the Emerald Crystal, its bright green glow spreading out on all sides.

Her eyes lit up. "Wait, you found the Emerald Crystal?" the Alliance captain asked, turning to Yomatri.

"Yeah, wait, why?"

Captain Zeron clicked her tongue and bumped fists with him. "That's what I like to hear! I knew you had it in you, kid." Miyuki and the others shared a laugh. Pointing at her squad-mates, Zeron asked, "Are they going to watch over the council room?"

"Yes," responded Master Zorhins. He turned to the group, then said, "Here, let's go everyone."

✡✡✡

Minutes later, the group walked through a large network of interconnected hallways just outside the main lobby. Along the walls were various dorms where Aridnemekian families lived. Children raced through the narrow halls, while groups of teenagers conversed with one another in their language just outside their rooms.

Standing near the four brothers, Yomatri glanced at them, noticing they were rather quiet. He watched as his friends observed the other Aridnemekian teens in the hall and listened in on some of their conversations.

"Hey, buddy ol' pal, this might be where you and your brothers will be living soon," Yomatri whispered to Sage who smiled with what seemed to be relief.

Miyuki asked, "Captain Zeron, was this what you were talking about when you first met us? Is this where the hundreds of Aridnemekians live on this island?"

"Yes, exactly. In the dorms, children live with their

parents and essentially, they're free to do whatever they want—until curfew, of course."

Beta interrupted, "Can I ask how many Aridnemekians exactly live here, on the island? I remember someone said it before, but I forgot."

The Alliance captain continued, "Almost seven hundred, I want to say. But not all of them live here in these dorms. You know, some of them—like technicians—live in other parts of the island, like the basement for example."

"Hey, I have another question, Captain," said Miyuki. "When did you realize you were missing that map of yours, that me and Yomatri had? I know you used it to communicate with us so we could meet you and your pilot at that closed-down movie theater."

"I actually noticed a few hours after my team and I left Yomatri's house. But we couldn't turn back because Master Zorhins urgently needed us here at the island. You still have it with you, though, correct?"

"Yep. Here, lemme get it." Pausing, Miyuki reached into her backpack and handed the parchment to the Alliance captain.

"Thank you, guys."

"Captain, do you know what those strange lights in the sky were when we first met?" asked Yomatri. "You had to have seen them. I know when Miyuki and I were heading back to my house, we saw a bunch of colors in the sky—like blue, green, red, and some other ones too."

"Yes, I know what you're talking about. I believe they were energy fields from the twelve crystals. Did something strange happen to you and Miyuki that night, you know, before we actually met?"

"Yes, actually!" Miyuki interrupted. "Me and Yomatri went out skating and nearly died believe it or not. There was an accident and we both collapsed into this lake, but somehow we were both saved. And then our clothes like dried all by themselves. It was super weird."

"Do you think it was that night that we obtained our elements?" Yomatri asked Zeron.

"I'm sure of it. It's the only possible explanation. The energy fields from the rods must've helped you both quickly adapt to the danger. In turn, you both were able to free yourselves from the water."

"I knew it!" Miyuki said to Yomatri.

"Okay ... you were right," he responded, playfully rolling his eyes.

Eventually, the group arrived back outside to an area along the west side of the island and followed a narrow snow-covered path lined with bushes and other plants.

"Hey, Emma," said Miyuki, "can you tell us who that man was that invaded Manhattan? I remember you saying you've been hearing a lot about me and Yomatri lately."

Emma answered, "Yes. His face was shown on the news in hundreds of videos recorded by civilians. His name is Shinzuki—a powerful sorcerer of the Aridian Army. Back on Aridnemeki, he was always causing trouble throughout the twelve kingdoms. He's wanted by the Alliance for countless war crimes."

Yomatri added, "He's super tough too. Me and Miyuki nearly lost the first time we battled against him."

Captain Zeron spoke up. "That's okay, Yomatri. At least you guys worked together and managed to defeat him. Here on Ember Island, you can hone your combat skills and train whenever."

After walking through a small wooded area, the group stopped near a large snowy field enclosed by tall trees.

"What is this place?" asked Beta.

"This is just one of the many training courtyards here on Ember Island," said Master Zorhins.

Yomatri stood frozen, his mouth hanging agape as he thought of training at space camp and felt that old thrill. His attention back on the present, the teenager scanned the courtyard closely.

On the inside, groups of teenaged trainees sparred against one another with swords, scimitars, and daggers carved out of wood. Leaders and mentors watched over the teens while small fires burned throughout the courtyard. Scattered around those training were colorful Hero Alliance banners staked into the ground.

Captain Zeron opened a waist-high wooden gate and Miyuki and the four brothers raced inside, pausing near a wooden hut for a better look.

The Alliance captain turned back. "Are you coming, Yomatri?" she asked, seeming confused that he still stood by Master Zorhins.

"Yeah, I just have to ask Master Zorhins something."

Captain Zeron nodded, then turned away as she headed into the courtyard. Meanwhile, the Alliance leader faced the young teen, who seemed lost.

"Everything okay, kid?" he asked.

His arms crossed, Yomatri shook his head. "Yeah ... I was just thinking for a moment. I don't know, this just came up in my head—like I've been thinkin' about everything that's been going on lately. Like for example, the battle with Shinzuki and when me and Miyuki launched that attack on that abandoned warehouse back in Westchester."

"Yes, that was very brave of you both. I think you and Miyuki make a great team."

"Yeah, Miyuki—she's an awesome partner. I don't think there's anyone else I'd have by my side, honestly. But now that I'm thinkin' about it, like even when we were searching for the Emerald Crystal, there's been many times where she's actually saved my life."

"What do you mean?" Master Zorhins asked, his eyes fixated on the teenager.

"Like I remember when we were goin' up against Shinzuki—I was totally helpless—and he threw a punch at me or whatever, and Miyuki came to the rescue and defended me with a shield of hers. And then she helped me from the ground and we took him on together."

"I see," the Alliance leader said, tapping his chin.

"Yep, and then, during the battle at the warehouse, I remember this missile was comin' at me and I guess I was distracted or something, but she ended up tackling me outta the way and saved both our lives."

"That's really impressive of her. Did something happen during the search for the Emerald Crystal too?"

"Yes, actually! I almost fell into a pit in this really dark cave that we were in and Miyuki jumped in and tugged me back. And then, like a few moments later, she tackled me out of the way of these rocks that crashed to the ground and could've killed me. It was really scary."

There was a brief silence.

"Well, you know what all this means, right?" asked Master Zorhins. Yomatri glanced at him curiously. "It means that she really cares about you. I mean, I don't necessarily know how long you've both known each other, but her actions say a lot."

"Yeah, I get what you're saying. I don't know, though. I mean, I know we found the Emerald Crystal and everything, which is a good thing. Maybe I'm just overreacting, but sometimes I feel I'm not up for this whole 'saving the world' thing like I should be."

"You don't have to say that," the Alliance leader said, shaking his head. "If you think about it, she couldn't have done all this without your help. Yes, she's saved your life many times, but I'm sure there's been at least one or two moments where you helped her perhaps. The way I see it— she needs you just as much as you need her."

"That's a good point."

"Even though you're a hero now, doing what you did is not easy. As I said before, you guys are a team and you both work incredibly well together. And for the record, for someone who was so hesitant on saving the world at first, you've got a lot of guts, kid—that's for sure."

Yomatri grinned. "Did Captain Zeron tell you about that—how I was sorta skeptical at first?"

"Yes, but she was just joking about it," the Alliance leader smirked. "Look, I won't tell Miyuki about any of this, but I just want to say, don't let this get to you. Being a hero is not a simple task and for sure, there'll be tough challenges in the road ahead."

His expression hopeful, Yomatri replied, "Thank you, sir. What you said really means a lot."

The Alliance leader patted him on the back. "Here, come on. Let's go into the courtyard."

Moments later, the two joined Miyuki and the others near the wooden hut. Together, the group watched as a teenager with short brown hair wearing protective garments vigorously clashed swords with another Aridnemekian.

Yomatri's eyes focused on their quick movements. The sound of wood clacking together filled his ears. After a short exchange of swordplay, the dark-haired teen had won the round.

Turning to Master Zorhins, Yomatri pointed. "Master, who is that?"

"That's Hano (Han-OH)—a strong, agile teenager. Every evening after lunch, he trains out here with kids his age and even older. He teaches them what he knows and helps them improve their combat skills. He's one of the best trainees on this island I know. It wouldn't be wise to underestimate him."

Yomatri gave the Alliance leader a solemn nod.

Hano turned his attention to the group. He rested his wooden sword against a tree and ran over to them. Offering a hand to Yomatri, he said, "Hey, I know you! Your name's Yomatri, right?"

"Yeah, wait, how'd you know?"

"How could I not? I heard a lot about you with the whole battle in Manhattan a few days back. Almost everyone here knows your name. I'm Hano."

The teens shook hands.

"Nice to meet you," Yomatri said, pausing to introduce his friends.

After exchanging greetings, Hano continued, "You're really popular around here on this island, Yomatri. There's no doubt you're a good fighter. But let's see how powerful you really are."

He seemed hesitant before responding. "Wait, I'm confused. What are you saying?"

"Face me in a little training exercise. First one to get to three points wins. You'll need some protective armor. This can be your first real test. Whoever wins buys the other guy a free lunch."

"I don't have any money on me, sorry," Yomatri replied, nervously rummaging through his pockets. "And I didn't really, um, come here to fight."

Hano rolled his eyes, a half-smile on his face. "Come on, man. Don't be like that. You're stronger than you think. But that doesn't really even matter. I bet I could beat you without even trying."

"Yomatri, don't worry." Captain Zeron chuckled. "We can make accommodations for the whole lunch thing if you're willing to fight."

"Hmmm … sounds like a challenge there. I also have something to add, on Yomatri's part," said Master Zorhins. The teenager focused nervously on the Alliance leader. "Yomatri, if you win this small test with Hano, I too will reward you."

His brow creased, Yomatri glanced at Miyuki and the four brothers, then returned his attention to Master Zorhins. "What do you mean by that?"

"I overheard you speaking with Sage earlier. And I remember you saying that he and his brothers helped you back in Westchester and that they were prisoners once before. I'm assuming that they don't have homes yet. Is that correct?"

Beta stammered, "Are you saying that you'll—"

The Alliance leader nodded, then turned to Yomatri. "If you win, I will offer Sage and his brothers a home, here on Ember Island."

The eyes of the four brothers lit up.

"Yomatri!!" Beta yelled excitedly.

Mako continued, "You have to take on this challenge! That would be the best gift ever. You can totally win this!"

Yomatri paused to consider his friends' words, then turned confidently to the Alliance leader. "Alright, you've got it, Master Zorhins. We're on."

Beta and Mako erupted in a series of cheers to which Miyuki and Yomatri smiled.

✫✫✫

Later, the six teens regrouped with Hano at the edge of the courtyard near the water. Now dressed in protective armor and a defensive helmet, Yomatri was ready to battle. Standing nearby, Miyuki and the others watched closely.

From around the courtyard, other Aridnemekian

spectators joined to observe the fight. In the center, the two teens prepared combat stances, standing several feet apart. Between them, a referee dressed in a dark winter coat stood firm as he snapped two opposite colored flags.

Yomatri took a deep breath, eyeing his opponent.

"Are you ready to lose?" asked Hano.

"I wouldn't say that," Yomatri assured. Hano crept toward him with a taunting smirk. Yomatri edged backward.

Hano delivered a powerful side-kick which Yomatri blocked. Together, they traded fierce punches and kicks, dodging just in time.

Again, Hano kicked at his opponent, barely missing him. Yomatri leaped back onto his hands and sprung quickly to his feet. Swinging, he and Hano dodged powerful blows with precision.

Yomatri threw a punch as a heap of snow lifted from the ground and shot towards his adversary. Swiftly, Hano dodged the attack and fired a burst of shadowy energy at his contender.

Tiny bits of snow quickly formed into a thick, defensive ice shield in one of Yomatri's hands. Having shielded himself from his foe's attack, he charged forward, using his other hand to strike with repeated punches. At one point, Yomatri caught Hano by the arm and forced him backward, facing the boy with a fearless scowl.

Hano immediately responded, hurling a second energy rocket at Yomatri. In a flash, Yomatri slid down into the snow, dodging his opponent's attack. As he rose to his feet, the teen turned around, his heart racing. A third energy blast slammed into his shield, causing it to crack.

Without hesitation, Hano fired yet another missile, and Yomatri's shield exploded into pieces. Blown off his feet, the teen painfully crashed onto the ground. He got up slowly and swallowed hard, eyeing Hano closely.

The referee standing in between them lowered a red flag, awarding a point to Hano. In the crowd, Master Zorhins and Captain Zeron studied Yomatri with tense brows.

Having won the first round, Hano inched backward and returned to his starting position as his opponent did the same. He nodded respectfully to Yomatri, who began the second round by launching a water missile at his adversary. Hano jumped out of the way, but upon standing, immediately blocked swift punches from Yomatri.

As the two of them sparred, Master Zorhins' eyes widened. Miyuki watched Yomatri nervously, and her friend continued to fight, sweat shining off his face.

Both of them traded rapid punches and kicks, swiftly parrying each other's strikes. At one point, Yomatri spun around and socked his opponent in the jaw, knocking him to the ground.

In the crowd, Miyuki shared stunned looks with the four brothers, noticing Yomatri easily won the second round, tying the score one-to-one.

Helped up by the referee, Hano eyed his opponent wearily. After taking a deep breath, he began the third round by charging at Yomatri, kicking snow all around him. He attacked with strong punches and kicks.

Knocked to the ground, Yomatri narrowly avoided another deadly punch by rolling out of the way, then swiftly spun back onto his feet. The teens continued to trade vicious blows, and at one point, Yomatri took his foe by surprise, swiping gracefully at his legs.

Hano collapsed down into the snow. As he looked up, his eyes met Yomatri standing over him with raised fists. The referee lowered a blue flag, awarding a point to Yomatri, the score now at two-to-one.

"Yeah, Yomatri!" Miyuki yelled, cheering wildly.

Looking over to her, Yomatri smiled, then turned and helped Hano from the ground. The teens inched several feet apart, preparing for the fourth round.

Hano charged at his opponent with a leaping kick. Yomatri sidestepped the attack. Determined, he forced Hano backward and cast his arm outward. Bits of snow from the ground quickly gathered into his hand and formed into a sturdy ice sword. He swung at Hano, narrowly missing him.

Again Yomatri slashed with his weapon, but Hano ducked and struck with a solid blow, knocking him to his knees. Yomatri dropped his sword, and Hano quickly grabbed it. Advancing, he kicked his opponent to the ground as the crowd erupted into cheers.

Nearby, the referee lowered his red flag, awarding a point to Hano. Lying back exhausted, Yomatri knew there was just one more round to decide the winner. Panting, he slowly rose to his feet while Hano reassumed his starting position.

Yomatri swallowed hard and knitted his brow, then created another defensive shield from the snow with his elements. In his other hand, he formed a spiky mace and stood firm. Unamused, Hano lunged at his opponent, sword in hand.

Their weapons clashed as the two teens fought, striking hard with each hit. At one point, Hano had gained the upper hand, knocking Yomatri's weapon from his grasp. Courageously, the teen defended himself as Hano's sword collided with his shield.

Yet again Hano attacked, this time with a powerful, swift strike, shattering Yomatri's shield to pieces. He advanced quickly and kicked his opponent to the ground, sending him skidding backward in the snow. Hano charged at his contender and swung aggressively with his sword.

Seeming to occur in slow motion, Yomatri thrust his arms out in front of him as a pillar of thick ice rocketed from the ground, defending him. The teen scurried to his feet, raising his fists as he eyed Hano closely.

His face glistening with sweat, Yomatri advanced and fired repeated water attacks at Hano, throwing him off balance. In one final move, he leaped up and spun around to deliver a heavy kick to his opponent's chest.

Dropping his weapon, Hano crashed to the ground, defeated. Around the two exhausted teens, Miyuki and her friends cheered wildly along with the crowd of Aridnemekians.

Eyebrows raised, Yomatri glanced over at Master Zorhins and saw he was beaming. Beside him, the referee lifted his blue flag high, and Yomatri pumped his fist into the air, triumphant.

Emma and Captain Zeron looked on, impressed.

Turning back to Hano, Yomatri helped him from the ground. As the crowd continued to cheer, he slung the boy's arm over his shoulder.

"Ah, that was just beginner's luck." Hano smiled slyly. "You won't be so lucky next time."

"Yeah, maybe, I guess." Yomatri chuckled.

Miyuki rushed over and gave him a tight hug. "Yeah, Yomatri! You did great!"

"Awww, thanks."

Yomatri turned to the four brothers, giving them each a relieved high five. Then he turned back to Hano and bumped fists with him.

✿✿✿

Later, Yomatri and his friends regrouped in the network of interconnected hallways just outside the main lobby. Groups of Aridnemekian teenagers were nearby, conversing with one another in their language.

Miyuki and the others followed Captain Zeron and Master Zorhins to a dorm at the end of one of the halls. The Alliance captain took a keycard from her pocket and unlocked the door, then glanced at Sage and his brothers who were the first to walk in.

Miyuki and Yomatri entered soon after and watched as the faces of the four brothers lit up with joy and relief.

The teens closely examined the large room which included two bunk beds, a series of shelves where board games were stored, a flat-screen TV mounted on the wall, and a mini-refrigerator in the corner.

Mako and Beta rushed over to the fridge and opened it, finding that it was filled with an assortment on ice-cold drinks and snacks.

"Whoa!!" they both said, each taking a beverage and snack from inside.

Nearby, Zatch hurried over to one of the bunk beds and buried his face in a soft blanket. Miyuki and the others laughed, then turned their attention to Sage, who used a remote to turn on the TV. He gasped, a variety of colors from the screen shining off his face.

Briefly, he turned back to the others. "You guys, this is amazing! Thank you, we really appreciate it."

"Yes, thank you," his brothers affirmed.

"Well, it's all for you guys as promised," said the Alliance captain. Standing nearby, Miyuki and Yomatri looked on happily.

"You guys deserve it, for everything you've done," Master Zorhins insisted.

One by one, the brothers rushed toward Yomatri, then Miyuki, giving them each a warm hug. Afterwards, they all thanked them both repeatedly.

"Wait, I thought you weren't the hugging type," Miyuki said to Zatch with an unsure look.

"I typically don't like to do the hugs, yes, but this deserves one."

Miyuki gave a smirk, then turned to Captain Zeron. "You guys must've given them like the best dorm on the island or something. I mean, this room is lit!"

The Alliance captain grinned but appeared confused. "Wait, I don't understand," she said, her arms crossed. "You're saying that the room is on fire?"

Miyuki snickered and shook her head. "No, no—never mind! Forget what I said. It's a long story."

Master Zorhins turned to Yomatri. "You did great out there, kid. I'm impressed."

"Thank you, sir. Maybe I can get that free lunch next time I come here or somethin'?"

"Yes, of course."

Miyuki checked her smartwatch. "Hey, Yomatri, we should get going, don't you think?"

"Oh yeah, you're right," he responded as the brothers embraced him and Miyuki yet again. "Man, I'm gonna miss you guys."

"Me too," Miyuki added.

"Don't worry," said Sage. "We will see each other again. I'm sure of it."

"Are you guys gonna be alright?" asked Yomatri. "You know, this is your home now."

"Yes, we should be fine," Mako insisted. "You have our thanks."

"I'll be back in just a bit to check on you guys and make sure you've got everything," the Alliance captain said to the brothers. "We're just gonna take Yomatri and Miyuki home now."

Sage and his brothers nodded and waved good-bye as Captain Zeron and the others stepped out into the hall, gently closing the door behind them.

Suddenly, Hano appeared and approached the group.

"Hey, Yomatri!"

"Oh, hey, man. What's up?"

"Good thing I found you before you left. I just, uh, wanted to congratulate you. I mean, what you did out there today was really impressive. We'll definitely have to face off again sometime."

"Thanks, dude. I'm always up for another one." The two teens shook hands. Then Yomatri turned as he and Miyuki began to follow Captain Zeron and Master Zorhins while waving good-bye. "I'll see you soon, though, Hano!"

"Yes, my friend. Safe travels."

Minutes later, the heroes regrouped at an outcropping near the water. A large black Alliance jet was parked several feet away.

"Yomatri and Miyuki, two of my pilots will take you both back to New York," said the Alliance captain. "We should get you guys home soon, like Miyuki said."

"Okay, sounds good," said Yomatri. "But hey, you guys, I really had a lotta fun here today. Honestly, thank you for showing me and Miyuki all this. I'll have to come back and visit sometime."

"You're always welcome," Captain Zeron replied, then paused. "Oh wait, I almost forgot. This is for you guys."

The Alliance captain reached into her pocket and took out a small round gadget with a tiny red light in its center. On the sides of the device were various buttons and switches. She handed it to the teenagers.

Miyuki took the object and studied it with Yomatri. "What is it?" she asked.

"It's almost like a cell phone—a really neat communication device. With it, you can contact myself or

Master Zorhins if you ever need to. It'll also help in the future for getting you guys to and from Ember Island. Oh and uh, it's got a built-in tracking system, so we could easily locate you guys if something were to ever happen to you."

"Heyyy, that's neat, Captain! Thanks," said Miyuki. She paused as the red-haired man with the wooden arm suddenly appeared. In his hand was the Emerald Crystal.

Yomatri pointed at him, confused. "Wait a sec. What's goin' on? Why's he got the crystal with him? I thought you guys were gonna lock it up or something."

Master Zorhins turned. "I've changed my mind, Yomatri. I know this might seem rather strange, but I'd like you to hold on to the Emerald Crystal for now. Keep in mind, though, that this is a very important object and it'll be a big responsibility of yours, so I want you to take good care of it."

"Wait, I'm confused. What do you mean?"

"You're probably thinking that I don't want it. But that's not the case. I just think that this will be a great opportunity for you to learn a bit more about it perhaps," the Alliance leader responded. The red-haired man handed him the ancient rod.

"Are you serious?!"

Smiling, Master Zorhins handed Yomatri the rod. "You and Miyuki make a great team, as I've said before, and I trust you both very much. Maybe the crystal will reveal a connection you have with your powers or perhaps it will teach you things I cannot. Only time will tell."

"That's a good way to put it," the Alliance captain said, tapping her chin.

Breath taken, Yomatri replied, "Okay, yes, yes—I'll do my best to keep it safe for you, sir! Promise." He turned to Miyuki and smiled at her, then shared warm hugs with Captain Zeron and Master Zorhins.

Afterwards, the teens made their way to the Alliance jet, waving good-bye as they did. Once inside, they each strapped themselves in while the ship's boarding door slowly slid shut.

Master Zorhins and Captain Zeron looked up, watching as the jet lifted off and pivoted its metal wings to its sides. Within seconds, it had soared off into the dark winter sky.

CHAPTER THIRTEEN:

A NIGHT UNDER THE STARS

Amid a swirl of billowing dirt and snow, the Alliance jet had returned to New York City, landing in the parking lot of the closed-down movie theater. In the cockpit, one of the pilots flipped a gear switch, putting the jet in park. Afterwards in the ship's cabin, the teenagers unbuckled their seat belts and returned their headphones to a nearby shelf.

"Hey, we made it! We're home!" Miyuki cheerfully said while stretching.

"We're home!" Yomatri repeated, pumping his fists in the air. They each took their backpacks from the floor of the cabin and headed toward the exit of the jet.

Turning back, the teens waved good-bye to the Hero Alliance pilots. A boarding door to the jet's cabin slammed shut moments later, and within seconds, the ship was off and heading back toward Ember Island.

Walking to the car, Miyuki noticed that her father's SUV was still in the same place and everything around her seemed to be okay. She and Yomatri entered the vehicle.

"Oh my gosh, wasn't that so much fun?!" Miyuki asked, watching as her friend threw his backpack in the backseat. "It was so nice to see Captain Zeron again and finally meet Master Zorhins. Hano seemed pretty cool too."

"Yeah, they were all really nice to us! The whole thing was just incredible. It really surprised me how large that island was. There's still so much I wanna see."

"I wouldn't worry. I'm sure we'll be back there in no time," Miyuki insisted. She checked her phone and looked at the time. "So, now that we're back in the city, what do you think we should do? We still have a lot of time on our hands. I mean, it's only a little after four o'clock."

There was a brief silence.

"I don't know ... ummm ... do you wanna hang out together?"

"Sure, why not? We can go wherever you want. I'll pay for you."

"Wanna go out for pizza and games, I guess? I don't know ... I'm just tryna come up with ideas."

Miyuki snickered and struggled to keep a straight face. "That sounds a little childish, don't you think, Yomatri? I mean, let's be real—we are teenagers."

"Oh, come on! It'll be fun. You and I can be kids just for once—today. You never know ... maybe together, we'll experience something new."

Miyuki shook her head, grinning. "Okay, what the heck. Let's go have some fun then. I have a nice place in mind that we can go to."

Relieved, Yomatri watched as Miyuki started the car. Within seconds, the sleek white SUV exited the parking lot and then joined the city streets, filled with heavy traffic. Lines of different automobiles—cars, taxicabs, buses, minivans—snaked through the narrow city streets.

Many vehicles were nearly bumper to bumper with each other. Headlights flashed sporadically, some cars only moving a few feet at a time before being forced to brake again. In several vehicles, some people texted while others spoke on the phone.

Eventually, the teens arrived back in a major part of Manhattan known for excitement and fun. Miyuki wanted to treat Yomatri to something nice, and she thought having dinner at a well-known pizzeria was a good idea. She found a space several blocks down from the pizzeria and parallel parked.

After getting out from the car, she headed toward the restaurant. Yomatri quickly ran after her and grabbed her by the wrist.

"Wait, what are you doing?!" Miyuki asked with a grimace.

"I just thought of something! We can come back here later. Let's go have some fun for now," Yomatri insisted, his face beaming. "Come on!"

"You tricked me!" Miyuki yelled as her friend started running, still holding her by the wrist. Though she was a bit mad, Miyuki went along, blushing heavily.

In the cold, the two teens walked hand in hand on the icy sidewalks. Together, they passed by many people and eventually arrived at a food vendor where fresh hotdogs were sold. Miyuki purchased two, and they ate them together on a nearby bench.

"Hey, these are good, aren't they?" asked Yomatri.

"Yeah, I'd say so." Miyuki smiled at her friend and then shyly looked away.

Later that same day, the teenagers headed to a music store whose windows were covered with bright Christmas lights and colorful posters. In the back, they each mock-played several instruments loudly.

Miyuki slammed a pair of cymbals together while Yomatri pounded wildly on a set of drums, making crazy sounds and disrupting the peace of the customers. He then transitioned to a guitar, strumming like a lunatic.

Miyuki grinned.

Suddenly an old clerk appeared, insisting that if they didn't stop he'd kick them out then and there. Yomatri and Miyuki, their inner-kid personalities in high gear, laughed hysterically, ignoring everything he said.

After taking a set of flutes from a nearby shelf, the teenagers joined each other in a tune, playing loudly while they laughed even harder.

The clerk glared, his knuckles whitening as he held both fists at his sides. Trying to put the instruments back, the teens had accidentally knocked over a large bookstand, irritating the clerk even more.

Wide-eyed, Miyuki glanced at Yomatri, realizing it was time to leave. Together, the teenagers ran while the clerk chased them outside, swatting at them with a dusty broom, annoyed at their foolishness.

Racing down a crowded sidewalk, Yomatri and Miyuki tried to blend in the stream of people to hide from any police officers. Amidst the constant chatter from surrounding pedestrians, the teens picked up their pace.

Within minutes, the two of them arrived at a large clothing store, its racks filled with assorted fashionable apparel. Over the intercom, a funky hip-hop song played, which they both recognized.

Searching through the clothing racks, Miyuki found an abnormally large Santa hat for kids that looked very funny and oddly fit her. She put it on, smiling at her friend who tried on a goofy-looking knit hat himself.

Miyuki then noticed a blue scarf hanging on an empty rack. After trying it on, she turned to Yomatri.

"You're so silly," Miyuki said, shaking her head. "But hey, listen—I actually kinda like this scarf."

"You should buy it," Yomatri insisted.

Giggling, she replied, "Maybe I will."

✫✫✫

Against a light snowfall, the teenagers returned to the famous Manhattan pizzeria they'd initially meant to visit. Immediately as they walked in, the combined smell of cheese, tomatoes, sausages, and freshly-cooked pizza filled the air. At a small bar decorated with flashy lights, crowds of New Yorkers watched a football game shown on a large flat-screen TV.

Nearby, dozens of customers helped themselves to soda and other tasty drinks, and throughout the restaurant, people laughed and chatted as they ate. Holding hands, Miyuki and Yomatri were seated at a table in the middle of the restaurant by a tall brunette hostess.

While they settled in, the teens examined the menus.

"Oooo—everything here looks so good!" Miyuki said, her face beaming; she noticed choices for deep-dish pizza, pastas, salads, and more.

"What do you think we should order?"

"I don't know, uhh ... do you wanna split a pizza?"

"Won't that be a lot for just the two of us?"

Miyuki clicked her tongue. "You're right. Let's order a small. I think we can handle a small." She laughed. "Are you okay with sausage and pepperoni on yours?"

"Yeah, that's fine," Yomatri said, then paused. "Hey, I just thought about it ... I should probably text my parents and let 'em know where I'm at. They're probably wondering where I am."

"Yeah, that's a good idea," Miyuki responded, watching as her friend pulled out his mom's phone and sent a quick text message to his father. Suddenly, a waiter came over and Miyuki placed their order. After the server had gone away, she continued, "You look tired, Yomatri. Are you sleepy?"

"A little bit. It's just been a long day. That fight with Hano kinda wore me out to be honest." He chuckled. "But I had a lotta fun, though. I really liked hangin' out with you. We should do this again sometime."

Smiling, Miyuki blushed. "Yes, we should! That music store was really fun. You think that guy who attacked us with the broom hates us?"

"Oh yeah. We'll probably never be able to go there again."

After a short dinner, Yomatri glanced out a nearby window and noticed how dark the sky was getting, but that didn't stop him from having more fun with his friend. He and Miyuki entered an arcade inside the pizzeria.

Together, the teens played various two-player games and raced one another on driving simulators. As time went on, they also enjoyed several rounds of skee-ball and basketball.

Miyuki later played a digital dance game with bright, multicolored lights. At one point, Yomatri joined in and challenged her. As they played round after round, bystanders began to watch. More people crowded around them by the second and they each got better and better as the night went on.

Miyuki was superior in the end. "How was that?" she tiredly asked, stepping off the dance platform.

"That was impressive! You did great."

✫✫✫

Almost an hour later, all of their fun had finally come to an end. Together, the two teenagers headed towards the entrance. "Thank you, guys!" Miyuki waved back at the pizzeria's staff as she closed the door behind her. Turning to Yomatri, she said, "Hey, that place was so much fun! We should definitely go there again."

"Yeah, I'd say so. Aren't you glad that we hung out?"

"Yes … you were right," Miyuki replied, playfully rolling her eyes. She took Yomatri by the hand as they continued down the sidewalk.

"Hey, can I ask you something?"

"Yeah, sure. What's up?"

Yomatri glanced aside bashfully, then returned Miyuki's gaze. "I mean, our lives have changed so much in the past few days, honestly. Look, we nearly *died* the first day we met.

We got recruited by these warriors from another planet, you and I worked together to defeat a deranged sorcerer, and we saved the four brothers from that prison or whatever in Westchester!"

"Sounds like the weirdest story ever, doesn't it?" Miyuki giggled but then grew more serious. "But yeah, I know what you're saying. It's been really crazy lately. We met at a bakery of all places. And if you think about it, I mean, we've been on this adventure together since the beginning."

"Yep, and to top it off, we got to visit like the best island ever!"

"Yeah ... I honestly would've never expected any of this to happen, and to meet you," Miyuki said; she started to redden.

"Do you still consider me that funny-lookin' space kid from the news?" Yomatri grinned.

"No, no, you're fine!" Miyuki replied, sharing a hysterical laugh with her friend.

"Well, I have to ask: what do you think about everything that's been goin' on lately?"

"What do you mean?"

"Like how's it been for you so far, now that you're a hero and all?"

Miyuki paused to think. "Umm ... it's been a little weird adjusting, I'll have to admit. I've been having to keep this whole 'hero thing' a secret from my parents all this time, just like you—even though they're out of town. And I don't really wanna tell any of my classmates either when I go back to school. I wouldn't want them to think I'm a freak or something."

Yomatri shook his head. "You're not a freak, Miyuki. You're awesome! I'd say you're one of the coolest people I know."

She smiled adoringly at him. "Awww, thanks. Hey, I have a question for you now: are you worried at all about what might happen?"

"A little bit, yeah. Now that the four brothers are gone and Shinzuki's been captured, I'm not really sure what to do next or what to expect. How about you?"

"I feel the same way really. I don't know ... it kinda feels like you and I are on our own for now," said Miyuki, walking past many snow-covered trees along the sidewalk.

"Do you ever think we made the wrong decision in choosing to help Captain Zeron and the others?" Yomatri asked, seeming curious.

Miyuki furrowed her brow. "No, no ... why do you say that?"

"I don't know. Master Zorhins and I were talkin' on Ember Island today, and you actually came up in our conversation."

"Really? What'd you guys say?"

Yomatri seemed hesitant before responding. "We were, um ... just talkin' about everything that's been going on lately—like the battle with Shinzuki, the attack in Westchester, us finding the Emerald Crystal ... and uh, I just kinda told him, that there's been many times where you actually saved my life."

"When—what did I do?" she asked, looking confused.

"Like for example, during the battle in Westchester,

you tackled me out of the way of an oncoming missile. And then when we were looking for the Emerald Crystal, it was you who kept me from falling into that pit and you who saved my life when those rocks crashed to the ground and nearly killed me."

Miyuki's eyebrows rose. She paused to think. "Well, yeah, because I mean, you're my friend and I care about you. I know there's been many times where things were really tough—like you said, when we were searching for the Emerald Crystal. And the battle with Shinzuki wasn't all that easy either. If you think about it, both of us nearly lost our lives. Don't sweat it."

The teens came to a stop in front of the SUV.

"I don't know. I told Master Zorhins this too—that sometimes, I just feel I'm not up for this whole 'saving the world' thing like I should be."

Miyuki sighed. "No, no, you don't have to feel that way. It's okay, honestly. I think we're doing fine. I mean, we're only this far in our journey and we've already found one of the twelve crystals! That's pretty impressive, Yomatri, don't you think? Seriously, don't worry. I've got your back. You and I are in this together."

A smile slowly formed on Yomatri's face as he stared into Miyuki's eyes. He shook his head, then said, "You're right. Maybe I was just overthinking."

Together, they shared a warm hug.

Miyuki patted him on the back. "Here, come on. I'll take you home."

✧✧✧

Later that night, the teens had arrived back at Yomatri's house in Forest Hills. When Miyuki stepped out of the vehicle, she walked around it so they could hold each other's hands.

"Hey, Yomatri, I've gotta say I really had a lotta fun with you today. This is honestly the most fun I've had in a while. Thank you for making this one enjoyable day," Miyuki said, smiling coyly at him.

"Yeah, no problem. I had a lotta fun with you too. You were right—we've been friends from the beginning, since I landed back on Earth." He and Miyuki stared into each other's eyes. "Are you gonna be okay driving home?"

"Me? Oh yeah, I'll be fine; don't worry. I don't live too far from here anyways," Miyuki responded, flashing an adoring grin; she inched toward him.

Yomatri smiled back nervously as they both leaned in close, briefly touching foreheads. The teens closed their eyes and pressed their lips together, sharing a gentle, steady kiss. Both of them began to blush, and Yomatri caressed Miyuki's cheeks with his thumbs. At the same time, she held him by the waist.

Again, the teenagers eagerly pressed their lips together. Shortly after, they parted and held each other's hands. Seeming shocked, their eyes met again as they shared an excited laugh.

Smiling, Miyuki glanced up at the dark winter sky, now filled with bright stars. Then she returned her attention to Yomatri and said, "I'd better get going."

"Yeah, it's getting late. But I'll, uh, see you soon."

Together, the teens shared a parting gaze, waving

good-bye at one another while knowing that, once again, everything in their lives had changed.

CHAPTER FOURTEEN:

BUILDING BONDS

Sitting at a desk in his dorm on Ember Island, Sage drew many doodles in a small sketchbook. Suddenly, he paused and looked up, hearing a knock at the door. His brow furrowed as he got up to answer it, only to be standing face-to-face with a tall redhead wearing blue and yellow armor that resembled a knight's—*Captain Zeron.*

"Hi, Captain. What are you doing here?" Sage asked with raised eyebrows.

"I came back to check up on you, remember? Is it alright if I come in?" the Alliance captain responded.

"Yes, that's fine," said Sage, watching as she closed the door, then took a seat on one of the bunk beds. He sat beside her only moments later.

"How come you're all alone? Everything alright?"

"Yeah, I'm okay. This room is really nice and everything—again, I want to say thank you. It's just that my parents have been on my mind a lot lately even though it may not seem like it," Sage replied. He looked down sorrowfully, then shook his head. "It's hard to believe that it's only been a few years since the attack, too."

The Alliance captain eyed the teenager with a sad expression. "I remember your brothers told me about that the moment I first met you all. I was surprised, actually, because I know most people aren't so quick to open up about stuff like that. And I bet it must be very hard for you guys." Gently, she rubbed his back. "But it's okay to miss them. That's entirely normal. Is there anything I can maybe do to help?"

"I'm not really sure," Sage responded. He sighed disappointedly. "Now that I'm here on Earth, what I used to call home back on Aridnemeki feels so far away. And I can't do anything to change that."

"I know what you mean. It's been hard for all of us, really—having to come to an entirely different planet and rebuild, start anew. But that doesn't necessarily mean that things can't get better!"

"What do you mean?"

"Maybe I worded it a little funny," said the Alliance captain; she smiled briefly, then paused to gather her thoughts. "Yes, you and your brothers were imprisoned by the Aridian Army for what may have seemed like forever, but just take a moment and look back on what you've achieved so far."

"I don't, uh, understand."

"Well, for one, you and your brothers teamed up with Miyuki and Yomatri and managed to free yourselves from the abandoned warehouse in Westchester."

"Yeah, Yomatri and Miyuki—they're great. I can tell they're really caring people. I mean, they both offered my brothers and I food and took us into their homes without question."

"That's good to hear. That actually brings me to my next point: you now have a home where you can live freely and have fun with people from your home planet. Even better, you can now say that you're on a mission to help the Alliance save the world."

Sage paused, grinning as he considered her words. "I guess I never really thought about it that way. Maybe you're right."

"Exactly! I think your parents would be proud of you," the Alliance captain said, then paused. "You don't have to feel ashamed about your past. What matters is the person you are today. And you're not alone either, even if you think you are."

Sage chewed his lip. "Even to this day, though, it just seems like the Hero Alliance and the Aridian Army are always fighting and nothing ever gets resolved."

"You have a point, for sure. Perhaps right now it doesn't look like anything's changing, but I'm sure things'll get better as time goes on. Personally, I never wanted to have to fight in a war during my life either. It definitely takes a toll on you. I just hope that one day, it all comes to an end."

There was a short pause.

"Are you afraid to die in battle, Captain?"

The Alliance captain stared back, her expression uneasy. Looking away, she began to blink pensively. "Yes. And with every battle I've fought in, there's been moments where I feared for not only my own life, but also for the lives of my comrades," she said, meeting his gaze.

Sage nodded thoughtfully.

"Listen, I promise you that things will get better for you and your brothers. Just … give it some time. You're a good kid with a lot of potential, and I believe in you."

A smile slowly touched the corners of Sage's mouth. With tears welling in his eyes, he pulled Zeron into a warm embrace.

"Thank you, Captain."

✫✫✫

At home while on his way to his bedroom, Yomatri stopped at the doorway to his parents' bedroom and peered inside. With Luke sound asleep, Miya sat on the edge of the bed, a book in her lap and a cup of tea in one hand.

Suddenly she looked up and saw her son.

"Oh, hi, honey. I was just getting ready to call you actually. Was startin' to get a little worried," Miya said softly, setting her cup of tea down atop a nightstand. "Where've you been all this time?"

"I was just, uh, hangin' out with Miyuki—in Manhattan. It was awesome. We had a lotta fun," Yomatri whispered, then paused. "But I remember sending you guys a text message. Did you not get it or something?"

"Maybe, I don't know. I probably didn't notice it since I've been sitting here reading so long," Miya replied; she set her book aside and pulled out Luke's phone from her pocket and checked the settings. "Ohhh, I see what happened. I had his phone on mute."

Yomatri shook his head, grinning. "You know, Mom, you seem to worry a lot. But you don't have to. I can handle myself. Miyuki and I were just spending the day together— honestly. That's all."

"Well, I guess I wouldn't really be the mom you know

and love if I didn't worry about you all the time," Miya said with a smirk, then paused. "Maybe you're right, though. I do seem to keep forgetting that you're getting a little older now."

"It's okay, don't worry about it. But hey, I'm gonna get some sleep. You need anything before I go?"

"Nope, I'm good, honey. Thank you, though. Have a good night!"

Yomatri waved good-bye and gently shut his mom's door, then headed to his own room just down the hall. As he entered his bedroom, he flipped on the light and set his mother's phone down on the desk.

The teenager paused, noticing a remote lying next to his laptop, and decided a little TV before bed wouldn't hurt. After turning on the television, he sat on the edge of his bed and lowered the volume. Yomatri flipped through many channels, then all of a sudden, stopped on *Channel 6 News*.

"What's going on?"

He leaned in close with the white of the screen glowing in his eyes. A woman with short brown hair spoke over a breaking news report:

> *... It was only hours ago when a dangerous inmate managed to escape from this prison here in Brooklyn in an attack which left three officers dead and several others injured. Reports are still coming in, but investigators have concluded that this is the same man who was responsible for the invasion of*

Manhattan that occurred early last week. While his motive still remains a mystery, police are asking that New Yorkers everywhere be on high alert until further notice . . .

This was more than Yomatri wanted to hear. Immediately, he turned off the TV and sat still, staring off with a look of disbelief in his eyes.

"I don't, I don't believe this."

The teenager shook his head, then buried his face in his hands. After taking a deep breath, he looked up and rested his chin against his fists. Yomatri continued to stare ahead, blinking pensively.

✫✫✫

On Ember Island, in one of the many interconnected hallways, Sage paused as he and Hano bumped into each other. "Whoops . . . sorry!" they both said.

"Oh, hey! There you are. I've been looking all over for you," Hano started. "What are you doin' up so late? You must be exhausted after such a long day."

Sage rubbed his eyes and yawned. "I am. I was just going to grab a small snack from the mess hall and then go to bed. The ones in my room taste a little funny to be honest. Maybe it's just me. But anyways, why do you ask? Did you need me for something?"

Hano placed his hands on his hips. "Well, look, I know this might sound a little weird, but lately I was thinkin' about what happened in the courtyard today between me and your friend, Yomatri. By the way, big congrats to him for winning."

Sage looked confused. "What are you getting at?"

"I was just wondering if I could get to know you guys a little better as a group. Maybe all of us could have dinner at a small restaurant or somethin' in New York."

"That'd be fun. But wait a minute. You've been to the outside world before?"

"Yes, only three or four times, though. It's not so bad actually. Very easy to blend in. Now that I think about it, I've got a pretty cool place in mind we could go to if you guys are up for it."

Sage paused for a moment, considering Hano's words. "Okay, I'm in. I'll be sure to let the others know and then I'll get back to you. Is that okay?"

Hano replied, "Yes, great! I'm looking forward to it."

CHAPTER FIFTEEN:

A LOST FRIEND

A few days later ...

"I hope you guys like eating! This restaurant—I mean, I've only been there twice, but it's reeaally good," said Hano, wearing a black jacket and jeans. He walked beside Yomatri and his five friends down a narrow city street illuminated by bright lights with stores and shops along its sides.

Miyuki's eyebrows rose. "That sounds promising. What kind of food does it serve?"

"All sorts of stuff: noodles, rice, vegetables, and uh, a dish I think you guys call 'sushi'?"

"Yep, that's right," replied Miyuki. "That's super cool, though."

"Wait, so, Hano, how many times have you been to the outside world before?" Yomatri asked. "It seems like the Alliance really trusts you."

"Yes, I love it! It's a big honor. There's so much to see and do here in New York. But to answer your question, only about three or four times. Nothing too extravagant— just sightseeing and a little shopping here and there. Maybe that'll change down the road."

"Would you say there's a little more freedom here in the outside world, you know, in New York?" asked Miyuki.

"Definitely! I mean, Ember Island—it's by no means a prison, but sometimes it's just nice to get out and experience new things."

"That's a good way to put it."

"Hey, Yomatri," said Sage, "can I ask why you have your, eh, backpack with you?"

"Oh, uh, Hano told me to bring it. I guess me and him were gonna head back to Ember Island after dinner and train for a bit. And then I was gonna go home afterwards. I've also got the Emerald Crystal with me, so that'll be fun to play around with."

"Ah, okay, no worries—just wondering."

Moments later, the group arrived at the entrance to a large two-story restaurant, its windows filled with strands of decorative lights that shined vibrantly in the nighttime air. Immediately as they entered, they noticed waiters and waitresses dressed in fancy black uniforms assisting guests left and right.

An assortment of multicolored paper lanterns hung from the ceiling, illuminating the dimly lit restaurant. Customers enjoyed their meals and chatted in between while busboys quickly scrubbed down table after table. The smells of rice, fried noodles, meat, and seafood permeated the air.

After briefly looking around, Yomatri and his friends turned their attention to a group of chefs who were preparing various meals behind large metal grills. With poise, they quickly chopped vegetables and other ingredients, flipping them afterward as smoke billowed in their faces. In the back, more chefs prepared fish, noodles, and shrimp on stoves, using a set of spatulas to cook.

A group of enthused customers watched from behind a counter as the men continued cooking. While some people recorded videos, others held up their phones, snapping selfies in front of the hot grills.

Suddenly, a brunette waitress came over to Yomatri and the others, carrying a handful of menus. "Hello! Is this a party of seven?" she asked.

Hano took a quick head count of the group. "Yep, this is everyone. We're all here. I forgot to mention, though—we had a, um, reservation for 8:30."

"Oh. Umm . . . one moment." The woman checked a nearby computer, then crossed out a name on a small notepad. "Alright, you're all set. Follow me if you would please," she said, smiling, as she led the group over to a large table near the front. In its center was a round serving tray and a pair of chopsticks for everyone.

Miyuki took a seat beside Yomatri, who rested his backpack against the table. "Okay, I gotta give you some credit, Hano," the girl said. "We haven't even eaten yet and this place has already lived up to what you said!"

"Thanks, I'm happy to hear that. I'm sure you guys will love the food."

✡✡✡

Later, surrounded by various dishes and bottled soft drinks, the seven teens tried different foods while chatting in between.

"Is that what I think it is?" Miyuki asked, pointing her chopsticks at a tray of sliced meat.

Hano grinned. "Yep, it's 'duck', I think you guys call it? It's really good, I swear! Try it." He took a sip of his soda.

Miyuki glanced at Yomatri with raised eyebrows.

"Yeah, that's definitely gonna be a 'no' for me," Yomatri said, laughing hysterically.

"Oh, come on! If I try it, you have to also."

Yomatri shook his head, then paused as he felt his mother's phone vibrating in his pocket. He pulled it out and answered: "Hey, Mom. What's up?"

While Miyuki and the others chatted in the background, Miya responded on the other end: "Hi, sweetie! Was just checkin' up on you. Is everything alright? Are you having fun with your friends?"

"Yeah, yeah, I'm fine. We're just havin' dinner at some sushi restaurant or whatever in Manhattan." He turned, motioning to his friends to lower their voices. "We'll have to come here sometime—you, me, and Dad."

Yomatri looked off, distracted, only half-listening to his mom. At one point, he returned his attention to the table, noticing Hano eyeing his backpack.

"Yeah, for sure! You'll have to get the name of it from your friends," Miya insisted. "But it sounds like you're having a lotta fun. I won't hold you too much longer."

Yomatri took the phone away from his ear for a moment and then asked, "Hey, everything alright, Hano?"

He shook his head. "Yeah, yeah, I'm okay—sorry, I was just thinkin' about something."

Moments later, Hano glanced up as a waiter with various strange tattoos on his arms suddenly walked past the table. Briefly, he locked eyes with the man and without his friends seeing, gave a hand signal to him.

The waiter nodded, then turned and gave a thumbs-up to a chef in the back kitchen. Hano returned his attention to the table, and again stared at Yomatri's backpack leaning nearby.

Sage noticed and spoke up. "Hey, you alright?"

"Yeah, I think it was just somethin' I ate," Hano said, gently rubbing his stomach with a grimace. "But I'll be fine, honestly; don't worry."

All of a sudden, a fiery explosion came from the direction of the back kitchen, the force of the blast knocking Yomatri, his friends, and those around them to the ground. Pots and dishes clattered against the floor, and one by one tables toppled over as an emergency siren had gone off.

Yomatri dropped his mother's phone, leaving her screaming in disbelief in the background. Miyuki and her friends glanced at each other, their faces a mixture of worry and confusion. Waiters and waitresses screamed over the commotion, demanding that everyone evacuate the restaurant.

"What's going on?!" Yomatri shouted, staggering to his feet. Customers were rushing past him, heading toward the front door.

Flames grew and licked the back kitchen's walls.

Miyuki and the brothers rose. "I don't know! It sounds like something from that kitchen over there!" she said, pointing. "We've gotta help those people!"

"You guys, I'm gonna go and get help!" Hano shouted, pointing back toward the front doors.

"Wait, no, Hano, we don't need you to do that!" Yomatri yelled. A second, smaller explosion went off in the kitchen, distracting him and his friends.

"Whatever—it's fine!" Miyuki stammered. "Let's go and help those people."

With his friends distracted, Hano quickly took Yomatri's backpack from the floor and slung the bag's strap over his shoulder. He then turned away and sprinted out of the restaurant while Miyuki led her friends to the back kitchen.

The brunette waitress and her coworker came up from behind and stopped them. "Please, don't go back there!" one of the ladies begged. "I know you're only trying to help, but we have to leave!"

"It'll only be a few minutes, I promise! We can't sit here and do nothing," Miyuki responded.

The brunette woman shook her head, then rushed to a nearby phone and dialed 911 while her coworker escorted injured patrons outside. Afterwards, they both quickly headed out the front door with the remaining customers.

Miyuki and her friends burst through the back kitchen door. Inside, thick black smoke billowed up, the air close and hot.

Pausing, the teens noticed several chefs and other employees who worked together to clear the flames; some used fire extinguishers while others filled buckets and pots with water and emptied them on the fire.

Yomatri and the four brothers made their way through

a cluster of spilled-over pots and pans, coughing repeatedly. Together, they used water buckets to help the employees clear the flames. After the fires had diminished, Yomatri ordered the remaining workers to evacuate the restaurant.

Most did as instructed and were heading out the back door when others suddenly removed their chef's uniforms, revealing protective armor underneath. One after another, the men quickly armed themselves with sharp knives and other utensils to use as weapons.

The six teens gaped, shocked.

"What's going on?" Yomatri asked, edging back with raised fists.

"I don't know!" Miyuki responded, shaking her head. Immediately, she dodged a knife attack from one of the men. Pushing him aside, she grabbed a metal pot from an overhead rack, then swung at him as if wielding a tennis racket.

Miyuki bashed the man across the face, knocking him out, then turned and kicked another assailant to the ground. Not even a second later, she was up against a third employee, who swiped at her with a rolling pin.

Bracing herself with the pot, Miyuki used it as a shield. Her attacker swung again and again. Wincing, the girl managed to knock the weapon from the man's grasp with a swift strike as she pushed him into a counter. In one final move, she kicked her opponent square in the chest, wiping him out.

Nearby, one of the employees lashed at Yomatri with a large sharp knife. Missing him, the man kicked the teen who fell backward onto the ground. Yomatri dodged another swipe of his opponent's blade, then sprung up and knocked his foe unconscious with two swift jabs.

The teenager turned as another employee came at him, wielding a copper frying pan. The man swung, but Yomatri ducked. His heart racing, Yomatri grabbed his opponent by the arm and swung him in a circle before slamming his head against a metal countertop.

A third employee lunged at the teen with a long wooden spoon. Yomatri dodged the attack and socked the man in the jaw. Advancing, he spun around to land a powerful roundhouse kick on his opponent, sending him crashing into a wall.

One of the previous attackers started to rise, but Yomatri knocked him back down with a brutal kick to the face. He turned and ran across the kitchen to exchange blows with a fourth man.

At one point, Yomatri's opponent threw a forceful punch, and the teen crashed backward into an empty trash can. Yomatri glanced up, wide-eyed, as the worker rushed toward him, now wielding a greasy spatula.

In a flash, Mako came to Yomatri's aid, hitting his foe over the head with a glass cutting board. The man collapsed to the ground, and Mako tossed his weapon aside, then quickly helped his friend up.

With raised fists, the teens stood side by side, closely eyeing two more armed employees. Dodging a knife attack, Yomatri grabbed his opponent by the shirt and swung him into the other employee. The two men collided against a cabinet full of dishes and measuring cups.

A third worker had emerged from the shadows. He took Mako by surprise, knocking him back into a counter full of serving trays with a swift kick. Clenching a metal ladle, the man grinned and swung fiercely with his weapon.

Sage came to the rescue, ramming a metal cart into his brother's assailant, who crashed wildly to the ground, hitting the floor face-first.

Panting, Yomatri paused, the fire alarm still ringing in the background. He stood bent halfway down, his hands on his knees. With sweat dripping from her forehead, Miyuki leaned back against a vertical column, trying to catch her breath while the four brothers did the same.

"Okay ... so we got the fires cleared. I'm not totally sure what just happened, but I think we're alright if these guys don't wake up for a while," Miyuki said. "What do you guys think?"

For a moment there was silence. The teenagers eyed one another, hoping someone would speak.

"Wait, hold on a sec," said Yomatri. "Does anyone notice anything?"

Mako looked confused. "What do you mean?"

"Hano's been gone this whole time and he's still not returned with any help. I mean, I know he went to get the police or whatever—at least that's what he said he was gonna do—but we fought that battle ourselves."

Miyuki furrowed her brow. "I still don't understand. What are you saying?"

"I know this is gonna sound weird, but part of me feels like he's betrayed us," Yomatri explained. "Think about it. I remember him staring at my backpack while I was on the phone. His eyes were like glued to it. He knew the Emerald

Crystal was in there! Wait, now that I think about it, where is my backpack anyway?"

"Yomatri, now stop for a minute," Miyuki insisted. "You really think that innocent kid deliberately did all this to betray us and get away?"

"Yes! And he's not innocent! He's a thief! A spy—something!" he yelled, slamming his fist down onto a metal table. He shook his head, then said, "Oh, how could I be so stupid? I wasn't watching him close enough!"

"Well, don't panic. Let's at least try and look for it really quick," said Miyuki.

Together, the teens ran back into the main dining area, returning to the table they were seated at. Frantically, they searched underneath it and looked on the seats, still not seeing the backpack.

Leaning down, Yomatri picked up his mother's phone from the floor nearby and placed it in his pocket. He and his friends paused, each of them taking a deep breath.

"At least I found my mom's phone."

"This is bad. I'm sorry, but I kind of agree with Yomatri," Sage said, glancing at the others, his eyes growing worried. "He sort of did the same thing to me. I also noticed him looking at it when we were eating."

"You guys, he made it seem like he was on our side," said Yomatri. "That's why I didn't think anything of it. And he just seemed so nice about it, after I caught him staring at my backpack, that I didn't think anything of that either!"

"Okay," Miyuki broke in, "I think you guys are right. I bet he's got it. But if that's the case, we can't just stand here and do nothing. We've gotta find him."

"You're right," Yomatri insisted. "We probably don't have that much time to catch him. Let's get outta here, you guys." As he headed for the exit, his friends wearily followed along.

Moments later, the six teens joined the flood of civilians and restaurant staff outside. Parked along the sidewalks were numerous fire trucks, police cars, and ambulance vehicles with flashing red lights.

Paramedics quickly attended to the wounded with stretchers laid out nearby. Police officers questioned witnesses, while firefighters directed groups of people to nearby shops where they could be safe for the time being.

Yomatri scanned the area, noticing the streets surrounding the restaurant were blocked off, but that wouldn't stop him and his friends from trying to track down Hano. After a moment, he'd locked eyes with the brunette waitress and her coworker from before. Miyuki and the four brothers followed as he ran over to the ladies.

"Hey, there you are!" said the brunette woman, sighing with relief. "Thank God you guys are safe. What happened in there? Is everyone alright?"

"Long story. Listen, did you see a teenager about my height?" asked Yomatri. "He's got short brown hair almost like mine, and he's wearing jeans and a black jacket, I think."

"Yes, and he's also carrying a backpack," Mako added.

The waitress struggled to think. "Wait, do you mean that kid who was sitting with you?"

Yomatri's eyebrows rose. "Yes! Him."

"Okay, umm … I think I know who you're talking about," the woman replied, tapping her chin.

"Did you by chance happen to see where he went?" Miyuki asked. "We really need to find him."

"Yes," the woman answered. "I remember seeing him going in the direction of the subway—over there," she said, pointing down the street.

The teens glanced over.

Turning his attention back to the woman, Yomatri sighed with relief. "Oh, thank you, thank you!" He then turned to Miyuki and the brothers. "Come on, let's go, you guys."

The waitress and her coworker looked on as the teenagers raced down the narrow city street, soon disappearing into the crowds.

☆☆☆

In an underground subway, Hano hurried down a flight of stairs, passing by many panicked individuals. With each step, he tried to distance himself from the restaurant as much as possible.

Amidst terrified screams and chatter, he confidently continued forward. At one point, he stopped at the corner leading to a long hallway and checked his wristwatch.

Minutes seemed to pass by like seconds and Hano grew worried. "Ahh ... where is he?" he asked himself, frantically looking around. "I thought he'd be here by now!"

Again he scanned the crowds of people rushing past him. Frustrated, he threw up his hands and took off in the direction of a sign pointing towards "departing trains."

Meanwhile, Yomatri and his friends raced through a

large crowd some distance behind him. Eventually, after rushing down the flight of stairs, they approached a platform where hundreds of commuters waited to board an oncoming train.

Sidestepping past commuters, Miyuki and her friends strained to look over the sea of people.

"Anyone see him?" Yomatri asked as he and the others reached the platform where they waited for the oncoming train, now only fifty feet away.

More and more people strode past the teens.

"Not yet ... ," replied Miyuki; she was looking all around, desperately trying to scan each individual.

At last, the train slowly came to a stop as people quickly boarded and exited. Over the PA system, a brief recording played stating that it would leave in just one minute.

Yomatri entered a car toward the back of the train. He peered left and right, still not seeing Hano. For a moment, Sage and his brothers split up while staying in close proximity to one another.

"There's too many people. We're never gonna find him," Yomatri told Miyuki.

"Ahh ... just keep looking!"

Yomatri got off the train, and again glanced to his left and right. He saw nothing. The remaining commuters hurried on board, knowing that the doors would soon close.

One final time he turned left, spotting, down one car, a dark-haired teenager wearing a black jacket boarding the train. Yomatri pointed while trying to keep his voice down. "There he is!" His friends turned. "You guys, get on the train before the doors close!"

The teens quickly boarded the crowded car while trying to keep a close eye on Hano. A short moment later, the doors behind them shut and they were off.

Moving carefully around the passengers, the teens tried to remain calm. Some of the people without seats held onto overhead latches and metal poles in the center of the train car as the vehicle continued forward at a steady pace.

In the next car Hano held an overhead latch, standing beside a woman holding a coffee cup while she spoke on the phone. Meanwhile, Yomatri and Miyuki had reached the end of their car, the four brothers following close behind. Gently, Miyuki opened the door to the next and continued onwards.

All of a sudden, the door connecting the two cars had slammed shut behind them. Miyuki and Yomatri turned back, growing worried as they tried unlocking the door but without luck.

Mako and his brothers pounded on the door, but nothing seemed to help them now. Yomatri and Miyuki turned back around, locking eyes with Hano, who remained still.

"Everyone, I need you to listen to me!" Yomatri yelled to the bystanders, who glanced over at him. "I need you to come back to where I am and hide behind the seats or anything there is!" Pointing at Hano, he continued, "That boy over there's up to no good. He has to be stopped. This isn't a game! Please listen to me!"

Immediately the panicked civilians rose up from their seats, screaming. One after another, they headed over to the teens—some dropping their coffee, cell phones, purses, and other belongings.

With three-fourths of the car now free of space, Yomatri paced slowly toward his friend. "Hano!" he yelled. "Wh—why are you doing this? I thought you were one of our friends. It was you who started that fire back in the restaurant, wasn't it?"

Hano glared at him with a tight smile. "I didn't really expect you to catch up to me. Hmph. I'm impressed."

Miyuki's eyes grew tense. "It's over, Hano! Give us the backpack! You know it doesn't belong to you! You *aren't* the person we thought you were!"

"You're right. I'm not." Hano pulled out a tiny device from his pocket and pressed a button as everyone watched—the device had quickly expanded into a sharp metal sword.

With raised fists, Miyuki and Yomatri stood beside each other, their expressions uneasy. Hano quickly advanced, slashing at Miyuki. The girl dodged the sword, hopping over an empty seat, then came face-to-face with him.

Again she dodged a sword attack and caught her opponent by the wrist, his blade mere inches from her face. Miyuki forced him backward and Hano crashed into one of the metal beams, dropping his weapon.

Yomatri charged forward and threw a punch at the boy, who defended, bracing his arms up against his face. Immediately Hano responded, attacking with swift jabs and kicks.

Yomatri blocked each fevered attack, then kicked him in the chest, knocking him backward. Miyuki grabbed Hano by his jacket and slammed him into an empty seat.

The group of passengers cheered as Hano dropped to the floor but managed to retrieve his weapon. He sprung back up and lashed at Miyuki and Yomatri yet again, narrowly missing them.

Miyuki punched at Hano, who blocked her strike. He feinted with his sword, then delivered a heavy blow to the girl's side, knocking her back. Miyuki grimaced. Advancing, Hano kicked her to the floor of the train.

Wide-eyed, Yomatri dashed behind a seat, dodging his opponent's sword. Rising, he threw a punch at Hano but missed. Hano had gained the upper hand and slashed once more with his sword, cutting his former friend along his left arm.

Yomatri screamed in pain and clutched his arm, blood dripping onto the floor. Behind him, the group of passengers grew worried. Hano continued and released a powerful frontward kick, knocking his opponent down.

The teen collapsed to the ground, baring his gritted teeth. Hano stepped closer toward Yomatri and stared down at him, his chest heaving.

All of a sudden, one woman sprung up and charged toward Hano. She swung at him with her purse, but the teen forced her back with a magical force, hurling her into a wall.

"Aaahh!" the woman cried.

Other civilians rushed over to help her.

Yomatri slowly rose, mustering up just enough energy to fight back. In one swift motion, he bashed Hano across the face with his other arm, then kicked him in the chest.

As the train turned sharply, both teens crashed back against empty seats. The vehicle resumed on a straight path seconds later, and Hano quickly rose to prepare his next move.

Viciously he slashed at Yomatri who barely managed to dodge each and every attack. At one point, as Miyuki did before, he caught Hano by the arm and forced him backward.

Yomatri advanced, swiping the sword out of his opponent's hand. Hano retaliated, trading fierce blows with his former friend. Again Yomatri kicked Hano square in the chest, knocking him down the center aisle of the train car.

Behind him, the group of panicked civilians watched tensely. Some of them turned as the four brothers suddenly entered the train car, having finally gotten the door open. Hano picked up his sword and slowly rose to catch his breath while Yomatri helped Miyuki up from the ground, hoping there was still a chance to talk.

Panting, Yomatri pleaded, "Hano, what happened to you? Why ... why are you doing this? Do you really want a war with the Alliance or something?"

Hano glared at his former friends, tightening his fist. A swirl of dark energy circled around his hand. "You don't understand, Yomatri. All I can say is that you'll never regain possession of the Emerald Crystal!"

Immediately, he turned and smashed open a glass window with his hand—the shadowy energy swirling around his fist helping him absorb the punch. Quickly, he then jumped out as a heavy wind blew through the train.

"He's getting away! We've gotta stop him!" yelled Miyuki.

In the driver's cab, the conductor shouted as sparks

flared from his control panel. He glanced at the speedometer, noticing the train had suddenly moved to top speed all by itself.

Instantly, everyone aboard was jerked backward and violently thrown. Civilians crashed into one another, as did Yomatri, Miyuki, and the four brothers. The conductor tried to brake, but nothing seemed to work. He honked his horn repeatedly.

The overhead lights began to flicker but soon blew out, now leaving all the train cars dark with only their emergency lights glowing faintly. Missing its stop, the train rushed by a platform where passengers were waiting to board.

As it skidded along the side of the platform, sparking against the concrete, many onlookers jumped backward. People screamed as the train shrieked past. Some of them ran into the next room, hiding behind benches and walls. Others ran, desperately trying to find the nearest exit.

Armed police were among those in the crowd. Together, they worked to try and maintain the pandemonium while evacuating civilians to safety. Inside, Yomatri and his friends feared the worst. All of them were on the floor hanging on tightly to empty seats.

Inadvertently the train had left its track, skidding off the metal railway as hot sparks flared from underneath its wheels. Everyone screamed as it turned a long corner at high speed, approaching a tunnel.

It was then that the vehicle completely spiraled out of control and slammed against the side of the tunnel, sliding up and down. Eventually its speed had reduced as all the civilians onboard hit seats, windows, metal beams, and the walls.

As the train slowly screeched to a halt, chunks of metal and concrete smashed through glass windows, crashing violently into the cars.

✿✿✿

In near-darkness with thick smoke wafting close, Yomatri woke up with a start—gritting his teeth as he pushed a large chunk of rubble aside. He coughed and coughed, then glanced over at Miyuki. Her face was blackened by smoke and her body was slumped back against the side of the train.

Turning, Yomatri looked over at the brothers but was unable to get a read on their condition. The four of them all had their heads facing downward, their hair disheveled. Staggering to his feet, Yomatri desperately tried to wake his friends by shaking them, but nothing seemed to work. Fearing the brothers were dead, his heart began to pound.

The teenager paused and took a look at his surroundings. Many of the train's windows were shattered open. Its plastic seats were torn apart and the floor was riddled with small dents and cracks.

Dozens of civilians were lying all around, some against the walls, awake, while others remained unconscious. A few of them seemed unable to stop screaming in anguish. In his head, Yomatri could hear a faint ringing noise. It annoyed him, but he tried not to focus on it.

Briefly, he peeked out a broken window and checked to see if everything outside was okay, mostly only seeing the blackness of the tunnel. Amidst a long trail of rubble and concrete, smoldering flames burned outside, providing some light.

All of a sudden Miyuki woke, coughing and choking from the thick black smoke in the air. With little strength, he lifted her body, carrying her in his arms; she was now unresponsive.

"Oh man ... please be alright, Miyuki," Yomatri said worriedly, gritting his teeth.

Meanwhile, Sage and his brothers had gotten up one by one. Sluggishly, they leaned against a set of seats, struggling to find enough energy to move. Yomatri turned and glanced back at them, giving a smile of relief.

He wrapped one of Miyuki's arms around his neck, then headed out an emergency door. Looking left and right, he saw nothing. Yomatri walked over to the other side of the tunnel and gently rested her against the stone wall. He then brushed strands of her curly brown hair aside, trying to wake her. No response.

For a moment, Yomatri paused, focusing closely on the sound of faint footsteps. Eyebrows raised, he turned his head as he waited again, this time, the footsteps getting much closer.

All of a sudden, a bright flashlight shined throughout the dark tunnel. "Hello? Is there anyone out there?" a voice called. "If you can hear me, please stay where you are! We're going to help you."

Yomatri gasped, the white light glowing on his face. A wide smile formed on his lips as he gathered just enough energy to clap and alert whoever held the flashlight.

"Hey!!! Over here!!" the teen shouted, his voice cracking. He began to cough.

Yomatri clapped and clapped, louder each time, hoping that someone could hear him. With each passing second, the teen's face grew more worried. He feared he wouldn't be heard or seen, and that his friends would be left there to die.

Looking all around, Yomatri desperately tried to find something to make noise with. His eyes shifted to the ground where he ran his fingers through the dirt, eventually finding several tiny pebbles.

Without hesitation, Yomatri threw them against the side of the train. *Tack. Tack. Tack.* Pausing, he looked back at Miyuki, growing more worried by the second. Yet after glancing toward the light again, his expression changed in a matter of seconds.

Out of the darkness, a small team of firefighters had appeared! Wide-eyed, Yomatri dropped to his knees beside Miyuki, his mouth hanging open.

After a moment, the emergency crew had reached his position. A female firefighter rushed over to help him while her team headed inside the train to help his friends and everyone else.

The woman helping Yomatri looked him in the eyes. "Hey, kid, are you alright?" she asked. Glancing over to Miyuki, she continued, "What's goin' on with your friend?"

He coughed again and again. Wearily, he replied, "I think she's unconscious, I'm really sure, though. But she really needs some help."

"We'll need to have her checked over," the woman insisted. "What about you? Are you okay? Can you walk fine?" Yomatri didn't respond. His body shook and shook. "Look, I know this is pretty hard for you right now, kid, I do. But I just wanna let you know, it's gonna be—"

Exhausted, he fell into her arms and gave her a tight warm hug, tears streaming down his cheeks. The woman was shocked; she didn't know what to do but accept the boy's hug. Gently, she rubbed his back and rested her cheek on his shoulder.

In his heart, Yomatri had trusted Hano as a friend, but today he knew that bond of friendship was undoubtedly broken. Knowing his former friend had hurt a lot of people today, he couldn't let him get away with it. He *wasn't* going to let him get away with it.

As painful as it was not having the Emerald Crystal any longer, Yomatri knew he had to get the ancient rod back. It was either that or his promise to the Hero Alliance would be forever broken.

CHAPTER SIXTEEN:

HEALING WOUNDS

High above thick white clouds, a black Hero Alliance jet soared over New York Harbor toward Ember Island. Inside, Miyuki slept on the floor of the cabin beside Yomatri and the four brothers, all of them with soft warm blankets draped over them. Outside, the moon shined brightly over the water amidst the gathering darkness of the winter sky.

In the cockpit, Master Zorhins piloted the ship, scanning the sky ahead. Seated beside him was Captain Zeron who examined a tablet displaying geographic information. Turning to the Alliance leader, she asked, "How far are we?"

"About ten minutes out from home base. We should make it there in no time. Do you know what time it is by chance?"

"Uhh ... it's almost 4 a.m."

The Alliance leader nodded. "How's the team doing back there?"

With a worried look, Captain Zeron glanced back at the sleeping heroes, then returned her attention to Master Zorhins. "Hard to say. I mean, they're all sound asleep—probably really exhausted after what happened. We'll need to heal their wounds as much as possible when we get there."

"Any word on Yomatri's or Miyuki's parents?"

"No, nothing yet. Miyuki mentioned that she never told her parents about the derailment or about anything that's been going on lately, I think because they're out of town. Yomatri—I'm not so sure about. I haven't been able to talk to him since the incident which, by the way, is all over the news."

The Alliance leader sighed. "Ahh ... that's not good news. There's nothing we can really do about it now, though. I feel bad for the kids. They definitely took a big hit."

"Yeah. I'm just happy they all made it out alive. But luckily, the authorities haven't released the names of anyone yet—civilians, perpetrators of the attack, or even Yomatri and the others. Looks like the story's still developing."

Captain Zeron watched Master Zorhins who nodded and rubbed his eyes wearily. Her expression solemn, she turned away and looked ahead, staring at the dark sky out in front of her as the Alliance jet continued calmly over the harbor.

✵✵✵

As dawn arrived, a white light shined above Yomatri, dressed in a black shirt and jeans, now lying back in a soft linen hospital bed. Slowly, his eyes fluttered open. He rolled his head to the left, noticing an illuminated figure which, once his eyes had adjusted, turned out to be a doctor wearing a stethoscope around her neck.

Glancing to his right, he saw Miyuki conversing with another doctor who stood over a metal tray filled with various medical tools. Yomatri's gaze then shifted toward the ceiling, where he briefly stared at an overhead light.

Suddenly, a gentle hand touched his shoulder. Yomatri turned, seeing Miyuki looking down at him, only wanting to make sure he was okay. Her hair tied back in a ponytail, she was dressed similar to her friend, wearing a black fleece and jeans. On her neck and hands were several small scars.

Looking confused, Yomatri stared into his friend's round green eyes. With little strength and some help from her, he managed to sit up on the bed. After rubbing his eyes, he turned and studied the two doctors who conversed with one another in an Aridnemekian language.

Again Miyuki tapped him on the shoulder and his attention snapped back to her.

"Hi, Yomatri," she said with a warm smile. He eyed her closely. "Those two women over there are doctors. They're here to help you, like me."

Yomatri still seemed lost. His voice weak, he asked, "Wait, what do you mean? Where, where am I? Where are we, Miyuki?" He cleared his throat and began to stretch.

"On Ember Island. Captain Zeron and Master Zorhins helped get us here. I immediately told 'em about what happened, and they saw that we needed help, and now ... we're here. You don't have to worry, though. Everything's okay."

Yomatri shook his head. "Wait, hold on a minute. I remember falling into the arms of a firefighter—in the tunnel. And you, you were unconscious ... and the same with the four brothers. What happened to everyone? And what time is it?" he said, his voice rising with worry.

"It's morning," Miyuki responded. "Look, I know it

all doesn't make sense right now, but you fell unconscious shortly after falling into the firefighter's arms. I know this 'cause I actually woke up just a few minutes after the train crash."

"Wait, so, how'd we get here then?"

"We were taken to a hospital along with everybody else who was on the train. But I didn't let the nurses that took care of us call your parents or mine. When they weren't in the room, I actually contacted Captain Zeron with that little communication device she gave us when we first visited the island—you remember, right?"

"Yeah."

"Yep, so I guess she and Master Zorhins went in undercover to the hospital we were at, and they managed to sneak us out before anyone noticed—the four brothers too. And then they took us here a few hours after midnight on a jet. That's all I remember really."

"Okay ... I mean, that all makes sense, but why don't you look exhausted or injured at all? And what about Sage and the others? What happened to them? Are they fine?" He began to panic.

"Yes, yes, Yomatri. Please calm down," Miyuki answered, gently resting a hand on his shoulder. "They should be fine. I think they're sleeping right now. The doctors on Ember Island healed them up first, but they still have a few injuries, like me."

"Phew. That's good to hear."

Miyuki paused to show him the scars on her hands and neck. "I'm still really tired, actually. I haven't had much sleep. And it's a little hard to move, but I'm okay for the most part. My head feels fine too, which is sorta weird 'cause for a second, I thought I had a concussion. The doctors said the same thing—they didn't find any signs of one."

Yomatri looked confused. "That is really weird. But I mean, good thing you're okay."

"Yeah, I don't know if it's somethin' with my powers or what. Maybe some new ability? I have no idea. But now I'm just helpin' the doctors in any way I can to heal your wounds. We're all getting better, but it'll take some time—probably at least a week to heal."

Briefly, Yomatri examined his arms which were riddled with red scars, many of them bandaged with medical tape. He then looked his friend in the eyes and smiled. "Hey, thank you, Miyuki. I really appreciate it, honestly."

She blushed. "You're welcome. I'm just really glad you're safe." Smiling back, she walked over to a nearby counter filled with spare clothes, a thermometer, several rags, and a cup of orange juice. Returning to Yomatri, she passed him the cup of orange juice. "Here, drink this. The doctors said you need to drink a lot of fluids and get some rest, and that you don't need to strain your body any further. They recommended the same for me."

"I dunno how that's gonna work out. We've gotta get that crystal back." Yomatri took a sip of his drink while Miyuki leaned against the counter, her arms crossed.

"Yeah, me either. I just can't believe Hano did this to us," she said, shaking her head in disbelief.

"I agree, but we've gotta stop him. I just ... don't really know how. It's like part of me doesn't even know what to do anymore."

Miyuki knitted her brow. "What are you saying?"

"I don't know. I feel like we were on a really good run when we discovered the crystal back in that cave in Westchester. And then I made the mistake of trusting him and we became friends, which allowed room for all this to happen. I just didn't see that he was gonna betray us."

"I know, I know. Neither did I. Not even the four brothers. But don't beat yourself up. If you think about it, that rod was really a responsibility for all of us—not just you. And now we have to work together to fix this."

"Maybe the best option right now is to just recover and not lose hope."

"That's a good idea. Yes, what happened is unfortunate, but we can't let this one incident faze us. We've gotta keep fighting."

The teens smiled at each other with renewed hope.

After a moment, Miyuki turned around and began arranging items on the counter. "I'm assuming you haven't told your parents about what happened yet, right?"

"Of course not. They'd freak out if I did. But the more I think about it, I'm kinda realizing that I'm gonna have to at some point," Miyuki responded, shaking her head. "I'm just gonna call them later today and explain everything, probably when I get home. I'm sure they'll understand given what happened."

"I'd think so too." He glanced aside, then said, "I'm honestly not sure how to go about tellin' all this to my parents either. I just hope they didn't like call the police or do something crazy."

"I'm sure it'll be okay. Your mom seems really nice and understanding." She turned back around. "Let's do this: today I'll tell my parents about everything that's happened so far to us and you do the same. Deal?"

"Deal."

Miyuki walked over and gave him a gentle hug. As she rested her cheek on his shoulder, she rubbed his back, blinking pensively.

Abruptly, Captain Zeron and Master Zorhins entered the room and the teenagers turned. "Hi, guys," said Master Zorhins. "How are you, uh, both doing?"

"We're okay … just recovering," Miyuki responded, leaning beside her friend.

"That's good to hear. It's good you both are alright."

"Yeah, you guys definitely had us worried for a moment," said Captain Zeron.

"Are the four brothers okay?" Yomatri asked, curious.

"Yes, they're fine right now. Their bodies are slowly healing. By the way, Yomatri, has the doctor told you that you should get a lot of rest, drink many fluids, and—"

"Yeah, Miyuki told me already. She's got me covered." He turned as they each grinned. "Have either of you heard any updates from the news yet? I'm really anxious to know."

"Not recently, no, but we can check." The Alliance captain grabbed a remote from the counter and turned on a flat-screen TV mounted along the wall.

Miyuki and Yomatri watched as she changed to *Channel 6 News*. A female reporter with short brown hair spoke before horrifying images of the train derailment:

> *... At this point in time, there is still no one who has claimed responsibility for the attack that occurred on a subway in Manhattan late last night. Though, we've recently heard from some of the wounded and they were able to provide a brief description of a potential suspect: a Caucasian teenage male who was last seen wearing a black jacket, jeans, and a green shirt. However, he has currently not been identified by police. Officials are asking anyone with related information to please come forward as the investigation continues. We will continue live coverage of this horrific event after this short commercial break ...*

Yomatri and the others looked away from the screen.

"Well, they haven't said anything yet ... about you guys at least," said Captain Zeron, "which makes sense, I guess, because the attack isn't even a day old. Hopefully, it stays like that and the news doesn't mention Miyuki's or Yomatri's name. That wouldn't be good, especially since you guy's parents are worried sick, I assume."

"Yeah, it's funny—me and Miyuki were just talkin' about that," said Yomatri. "I guess we're just gonna tell our parents about everything that happened when we go home today. Sooner or later, they'll find out anyways."

"That's totally okay. We can take you guys back to New York with one of our jets whenever you're ready."

"For sure," Yomatri said, then paused. His expression grew worried. "Have you guys heard that Shinzuki recently escaped prison?"

"Really? I didn't even know that," said Miyuki.

Yomatri looked her in the eyes. "Yeah, I'm sorry. I don't know why I didn't tell you and the brothers earlier when we were hangin' out at the restaurant."

"It's fine, don't worry."

"We did hear about the escape, yes," Master Zorhins interrupted. "Very sad what happened. And now we've got Hano to worry about, which makes things a little more complicated. But our priority is getting the Emerald Crystal back. Nothing else."

"I guess there's no way we're getting through this peacefully then," said Miyuki. "My bet is that Hano and Shinzuki are probably working together by now since they share the same interest—the Emerald Crystal. And we know that the more power they get their hands on, the stronger they'll become."

"Do they even know each other, though?" asked Yomatri.

"I don't know," Miyuki responded, shrugging her shoulders. "I mean, we know they both work for the Aridian Army, but I wouldn't doubt it."

"Well, we'll just have to fight back with all we've got then," Master Zorhins insisted.

There was a short pause.

"And we'll be there to help," a voice said. Miyuki and the others turned their heads to see Sage and his brothers standing in the doorway to the infirmary. "I can't thank you both enough for saving our lives. It means the world to us. My brothers want to thank you, too."

Overwhelmed, Miyuki rushed over and hugged Sage tightly. He accepted her hug, feeling relieved himself. Captain Zeron and Master Zorhins smiled at the cheerful heroes, whose spirits were high now.

Getting up from the bed, Yomatri walked over to the four brothers and gave them each a warm hug. He smiled to himself, realizing that even through the darkest times, he and his friends could still manage to be a team and help one another out.

It seemed that their priorities were set, and it was now time to regain possession of the Emerald Crystal.

✫✫✫

Later that same day in Forest Hills, Yomatri walked up the cobblestone driveway of his house with his friends following close behind. As the group finally made it to the icy front porch, Yomatri's heart began to pound.

He took a deep breath.

"Don't worry, everything's gonna be okay," Miyuki insisted; she held his arm tightly, her other arm wrapped around his shoulder. "You'll do great. Can you make it from here?"

"Yeah, I should be fine. I'm just really nervous. I don't know what they'll think."

Miyuki clicked her tongue. "Umm ... just, uh, tell 'em about what an awesome job you did of saving all our lives yesterday! They'll be really proud of you for that. If you need us, just call us inside or something."

"Okay, okay. Hopefully she doesn't go nuts on me. I'm goin' in."

Miyuki let go of her friend and watched him nervously, making sure he was actually able to walk on his own. Gently, Yomatri opened the front door and slowly entered the house.

"Hey, Mom, I'm home!" he called out.

A worried-looking Miya, wearing a dark shirt and jeans, stepped out from the kitchen. Suddenly seeing her son, she gasped, then rushed forward and embraced him.

Shaking, she held him tightly, tears streaming down her cheeks. "Oh my God, Yomatri!! Please don't ever scare me like that again! Where've you been?" Miya examined him, noticing the bandages on his arms and minor cuts on his hands. "What happened to you?!"

"Wait, first, please don't tell me you called the police," Yomatri responded. He and his mother turned as Luke entered the room.

His father sighed with relief. "Oh, thank God you're here, kiddo. What happened to you?"

"It's ... a long story. But I can explain."

Miya turned back to her son. "No, no, sweetie, I didn't call the police. But I was really close to it! I just thought, 'He has to come home soon.'" Wiping tears from her eyes, she smiled, her face beginning to turn red. "You had me so worried! I heard these loud bangs and screaming on the phone. And you never called me back or anything."

"I wanted to, but I couldn't really with everything that was going on. Did you guys not hear what happened?"

His parents shared confused looks, then Miya turned to her son. "No? Wait, what do you mean?"

"Here, come look," Yomatri responded, grabbing his mother by the wrist; she and Luke followed him into the living room. His parents curiously watched their son, who turned on the TV and quickly navigated to the news channel, where a report pertaining to yesterday night's train crash was playing.

Images of numerous paramedics attending to the wounded had appeared on the screen. The news report slowly transitioned to dark, frightening images of the damaged train which lay empty in the spooky underground tunnel.

Miya and Luke glanced nervously at their son, then returned their attention to the report. More images were shown—some depicting firefighters clearing flames from the derailed train. Other photos showed police officers and forensic analysts investigating the destruction.

Suddenly, a photo of Yomatri running down a busy city street near the sushi restaurant had appeared on the screen.

Luke and Miya's eyes widened.

Miya pointed at the TV and stared at her son with a shocked expression. "Hold on a minute. Yomatri, what is this? What's going on? Why's your face all over the news?" she asked, her voice rising with each word.

"Mom, alright, before you freak out, let me explain," he begged.

"No, you let me explain something here!" Miya yelled, pointing a finger at her son. "When did all of this happen? And where've you been all this time? You told me you were going to hang out with your friends and then I see your face on the news with all of this destruction!"

Luke lowered the TV's volume while the news report continued. Yomatri pleaded, "Mom, you're not understanding ... just lemme explain."

"No, I don't think you're understanding!" Miya continued. Pointing at the TV screen, she asked, "What's up with that photo of you runnin' down the street or whatever? How badly were you injured? Did you go to the hospital?"

"Yes, I went to a hospital. Long story short, I'm fine. Mom, can I please just—"

Miya stepped closer to her son. "I'm just saying I care about you. I worry about you. That's why I'm always wondering where you're going or who you're with. Are you sure you're alright?"

Yomatri gave his mother a reassuring nod. "Yeah, Mom, I'm fine. Please—just listen for a second." Confused, his mother stared at him with a distorted expression.

Luke looked on, curious.

After a brief silence, Yomatri continued, "Yes, you're right. I probably shouldn't have gone out so late with my friends. Yes, I should've called you back and told you about what was going on. And yes, it may be my fault that all this happened! But there's more to the story and I need to tell you."

Miya crossed her arms and took a deep breath. "Alright, Yomatri, I'm listening."

As he was about to respond, Miyuki and the four brothers raced into the house and entered the living room. Perplexed, Miya eyed her son's friends but said nothing.

"Oh, hi. Sorry," Miyuki said to Miya, her expression a mixture of confusion and awkwardness. "We just heard yelling … and it was getting really cold outside … and we thought we'd, uh, come in."

Yomatri glanced at Miyuki with a smirk, then locked eyes with his mother. "Alright, Mom, lemme explain. I think it was on Christmas day—Miyuki and I were approached by this group of alien heroes or whatever from another planet. And basically, they told us that we need to save the world. They said that the Earth is under a great threat and that to save the world, we need to gather these twelve ancient crystals, right?"

"Oh boy," Luke said to himself, shaking his head.

Miya stared at her son, unamused.

"Look, I know this is probably one of the silliest stories you've ever heard and it might not make sense right now, but just hear me out!" Yomatri paused to gather his thoughts. "I'm pretty sure it was that same night—Miyuki and I went ice-skating beforehand. There was an accident and we almost fell into this lake or whatever, but somehow we both came out being able to control water."

Luke asked, "Wait, really?"

"Yes, and so a few days later, the city was attacked by this deranged sorcerer or whatever—really messed up dude," replied Yomatri. "You remember that, right, Mom? When you and I were watchin' the news that one day and then Miyuki came over like right after?"

"Yeah, I remember."

"Well, that's why I was acting so weird. And no, it was not 'the itch.'"

Miyuki snickered, causing Mako and his brothers to also laugh. Ignoring his friends, Yomatri continued, "I guess what I'm trying to say is I didn't really wanna tell you guys about anything that had happened."

"I was wondering why you were actin' so strange that day," Luke said, trying not to laugh. "Boy, you were being super weird. But I guess it all makes sense now."

Miya glanced at the four brothers, then returned her attention to her son. "Okay, so where did they come into this little story of yours?"

Yomatri replied, "Yep, so me and Miyuki raided this abandoned warehouse in Westchester where the bad guys were sorta keepin' these people prisoner. And then after this huge fight, we actually ended up finding one of the twelve crystals—the Emerald. You remember that night when me and my friends came home and you and Dad like started interrogating us?"

"I do remember that now that you mention it," Luke interrupted, snapping his fingers. "It was around the time we had that New Year's party. Man, you guys were even stranger then."

Yomatri and his friends giggled.

Miya responded, "Wait, hold on. What are you talking about 'raided'? What, did you go to war and come back or something?"

"No, no, Mom. I don't really know how to explain it, but yes, Miyuki and I sorta led this attack that helped free these four," he responded, pointing at Sage and his brothers. "But then later on, we met this guy named Master Zorhins—coolest dude in the world."

"And what does he do exactly?" asked Miya.

"I was just about to get to that. Basically, he's the leader of these heroes who are tryna help save the world. We even met a kid my age named Hano. And then we became friends ... but he ended up betraying us."

"Yomatri's right," Miyuki interrupted. "Hano's actually the person who caused all of the destruction in the subway last night, and at the restaurant where we had dinner."

"How did he betray you guys?" asked Luke.

"He acted like he was on our side and he took the crystal that we had away from us," Miyuki explained. "There was a battle at the restaurant, but we managed to follow him into the subway where he caused the train to derail. It seemed like he had it all planned."

"Yep, so now that leaves us here." Yomatri turned to his mother. "We're all trying to work together to get the crystal back before Hano becomes too powerful."

Her arms crossed, Miya still looked unamused. "I'm still havin' a hard time believing this story of yours. I mean, can you at least show your father and me that you have these special powers you mentioned?"

"I guess so, but how?" her son asked. A thought suddenly clicked in his mind as he continued, "Wait, don't answer that! I've got just the idea."

The teenager went into the kitchen and grabbed a tall glass from one of the cabinets, then filled it with water. Returning to the living room, he set the glass down on the coffee table.

Everyone else watched confusedly.

"What are you doing?" Miyuki asked, curious.

"I'm gonna show you, just be patient my little

grasshopper," Yomatri replied, grinning. He stood up straight and rubbed his hands together, then glanced at his parents. "Okay. You guys are gonna love this!"

After taking a deep breath, he held out both hands, the water rising as he summoned it from out of the glass. Luke and Miya looked on, wide-eyed. Yomatri continued, churning the water left and right.

The teenager then dragged his left hand upward, separating the body of water into two. He waved his right hand in a circular motion and watched as the water spiraled in a circle in midair. Lastly, Yomatri gently lowered both of his arms, releasing the water back into the glass.

"Oh, my God!!" Miya yelled, covering her mouth with her hands.

Luke traded a surprised look with her, then locked eyes with his son. "Okay, now that's pretty cool actually."

"I told you guys! I wasn't lying," Yomatri smirked.

Miya took a deep breath, then lowered her head and relaxed. "Well, now I feel all bad," she said, starting to smile. Leaning against her husband, she continued, "This is actually kinda interesting, you guys. Yomatri, why didn't you tell me about any of this sooner?"

He paused to gather his thoughts. "I don't know. I guess I was just, uh, really worried of what you'd think."

"No, no ... I mean, you went to space camp and that was really awesome and futuristic!" said Miya; she cocked her head with a knitted brow. "Why would this be any different?"

Yomatri shrugged his shoulders. "I'm not sure. I wasn't, uh, expectin' you to respond like this."

His mother continued, "Well, I didn't really know you were connected to all this stuff that's been happening on the news lately. You do a good job of hiding things from me, actually, which we'll have to talk about later. But I'm happy for you. I couldn't be prouder. I mean, you're helping people for the good, and I just wasn't understanding of all this. I'm really sorry, you guys."

Miya turned to her son's friends, making sure they'd heard her apology and acknowledged it.

Miyuki smiled. "It's okay, don't sweat it."

"Was there anything else you maybe wanted to know?" asked Yomatri.

"Well, I've got a million questions, but let's just start slowly, I guess. Here, come on," Miya insisted. She grabbed Luke's hand as he followed her into the dimly lit kitchen. The six teenagers did the same. "Yomatri, if you were wondering, I'm gonna be making lasagna pretty soon for dinner tonight."

"Mmmm, yummy!" Miyuki said, noticing various ingredients on the kitchen counters: a box of noodles, different packages of cheese, tomato sauce and more. After a moment, she and the four brothers sat down at the dining table.

Leaning against the refrigerator, Luke eyed his son. "I gotta say too, kiddo—this is a pretty interesting story. I'm proud of you too. It seems like you've done well so far, even though I know it was probably hard to prevent a train from crashing. But I'm happy you did your best to stop that guy."

"Thank you. That means a lot, Dad."

"Of course. How do you plan on gettin' that crystal

back, though? And stopping him? That 'Hano' guy you mentioned."

"We're not, uh, really sure, honestly," Yomatri responded, glancing at his friends. "We're tryna figure something out, though."

Meanwhile, Miya turned a dial on the stove to a lower temperature. Then she turned and motioned to Luke and asked him to come upstairs. On the way, she said, "Hey, Yomatri, just promise me if something like this ever happens again, you'll try to let me know where you are or what's going on."

"Promise." He nodded. "Where are you guys going by the way?"

"We'll be back in a sec, don't worry."

While his parents headed upstairs, Yomatri chatted with his friends at the kitchen table. Miya and Luke entered their bedroom, closed the door, and faced each other.

"What's up, honey?" asked Luke.

"I don't know," Miya replied, running her fingers through her long brown hair. "I wasn't trying to be rude or anything ... I just ... needed a break. Everything's fine. It's just a lot to take in all at once, you know?"

Lowering his eyes, Luke sighed and shook his head. "Yeah, I know what you mean. I really had no idea Yomatri was doing any of this either."

Miya wrapped her arms around her husband and rested her head against his chest. "I don't know. I mean, it's really cool that he's out saving the world and everything. And he seems to be having so much fun with his new friends— which I love, don't get me wrong—but I'm just worried for his safety now."

"Yeah. Anything could happen to him now. Sooner or later he might become a public figure and things could get even worse," said Luke, resting his head against his wife's. "What do you think we should do?"

"We've gotta keep him protected and just watch over him, I guess. I'm not really so sure."

CHAPTER SEVENTEEN:

LOVE IN THE SHADOWS

Downstairs, as the four brothers continued chatting with each other in the kitchen, Miyuki and Yomatri separated from them to talk in private.

"What's up? What did you wanna tell me?" asked Yomatri.

Miyuki checked her smartwatch, then looked him in the eyes. "Hey, now that everything's cool with your parents, do you think we could, um, go somewhere together in Manhattan?"

"Sure, but where?" Yomatri asked, crossing his arms.

"Oh ... just somewhere fun," Miyuki smirked. "You should ask your parents if it'd be okay for you to come hang with me."

"But I don't even know where we're going exactly. What am I supposed to tell them?"

"I'm not sure. I guess you could, uh, say something like 'my good friend Miyuki wants to take me somewhere fun in Manhattan'," she responded, playfully nudging him. "Maybe not those exact words, but you get what I mean." She giggled.

Yomatri shook his head, grinning. "Okay, okay."

"Hey, one quick thing before you ask 'em: are you sure

you're okay from the train crash and whatnot? It'll be a lotta walking."

"I'm a little sore here and there, but I should be fine. I'm gonna get some rest later, though, for sure." She nodded. "I'll, uh, be right back." He turned away and headed upstairs to his parents' bedroom, tripping on the stairs.

"What happened?" Miyuki whispered, looking up towards the second floor.

"Nothing! I'm okay, I'm okay," Yomatri replied, his face reddening. He turned away and knocked on his parents' door.

After a short moment, Miya and Luke appeared.

"Hi, Yomatri," said Luke.

"Hey, are you guys alright?"

"Yeah, we're fine ... just talking," Miya responded. "Why, what's up?"

"Well, Miyuki just said that she wanted to take me somewhere in Manhattan if that's okay with you guys. I don't know where exactly, but I guess it's supposed to be like a little surprise or somethin'," Yomatri replied, slowly regaining his breath. As his parents were about to respond, he interrupted, "I'll totally let you guys know if anything goes wrong this time! Promise."

His parents shared worried looks, but after a moment, they became more relaxed. Luke returned his son's curious gaze and replied, "Sure, that should be fine, kiddo."

Yomatri sighed with relief. "Awesome! One more thing: is it okay if she comes over for dinner later? Maybe this would be a good chance for you guys to get to know her a little better?"

"Yes, that should be fine, sweetie," Miya answered.

"Great! Thank you so much, you guys—really. I'll be back in a bit," her son responded. He waved good-bye, then headed back downstairs, stopping beside Miyuki. "Okay, good news. They said it'll be fine."

"Sweet!" the girl replied, looking up from her cell phone. She placed the device in her back pocket and grabbed her friend by the wrist as he followed her into the kitchen, stopping near the four brothers. "Hey, you guys, Yomatri and I are gonna go hang out together in the city."

"Interesting," Mako said, tapping his chin. He glanced at his brothers. "No, I'm just kidding. That's okay. We were actually getting ready to head back to Ember Island anyways."

Miyuki looked concerned. "Do you guys know how to get back to Ember Island from here on your own?"

"Don't worry, we've got it handled. The Alliance can help us if we get lost. We've got one of these to help," Mako answered, showing her a small round communication device with buttons on its sides.

"Yes. We can catch up with you guys another time. No worries," Sage added. "We're still a little tired."

"Alrighty, sounds good, I guess."

As the brothers got up from the chairs to the dining table, Miyuki and Yomatri embraced each of them.

✵✵✵

On a packed bus later that evening, Miyuki stared out its frosty windows, noticing a variety of shops along the snow-covered sidewalks—a supermarket, clothing stores, a comic book shop, and a few tiny restaurants mixed in between. She turned to Yomatri who was asleep beside her, his head resting on her shoulder.

As the bus gently came to a stop at a busy street corner, Miyuki scanned ahead. Many of the passengers had gotten up and headed toward the exit. Glancing back at Yomatri, she watched as his eyes slowly fluttered open, rising to meet her gaze.

Miyuki flashed an adoring grin. "We get off here."

Yomatri lifted his head and rubbed his eyes wearily, then looked at her. Miyuki stood up and walked toward the front of the bus. Her friend got up moments later and followed her outside.

Snowflakes were falling and Yomatri looked all around, noticing the hustle and bustle of people from all walks of life. His attention shifted to Miyuki as she began down the sidewalk.

"Where are we going?" he asked curiously.

Miyuki glanced back, placing her hands in her pockets. "Just follow me ... you'll see!"

Almost fifteen minutes later, the teens arrived at a major commercial intersection in the city, filled with flashy, colorful lights. Tall skyscrapers covered in thick snow loomed high above, some displaying large electronic billboards of businesses, food, music, upcoming movies, and more.

On the streets, cars and taxicabs went in all directions, honking repeatedly at one another. Hundreds of people chatted with each other and it seemed that everyone was enjoying their time.

The teens came to a stop.

Eyeing Yomatri, Miyuki asked, "What do you think? Have you ever been here before?"

"Yes ... I remember this place," he replied, continuing to look around.

"What do you mean? You were here when you were younger or somethin'?"

"Yeah. My parents used to take me here all the time when I was little. I remember they actually took me here the day before I left for space camp. It's called Times Square, I think, right?"

"Wow, that must've been exciting! But yeah, you're right—that's the name of it," Miyuki responded; she took out her cell phone and pulled Yomatri close. "Hey, we should take some pictures together. What do you think?"

"Okay," he responded, beginning to blush. Eventually, he became more relaxed as he and Miyuki took multiple selfies and later captured photos of themselves posing in front of different stores and billboards.

☆☆☆

Later, the two teens walked amongst thousands of pedestrians. Miyuki glanced at Yomatri, who seemed to be lost in a deep thought. "Everything alright?"

"Yeah, I'm okay. I just remember like during the summer, my mom and dad would always take a bunch of pictures of me, like you and I did before. And sometimes, if I was really good, they'd buy me like a bag of popcorn or whatever kind of candy I wanted," he laughed. "I used to cause a lotta trouble—always running around for no reason. Sometimes I'd get lost, but my parents never got mad really."

Miyuki smiled. "Awww, that's really sweet."

Yomatri traded a look with her, then glanced off, pausing to gather his thoughts. "I really miss those days actually … and hangin' out with my parents. Now that my life's changed so much recently, it's like I never get to do that anymore. I've been so caught up with all this Aridnemekian stuff that I haven't really spent much time with 'em."

"It's okay; don't beat yourself up. I mean, I'm sure when we get the Emerald Crystal back and make things right with the Alliance, you'll be able to hang out with them much more."

Eyeing Miyuki, a smile slowly formed on his face. Suddenly, his mother's phone vibrated in his pocket. He quickly pulled it out and answered: "Hello?"

Miyuki looked on, her expression curious.

"Hi, honey!" Miya said on the other end. "Your dad and I just wanted to check up on you—see how things are going. Where did you and Miyuki end up going?"

"Oh, uh, we're here in Times Square, actually. Remember that place you and Dad used to always take me to when I was really little?"

"Yeah, yeah, I know what you're talking about! We'll have to go there again sometime—the three of us. Hey, listen, I also wanted to let you know that dinner's almost ready, so hurry back soon if you can."

"Alright, awesome! I know I asked this before, but are you sure you're okay with Miyuki coming over for dinner tonight?"

Miya laughed. "Yes, sweetie. It's fine, honestly."

Yomatri paused, noticing Miyuki giving him a weird look. "Okay. Hey, uh, hold on a sec, Mom." He took the phone away from his ear and turned to his friend.

"What's goin' on? Is everything alright?" Miyuki whispered, sounding unsure.

"Yeah, yeah! Everything's fine. Would you like to come over to my place for dinner with my parents?"

"Sure, I'd love to!" she replied. Yomatri gave a thumbs-up, then brought the phone closer to his ear. "Hey, Mom, I've gotta go, but we'll be back home pretty soon."

"Alright, honey. Have fun!"

After he got off the phone, Yomatri pumped his fists into the air. Looking confused, Miyuki smiled as she did the same. The teens burst into laughter and for a moment, they each began playfully hitting one another. At one point Miyuki fell to the ground, landing on her butt.

Yomatri snickered, his eyebrows raised. Placing his hands on his cheeks, he asked, "Oh my God! Are you okay?"

"Yeah, I'm fine! Here, help me," Miyuki responded, laughing hysterically; she threw her hand out and he pulled her up from the ground.

Yomatri held her close, supporting her by the shoulders and waist. "Oh man, you're so silly," he said, shaking his head with a grin.

✡✡✡

Later in Forest Hills, Yomatri unlocked the front door to his house. He and Miyuki slowly entered. After taking off their shoes, they headed into the kitchen where Luke helped set the table. Miya took a pan of cheesy, meaty lasagna from the stove and rested it on a nearby counter, then removed a pair of oven mitts.

"Hey, Mom," Yomatri said, stopping to give her a kiss on the cheek. The aroma of cheese, garlic, peppers, and tomatoes filled the air.

"Hi, honey," she replied, glancing at Miyuki who waved. Miya continued, "You guys can go wash your hands and come eat."

"Alright."

While the teens headed for the bathroom, Miya helped Luke finish setting the table, which included a salad bowl, napkins, plates, silver eating utensils, and a small dish of buttered garlic bread. Afterwards, she reached into the fridge and set down a bottle of water for everyone onto the table.

Miyuki and Yomatri returned and sat next to each other at the dining table. Eventually, Luke and Miya joined the teens, sitting across from them.

"Mmmm ... everything smells so good!" Miyuki said, rubbing her hands together. She turned to Yomatri and whispered, "Man, your mom really knows how to cook!"

Luke and Miya chuckled, overhearing.

Yomatri smiled, then prepared a slice of lasagna for his friend, using a knife and fork. Miya and Luke each started with a plate of fresh salad topped with tomatoes, carrots, and cucumbers.

"Hey, I just wanted to say thank you guys for having me," said Miyuki.

"Absolutely! Yomatri's told us a little about you and you seem like a pretty nice kid," Miya responded. "Do you live here in Queens or another part of the city?"

"Yep! I actually live with my parents in an apartment in Sunnyside. And I go to school at Arrowsmith High, which isn't too far from my place. But I love it!"

"That's good to hear," said Luke. He and everyone else paused to continue eating.

"Hey, Mom, Dad, are you guys sure you're okay, like with the story and everything I told you about earlier?"

"Yeah, we're fine," Miya replied, trading a look with her husband. "I'm just happy I didn't pass out when you told me about everything. It was definitely a lot to take in all at once, but, you know, we're hangin' in there."

"Well, that's good at least," her son said, then paused. "I just thought of something I forgot to mention in my story. Probably not that important at this point anyways, but you guys remember when I was 'play fighting' in the basement a few days back?"

Trying to keep a straight face, Miyuki interrupted, "Oh, I know what he's talking about."

"Yeah, I remember that," said Luke. "Wait, why, what's up?" His wife looked on, confused.

"I wasn't *actually* play fighting." Yomatri chuckled and shook his head. "I was testing out the Emerald Crystal, like tryna see what it could do. And I don't know what I did wrong, but it like spiraled outta control and hit the wall a few times. Didn't damage anything, but that's what all those loud bangs were."

Miya lowered her fork, grinning, as she pointed at her

son. "I knew somethin' was up, you little liar! I was like, 'There's no way those chairs falling in the basement caused him to scream like that'! You were pretty loud there too, honey."

Luke and Miyuki shared a laugh.

Yomatri shrugged his shoulders. "Hey, I was legit terrified, what can I say?" After a brief silence, he continued, "I know I asked you this before, but was there anything else you guys maybe wanted to know about my story from earlier?"

Again Luke and Miya glanced at each other. Miya took a sip of her water, then said, "Yes, actually. I was just wondering who exactly were the people that supposedly want you to help save the world? I know you briefly mentioned them before."

"Ohhh ... how should I explain this?" Yomatri said, tapping his chin. "It's like a big group of 'em—they're warriors who fight for, you know, things like peace and prosperity. They call themselves the Hero Alliance. And right now, they're in a big war with a bunch of bad guys known as the Aridian Army."

Miya and Luke held amused grins, but eventually grew serious. "What exactly does the Aridian Army want? Do you know?" asked Miya.

"I would say ... to rule the world?" Yomatri responded, sounding unsure.

Miyuki added, "Yep, and to do that, they're tryna beat the Alliance in gathering all of the twelve crystals."

"I remember you guys mentioning somethin' about that," said Luke. "But didn't you also say that you and your other friends actually found one of 'em somewhere? And then I think Miyuki said like, if you get the other eleven, you or whoever will obtain this tremendous amount of power or something."

"Right. I mean, as far as we know, they're basically like these indestructible rods," Miyuki responded. "I'm honestly not sure what they're made of. Probably some sort of space rock. But each one has its own special power. Like for example, the one we found holds the power of earth."

"So ... what? It can control like rocks, dirt, sand—that kind of stuff?" asked Luke.

Yomatri snickered, shaking his head. "Yeah, Dad, but there's more to it than that. It's actually really powerful, come on now."

Luke crossed his arms and paused to think. "Well, hey, that's pretty neat actually! I mean, that'd probably be like the best gardening tool ever, right?"

"I love how he's getting into this," Miya smirked; she winked at the teenagers and took a bite of her food. After a brief silence, she continued, "Okay, so before, I know you guys mentioned this 'Hano' person. Who exactly is he, though?"

"We're not really sure, honestly," Miyuki said, sharing a confused look with Yomatri. "He could be a spy or something for the bad guys."

"Probably. That'd make the most sense, I think," Luke insisted.

"Well, he did intentionally bomb a restaurant like you guys mentioned. And he caused all that chaos in the subway," said Miya. "And he was also part of the reason why that train in Manhattan derailed, right?"

"Yep, exactly," Yomatri answered solemnly.

✡✡✡

Miya had just finished washing the dishes in the sink. As she dried her hands on a paper towel, Luke returned from outside after emptying the garbage. He reached into the fridge and grabbed another bottle of water, then turned to Miyuki and Yomatri at the dinner table.

"Hey, you guys, we're gonna head off to bed," said Luke. "And again, it was really nice having you here for dinner tonight, Miyuki."

"Yes, it was!" Miya added. "You'll have to come over again sometime."

"Yeah, totally! This was really nice. Thanks again for having me," she replied. Luke and Miya waved good-bye, then headed upstairs to their bedroom. Miyuki turned back to Yomatri and said, "Your parents are really sweet."

"Yeah, they're awesome. You gotta love 'em, right?"

Miyuki grinned; she rubbed her eyes wearily, then began to stretch. "Man, it's been suuuch a long day. I had a lot of fun, though—don't get me wrong. And I just remembered I'll be startin' school again pretty soon. But I guess that's the least of my worries, right?"

Yomatri didn't answer. He sat with his arms crossed, his expression thoughtful.

"Hey, what are you thinkin' about?" asked Miyuki.

Yomatri shook his head as he came back to his senses.

"Oh, uh, nothing really ... just the whole situation with Hano and the crystal, I guess. I know I probably said this before, but I just hope we can get it back 'cause I know the Alliance really needs it."

Looking down to examine her fingernails, Miyuki responded, "Yeah, I know what you mean. I guess this is just part of being a hero, you know? Facing challenges like these."

"Probably. Part of me kinda feels like he took it easy on me when we were battling it out in the courtyard on Ember Island—like he wasn't actually trying his hardest."

Miyuki looked up. "Why do you say that?"

"I don't know. Like I can just remember there were moments when he seemed to make mistakes on purpose. I think it was in the second round, he was up one point, and then he left himself wide open for a punch to the face."

Miyuki's eyebrows rose. "I kinda remember that too! But wait a sec. What exactly are you getting at?"

"Well, I mean, not only that, but there was also a moment in the third round where I easily finished him off by swiping at his legs. By that point, I think I was up two to one. Most people—especially a fighter like him—wouldn't just let their guard down that easily."

"Yes, to a certain extent."

"Look, what I'm trying to say is that I think it was all for show, even though he was acting like one of the good guys."

"Possibly ... I mean, I don't wanna bring you down or anything, but you might be onto something. I'm just honestly not sure."

"Well, take a sec and think about it. In the grand scheme of things, he was supposed to be viewed as this 'incredible' mentor for the other students on the island. But here I come in and just win, like that?" Yomatri snapped his fingers. "It doesn't add up."

Miyuki shook her head, then replied, "No, no, you're definitely bringing up some good points. I guess what scares me the most, now that you're bringin' all this up, is just the thought of what he's actually capable of—especially now that he's got the crystal on his side."

Yomatri nodded. "We're just gonna have to be extra careful from here on out and see what happens. I feel like that's really our only option at this point. We have to give it our all."

CHAPTER EIGHTEEN:

A VOICE IN THE NIGHT

One Week Later ...

L ate one evening, Yomatri sat beside his parents on a couch in the living room, watching a movie on the large flat-screen TV. In his lap was a big bowl of buttery, salty popcorn with a cold drink to his left. Miya and Luke leaned against one another and shared from a small bag of chocolate while lights from the screen flickered repeatedly.

As the movie went on, they pointed with excitement. In one scene, a dark-haired man equipped with a parachute jumped from an exploding plane. The surround system echoed with loud bangs throughout the entire house.

Eventually, Yomatri glanced at the wall clock and saw that it read 11:00 p.m., then leaned over to his parents. "Hey, you guys, I'm gonna head to bed. Just gettin' a little tired."

"Okay, that's fine. We'll be up there in just a bit." Miya checked her wristwatch. "I think the movie's almost finished anyways."

"Leavin' movie night early ... I see how it is," Luke joked. Yomatri grinned and got up from the couch, handing his parents the bowl of popcorn. "Nah, I'm just messin' with you, kiddo."

"I know, I know. This was really fun, though! We'll have to do it again sometime," he replied. "I'll see you guys tomorrow, right?"

"Yeah, I should be here," Miya insisted, exchanging a glance with her husband.

"I won't. I'll be at work." Luke frowned. "But hey, if you wanted to do somethin' maybe when I get off, I'm all for it."

"Yeah, that sounds good, Dad. I'll let you know if I think of anything." Waving good-bye, the teenager turned away and headed upstairs to his room.

"Have a good night!" said Luke and Miya.

In his room, after shutting the door, Yomatri jumped into bed and closed his eyes, trying his best to fall asleep. After an hour that seemed to go by quicker than normal, the time on the digital alarm clock atop his nightstand struck midnight.

Yomatri began to hear hundreds of individuals chatting with one another in an underground subway amidst oncoming trains.

A voice spoke loudly over a PA system while footsteps shuffled from all directions. Cellphones rung repeatedly and televisions mounted along the walls added to the noisiness of the subway. The smell of coffee wafted heavily through the air.

Yomatri, Miyuki, and the four brothers paused to board an oncoming train. Many people quickly entered and exited the vehicle, but after what seemed like seconds, the train's metal doors slammed shut.

Inside, Yomatri and his friends looked all around, trying to locate Hano—searching one train car after another. Together, they studied each and every passenger, hoping he'd eventually appear. Nothing.

Yomatri took the lead, and his friends followed, walking up and down a cramped car. They examined more and more passengers by the second.

At one point, the train took a sharp turn and Yomatri bumped into a dark-haired woman, knocking her phone and coffee cup out of her hands. Annoyed, she looked up at him, then bent down to make sure her phone was okay, but the entire screen had shattered.

"Aahhh—you idiot!" the woman shouted. She lunged at him, desperately trying to ring his neck. Grabbing it tightly, she dug her fingers into his skin.

Beginning to choke, Yomatri tugged the woman's wrists and tried his best to muscle her off of him, but she was too strong. His heart pounding, he watched as the woman's eyes turned completely black; her skin slowly began to melt away.

Yomatri dropped to his knees and looked around in disbelief. His attacker suddenly vanished into thin air. Clenching his neck, he coughed and coughed, struggling to gasp for air.

After a moment, he glanced back and quickly became confused—all of his friends were now lying on the ground. Immediately, he tried to grab their hands, but it seemed that an invisible force field prevented him from doing so.

"Yomatri!!" Miyuki cried, reaching after him. Sage and his brothers did the same, but no matter how hard they tried, nothing seemed to work.

His eyes wide with terror, Yomatri watched as the five of them slowly began to disappear in a cloud of darkness. Turning back around, he looked out in front of him, noticing dozens of lifeless bodies lying motionless on the floor of the train—his fellow passengers.

Out of nowhere, a blistering bolt of shadowy energy came at him. Yomatri dodged, falling backward. He looked up, noticing a hooded assailant—Shinzuki—wielding a sharp, pointy scepter.

The sorcerer glared at the teenager, his eyes burning with hatred. Suddenly, from the shadows, Hano appeared, the Emerald Crystal in his hands.

"That's not yours!!" Yomatri yelled.

Menacingly, Hano slowly sauntered toward Yomatri. Staring into the boy's eyes, he stretched his hand out in front of him.

Yomatri's vision was overtaken by haunting images: his mother screaming for help, his father begging for mercy, and many individuals shouting in panic. With his hand, Yomatri reached out and tried to save them all, but it was useless. His vision had returned to normal.

It was then that Hano slapped the teenager's hand away and lashed out with the Emerald Crystal.

"Aaahh!!" Yomatri screamed as he jumped from his bed, breathing heavily. Tiny drips of sweat ran down the sides of his face.

"Yomatri? What's wrong?" his parents called out from down the hall. Miya and Luke rushed out of their bed, spilling their bowl of popcorn onto the floor. Together, they burst open their son's door and ran inside. "What happened?!"

Yomatri didn't respond. Shaken, he looked up at his parents, who hurried over to the side of his bed. Miya turned on a small lamp resting on her son's nightstand. Yomatri came to his senses and placed his hands over his face. "It was like a nightmare or something. I can't really describe it. It—it's too painful!"

"Are you okay? Should I get you something?" Miya asked, placing a hand on his forehead. "Oh my God, you're burning up!"

"I'm alright ... just really hot," he responded, his heart

beating fast.

Miya turned to her husband. "Luke, honey, get him a glass of water, would you please?"

"Yeah, sure," he replied. Minutes later, Luke returned with a glass of cold water in hand. "Here, drink this, buddy. It'll help cool you down." Yomatri took the glass and began to drink. Luke continued, his expression grave, "What exactly did you see in your dream?"

Yomatri was silent, looking off to one side as he paused to gather his thoughts. "I remember I was on this train. My friends—they were screaming my name. And I saw you both too. You guys were shouting for help or something, but I couldn't get to you," he said, wiping tears from his eyes. "And all of the people on the train—they were dead—and I didn't really know what to do!"

Miya and Luke stared at their son, their jaws hanging open. "Oh my God ... that's terrible," said Miya. "What else happened? Do you remember?"

Yomatri, still sweating, gulped down more water. "I saw Hano ... and the sorcerer guy, he was there too. They had the crystal I was tellin' you guys about—the one they stole from me and my friends. But no matter what I did, I couldn't get it back!" He shook his head. "I can't really remember much else after that. Ahh ... I feel so bad."

"No, no, you don't have to feel that way," Luke said, gently touching his son's shoulder. "It was just a dream. That's all that matters."

Miya added, "Yes, honey, it's okay; don't worry. You're safe now."

Yomatri glanced up at his parents. His lips began to

quiver and his eyes filled with more tears.

Miya, a look of sorrow on her face, took her son by the arms and pulled him in for a hug. Luke joined in and tried his best to comfort him.

His eyes closed, Yomatri held on to his parents tightly, knowing this was a night he'd never forget.

CHAPTER NINETEEN:

A DARK HOUR

A winter glow was spread across the city as stretched beams of sunlight broke through, brightening skyscrapers and other tall buildings. In the streets below, hundreds of people walked along the bustling sidewalks while cars and taxicabs honked at one another in the distance.

At home in Forest Hills down in the basement, Miya had finished putting a load of dirty clothes into the washer. She turned and placed a bottle of detergent back into a nearby closet and then paused.

"Okay, so that's out of the way ... now I need to check up on Yomatri," she said to herself. After turning off the light in the laundry room and shutting the door, she headed up to her son's bedroom.

Peeking through a cracked door, Miya found that he was sound asleep with a warm blue blanket draped over him. He snored with his mouth wide open, which she found adorable. Gently, she opened the door and quietly inched inside.

Miya scanned her son's room which was filled with smelly clothes, old dishes, and several baskets of laundry that needed to be taken downstairs. She shook her head, then opened the curtains along one of the walls to help shed some light into her son's man cave.

Suddenly, Yomatri began to stir. Moving slowly, he turned towards the light in his peripheral. After brushing off the blanket, he began to sit upright.

Miya walked over to him as he rubbed his eyes.

"Hey, sleepyhead. You look a mess," she laughed, gently rubbing his spiky brown hair. "It's good you're finally awake."

Yomatri continued to rub his eyes. "What time is it?"

Miya checked her wristwatch, then glanced around her son's bedroom again. "Almost one o'clock. You should really clean up in here. It's a mess." Giving her son a pat on the back, she continued, "Come on, get up."

"Okay, I'll be downstairs in a sec."

Just over ten minutes later, Yomatri arrived downstairs. He entered the kitchen and paused next to a counter near the stove, noticing a plate wrapped in tinfoil. While his mother poured herself a glass of milk, he unwrapped the foil, seeing a blueberry bagel, a side of eggs, and three strips of fresh bacon.

"Is this for me?" asked Yomatri.

"Yep, I made you a little breakfast. All yours."

The teenager smiled as he threw the plate in the microwave and grabbed a fork from a nearby drawer. He then leaned against a counter and looked down, his expression thoughtful.

"How are you feeling ... after what happened last night?"

Yomatri shifted his gaze up to his mother. "I'm okay.

Wasn't really expectin' to have a nightmare like that, but I'm fine." Miya nodded solemnly. He continued, "Where's Dad? He's usually up by now, isn't he?"

"Yeah, he's at work, remember? It's Monday, and those are usually his busiest days," Miya replied, taking a sip of her milk. "But since it's almost 1, he might also be at that restaurant he sometimes goes to during his lunch break."

"Oh yeah, that's right!" Yomatri snapped his fingers. "He did say that he had to work today."

✵✵✵

Along a snowy sidewalk in Queens, Luke, dressed in a hooded black jacket and jeans, exited his car and walked toward one of his favorite places to eat—a famous restaurant called Stewart's Diner. Immediately as he entered, the smell of fresh butter burgers and salty fries filled the air.

At a long wooden counter towards the front, groups of customers sat together on bar stools, chatting and laughing while they enjoyed their meals. Above their heads were multiple flat-screen TVs, many of them depicting football and soccer games.

In the center of the restaurant were assorted tables and chairs. Numerous waiters and waitresses attended to guests left and right. Many of the diner's walls were decorated with awards, posters, antique items, and other vintage mementos. In one of the corners, a tune of smooth jazz played through a jukebox decorated with flashy Christmas lights.

After a short moment, Luke was seated along the edge of the front counter next to a pregnant woman and her two children. Minutes later, his waitress—a tall blonde in her twenties dressed in a fancy black-and-white uniform—came over.

"Hi, there! My name's Jaimie and I'll be your server today," the woman said, passing Luke a menu. "What can I start you off with, sir?"

"Just a water's fine." Luke smiled.

"Sure thing! I'll be right back with that," the woman replied as she walked away.

✫✫✫

At Arrowsmith High School, Miyuki sat in the back of her math class beside many of her classmates—some of them daydreaming while others chewed gum and drew on their desks with sharpies. Atop her desk was a notebook filled with various doodles and several pens and pencils; her backpack leaned against her seat.

Glancing at a wall clock, she noticed it was almost time for class to be let out, yet the teacher continued to talk and talk. At one point, she leaned over toward another classmate.

"When is this lady gonna shut her mouth and let us go? I can't believe she's already giving us homework and it's only the first day back from break."

Her classmate, a redhead with round glasses, grinned and tried to keep herself from laughing. "I know, I was thinking the same thing! She's sooo annoying. Hopefully someone'll fire her."

Miyuki sighed and crossed her arms. Leaning back in her seat, she glared at the teacher who continued babbling on and on about the importance of students turning in their homework but couldn't have cared less.

Again she glanced at the clock, then rolled her eyes. In just a few minutes, she would be free from prison.

✰✰✰

At home, Yomatri had finished his food. Walking over to the sink, he set his plate on top of several dirty dishes and watched his mother, who prepared herself a peanut butter and banana sandwich.

He looked disgusted. "You really like those? They're so nasty!"

"Yeah, I mean, they're not that bad. Very nutritious, actually." Miya chuckled, shrugging her shoulders; she licked her knife and placed it in the sink. Afterwards, she turned and began putting away the peanut butter and wheat bread.

Yomatri shook his head, then went upstairs to get dressed. Minutes later, he returned to the kitchen, stopping near the fridge while his mother wiped off a counter with a wet rag.

"Hey, Mom, are you doin' anything today?"

"I'm not really, uh, sure. Why, what's up?"

All of a sudden the entire house rocked violently, and Miya grabbed the kitchen sink with one hand and gripped the edge of the counter with the other. Yomatri took hold of the refrigerator, but then its door was thrown open by great force.

Bottles of soda, fruits, a package of eggs, and other items fell out of the fridge and crashed to the floor. Around them, everything else began to quake. More and more items fell to the ground—a paper towel holder, a bread box, several forks and knives, and even a coffee maker.

Yomatri watched as the small TV on the counter next to the stove went to black. At the same time, its power cable snapped from the wall and the TV itself crashed onto the wooden floor. Around him and his mother, the chairs to the kitchen table fell over with a clatter.

Not even a second later, the cabinet doors slammed open as dozens of glass dishes dropped out, shattering into hundreds of pieces. Pots and pans clanged as they hit the floor. Above their heads, an ornate chandelier wobbled violently while other lights in the house flickered.

Her eyes widening, Miya looked up at the ceiling and feared the worst. Suddenly, everything came to a stop. A deathly, uncomfortable silence filled the room.

Standing in shock, Miya and Yomatri's eyes met.

"What was *that*?!" Miya yelled, breathing heavily as she glanced around.

With tiny beads of sweat dripping from his forehead, Yomatri shifted his gaze behind his mother where in the living room, the large flat-screen television was somehow still on. Quickly, he raced over and grabbed the remote from the floor.

"What ... what are you doing? This is no time for TV!" Miya snapped.

After taking several deep breaths, Yomatri managed to regain control of himself. He turned to the news station, trying to find an explanation for what just happened.

"Oh my God," he whispered to himself.

The screen showed a snowy street in Queens with a large number of abandoned vehicles and taxicabs scattered about. Parked along the sidewalks were various firetrucks and police cars with flashing lights. Other clips showed civilians running in horror while explosions could be seen erupting in the distance.

Yomatri knitted his brow. He turned as his mother rushed over to him. After sharing worried looks, they both turned their attention to the TV.

"What's happening?" asked Miya.

"I don't know—something really crazy for sure."

Miya shook her head in disbelief. As continuous images of mayhem and destruction were shown, a reporter's voice bellowed:

> *... It appears the NYPD and fire department have been called in to help, but clearly, it is too much for them to handle. The authorities are currently doing their best to get everyone to safety and they've asked that everyone remain calm as they attempt to get the situation under control. If there's anyone out there who can help, they ask that you please provide immediate assistance ...*

"What, are we under attack or something?" Miya asked. Yomatri shook his head and turned away as he raced upstairs to his room. "Wait! Where are you going?"

"Hold on a second!"

In his bedroom, Yomatri reached into his closet and began searching for his backpack. Breathing heavily, Miya finally caught up to him. She stumbled against the door but managed to keep herself up, watching her son from behind.

Seconds later, Yomatri found his backpack and one of his most beloved weapons he'd used in space camp—a rusty, battered metal staff. He clicked a tiny red button on the weapon and watched as it retracted to a length half its original size.

Tossing his staff and backpack onto the bed, he then turned around to face his mother.

"What are you planning to do—go out into the city and help?!" Miya yelled, watching as he hurried to get ready, putting on a hooded jacket and a pair of black gloves.

"Yes, I have to!"

"There's no way you can go out there! You have to stay here! It's too dangerous!"

Yomatri lifted his head and stared at his mother with an outraged look. "I can't just sit here and do nothing! I've gotta help those people out there! They need me."

Miya sighed angrily and shook her head. "Alright, fine!"

After tying his shoes, Yomatri paused, studying his mother with a puzzled expression. "What, you wanna come with me?"

"No, no, it's okay! Just go ahead! I'll probably catch up with you somewhere! I'm gonna try to find your father!"

Yomatri eyed his mother uneasily and then pulled her into an embrace. Tears began to well in Miya's eyes. Turning around, he took his staff and backpack from the bed.

After slinging the bag over his shoulder, the young teen

raced back downstairs and headed outside, knowing it was imperative that he get into the city as quickly as possible.

Standing alone, Miya took a deep breath and nodded. "I can do this," she whispered. Within seconds, she hurried downstairs. After finding her car keys and putting on a winter jacket and shoes, Miya ran out of the house.

✶✶✶

In a bustling hallway at Arrowsmith High while on her way to lunch, Miyuki and several of her classmates paused after feeling a sudden, strong jolt. Miyuki glanced up at the ceiling and then at those around her, their faces looking shocked and confused.

Suddenly, overhead fluorescent lights began to flicker as the ceiling shook violently. Immediately, the students in the hall turned and began fleeing toward the exit doors, jostling as they did.

Against a storm of screams and shouts, Miyuki joined the others. Looking back, she tried to locate her friends but couldn't see them. Having been pushed along with the crowd, Miyuki turned around and rushed outside.

Together, she and many others regrouped near a wooden bench next to multiple students wearing horrified expressions. Eventually, the students watched as a large number of police officers, firefighters, and paramedics had arrived on the scene.

"What's goin' on?" asked a lanky teenager with curly black hair.

"I don't know, man! This is crazy!" said another student.

With a tense brow, Miyuki scanned the area. Around her and a few of her classmates, several students stopped to catch their breath while others were being examined by paramedics and emergency responders. Pulling her cell phone out of her pocket, she tried to call Yomatri, but there was no reception.

Miyuki grew frustrated and shook her head. Suddenly she looked up, as the sound of constant explosions erupting could be heard in the distance. Miyuki and her classmates grew even more worried.

"What was that noise?!" one girl cried.

"There's gotta be a way to find out what's happening," Miyuki whispered to herself, gritting her teeth. She glanced back at her classmates, then turned away and broke into a sprint, heading away from the school.

"Wait, Miyuki!" one student called after her. "Where are you going?"

Miyuki continued on, running as fast as she could in an attempt to get into the city.

☆☆☆

On Ember Island, in a lounge area at the top of a flat summit, Sage and his brothers watched the news on TV with many Aridnemekian teenagers. They were horrified by what they saw, having some sense as to why this was happening.

As the news report continued to show frightening images of a city in peril, the four brothers could no longer sit and watch. Sage motioned to the others, who regrouped with him in a corner of the room.

"Oh, this is horrible. We've got to do something about this," he insisted.

"Yes, we can't stay here. We have to go to the city and help those people!" Beta affirmed.

"Then we'll need to move fast," said Zatch. "We don't have much time. Miyuki and Yomatri probably need our help."

"Alright, guys, let's get ready then," said Sage as he, Beta, and Zatch began to head off.

"Wait!" Mako yelled. His brothers turned. "What about Master Zorhins and Captain Zeron? Shouldn't we tell them that we're leaving?"

"No, there's no time for that!" responded Sage. "They're probably going to be mad we're stealing a ship, but regardless, we have to move."

"How will we get there?" Mako asked, glancing at his brothers.

There was a short pause.

Zatch snapped his fingers. "I've got an idea! We'll need to somehow open up the portal to the city, though, for my plan to work. And a ship. We're gonna need one of those too."

"I think I can help with the portal," said Beta. "I sorta have an idea of how it works."

Sage nodded, then turned and led the way as his brothers followed him out of the lounge. Together, the teens raced to their dorm to prepare for battle.

Moments later, they'd returned back outside to the top of the flat summit. The brothers ran toward the center of the mountaintop, noticing a large mechanism made up of interconnected metal parts, its aperture in the shape of a circle. In front of the aperture was a sphere-shaped receptacle.

Panting, Mako asked, "Alright, so how do we turn this thing on?"

"Yes, so follow my lead! We'll first need to combine our elements into this canister here," Beta instructed, pointing. "It'll temporarily store the energy, but only if we do it all at the same time."

His brothers traded unsure looks, then after a moment, the four of them surrounded the receptacle. Working together, they each fired beams of elemental energy upon it: fire, electricity, earth, and water.

"More power!!" Beta yelled. He and his brothers strained with effort as they followed along, increasing their elements' intensity. Inside the canister, the four elements fused together, becoming a ball of rainbow-colored energy.

Sage's eyes widened, bright light shining off his face. "Wait, it's working, isn't it? At least it looks like it is?"

"Yes, yes! There's still one more thing we have to do, though. Here, Zatch, come help me!" said Beta. He raced over and slipped one of his arms into a metal apparatus connected to the spherical receptacle.

Zatch did the same to a second one close by, then asked, "What now?"

"Alright, so this acts just like a lever! You can turn it left and right. Make sense? If we turn it hard enough, it might be just enough to force open the portal!"

"I understand."

Beta continued, "We each go right on three! One, two, three!" Both he and Zatch turned the mechanism to the right, pushing as hard as they could.

The brothers watched—a beam of rainbow light shot out from the canister and into the portal's aperture. It shined brightly, eventually opening up a view of the outside world, the city of New York far out in the distance.

"YEAH!!" the brothers cheered, pumping their fists in the air. Beta continued, "Alright, we'll need to move fast! It's only gonna stay open for a short time, I think."

"Let's get to the ship then!" Sage instructed.

Only moments later, a large Alliance vessel raced through the opening, headed towards the city.

✬✬✬

In Queens, a massive invasion threatened the human race. Many of the streets were clogged as people continued abandoning their cars. Against a light snowfall, several individuals from nearby shops ran outside, horrified by what they saw.

A band of savage marauders with war paint drawn on their faces swarmed the city streets. Many of them wore protective metal armor over tattered leather robes.

Others looked like goblins, some with horns and sharp yellowed teeth. Each was armed with medieval-style weaponry that included spears, swords, scimitars, maces, and crossbows.

As several soldiers began to fire arrows, many people took cover and fled screaming in the opposite direction.

Although the thick snow made it difficult, the terrified civilians ran faster and faster, desperate to get away.

Along the crammed sidewalks, police and firefighters arrived on the scene, rushing out of their vehicles, sirens wailing. The authorities motioned to the fleeing civilians, trying their best to evacuate them to safety.

While the fire department began to take over, the police assembled into small groups. As a team, they drew their sidearms and fired upon the invaders.

Bullets ripped through the air. Many of the soldiers quickly defended themselves, forming shields with their elements. While the officers paused to reload, the enemy seized the opportunity to take the upper hand.

Blasts of shadowy energy knocked a few officers off their feet, hurling them back so they crashed to the ground. More enemy shots rained down, striking the snow and various cars in the streets. Multiple explosions erupted, thick black smoke rising up.

One after another, officers rushed to help each other up, then continued fighting. At the same time, civilians continued to run away amidst small fires and piles of wreckage and debris.

Overwhelmed, the police tried their best to hold off the advancing soldiers, but nothing seemed to stop them. More and more enemy invaders appeared from the shadows.

As the battle in the streets continued, at Stewart's Diner, many of the TVs went to black while on several counters, glass cups and dishes rattled violently. Luke and other panicked customers hurried over to a row of front windows and peered outside.

One woman spotted something horrific as she pointed—a group of civilians had been slain by spears and swords. Customers cried out and turned away, fleeing toward the back of the diner. At the same time, waiters and waitresses tried their best to keep everyone calm.

Luke turned and shouted across the restaurant, "Hey, everyone! We need to lock the doors! We have to keep those soldiers from coming inside!" Around him, waitstaff scrambled to each and every entrance and hurriedly locked the doors.

Suddenly, the waitress who'd served Luke rushed toward him. "What should we do now?" she asked, her voice unsteady. Beside her were other employees looking exhausted and scared.

"Anything you can to keep these people safe! Whatever you have to do!" said Luke. He paused for a moment to think, then began moving tables. "Here, I've got an idea! We can use the tables as a defense. Set them down on their sides as cover and use the chairs to help blockade the doors."

Without hesitation, the diner employees followed along. Working as a team, they tossed the tables down on their sides, positioning them to form a defensive wall in the center of the restaurant. Other workers gathered several chairs and set them in front of the doors.

Panting, Luke glanced around at the nervous customers—a mixture of men and women, children and older adults. "Alright, I need everyone to get behind the tables!"

Everyone hurried to do as told. Several customers huddled in groups to conserve space. Luke watched closely, noticing the tables were so big they covered nearly everyone.

Suddenly, a waiter with spiky black hair touched his shoulder. "Hey, is it alright if I close the curtains so we won't be noticed?"

Luke replied, "Yeah, that's fine! As long as we're out of the enemy's eye, do whatever's necessary."

The waiter nodded and then motioned to some of his coworkers. Meanwhile, a team of servers pushed eating utensils onto the floor, desperate to get them off elevated surfaces. Minutes passed like seconds and most of the employees had completed their assigned tasks.

Luke shouted, "Okay, you guys—I need you all to listen closely! The enemy's steadily approaching! We've got all the customers behind the tables! Now it's your turn!"

After the last few curtains had been lowered and all utensils were off the counters and tables, the employees did as they were told. Moving quickly, they hid behind the tables among the customers.

Luke was the last one to join them. He dropped down beside the pregnant woman from before, and her two kids, taking hold of a metal serving tray for protection.

The woman, looking exhausted and stressed, stared into Luke's eyes.

"Is everything going to be okay, mister?" one of the kids asked.

"Yeah, pal, it's gonna be alright ... stay by Mommy! Don't worry!" Luke insisted as drips of sweat streamed down his forehead.

Outside, the attack on New York continued.

CHAPTER TWENTY:

FALL OF THE HEROES

While firefighters continued directing fleeing civilians to safety, more police officers had joined the fight in the streets, taking up defensive positions behind cars and piles of wreckage and debris.

Together, they fired at the enemy invaders, but their opponents only continued to defend themselves with shields crafted from their elements. A band of marauders pressed forward, decimating officers one by one. Blasts of shadowy energy and bullets roared back and forth as multiple explosions erupted around the police.

At one point, while a team of masked soldiers paused to reload their crossbows, another troop hurled grenades in the direction of the police. Officers rushed to take cover. Explosions ripped through numerous abandoned vehicles, tearing them apart like toys.

In various stores and shops along the sidewalks, hundreds of people watched the carnage outside, growing more frightened by the second. At a busy intersection, one officer was violently thrown into a pile of rubble. Another had been killed by three arrow shots to the chest.

Civilians continued to flee the mayhem, running as fast as they could in the snow. Meanwhile, Miyuki—her curly brown hair billowing—raced down a neighboring street.

Amidst small fires, she dropped down behind a damaged taxicab for cover while catching her breath.

Cautiously, she peered over the back end of the vehicle. Her eyes wide, she watched as more police were killed in the distance. Rising to her feet, she turned and locked eyes with a masked soldier armed with a bow and arrows.

The man fired at her but Miyuki ducked behind the taxi, then quickly sprung back up and hurled a water rocket, wiping him out.

Having been spotted by another soldier, Miyuki turned and hurried away. Arrows pierced several nearby cars, barely missing her. Whirling around, she fired a powerful burst of water at her pursuer, sweeping him off his feet. Miyuki continued on. Turning a street corner, she raced behind a brick building to take cover yet again.

Across the street, while enemy fire blasted the snow around them, a group of police stopped and looked over, noticing her. "Hey, kid!" one officer shouted. "You've gotta get out of here! It's too dangerous!"

Miyuki covered her head. Explosions continued all around, rocking the ground beneath her feet. While several officers reloaded their weapons, she peered around the corner and glanced further up the street. Her eyes focused on another intersection several hundred feet ahead.

Accompanied by a small unit of soldiers, a tall hooded figure had emerged from the shadows, a pointy scepter in hand. Clouds of black smoke began to thin and Miyuki squinted at the mysterious figure, recognizing him almost immediately—*Shinzuki.*

"Oh, no," she whispered, her lips trembling.

His face obscured by a dark leather mask, the sorcerer surveyed the battlefield before him, looking pleased. Next to him, Hano suddenly appeared.

Wearing a jacket, jeans, and a backpack, the young teenager brandished a sharp, jagged object that shined with a bright green color. In a matter of seconds, the two of them had disappeared in the crowd of fighting bodies.

Miyuki shook her head, then left her hiding place and ran further up the street. Multiple officers stopped firing and lowered their weapons. The men shouted at her, but she continued on. Running toward a trio of armed marauders, she ducked as one lunged at her with a metal spear.

With poise, she snatched the weapon from the man's grasp and kicked him aside. Miyuki turned just as another soldier rushed at her with a sword.

Dodging her opponent's blade, she swiped at him but missed. She panicked. From behind, the third marauder kicked her to the ground and glared, his eyes filled with hate.

Lying in the snow, Miyuki glanced up fearfully. One of the men stabbed at her with his weapon.

In a flash, a forceful hit to the jaw knocked the invader several steps backward. Wide-eyed, Miyuki watched—a teenager with spiky brown hair wielding a battered metal staff had spun around to deliver a powerful, finishing blow to his opponent.

"Yomatri!!" she yelled, grinning widely. The boy turned and raced toward the other invader, knocking him off his feet with a swift, solid strike of his weapon.

Panting, he rushed over and helped his friend up, both

of them sharing a look of relief.

Miyuki asked, "Hey! Where'd you come from?"

"Long story—I can explain later. Are you alright?"

"Yeah, I'm fine."

"What's the plan?" asked Yomatri.

"We've gotta continue helping the police and try to hold off the soldiers for as long as we can. It's our only chance of winning."

The teens turned and looked ahead, noticing a large team of enemy combatants charging toward them. Many of the officers, their guns still lowered, looked on nervously.

Readying his weapon, Yomatri clenched his teeth. Miyuki stood beside him, fists raised. With his staff, he blocked fierce blows from his attackers and dodged a sword while Miyuki fended off multiple troops, using a variety of strong water attacks.

Skillfully, Yomatri defended as more soldiers came at him, parrying blows and scattering shots of dark energy in all directions. As one man lunged at her with a sword, Miyuki responded quickly, forming a thick, defensive shield made of ice.

Again, the soldier lashed at her, making her waver, but she managed to stay afoot and fight back. Turning, she bashed her opponent across the face with her shield, then continued on to the next.

Meanwhile, Yomatri managed to dispatch one marauder with a solid strike to the torso. A second stabbed at him with a scimitar, which he gracefully dodged before twirling around, landing a powerful blow to his opponent's face with the end of his staff.

A third soldier wielding a spiky mace swiped at the teen, their weapons clashing. Grimacing, Yomatri forced the invader back and swiped at his opponent's shins, knocking him down. He turned left, his eyes widening as a spiraling bolt of shadowy energy slammed into him, sending him skidding backward in the snow.

"Yomatri!" Miyuki yelled. A masked assailant quickly brandished a metal spear, taking her by surprise as he swung, clubbing her with the end of his weapon.

Miyuki screamed in pain and dropped to her knees.

Now without his staff, Yomatri sprung back up, his heart pounding. He dashed toward his friend's attacker while encasing his arms in thick ice. As he punched and kicked, the man easily carried his strikes, defending with a shield in his other hand.

At one point, the soldier forcefully kicked Yomatri in the chest, knocking him back to the ground. He then slashed with his spear, attempting to deliver a finishing blow, but a water rocket from Miyuki sent him crashing down.

The girl picked up her friend's staff from the ground, then rushed over and helped him up.

Yomatri took the weapon, then asked, "Are you okay?!"

"Yeah, I'm alright. We have ... to keep fighting."

"There's too many of them! There's no way we can take them all on." He and his friend were driven back.

Blasts of dark energy stormed past their heads and officers taking cover desperately called for help over their radios. Miyuki and Yomatri watched as suddenly, a group of masked assailants ripped incendiary grenades from their utility belts and hurled them at their opponents.

Police officers ran wildly and ducked.

"No!" Miyuki cried. "We have to help them! They're going to be killed!" Teams of enemy invaders began to advance. A fiery explosion had wiped out several police.

Against raging flames and a flurry of billowing smoke, a commanding female officer turned and shouted to her comrades, "Retreat! We have to fall back! Get everyone out of here immediately!" Around her, groups of officers turned away and fled.

Miyuki eyed Yomatri, her expression a mixture of shock and worry. With police and citizens running on all sides, Yomatri stared back uneasily. "Miyuki, we have to leave! We can't stay here!"

Hiding back tears, Miyuki took his hand as they each turned away and joined the retreat. Running from the soldiers, they both glanced back in horror. Their hearts pounded as they feared they'd soon be captured.

Forcing their attention away, the teens continued to follow the officers and eventually turned a street corner. Civilians raced into nearby stores and shops along the sidewalk while police attended to their wounded comrades.

Other officers stopped to catch their breath and plan. Miyuki and Yomatri stared nervously at each other again, knowing the worst was yet to come.

CHAPTER TWENTY-ONE:

THE BATTLE FOR NEW YORK

Enemy fire continued to streak past the heroes' position. Panting, Miyuki shifted her gaze behind Yomatri where officers continued assisting their wounded comrades. One exhausted officer with rips in her uniform reached over and grabbed a radio lying in the snow.

Her forehead beaded with sweat, the woman pleaded, "Is there anyone out there who can help us? This is Officer Whitney! We're takin' a lotta heat from the soldiers! I repeat: are there any officers in the surrounding area that can provide assistance? Does anyone copy?"

The officer waited nervously, but the only answer she got was a muffled, unintelligible response.

Yomatri, Miyuki, and the police and firefighters eyed one another with worried looks. Again the officer spoke into the radio: "I'm sorry! I ... I didn't understand! What was that? Please repeat!"

A silence filled the air as the officer paused; she lowered her head and glanced around at everyone else, all of them sensing that no one was coming.

"Oh no ... this is bad," Miyuki said, staring ahead with her mouth agape. Turning, she whispered to Yomatri, "There's gotta be something we can do!"

Eyeing her closely, Yomatri clenched his staff. He took

a deep breath and nodded, then slowly walked past her. Peering around the corner to see the adjacent street, his eyes widened as he noticed the army of enemy invaders had gotten much closer.

Miyuki joined him and looked ahead. "They're gonna wipe us out at any moment. We've gotta get outta here!"

Suddenly a shower of ice pellets rained from the sky, disorienting many of the enemy troops. The invaders groaned and shouted while some glanced up at the clouds but saw nothing.

Yomatri knitted his brow. "What in the world?" He traded a confused look with Miyuki, then returned his attention to the chaos out in front of him.

Marauders were readying their weapons and adopting battle-ready stances, but only seconds later, another storm of pellets came down, striking more soldiers. While some invaders rushed to help their wounded comrades, others closely surveyed their surroundings.

Still, there was no answer.

"What's going on?" asked Miyuki. Police and firefighters standing nearby glanced in her direction.

"Look!" Yomatri stammered, pointing up at the sky. Miyuki and everyone else's eyes followed.

In the distance, a bright speck of light came soaring toward the battleground. As it grew closer, it appeared to be a ship resembling a miniature stealth bomber. Armed with four cannons, the ship swooped in low, flying head on into incoming enemy fire.

A water missile spewed from one of its guns, wiping out a group of masked troops. Enemy arrows ripped through the air, striking the vessel repeatedly, but the ship stood strong as it continued—this time launching a heavy burst of fire, knocking out a group of soldiers.

Turning sharply around a building, the ship attacked again with full force, firing upon numerous invaders with shots of elemental energy. Explosions erupted all around, violently tossing up snow.

More enemy combatants fired on the ship using crossbows, but like before, their arrows bounced uselessly off the vessel. Yomatri and those nearby watched in wonder as the ship swooped in low yet again, attempting to prepare another powerful attack.

One commanding soldier gesticulated, quickly forming a ball of dark energy. He cast his hand outward and the blistering shadow bolt slammed into the side of the ship. Thick black smoke shot out from one of its wings, causing the vessel to spin out of control.

Having clipped the side of a building, it then crash-landed in a ball of flames just several hundred meters in front of Yomatri and the others. The heroes shielded themselves as bits of rubble and concrete shot up from the ground, pelting nearby buildings and shattering glass windows.

Eventually, the ship came to a complete halt in the middle of an intersection. The commanding soldier motioned to his comrades, who ceased their fire and looked on curiously.

Yomatri raced forward a few feet, then stopped in his tracks. Miyuki and several officers gathered behind him, their expressions worried. Amidst smoldering flames, Sage and his brothers slowly emerged from the wreckage, each preparing a strong combat stance.

Miyuki and Yomatri gasped, their eyes widening.

"Whaaat?!" the teens both said.

"You guys, that was amazing!" Yomatri yelled. "Are you alright?"

"Yes, we're fine; don't worry about us," Mako replied.

Miyuki glanced at Yomatri. "What do we do now?"

"We fight! We have the chance to take back the city." Turning back to the brothers, Yomatri continued, "You guys know what to do! Like I said to you once before: we're a team, and we stick together no matter what!"

Sage and his brothers glanced back, each nodding solemnly. As a team, the six teens charged forward and rushed into battle, taking cover from a barrage of enemy arrows. Yomatri knocked down one invader with a swipe of his staff, then leaped over a taxicab and swung, sending another to the ground.

Having landed safely, Yomatri turned. Another soldier lashed at him with a spear, but the teenager dodged the sharp blade, then spun around and knocked the man off his feet with a swift strike of his weapon.

Standing nearby, Miyuki fended off a team of marauders, using a mix of ice and water attacks to assist her in the fight. Yomatri joined in, taking on some of the men with repeated attacks from his staff.

More and more enemy troops closed in on the heroes while police and firefighters began further evacuating the area. Mako dashed forward and took a used crossbow from the ground, noticing it was half full of arrows. Aiming the weapon at an invader, he fired, the arrow piercing through his thick metal armor.

Wielding a spiky mace, another soldier came at him, swiping the crossbow from the teen's hands. He knocked Mako back with a heavy kick, sending him down into the snow.

Mako glanced up, his eyes wide. The man lashed at him with his weapon, but a blazing fire blast sent the marauder crashing down.

Sage rushed over and helped his brother up.

"Hey, thanks!" said Mako.

"Yeah. Come on, let's keep fighting!"

Mako turned and ran head on at a group of enemy combatants, his eyes aglow. He leaped up, channeling bursts of electrical energy into one of his hands. Upon landing, the teen punched the ground. Bolts of lightning shot up, blasting the men backward.

Nearby, while taking on a pair of masked soldiers, Beta spun around, shooting two quick bursts of water. One of the men blocked the attack with his spear while the other fired a heavy beam of dark energy, knocking Beta back into a wrecked car.

Snarling, the marauder continued, striking forcefully with a sword in his other hand. Beta dodged and the weapon pierced the vehicle, the sharp blade mere inches from his face.

From behind, Zatch manipulated the earth and hurled chunks of broken concrete at the men, wiping them out just in time. His face beaming, Beta raced to his feet and joined his brother.

Beside them, Miyuki continued to trade fierce punches and kicks with enemy troops, dodging just in time. At one point, like Mako, she stopped and picked up a used crossbow from the ground—using it to further trim the enemy's numbers.

Close by, a team of three soldiers charged at Yomatri, their swords and spears aimed. The teen gritted his teeth and dodged their weapons, then used his own to go on the offensive, striking with a whirlwind of swift attacks. Yomatri stabbed and slashed with his staff and soon came to a pause. Panting, he looked down: all of his opponents were laid out at his feet.

Miyuki glanced over. "Yeah, Yomatri!"

He gave a quick thumbs-up, then dashed behind a building for cover; Mako stood beside him.

"We're doing good," Yomatri said to the Aridnemekian. "Much better than I expected."

"Yes, my friend—we have to keep pushing them back!"

Yomatri gave a solemn nod, then headed back into battle. He clicked a tiny green button along the shaft of his staff, separating the weapon into two metal wands. He then clicked a yellow button, firing up an electrical charge in each wand.

An enemy soldier swiped at him with a spear, but Yomatri ducked the blade. Upon rising, he shouted, striking his opponent in the chest with one of his electrified rods.

Another marauder slashed with a scimitar and Yomatri dodged, then leaped up and delivered a spinning kick, knocking the man back. Having landed safely, the teen stopped to catch his breath.

"Wait a minute. What's goin' on over there?" he asked. His eyes focused on a restaurant several blocks down the street, its windows curtained.

Yomatri squinted, noticing a tall man in a hooded robe accompanied by five masked soldiers armed with spears. Clenching his electrified wands, the teen quickly grew worried.

Together, the men closed in on the restaurant, smashing open its glass front doors.

✫✫✫

Inside, the air was deathly silent. Luke's heart pounded as the marauders paced slowly toward him and everyone else. Still hiding behind the tipped-over furniture, the diner's staff and customers looked to him for help.

The men's heavy footsteps grew closer by the second.

While a few children began to cry, Luke eyed a small group of waiters and waitresses and nodded to them. Hidden by the furniture, they slowly crawled to the back kitchen, desperately trying not to make a sound.

Finally Luke emerged to face his new opponents. Arms raised, he inched toward the enemy invaders. "Alright, you've found us. We chose not to evacuate. What is it that you want?" he asked, looking worn.

"Ahhh … don't be afraid, my friend," the hooded man, Shinzuki, replied, his voice deep and menacing. He extended his arms, wielding his pointy black scepter in one hand. "You are merely doing what any man would've done in this situation. But as you can tell, my side has lost this battle."

Luke's eyes grew tense. "Get to the point, you creep."

The sorcerer paused before he continued. "Try to be the hero if you wish. It won't help. You and everyone else here will become my prisoners. If you try to resist, I assure you that things will not end well."

Luke closely watched the mercenary, studying his every move. At one point, he slowly lowered one of his hands and began to scratch his neck.

"What are you doing?!" one soldier snapped, readying his weapon.

Luke locked eyes with him. "What does it matter to you anyway? Only reason you guys are here is to cause pain and suffering. Why? How's that gonna help anyone?"

"It wouldn't make sense to someone like you," Shinzuki interrupted, gritting his teeth.

Luke turned to the sorcerer. "Hey, man, I heard a lot about you with the whole battle in Manhattan a while back. Heard you got beat pretty bad by two kids. That must really suck. I mean, what kind of 'bad guy' do you even think you are?"

Meanwhile, the waiters and waitresses had crawled out from the back kitchen and returned to their hiding spots behind the cluster of furniture. One after another, the customers armed themselves with metal pots and frying pans, while others prepared spatulas, ladles, and other utensils.

"What's that noise?" another soldier asked. Nervous, he briefly eyed Luke. After receiving no answer, he pressed forward. "Answer me!!"

Luke threw a punch at the man, but the invader dodged,

then sank a fist into his gut. Luke doubled over, and the man punched him again. Wincing, Luke glanced up at his opponent, who growled tauntingly.

The soldier hit him a third time with his fist. Luke gritted his teeth, and with no chance to recover, the first soldier advanced and swiped his spear, sending him crashing back into a table. Lying on his side, Luke clutched his stomach with a hand.

Pressing forward, the invader stared down at him, his chest heaving. "It's over for you!"

Shinzuki and the other soldiers looked on tensely.

All of a sudden, a pot was seen hurtling through the air. It struck the enemy combatant standing over Luke square in the forehead, knocking him out. Immediately, the diner's staff and customers pushed the furniture aside. Hurrying to their feet, they charged at their opponents head on.

The other invaders quickly responded, slashing at the civilians using spears, swords, and scimitars. Together, the team of New Yorkers stood strong, attacking and defending in turn.

The waitress who'd served Luke rushed over and helped him up as other staff members smacked the marauders with pots and pans; some were beaten senseless with wooden spoons, rolling pins, teapots, and bare fists.

Even a few kids helped, working together as if taking down a big bully. Some squirted bottles of ketchup and mustard in the enemies' faces, temporarily blinding them. Other children hurled hot sauce, salt, and pepper at their attackers to spice things up.

In no time, they'd defeated all of the soldiers except

one. Bravely, the last man took a firm stance and clenched his weapon, but in a matter of seconds, his luck had run out.

A figure with long dark brown hair rushed forward and bashed him across the face with a fire extinguisher, smashing his head into a wall. *Miya.* The soldier slowly dropped to the ground, the metal frame of his mask shattered open.

Leaning against a counter with a frying pan in one hand, Luke stared in astonishment. "Miya! Where'd you come from?"

The customers and staff lowered their weapons.

"Long story!" Breathing heavily, Miya tossed the fire extinguisher aside; she rushed over and tried to comfort him, suddenly finding herself unable to move. "What—what's happening?!"

Luke's eyes widened. He shifted his gaze to where Shinzuki stood. The sorcerer glared with a raised hand. Angered, Luke jumped up and swung with the frying pan, narrowly missing him.

"Honey, no!" Miya yelled. She dropped to her feet and turned to her husband with a worried look.

Luke swung with the pan a second time, but Shinzuki held him in place using his elements, a swirl of energy spiraling around one of his fists. The hooded invader twisted Luke's wrist, disarming him. He then grabbed his opponent by the throat with one hand, lifting him off his feet.

The diner's staff and customers watched in horror.

"Luke!" Miya screamed, her expression grave.

The sorcerer glared at him. "You've tried your hardest, but it just wasn't good enough."

Luke shifted his gaze behind Shinzuki where all of a sudden, someone came rushing toward him. Holding his electrified wands, Yomatri swiped at Shinzuki, who dropped Luke as he dodged the attack.

Again Yomatri attacked, but his opponent defended, quickly conjuring a shield with his elements.

"You again!" the sorcerer yelled.

With his other hand now free, Shinzuki fired a shadow bolt using his scepter and blasted the teen down onto the ground. Panting, Yomatri rose and the sorcerer advanced. He gesticulated, firing multiple streams of dark matter.

Yomatri braced himself with his wands, which absorbed his opponent's attack. In a flash, he spun around and lashed with his electrified rods, this time landing a successful blow to his foe's side. Shinzuki grimaced.

Immediately the sorcerer responded, using his elements to shoot glowing ropes of shadowy energy at Yomatri, restraining him by the arms.

"Oh, no!" the teen panicked. The staff and customers watched uneasily. Shinzuki glared down at Yomatri, his eyes burning with anger.

All of a sudden, Luke came from behind, hitting the sorcerer in the back of his head with a wooden cutting board. Yomatri dropped to his knees. Whirling around, Shinzuki knocked the weapon from Luke's grasp with a fierce strike, sending him to the ground.

The sorcerer advanced, firing a blistering energy bolt at Luke, who rolled out of the way just in time. Again the evil mercenary struck, narrowly missing him.

Luke scurried to his feet and began to run, but a third burst of energy knocked him off his feet. He crashed painfully onto the ground, then shook his head, a bloody gash on the side of his face. The sorcerer grinned, channeling dark matter into the head of his scepter.

It was then that Yomatri came from behind and lunged forward with his twin rods, striking the sorcerer in the back and shocking him unconscious. He watched tensely as Shinzuki slowly dropped to the floor.

The diner's staff and customers erupted in a series of cheers and applause.

Her eyes welling with tears, Miya rushed over and helped her husband up. "Oh my God, honey, please don't ever scare me like that again!" she said, embracing him, while giving a sigh of relief. "I'm so happy you're alive!"

Luke cupped his wife's face in his hands. "Yes, it's good to see you! I promise I won't ever do that again!"

Yomatri tossed his electrified wands aside and rushed over to hug his parents. "Oh man, it's good to see you guys." He paused for a moment to examine his father's wound. "Hey, Dad, are you alright?"

"Yeah, yeah, I'll be fine. Don't worry about me," Luke replied. His son eyed him uneasily with pursed lips.

A team of armed police suddenly entered the diner, briefly exchanging looks with everyone inside and studying their surroundings. The men then shifted their attention to Shinzuki who was propped up against a wall, unable to fight any longer.

Two police separated from the team and began to place

him under arrest. "Hey, is everyone here alright?" one of the officers asked. Exhausted, Yomatri and the others nodded.

"Good. We do need to get you guys to safety, though," said the second officer. "All of the civilians in the surrounding area have already been evacuated."

"Yeah," replied Luke. He turned to Miya, the staff, and the customers. "Alright, everybody, you heard what he said. It's time to move out. The police will protect you guys from here."

One after another, the diner's staff and customers stopped to thank Luke on their way toward the exit. He, Miya, and Yomatri each smiled, relieved.

☆☆☆

Later, everyone had regrouped outside. Luke, his wife, and son huddled together near the side of the diner.

"You did great out there, kiddo," Luke said to Yomatri. "That's a pretty neat weapon you got there too—the electrical batons."

"Thanks, Dad. You did great too. Had me worried for a sec, but I'm glad you're alright."

Overhearing a sudden rush of footsteps, the three of them turned to see Miyuki and the four brothers.

"Hey. There you are," Miyuki said to Yomatri, catching her breath. "What's goin' on?"

"Well, uh, Shinzuki's down." He turned to the four brothers. "Hey, if you guys wanna check with the police and see if they need help with anything, that'd be great."

Mako nodded. His brothers looked on attentively.

"Honey, I'm still a little worried," Miya said to her son. "You guys still need to find that 'Hano' kid, right?"

He creased his brow. "Yeah, no doubt. We still have one last thing to do."

CHAPTER TWENTY-TWO:

A LIFE ON THE LINE

Against the gathering darkness of the winter sky, Yomatri ran beside Miyuki down a narrow street littered with piles of rubble and debris. Passing by lines of abandoned cars, the teens closely surveyed their surroundings.

"Any idea where he might be?" Miyuki yelled; smoldering flames burned on the concrete nearby.

Panting, Yomatri replied, "No, not really! That's what worries me the most!" He held his electrified wands firmly, and together, the two of them continued forward.

At one point from behind, a blistering shadow bolt spiraled its way toward Miyuki. Immediately she jumped aside and tumbled down into the snow as the missile slammed into a brick building close by.

Miyuki rose to her feet, taking cover behind a wrecked taxicab. She screamed after her friend, who stopped in the middle of the street.

Turning around, Yomatri looked up at the sky. His eyes widened. A dark figure flew towards him at high speed, swinging fiercely with a sharp, jagged object. Yomatri clashed with the object, quickly using one of his batons to defend himself.

A burst of green energy ripped through the air, flashing

amidst gusts of snow. Yomatri was thrown to the ground, but Miyuki rushed over and helped him up. At the same time, the figure had landed several hundred meters in front of the teens.

Adjusting his vision, Yomatri locked eyes with his former friend, Hano.

"Your side has fought well today. I'm surprised," Hano said, catching his breath. In his hand was the Emerald Crystal. "But this isn't over just yet."

Standing close, Miyuki and Yomatri glared at their opponent, both smoldering with rage.

"You're nothing but evil!" responded Miyuki.

Hano dexterously twirled the ancient rod in one hand. Miyuki charged at him but was immediately forced backward by a shadowy force.

"Miyuki!" Yomatri yelled. His friend crashed violently into a parked car, knocking her unconscious.

A look of grim determination on his face, Yomatri turned back to face Hano. "You're gonna pay for that!" He charged forward and clashed weapons with his adversary, his wands sparking and crackling as electricity glided along the crystal's shaft.

"You'll never be the hero you were meant to be," said Hano. "It's over for you and your friend."

"I don't think so!" Yomatri replied.

Their weapons separated, and Hano swung repeatedly with the Emerald Crystal, driving his foe back on his heels. Now holding the rod in one hand, Hano used his other to unleash a torrent of dark energy.

Yomatri crouched and braced himself with his batons, remaining upright, but the force of his opponent's attack drove him back even further.

Again Hano hurled a barrage of dark matter at Yomatri, who slid underneath the energy stream. Upon rising, he and Hano clashed their weapons a second time, sending out a shockwave of destruction. Windows from nearby buildings shattered open on impact, glass raining down onto the street.

Meanwhile, Miyuki suddenly awoke. Her eyes focused on the duel as she lay prone.

Yomatri lunged with his electrified wands, but his opponent shielded himself with the crystal. Hano retaliated, backhanding Yomatri and spinning around to deliver a heavy blow to his side.

He struck again, socking the teen in the jaw, making him drop one of his batons as he barreled into an upturned car. Hano quickly advanced, now standing over him. He lashed out with the ancient rod but it was stopped midair.

"You'd better watch what you're doing," Miyuki said, gritting her teeth. Kneeling, she'd locked weapons with Hano, holding Yomatri's baton tightly with two hands.

Hano stared at her, shocked. Miyuki sprung up, forcing the weight of the crystal off the baton and attacking him fiercely. In a blast of sparks, Hano blocked each of her strikes, ducking and dodging in time.

With her opponent caught off guard, Miyuki quickly grabbed Yomatri's other baton from the ground and went on the offensive, attacking with swift, heavy strikes. At one point, she slashed at his leg, shocking him and making him drop to one knee.

Hano swiped at her, struggling to rise. Miyuki dodged, then lunged with the electrified wands; she missed as Hano rolled out of the way and slowly rose to his feet. Again and again he swung with the Emerald Crystal, now putting Miyuki on the defensive.

Miyuki leaped over the back end of a wrecked car as Hano barely missed, slicing right through the vehicle's thick metal. Miyuki somersaulted down into the snow, then turned to face her opponent.

A water rocket knocked Hano off balance.

Wide-eyed, Miyuki glanced over, seeing Yomatri running toward them. Again he attacked, the water missile surging forward, sending Hano back and causing him to drop the crystal.

Exhausted, Yomatri stopped beside Miyuki to catch his breath, both of them closely eyeing their opponent. Panting, Hano slowly got up to face the two teens. Tiny bursts of elemental energy crackled from the rod lying on the ground between them.

"You know that doesn't belong to you," said Hano, his panicked gaze shifting between Miyuki and Yomatri and the Emerald Crystal.

"It doesn't ... belong to you ... either," Yomatri replied. "Why—all of this? For what? You invade the city ... to hurt innocent people, for no reason. There has to be more to it."

"What I want doesn't concern you," Hano responded.

Yomatri wiped a speck of blood from his lip. "When I met you, I didn't think ... you were anything like this. What happened to you?"

"I simply chose the side that would help me achieve my destiny." Immediately he and his former friend rushed toward the Emerald Crystal.

"No!!" Miyuki shouted.

Reaching it first, Yomatri held the rod tightly with both hands and dodged a desperate punch from his foe just in time. He pointed the weapon at Hano as an enormous surge of green, elemental energy was summoned from the rod.

Miyuki was thrown to the ground.

At high speed, the cloud of energy swirled around the teens, growing larger and larger by the second. Yomatri's eyes began to glow a strong emerald color.

Bits of concrete ripped away from the street, and powerful blasts of magic shot out from the cloud of destruction, striking nearby buildings. Beneath everyone's feet, the ground shook with an intense roar, causing the street to crumble and break apart.

Her heart pounding, Miyuki watched Yomatri, who tried to contain the strong elemental force. More bursts of energy spiraled out of the cloud, burning signs and trees along the sidewalk.

Tears streaming down his cheeks, Yomatri began to hear voices from all sides:

> *We've missed you, buddy. We're really glad you're home.*

> *And for the record, for someone who was so hesitant on saving the world at first, you've got a lot of guts, kid—that's for sure.*

> *Seriously, don't worry. I've got your back. You and*
> *I are in this together.*

Yomatri's attention returned to the present. Purposely, he dropped the Emerald Crystal but had full control of its power. He took a firm stance, holding currents of swirling green energy at bay on both sides of himself.

Suddenly Hano fired a shadow bolt, which hurtled straight at Yomatri, who immediately responded, flinging his hands forward. A mass of elemental power slammed into Hano, and Yomatri shouted in anger, his hair and clothes billowing in the fierce wind. Miyuki shielded her eyes as a blinding light shot down from the heavens and ripped through the chaotic battlefield.

Yomatri stood still, the remainder of the mighty energy soon vanishing into the nighttime air. Slowly, Miyuki opened her eyes, hearing a trembling roar from within the clouds high above. The white light had cleared and Hano collapsed to the ground, unconscious.

Yomatri's eye color returned to normal. Drained, he fell backward, crashing onto the street. The Emerald Crystal, which slowly regained its color, remained still beside him.

Miyuki struggled to rise, but after some effort she rushed over, desperate to know if her friend was okay. Gently, she cradled him in her arms, calling his name again and again.

He was unresponsive.

At one point, Miyuki resorted to the only option she could think of—smacking him across the face—and instantly he came to. Yomatri coughed and coughed, trying to regain his breath.

The girl smiled.

"Miyuki! Hey! Are you okay? Why'd you slap me?" She pulled him into a warm embrace. "Why are you smiling? Was it something I did? Did I do something cool?"

"Yeah, I'm fine!" Miyuki took a deep breath. "And yes, you did somethin' really cool just now, I can tell you that."

The teens shared an amused laugh. Miyuki glanced over at the crystal, then returned her attention to Yomatri, finding him adorable.

"Wait, why are you holding me? Were we havin' a moment or somethin'?" asked Yomatri.

Miyuki looked shocked; her mouth opened wide.

"Umm ... I don't know. That's, uh, up to you, I guess," she responded, unsure of what to say. Looking away, she mouthed the drawn-out word "*wow.*"

Yomatri giggled. He took Miyuki's face and turned it toward him, eyeing her closely. Miyuki shook her head, then kissed her friend on the lips.

"What was that for?" Yomatri asked, surprised.

Miyuki blushed. Nervously she glanced down, then looked him in the eyes. "I don't know, I've been wanting to tell you this for a while now. I guess I just, um, didn't really know how to say it. We've been through a lot in these past few weeks ... and ... I just really like you a lot," she said, smiling coyly at him.

Yomatri smiled back. He and Miyuki eagerly pressed their lips together, sharing a gentle, passionate kiss. Miyuki cupped his face in her hands as he held her tightly by the arm.

Again, the teens kissed, parting shortly after. Their eyes met for a moment, and they both shared a relieved laugh.

"I like you a lot too," said Yomatri. Slowly, he sat up, mustering the last bit of his strength. Miyuki cautiously watched her friend, who glanced over at Hano and flinched. "Whoa! Wait, why does he look like that?"

Hano looked like an undead creature, his face and body covered in black dust.

Miyuki snickered but appeared confused. "I'm surprised you don't remember anything. We had this pretty big battle and see ... you did this really awesome thing with the crystal."

"Nope," he said, shaking his head. "I don't remember any of it, honestly. But I'm just glad that—"

Miyuki nodded solemnly. "Yeah. We won."

Yomatri stopped to survey his surroundings. Briefly, he stared at the Emerald Crystal, then continued to glance around. With a shocked look, he thought to himself: *did I really do all this?*

Miyuki shook her head, giggling at her friend's weird behavior, but he didn't seem to notice.

Suddenly, Yomatri's arms started to give way and he began to fall back down. Miyuki caught her friend, tightly wrapping her arms around him.

Together, the teens shared a long warm hug. Yomatri looked up at the winter sky while Miyuki rested her cheek on his shoulder. They were happy that all of this was over— for now, at least.

Around them, the street was littered with rubble

and debris; smoldering flames continued to burn on the concrete. There was a lot to clean up, but as long as Yomatri and Miyuki had each other, nothing else mattered.

"The Alliance is gonna be proud of us," said Yomatri.

Miyuki smiled. "Yep, that's for sure."

CHAPTER TWENTY-THREE:

A LONG JOURNEY AHEAD

At home the next morning, Yomatri and his parents sat together on a couch in the living room. The three of them were just finishing up a small breakfast of bacon and eggs while they watched the news on TV. Miyuki, with a cup of hot chocolate to her side, was seated nearby, her attention also focused on the television.

Police and firefighters worked together to clean up the destruction while forensic analysts investigated one damaged building after another. In the middle of one street filled with wreckage, the Alliance ship the four brothers used in the battle lay still, charred and smoking.

Pictures of Stewart's Diner were also shown on the screen. Many reporters from different news outlets spoke in front of the restaurant's smashed-open front doors, talking about Luke's heroism in keeping its staff and customers safe.

Miya smiled, setting a plate down onto the coffee table. She then glanced over at her husband, whose eyes lit up with happiness. "You did great out there, honey—takin' on that sorcerer or whatever he was," she said to him, gently rubbing his back.

"Good job, Dad," Yomatri said with a smirk.

"Thanks, guys," Luke replied, the bruise on the side of

his face now better than it had been.

Yomatri turned up the volume on the TV. He and everyone else listened closely as a female reporter relayed a brief message:

> *. . . It's quite evident that yesterday's extraterrestrial attack was a great challenge for the people of our beloved city, New York. Officials have commended the actions of the six teens who fought bravely to defend against the invasion. For many of us, it will take years to recover, but for now, all we can do is work together to rebuild and hope that something like this never happens again . . .*

A larger view of the city's destruction was shown as the camera panned outward. The news report transitioned to a commercial, leaving everyone staring at the TV, their expressions a mixture of shock and relief.

"I'm still blown away by everything that happened, you know?" Yomatri said, resting the TV remote against his chin. He glanced around at everyone.

There was a brief silence.

Miyuki took a sip of her hot chocolate, then replied, "Yeah, it's definitely a lot to take in looking back on everything."

"I agree. I'm just glad it's all over," said Luke. "But you guys should be proud of yourselves. I definitely know that wasn't easy defending the city like that."

"Thank you," the teens both said solemnly.

"What do we do now, though—now that the city's, you know, safe?" asked Miya.

Luke responded, "I honestly have no idea. The world's obviously gonna learn about the Hero Alliance and their war with the Aridian Army."

"That's true," Yomatri added, getting up from the couch, "but there's nothing we can really do about it at this point. Either way, Miyuki and I made a promise to the Alliance. And it's up to us to keep that promise."

Miyuki also rose and went over to Yomatri, taking her car keys from out of her pocket. "He's right. We have to go make things right with them."

"You guys are leaving now?" Miya asked.

Yomatri exchanged a glance with his friend. "Yeah. We'll be back, though. It shouldn't be too long." He reached down and grabbed his backpack and his beloved space-camp weapon, now back in the form of the rusty, battered staff.

"Well, here, lemme give you a hug, Miyuki," said Miya; she got up from the couch and embraced her.

Luke did the same.

"Hey, uh, I know I've only known you guys for a short time, but I just wanna say thank you for everything." Miyuki smiled warmly. "This is probably a bummer, but it might be a while before I see you both again."

Miya and Luke's expressions grew sad.

"Why do you say that?" asked Luke.

"It's nothing to worry about. It's just, with the new semester starting back up, I'll have to focus on school again

347

for the time being. My parents are definitely not the ones to accept bad grades," the girl answered, beginning to laugh. "Maybe I can come by sometime if Yomatri's nice enough to invite me over?"

"Oh, don't you worry. You're always welcome," Miya insisted. She wrapped her arms around her husband and leaned on his shoulder.

"Great!" Miyuki replied.

"I'll guess we'll, uh, see you guys later then," said Luke. "You kids be safe."

"You got it, Dad," Yomatri responded.

The teens waved good-bye, then headed outside, gently closing the front door behind them. Walking to her father's car, Miyuki stopped in her tracks on the front lawn.

Yomatri turned back and went over to her, curious. "What's wrong?"

Miyuki shook her head. Keeping her eyes down, she adjusted her friend's jacket. "Nothing. It's just ... I miss your parents already."

Yomatri glanced down thoughtfully, then raised his eyes to meet hers. "It'll be okay, don't worry. Like they said, you can always come by whenever. Maybe if you ever get a .break from studying?"

A smile slowly touched the corners of Miyuki's mouth as she reached up to give him a warm hug.

✫✫✫

On Ember Island, in one of the many lounge areas, Sage and his brothers sat at a round stone table, playing a game with several Aridnemekian teenagers. On the table were various piles of cards and circular chips of different colors. In front of each player was a bottled soft drink. Above everyone's heads, a series of lanterns hung from the ceiling, illuminating the dimly lit room.

"This is totally not how I expected things to go," Beta said, biting his lip. He glanced around at everyone, his fingers fidgeting on a two-card hand.

"Yeah. We're gettin' our butts kicked," Mako affirmed. "Is there any hope for us?"

"I don't know . . . ," said Sage. For a moment, he sat still, blinking pensively, then drew a card from a nearby deck.

The brothers paused and looked up, noticing Miyuki and Yomatri entering the lounge. Bystanders who were watching the game also turned.

"If you leave, you lose by default. No take-backs," said a slender teenager with goggles on his forehead, sitting on the opposite end of the table. Three other teens, one with a mechanical left arm, sat beside him.

In the center of the table was the pot—an assortment of silver coins and metal chips.

Sage returned his attention to the game, tapping his cards on the table. "I wouldn't say that." Pointing to himself, he asked, "Is it my turn?"

The teen wearing goggles on his forehead laid down his three-card hand, then angrily replied, "Yes, just go already! You're wasting my time! You and your brothers can't win."

Yomatri and Miyuki stopped beside the four brothers, overlooking the card game.

"Oh, hey, guys!" said Sage. He and his brothers glanced up at them and shook hands. "How'd you get here?"

"Hey! We just, you know, took an Alliance jet from Manhattan—the usual." Yomatri grabbed Mako's drink from the table and took a sip. "Hmph. That's not that bad, actually. Tastes almost like grape soda. What do we got goin' on here?"

Miyuki looked on, her face beaming.

Sage scratched his head. "Nothing really ... just, uh, me and my brothers winning yet again!" One after another, he set the cards in his hand down onto the table in a row.

The crowd of Aridnemekians standing around the table erupted in a series of cheers, applauding the four brothers, who each rose up looking relieved.

"YEAH!!" Sage exclaimed, pumping his fists into the air. Each member of the opposing team closed their eyes and hung their heads. Smiling, Miyuki and Yomatri joined their friends, following them out of the lounge.

Minutes later, the six teens regrouped at the four brothers' dorm just down the hall. Using a keycard, Mako unlocked the door and tossed a bag with the game's winning pot down onto a bed. He then returned back out into the hall, gently shutting the door behind him.

"What was that game you guys were playin'?" Yomatri asked the brothers. "That was awesome how you won even though we only saw like the last bit of it."

"It's something we used to always play back home on Aridnemeki. Our father was big into gambling so we kind of took after him," Beta said, chuckling.

"Yeah. By the way, Yomatri—and Miyuki too—we

were supposed to let you guys know that Master Zorhins and Captain Zeron were looking for you," said Sage. "Not really sure why, though."

"Oh," Miyuki responded, surprised. "Do you know where they are by chance?"

"Yes, this way." Everyone else followed him, turning the corner to another hallway. Down the hall, Captain Zeron and Master Zorhins suddenly appeared and stopped near the group. "Oh, hi. We were just about to come find you guys."

"That's alright, no worries," said the Alliance captain. "It's good to see you, Miyuki and Yomatri!"

"Thank you," the teens said. Miyuki asked, "Did you guys have something to show us?"

"Yes, we did. Please, come this way," replied Master Zorhins.

As the group walked, Yomatri conversed with Miyuki. "Hey, you never told me what your parents said to you after you revealed to them that you were a hero and whatnot. Were they sorta okay with things?"

Miyuki's eyebrows rose; she paused to think. "Umm ... they were a little taken back by it at first, like your parents, you know? It wasn't like they just said, 'Oh, she can control water and she's helping save the world now? That's cool.'" She giggled but then grew more serious. "There were definitely a lotta questions, but they're happy about what I'm doing. Everything that I have done."

Yomatri looked relieved. "Oh. That's good. Did you tell them about me at all?"

"I did! And surprisingly, they reacted a lot different

than how I thought they would. They actually wanna meet you."

Yomatri didn't respond. Bashfully, he glanced aside.

"What?" Miyuki asked, finding it hard not to laugh.

"Nothing," he replied. "I'm just, uh, thinking like, what if we become boyfriend and girlfriend one day? That'd be really cool, right?"

Miyuki blushed. "Yeah! I don't know, umm ... I'm not really opposed to it, honestly. It's obvious we both like each other. I mean, we both even said it."

Yomatri smiled, and he and Miyuki continued on.

✮✮✮

Later, near the entrance to a large underground cavern, water poured down, rushing past rocks to disappear down a dark cleft below. Miyuki and Yomatri followed the four brothers along a rough, uneven pathway. Above their heads, gigantic stalactites hung from the ceiling.

Yomatri held a cylindrical canister of light in one hand. It shined brightly as he raised it up toward his head, illuminating the darkness in front of the group.

Miyuki held a wooden torch, its fiery glow spreading out on all sides. "This is pretty cool," she said. "It's just like that cave we were in back in Westchester."

"Yeah, I agree," responded Zatch.

Yomatri and Miyuki paused frequently, studying an assortment of strange markings and symbols chiseled into the cavern's stone walls.

"Whoa!! What are these? Yomatri asked, frozen in

astonishment.

"This is incredible," Miyuki said, her mouth agape.

"They're pictures and symbols, words ... depicting the war back on Aridnemeki," the Alliance captain responded; she smiled at the looks on their faces.

"I love it," Miyuki said with a smirk.

Passing by numerous spider webs, the group progressed through the cold, shadowy tunnels made up of many different rock formations.

Eventually they made it to a dark, murky pool lit from a hole in the roof of the cavern. Large chunks of broken, smooth black rock surrounded the pool.

The teens paused nervously, studying the ominous water before them.

"What now?" Mako asked, curious.

"This is where we'll keep the Emerald Crystal safe for the time being, so we'll have a better chance at keeping it away from the enemy in the future," Master Zorhins explained.

Yomatri squinted, further examining the water. "You mean, we're gonna keep it here? In this pool?"

"Yes. I doubt the enemy would expect one of the twelve crystals to be there. Entering the water will be impossible as the pool will be sealed off by magic. A seal that only myself or Captain Zeron will be able to open."

"Ohhh, that makes sense. Like a protective barrier."

"That's correct."

"Is the Aridian Army aware that Ember Island exists here in this dimension, though?" Miyuki asked.

"That we're honestly not sure about," said the Alliance captain. "Though, it's quite possible that they might be now that Hano's turned to the dark side."

Yomatri handed the canister of light to Mako, who was nearby. He took a deep breath and pulled out the Emerald Crystal from his backpack, holding it tightly with two hands. It shined brightly, glowing its distinctive light green color.

Kneeling down, the teen gently dropped the ancient weapon into the pool. A bright green aura of energy emanated from the water and the rod sank slowly to the bottom of the pool. Yomatri stood up and edged back while still keeping a close eye on the water.

It was then that Master Zorhins stepped forward and gesticulated gracefully with both hands, conjuring a circle of glowing energy in front of him. Holding the energy circle at bay with one hand, he slowly twirled his other in a circular motion.

A series of interconnected geometric shapes formed inside the circle, followed by an assortment of strange letters and symbols. Miyuki and the others watched, breaths held.

Finally, the Alliance leader snapped his fingers and thrust his palms forward, propelling the sigil toward the pool. A blast of bright light flashed over the water, radiating outward.

Eventually, it vanished into the darkness of the cave with tiny bursts of magic shooting up from the water.

"That was incredible!!" said Miyuki.

Yomatri traded a surprised look with her, then knitted his brow. "Wait, what's going on? Why all the energy bursts?"

"Nothing, really. The water's just getting used to the spell I cast on it to keep the rod protected," the Alliance leader replied. "It is finished, though. The Emerald Crystal is now safe."

There was a short pause.

Miyuki glanced around at everyone, her expression concerned. "What happens now then?"

"I have a feeling this is where the fun begins," said Sage, tapping his chin.

Yomatri and the others grinned.

✬✬✬

Amidst a light snowfall, Aridnemekian children dressed in winter clothing chased one another back and forth across a large courtyard along the edge of the island. Some of the kids had snowball fights in the woods nearby.

Fires burned throughout the courtyard with several high-ranking Alliance officers and other commanders, including Captain Zeron, huddled around them.

A mixture of men and women laughed and chatted, feasting at an assortment of tables with drinks at their sides. At one table, the four brothers taught Miyuki the same card game they were playing before. A crowd of Aridnemekian teens watched closely. As some people sang joyous tunes and clapped, others pounded on drums and danced happily.

Beside a tree along the edge of the courtyard, where the mood was much quieter, Yomatri watched the celebrations excitedly.

Master Zorhins approached him from the side. "Having fun?"

The teen turned to face him. "Yeah, definitely! I absolutely love this place."

"Why's that?"

"There's so much to do and see here! It's like space camp all over again. It feels ... new and different."

"That's good. Do you ever miss space camp now that you're back on Earth with your parents?"

"Yes, of course," replied Yomatri. "I'm always gonna miss space camp. It's like my second home. My parents and I were talkin' about it once before, and at one point, my mom said that space camp is like something I can keep with me for the rest of my life." He smiled proudly.

Master Zorhins smiled back. "Your mother's right."

"Absolutely." Yomatri nodded. "But then again, like I said, this kinda feels like home, too—you know, Ember Island. And all the Aridnemekian stuff. And my new life as a hero. I know I was sorta skeptical about my abilities at first, but looking back on things, I'm really happy to be a part of all this, honestly."

"That's good to hear, kid. You and your friends have a lot to be proud of—especially working together to regain possession of the Emerald Crystal. That was a big victory for the Alliance. And for you. You've definitely grown a lot in the short time I've known you."

"Thank you, sir. That really means a lot. I'm excited to continue my learning and will try to do my best," the teen replied, looking out over New York Harbor. In the gray winter sky, the sun spread its fiery glow over the island.

A solemn look on his face, Yomatri began to reflect. At first, he, Miyuki, and the four brothers were only strangers to one another. He knew a lot had changed and through time, even more things would. The six of them had much to learn, and no one knew their fate.

A hero was born in the midst of these lessons, and like all heroes, Yomatri was anxious to face his next adventure.

A new day was upon him, and a long, epic journey ahead ...

About the Author

Javon Manning is an alumni of the University of Wisconsin–Milwaukee who studied Marketing and International Business. Ever since he was a kid, he's always had an interest in storytelling. In his free time, he enjoys traveling, drawing, playing video games, and spending time with loved ones. Javon resides in Milwaukee, Wisconsin with his family.

You can find him on Instagram at:

https://www.instagram.com/javon.manningauthor/

or e-mail: javonmanningbooks@gmail.com